BLAME IT ON THE BOGEY (MAN)

THE HIPPOSYNC ARCHIVES
BOOK 3

DC FARMER

WYRMWOOD
BOOKS

COPYRIGHT

Copyright © Wyrmwood Media Ltd 2024. All rights reserved.

The right of DC Farmer to be identified as the author of this work has been asserted in accordance with the Copyright, Design and Patents Act 1988. Names, characters, businesses, places, events and incidents are either the products of the author's imagination or used in a purely fictitious manner. Any resemblance to actual persons, living or dead, or actual events is purely coincidental. No part of this book may be reproduced in any form or by any electronic or mechanical means, including information storage and retrieval systems, without written permission from the author, except for the use of brief quotations in a book review.

First published 2017 as The Bewilderment by Wormwood books

This edition published by Wyrmwood Books 2024

A CIP catalogue record for this book is available from the British Library

eBook ISBN -978-1-915185-30-3
Print ISBN- 978-1-915185-31-0

Published by Wyrmwood Books.
An imprint of Wyrmwood Media.

EXCLUSIVE OFFER

WOULD YOU LIKE A FREE NOVELLA

Please look out for the link near the end of the book for your chance to sign up to the no-spam guaranteed Readers Club and receive a FREE DC Farmer novella as well as news of upcoming releases. HERE ARE THE BOOKS!

FIENDS IN HIGH PLACES
THE GHOUL ON THE HILL
BLAME IT ON THE BOGEY (MAN)*
CAN'T BUY ME BLOOD
COMING SOON
TROLL LOTTA LOVE
SOMEWHERE OGRE THE RAINBOW

CHAPTER ONE

EDGBASTON, BIRMINGHAM, ENGLAND

POLICE CONSTABLE KEVIN THOMAS trembled so much he'd spilled half his tea onto the cracked path that led from the rusty garden gate to the back door. A bitter December wind whistled down from the north, dropping the temperature fast, yet PC Thomas' trembling had little to do with the cold. His shakes were a consequence of having his living daylights go south, which is precisely what they were supposed to do when faced with something inexplicably horrific.

At six foot two and a regular for the divisional police rugby team, the sight of Kevin Thomas generally made the inexplicably horrific cross the road when it saw him coming. But what lay in wait in the cupboard under the stairs at Number 77 Vimy Way had done the trick all right, and no questions asked.

He hadn't thrown up. At least not so that anyone would notice. His partner, PC Andy Green, would probably not tell anyone even if he had, but not throwing up in this job was a matter of pride. He never lost his takeaway, not even in the eight-car pileup in the fog last autumn, when they'd accidentally been first on the scene and seen far too many pieces of human jigsaw scattered across the hard shoulder. He hadn't slept much for a week after that, but tonight's little episode on a quiet street in suburban Edgbaston was something else altogether.

The bitter ort of bile that burped into the back of his throat kept refreshing itself whenever the cupboard image flashed into his head. He gulped at the hot, sweet tea to wash it away. Just his luck to be the one to open that cupboard. He'd simply followed his nose, literally, and there was Cuthbertson, seventy-nine years old, in a grey cardigan and carpet slippers; moribund as a doorknob and huddled against the wall with an expression that would've not only curdled any nearby milk but turned it instantly into a pretty rank gorgonzola. He was not looking forward to describing all this to the lads back at the station.

Andy had radioed in for CID and a CSI team immediately after their cupboard discovery. Standard practice in all cases of unexplained death. But even now, an hour-and-a-half after finding the body, Kevin was still shaking. Andy'd sent him outside with a cuppa to calm his nerves. However, the only thing the tea helped calm as it dribbled shakily out of the cup was the moss in the cracks between the crazy paving slabs at his feet.

It was getting dark now. Kevin looked up into the Midlands sky at the fading red glow of a late afternoon sunset and saw little to console him. Across the street, a neon reindeer pulled Santa across a roof. An unwelcome reminder that it'd be Christmas in a week or two. He latched on to that merry thought. Tinsel and fairy lights and drunk teenagers passed out on the pavement at three on Saturday mornings who needed rescuing from freezing to death or choking on their kebabs. Oh yes, the season of goodwill to all men and sick on your boots. He ought to start thinking about Zoe's present. Not jewellery, she didn't want that. Maybe he'd ask her sister. Scarlett was never backwards in coming forwards with suggestions at the best of times—not all of them entirely appropriate either, especially after four vodka redbulls. Asking her would be a bit of a cheat but what the hell, better that than getting something Zoe hated...The thought froze in his head and he paused with the tea halfway to his mouth.

In the gloom, he could swear the door of the shed at the bottom of the garden was creaking open. He peered. Yes, definitely opening and out of it was emerging an athletic-looking man of average height in a dark jacket and white shirt followed by a woman, smaller but equally as sleek in a black suit and white blouse. Kevin watched warily as they looked around the garden and then caught sight of him. To his surprise, the man hailed him and started walking up the path. This was doubly odd to Kevin, whose experience of people in general was that they usually lost their amiability once they recognised the uniform. Most, in fact, turned sharply and sprinted the other way; this was Birmingham after all.

'Evening, Officer,' said the man when he was five yards away.

Kevin noted his age at not much older than his own. 'Did you just come out of that shed?' he asked, drawing heavily on his policing skills.

'We did,' said the woman in a surprisingly throaty voice, the type you often heard in Greek or Spanish flea markets, though the accent here was definitely British. Kevin wondered about adding 'sexy' to the 'throaty' but one look at her told him it was a thought he'd never voice in her company. She had a look about her that his old sergeant described as 'handy', as in 'handy to have around when the manure hits the windmill'.

'Early recce,' added the woman. 'Getting the lay of the land, you know.'

'Right.' Kevin put his eyes into narrowed suspicion mode.

'Oh, sorry. DOF,' said the man by way of explanation, and reached into his pocket for identification. Kevin regarded the folded black plastic wallet the man held up and took in a faded circle with a shield in the middle and the words, *Department of Fimmigration*, written in a slightly odd-looking font. 'I'm Agent Danmor, and this is Agent Porter. I gather you've been expecting us?'

Kevin put the cup down and wiped a tea-stained hand on his trousers. He had no idea who these people were but, being a good PC, had long ago realised he was always the last to know about anything operational. 'Yeah, right. We radioed everything in.' He offered a damp hand, which first Danmor and then Porter, shook.

Firmly.

'Are you the officer that found the body?'

'Yes,' Kevin answered.

'Sorry about that,' Agent Danmor said.

Kevin grimaced and his expression did not go unnoticed.

'Perhaps you'd care to show us?' Porter added.

'That's if you're sure you're up to it,' Danmor said.

'No problem,' said Kevin, though his brain screamed, *Noooo!* 'Follow me.'

He quickly ran through the events leading up to the discovery as he led Porter and Danmor through the house. A concerned neighbour rang in to report the fact that Mr Cuthbertson had not been seen for several days and there was a funny smell coming from under the back door.

'Never a great combination, those two,' Kevin muttered with feeling, and went on to explain how he and Andy Green had gone along expecting to find a collapsed pensioner and a battalion of well-fed flies. And that, together with a sickly smell like a butcher's shop at sunset in August thanks to the automated central heating, was exactly what they found. But they had not expected the added bonus of the freaky deleted scene from *Halloween 10: The Director's Cut* that awaited them.

Andy Green stood in the kitchen with the concerned neighbour as they passed through. They both looked on in silence when Kevin nodded and said, 'DOF.'

Neither appeared to be in any hurry to accompany him and the two agents.

Kevin explained that the undertakers were already on their way with orders to take the body straight to the mortuary for a post-mortem, but as of this moment, it remained as found. He paused in the passageway to run a finger around the inside of his collar. He was sweating, but his flesh felt oddly cold, like something on a fishmonger's slab. The suspense reminded him somehow of watching a late night showing of *The Exorcist* at the Odeon, knowing that the infamous head-rotating-on-a-body scene loomed. But here there was no convenient bucket of popcorn to hide behind and no woolly jumper courtesy of Zoe to bury his face in. He wanted to shut his eyes until it was over, but he couldn't. He was a policeman after all. This was what he did.

The door to the cupboard faced the kitchen only three steps along the passage.

'Here it is,' Kevin said hoarsely, reaching for the latch.

'Hang on a minute.' Danmor stooped to stare at the passage wall. Or rather at the dark oblongs hanging on the passage wall. 'These mirrors, none of them have been disturbed?'

Kevin shook his head. He hadn't realised they were mirrors. He'd thought they were empty picture frames. But Danmor used a pencil to lift the bottom of one far enough away from the wall and twisted it to demonstrate the reflective surface underneath.

'Okay,' Porter said. 'Where's the body?'

Kevin cleared his throat and undid the latch. The SOC boys had left it wide open but once they'd gone, Kevin had shut it again. 'He's exactly as we found him,' he said, looking back at the two agents, finger on the knob.

Danmor nodded for the door to be opened. The skin from the nape of Kevin's neck to the bottom of his sacrum contracted as if suddenly doused in arctic water. It was the face that did it. Upturned and hyperextended, one hand stretched out to ward off whatever it was that drove Cuthbertson into the furthest, darkest corner of this tiny space. The old man's mouth was twisted into a horrified grimace, the lips drawn back to show the dry plastic of his displaced dentures. But the eyes were the sour cream filling in the mortifying expression gateaux. They were dead fish eyes now, but it was the way that they bulged, the whites exposed, expressionless and yet somehow telling a desperate story of terror-stricken final throes. Kevin felt his stomach whirl. Something terrible had happened here in this dark little corner of this dark little house. He dragged his eyes away to the coats and hats and scarves and boots that the cupboard was designed to hold and concentrated on a pair of walking boots. It took a while for him to realise that he was holding his breath. He inhaled and sucked in the sweet, sickly smell of death.

'Not an image for his sweetheart's locket,' Danmor said darkly.

'Nothing's been moved?' Porter asked.

'Nothing,' Kevin replied, dragging his eyes around to look at the infinitely more acceptable visage of the DOF agent. Were those gold flecks in her irises?

'Thank you, may I...'

Kevin stepped back and stood, watching both agents go to work. They donned flesh-coloured gloves and Porter knelt to examine the body.

'There is a vestige of something here, I can feel it,' Porter said.

'And smell it.' Danmor pushed at the debris littering the floor.

'Happens sometimes,' Kevin explained. 'The soul isn't the only thing that tries to escape at the point of death.' He wrinkled his nose.

'There is that,' Danmor nodded. 'But I was thinking more about the ash leaves and oak bark. This, Constable Thomas, is a warding cell.'

Porter ran a finger across the floor. 'Chalk,' she said, examining the white powder residue coating her finger. 'Probably a circle. Incomplete now. His feet would have rubbed it away.'

Danmor nodded. 'Add that to reversed mirrors and you've got definite malevolence. I'll take some photos.'

Kevin frowned. 'Does this mean you two know what went on here?'

'Rough idea,' Danmor said. 'I'd say Mr Cuthbertson has been haunted by something very nasty.'

Kevin's face lit up with a wary smile. 'Did you say hunted or haunted?'

'Both apply,' Porter said. 'The signs are un-mistakable.'

The smile faded into mild confusion. 'Is that why he looks...so terrified?'

'Exactly. I suspect you'll find he died of a stopped heart. Pretty standard cause of death in malevolent terror.'

'Malevolent terror? Sounds a bit weird—'

'We need a little light in here,' Porter said, all businesslike. 'We brought headlamps. Would you mind helping us out, Constable?' She handed Kevin an elasticated band for his forehead.

Kevin hesitated only for a second. Unlike the one Danmor held, the lens on his looked strangely opalescent. 'How come mine's a funny green colour?'

'Red-free,' explained Danmor. Kevin shrugged and slid it onto his forehead.

'So this malevolent haunting and stopped heart business, is that what I should put down in my report?'

'Well, you could try,' Danmor said, and flicked on his light. 'But perhaps you'll find something a little less contentious. Here, let me switch that light on for you.' Danmor's fingers fiddled with the green lens and suddenly Kevin's mind went all rosy and warm as synapses uncoiled and neuronal connections unravelled and his face took on a beatific, contented look that came with not remembering what the nasty, unpleasant fuss was all about.

CHAPTER TWO

With the undertakers having come and gone and Cuthbertson removed from his dreadful prison, PCs Thomas and Green locked the door to Number 77 Vimy way and headed back to the station, their shift over.

'So, come on,' asked Andy, 'what did those immigration people want?'

Kevin thought about correcting him, something pedantic about the 'immigration' word, but for the life of him he couldn't think why. 'All they did was poke about a bit. They were efficient, seemed to know what they were doing.'

'Yeah? So did they know what made Cuthbertson look like he'd heard the hounds of hell scrabbling at the door?'

Kevin shrugged. 'Nah. Agent Porter reckoned on a heart attack. Sometimes sends people funny, she said. Spasm of the artery to the temporal lobe of the brain, apparently. Makes people think they see things when the end is near.'

'Really? Bloody hell. Amazing even how they know stuff, isn't it? So much for passing away quietly in your sleep. Sort of specialist forensic immigration team then, were they?'

'Seemed like it.' Kevin nodded, knowing it sounded about as likely as slug-flavoured crisps but letting it sail a good three yards over his head anyway. It seemed the right thing to do somehow.

'Who would've thought natural causes could end up giving you a face like that.'

'Yeah.' Kevin nodded again but quickly followed up with a frown. 'Funny thing is, I can't even picture him now.'

'Can't picture him? You went fifty shades of green when you first saw him. Mind you, he was a shocker alright, and I've seen a few.'

A vague awareness of dull horror lingered somewhere in the back of Kevin's mind but try as he might, he could not recall Cuthbertson's face, nor the details of the exchanges that took place between him and Agents Danmor and Porter. 'Maybe I'm suppressing the memory,' he said.

'And maybe my ladywear's a lollipop,' Andy responded.

'Ladywear?' Kevin scoffed.

'Yeah, as in hardware for ladies.' Andy looked across at Kevin, who was grinning. 'Bloody hell, that's the first smile I've seen all night. You really have forgotten the bugger's expression, haven't you? I hope to Christ my amnesia kicks in by the time I get to bed or there'll be no sleep for me.'

'Come on, you never lose sleep over anything.'

'Oh, yeah? And what do you know about it, Kevin Freud?'

'I had you down as Teflon coated.'

'You've got me all wrong, Kev.' Andy lifted his leg and let out a short, but very potent, airborne toxic event. 'Highly sensitive, me. Many's the time Denise has had to hold me in the wee small hours to stop me from sobbing.'

'If she's been holding you in the wee small hours it's not to stop you from sobbing,' Kevin said, wincing behind the sleeve of his coat and trying to stop his eyes from watering.

Andy laughed. 'Chance would be a fine thing now that she's five months gone. Prefers bloody marmite ice cream or chips slathered in marmalade.' He paused. 'Quite fancy some chips now I come to mention them. You?'

'Go on then. But no marmalade.' Kevin' eyes were still watering. 'And let's stop at that all night ironmongers to see if they've got any corks for that leaky porthole of yours.'

Kevin's report, when it hit the commander's desk, contained much the same information as he'd given to Andy and was in stark contrast to the one written by Matt Danmor. But then Danmor's was an FYO to the chief constable of West Midlands Police force. It spoke of Cuthbertson dying from adrenal overload due to a malign haunting and was marked for the top brass only. After all, they got paid for worrying about stuff like that, even if they had absolutely no idea of what to do about it. That was why they'd called in the DOF in the first place. Weird deaths, especially those where the deceased's expression was 'unusually grotesque' were called Munchers. Not with any tilt at mastication, but in relation to the famous painting known as *The Scream*, by Edvard Munch. One Muncher now and again might indeed be due to a confused person's temporal lobe playing horrible tricks. But when there is more than one, coincidence becomes a very nasty word in any policeman's vocabulary.

Cuthbertson was Muncher Number Three in as many months.

CHAPTER THREE

STEPINIT STREET, NEW THAMESWICK

ASHER LODGE STEPPED around a large and pungent lump of flesh peering down at him from under a beetled monobrow almost seven feet off the ground, and pushed open the door under the sign that read:

They Think It's Soul Over

He stood on the threshold, breathing in a heady coconut-tinged waft of imported air and taking in the carefully arranged ranks of flyers advertising exotic locations. Garish woodcuts of lush green alpine meadows with dancing milkmaids, or white sandy beaches lapped by azure seas adorned the walls. The words 'lush' and 'azure' were actually written and underlined in red on each one. On a desk in the middle of the room, two large signs in bold black on a cerise background positively demanded to be read:

Show them you care with this month's special—five years repayment on our deluxe pre-passing deal!

and,

Delay the pain for your dear departed with twelve months of paradise on an island of your choice!

Asher shook his head. He disliked hearse chasers. Admittedly, they weren't doing anything illegal, but places like this were knee-deep in soggy valley-bottom mud when it came to the moral, and mortal, high ground. He let the door shut behind him and heard the tethered cicada above it chirp to announce his presence. From behind a beaded curtain a man emerged. He grinned, showing more teeth than a photogenic shark in a face the colour of a ripe satsuma.

'Good morning, sir. Welcome to our 'umble hestablishment. Can I hoffer you some refreshment? Black tea p'raps? A nip of habsinthe?'

Asher let the salesman eye him up, knowing he'd see a man in his early thirties who could have done with putting on a little more weight, with drawn features accentuated by a halo of dark hair. He'd see pallor in his skin, but would have no idea that it had recently been a lot paler and that the dark smudges under sharp, cynical eyes were fading fast. All indicators, Asher knew, that could easily pass for grief in an establishment like this. He saw the man moisten his lips hungrily once he'd registered the signs. Business was business after all. But this wasn't the salesman's lucky day.

Asher smiled, reached into his pocket and took out his ID: a newish leather wallet containing a pewter badge depicting a stylised hawk above a many-branched tree and the letters 'FHIFAA'.

The orange-faced man's teeth disappeared under razor sharp, obsequious lips and his Adam's apple bobbed through a good two inches of travel as he gulped silently.

'Ah, Mr...sorry...*Hinspector* Lodge. How may I be of hassistance? If it's about our Crotapian bouncer on the door, I've been hassured that his visa's in the post—'

Asher held up his hand to cut him off. He leaned in to read the name badge pinned to the man's tunic and inhaled a sickly cloud of patchouli.

'I'm not here about the Crotapian, Mr...Malachite—'

'Please, call me Minty.' Malachite held out his hand.

Asher took it and shook. He felt his fingers gripped more tightly than was strictly necessary, but did not reciprocate. 'As I said, I'm not here about your employee, though you might want to have a little chat with him about personal hygiene. Quite apart from the smell, there was a rat-tail stump on his tie. That's… unpalatable.'

Malachite's smile returned to half power. 'Of course. Pilgrit gets a little peckish around this time of day.'

Asher glanced over his shoulder at the troll-like figure blocking out the light in the doorway. He looked capable of eating a small horse. Several of his compatriots had been prosecuted for doing exactly that. You didn't see many Crotapians acting as judges at gymkhanas anymore. Not since the blanket ban.

'They're a bit unpredictable, but they possess a certain presence, don't you think? Bit like hippopotamice.' Malachite let out a nervous little laugh.

Asher was still prepared to give Malachite the benefit of the doubt. After all, everyone needed to earn a living. But the irritating laugh grated. A lot. 'Exactly what need do you have for security? I don't see crowds clamouring to get in here.'

'It's not about stopping 'em getting in, it's more about encouragin' 'em to stay once they're 'ere.' Malachite winked. 'It takes time to fully appreciate the range of services we 'ave on hoffer.'

'I can imagine,' Asher said. 'But let me get to the point of my visit, Mr Malachite. I'm after information.'

Malachite's lips slid into downturned regret as he adopted a reverential tone. 'What we do 'ere, Hinspector, is hoffer a spiritual service. As such, we are bound by the same rules as the clergy, you know, client-priest privilege?'

'Spare me the lecture,' Asher said. 'We both know what really goes on here.'

'I can hassure you that our testimonials—'

'Are about as genuine as a cork wand. You may be able to fool the punters, Mr Malachite, so save the shoeshine for them.'

'Really, Hinspector, I must protest—'

'I know, for example, that you kept Mrs Gedorma Gascivon linked to an unmanned fortress off the coast of Northumbria for almost a year until she agreed to tell her son where she'd hidden the money.'

'I beg your pardon?' Malachite went into affronted mode with all the subtlety of a pantomime dame. 'I resent that suggestion—'

'It's not a suggestion. I know because she told me.'

Malachite's eyes widened. 'You're a necreddo? I didn't know they let your type into the…the…'

'Careful now,' Asher said, feeling the hairs on the back of his hands rise up and make his fists itchy. Never a good sign in his experience. 'You're neck-deep in horse manure as it is. You don't want to go completely under now, do you?'

Malachite's Adam's apple bobbed up and down alarmingly as he tried to swallow. Asher caught his eyes drifting towards a bone paperweight on his desk and guessed it was a porting artefact kept for such an occasion as this to facilitate a quick getaway.

'I wouldn't if I were you,' Asher said and flicked a small black scarab onto Asher's brocade tunic. 'There, now you're officially bugged. We can follow you anywhere.'

Malachite cleared his throat and drew himself up. 'Mrs Gascivon was a very stubborn lady. What we hoffer 'ere is an hopportunity for the recently departed to hexperience a little rest and recreation before they pass into the light. For many of them death is such a shock. We feel they hought to 'ave time to hadjust.'

'By anchoring them to a ruin somewhere with enchantments of dubious origin? Enchantments which are guaranteed to make them miserable?'

'Mrs Gascivon wanted somewhere near the sea.'

'Five yards from the beach is near the sea. Five miles off the coast is in it.' Asher shook his head. 'Look, I am not here to shut you down. And I'm not after names or places.'

Malachite's shoulders relaxed. 'So, what kind of hinformation can I 'elp you with exactly?'

'The Bewildered.'

'The Bewildered?' Malachite's voice shot up an octave. 'I wouldn't touch one with a punting pole.'

'Maybe not, but indulge me. What do you know about them?'

'Other than they're completely mad street people who argue with the man in the moon, you mean?'

'Good answer. Same as I'd get from anyone in New Thameswick. But the trouble is, you're not just anyone, are you, Mr Malachite?'

'Don't know what you mean.' Malachite's gaze slid away towards a poster of a cow wearing bells in a flower-dotted meadow.

'What happens to them when they die?'

'That is most definitely not my harea of hexpertise. I mean, we know they're 'omo sapiens that have slipped through the cracks and end up 'ere by mistake. And everyone knows it drives 'em a bit mad. What 'appens to 'em after they pop their footwear is not my concern.'

'Not your concern?'

'Habsolutely not.'

'Oh well, thank you for your time.' Asher pushed away from the desk.

Malachite looked stricken. 'Is that it?'

'Yes. You know nothing about Bewildered post-mortem soul transfer. I've made a note.'

'Right, good, hexcellent.' Malachite's panic gave way to a smile that beamed out in a can't-believe-my luck sort of a way. A triumphant smile that threatened to become a smirk at any moment. 'Delighted to be hof service, Hinspector Lodge.' Malachite coughed into his hand to hide his laughter.

Asher noted it. He had learned long ago to play the cards he'd been dealt. A skill developed out of good manners, a solid education, excellent diction and a respect for the law. All of which, if you did the maths, added up to 'prize pillock' in the republican eyes of New Thameswick's citizens. Someone with about as much street cred as a cardboard dagger. But being a pillock usually needed lack of insight as the clincher, and Asher had insight to spare. He knew what he was and he'd realised that if you let people believe you were a soft touch in the early exchanges, it meant you could easily sneak up on their blindside while they congratulated themselves for having outsmarted a twit. It was the chief form of entertainment for wide boys like Malachite. But the thing about cardboard daggers was that they could also give you a very nasty paper cut if you didn't handle them properly. They could even be fatal if the edge of that innocuous blade was dipped into something suitably poisonous.

Asher was neither a twit, nor a soft touch. And in general, people who believed that he was learned the hard way to hold onto their opinions until the dust settled. It had not yet settled in They Think It's Soul Over.

Malachite moved out from behind the desk and squeezed past Asher to hold open the door. He'd got as far as putting his hand on the handle when Asher said, 'Since you're in such a co-operative mood, Mr Malachite, I said I'd contact the Inland Revenants once I'd finished. They wanted a little chat. Funnily enough, you've been out the last eight times they've called.'

Malachite snatched his hand back as if the doorknob had turned into an Equatorian viper. 'The Revenants?' he repeated in a whisper.

'Yes,' Asher said. 'You keep a tight ship. I'm sure your books are in order. Shouldn't take them more than a couple of years to go through everything. They like to be thorough, as I'm sure you know. Like to leave no spiritual stone unturned. They've got some new arcane biocultware. They use mites to go over your books and then use mind-burrowing parasites to go over you... well, inside you actually. Find out all your dirty little secrets. You'd be surprised what people try and hide away in even the smallest, darkest, and most moist of crevices.'

Malachite turned a funny grey colour under the spray-on satsuma juice tan.

'Maybe I can ask around,' he said thickly.

Asher tilted his head to imply patience wearing a tad thin.

'Okay, we do talk about 'em sometimes,' said Malachite with an audible swallow. 'The Bewildered, that is. You know, me and my colleagues in the trade. Talk about 'em just like we talk about cockroaches. See the thing is, they're not on the books, not in the ledgers. I mean, where's the profit in that?'

Asher picked up on Malachite's derogatory description of the Bewildered and stored it away. 'So if you aren't interested in them, who is?'

'Do-gooders, mostly. You know. The right to die lot. I mean, truth is no one really knows what 'appens to 'em once they go, do they?'

'Only do-gooders?'

Malachite's eyes slid away. 'One or two others maybe. Look, I said I'd ask around, okay? Why are you so hinterested in a bunch of mad tramps, anyway?'

'Because…' Asher hesitated. He didn't like the chancer's glint he saw in Malachite's eye. He could almost see the scales shifting in the man's head, almost hear his inner voice wondering if there was the faintest possibility of coming out of this hairy scenario a couple of scruples ahead. But it really was none of his business. He didn't need to know there'd been a spate of killings. Not that anyone else in the damned city except Crouch gave a bag of cack about them. They all thought him mad to waste even one minute over it. After all, these were the Bewildered he was talking about here. Bloody nuisances. Human trash that constables were always clearing out from under filthy, tattered blankets and shop doorways of a morning, or arresting for screaming abuse at a horse after two flagons of begged, or stolen, axeberger wine.

But then no one else in the Department was a necreddo. No one else could hear the dead complaining about their treatment at the hands of slimy sods like Malachite and other dodgy transit shops like They Think It's Soul Over. And no one else heard the terrified screams of newly dead Bewildered almost every Thursday night like Asher did. It had been going on for weeks, and terrifying, harrowing, desperate screams they were, too. At first he'd thought them nightmares but now he knew that sometime within the following days he'd get a report from the constabulary about a body found in the river, or twisted and broken in an alley, or stuffed headfirst into a well. And he knew before anyone said anything that it would be one of the Bewildered.

Why they, of all of New Thameswick's vast array of citizens, could break through the psychic filters that stopped him hearing unwanted chatter from the dead when he slept, he had no idea. But break through they did. Asher had a vested interest in finding out who was killing them, if he wanted to get a good Thursday night's sleep.

His eyes refocused and fixed on Malachite.

'It's classified,' he said.

Malachite's smile froze. 'Right, well, I'll be in touch, Hinspector. But that means you won't be contacting the Revenants, yes?'

'I don't think we need to bother them…yet,' Asher said. 'I'll give you two days. And when I come back, that ugly brute guarding the door had better not stink like a ripe cheese.'

'I'll see what I can do. Only, if we give Pilgrit a bath, who's going to keep the flies away?'

The bad smell lingered in Asher's nose for a long time after leaving They Think It's Soul Over. It took a while, but slowly and grudgingly he realised it was a stench that surrounded the whole of the murdered Bewildered issue, and was not only confined to a smarmy post-mortem salesman and his Crotapian muscle.

He'd also been around death long enough to know that it was the stench of something very bad and very unnatural.

CHAPTER FOUR

JERICHO, OXFORD, ENGLAND

Hipposync Enterprises Catalogue Entry No. 34786
Philosophiae Naturalis, Principia Mathematica, NEWTON, Isaac.
1st edition, the rare and so-called export issue of 'the greatest work in the history of séance'. Published by Josef Streeter for the Royal Society, 1687. This is the sought-after three-line imprint, which includes the name of the bookseller, Samuel Smith. One of only 135 copies.
List price: £150,000

———

Roberta 'Bobby' Miracle read her entry and toyed, momentarily, with not replacing the word 'séance' with the word 'science', which is what was actually written on the typed description from which she was transcribing. She allowed herself a little smile; from what she'd heard of Newton's penchant for dabbling in all things supernatural, either word would have done nicely. Rereading the last sentence, she raised one dark eyebrow. £150,000 for a book seemed hardly believable. Even less believable was the fact that once entered into the sales catalogue of Hipposync Enterprises, there'd be a queue of collectors at least fifty yards long wanting to buy it. She still found that pretty amazing, but not as amazing as having that very book right next to her elbow on the desk as she entered its details. She considered it with mildly fearful eyes. It had no right to be worth as much. It was, after all, only a book. And yet someone thought it was worth that much because they were prepared to pay. And what exactly were they paying for? Words and knowledge and knowing that only 134 other people in the world had one like it. Less if you considered natural wastage like someone borrowing a copy from a library and never returning it so that it languished in a dusty attic. Or some eccentric member of the landed gentry using their copy for a doorstop and forgetting it was ever there so it ended up getting chewed to bits by a boisterous Labrador.

Fate loves its little jokes.

Bobby sighed. It didn't do to dwell on these things. It only made her feel weird. Still, a hundred and fifty thousand smackers worth of Newton's scribbles within spitting distance joined a long mental list of weird and wonderful things about Hipposync Enterprises. Things like the moment, two days before, when the boss, Mr Porter—cherubic, twinkling of eye and sporting an egg yolk stain the exact shape of New Zealand on his Fair Isle sweater—handed it to her.

'Pop this one on your pongcluetor, Roberta, that's a good girl. Time to top up the coffers, I'm afraid. Mrs Porter wants a new dinner set.' He finished the request with a chortle.

Pongcluetor was bad enough, but the chortle was the clincher. The list of people in Bobby's life who actually did chortle was a very short one and in terms of style, Mr Porter sat squarely at the top. She didn't generally approve of men calling her a good girl, either, but she made an exception for Mr Porter since he always prefaced it with her proper name and she genuinely thought he'd struggle to address her in any other way. She'd concluded, after the first two hours of her first day of the internship, that Mr Porter was a throwback from a different era, if not a different planet. An era that included rituals like a full English breakfast every morning, digestive biscuits with every cup of tea, twinkly eyes (as already described), a G&T at 6.00 pm, never commenting on another person's physical appearance, and a degree of eccentricity that would have had psychologists scrabbling for a pen and paper within five minutes of meeting him.

'Remember to make absolutely certain that this is the copy without the brandy stain on the inside cover,' he'd added—with a chortle—on handing her the book. 'Can't be sure myself. Not without me specs. I think it happened during a storm at sea. I'll be damned if I can remember where, though—you never knew where the blazes you'd end up with Daffy Darwin—though I do remember it was an excellent Calvados.' His eyes drifted off and for a second, Bobby swore she could hear the distant watery slap of a south sea swell against an oak hull. But then Mr Porter's twinkle re-engaged. 'I've got money on that one being in the loo at Porter Mansions. The stained one, I mean. Nothing like a spot of Newton to get you going first thing in the morning. If I'm wrong, let me know, and I'll swap 'em.'

Bobby had simply smiled and nodded and, like a drunken silk worm on its way home from the office party, managed somehow to follow Mr Porter's tortuous thread. She knew, even as she was doing it, that though her mouth was shaped into pleasant acceptance of his explanation, her eyes, more directly connected to her brain, were screaming, 'WTF?'

Buying and selling rare books was what Hipposync did and she'd been genuinely fascinated to learn about the business. They also, apparently, had a publishing arm, though she wasn't certain how long it reached even if she was fairly sure it didn't stretch to the sorts of literary fare found on the three-for-two tables at Waterstones, nor the daily deal on Amazon. *Voynich Revisited: A Contextual Analysis*, or *The Shardalas Chronicles of Apolostys* must have made someone's mouth water, but exactly who that someone was remained a mystery to Bobby.

'Keep up the good work,' Mr Porter had said, donning a voluminous coat with more pockets than a snooker table. 'I shall be back in a couple of weeks. Oh, and by the way, there'll be no hot food in the canteen while I'm away; I'm taking Mrs Hob… the chef, with me on holiday. She's good with my diet, you know. Keeps me regular. Kylah will, no doubt, look after you. We are off on a cruise, Mrs Porter and I.'

'Anywhere nice?' Bobby asked.

'The Adriatic, apparently. Thought I'd make a stop in Montenegro. Chap there says he has a copy of Lactantius' diary. Believe it when I see it. Toodle-oo.' He'd left the building with two 'business associates' in tow. Bobby wasn't sure what business Alf and Dwayne—which were the names she knew them by—were associated with exactly, but they looked very capable of doing it, whatever it was. At six foot four with dark eyes and a full beard, Alf looked like an evil henchman extra from any random British gangster film, while Dwayne, slight and sinewy, had more piercings than a…cushion made for pins. But they were also unfailingly polite as well as possessing a jolly, respectful humour that reminded Bobby of the brother of an old university friend who was a captain in the army, and Bobby found herself wondering if Alf and Dwayne might have been ex-forces, though she hadn't dared ask.

In fact, in the few short weeks of being at Hipposync, she'd decided that asking too many questions might not be her best approach. No one liked a nosy parker. And being liked was what it was all about at this stage of the give-us-a-job game. She knew Mr Porter quite liked her. But he was at the top of a small, tightly knit pyramid of management consisting of the Financial Controller, Miss Kylah Porter, niece of twinkly-eyes; and the sales director, Mr Matt Danmor. They were both young and dynamic, just a few years older than her own twenty-four years, and it was obvious they were in a relationship even though that was one of the things she hadn't asked about directly. In truth there was hardly any need. Judging by the odd sideways glance and the careful and studied efforts they made to avoid any impression of intimacy in the office environment, they might as well as both been wearing badges that read, *We're An Item*. Bobby had never seen gold-flecked eyes quite like Miss Porter's, and Mr Danmor's smile was a thousand-watt candelabra, but despite having both won prizes in the looks lotto, they seemed disarmingly and genuinely unaware of the fact. Seeing them desperately trying not to touch one another in the sardine tin environment of the tearoom behind reception was quite sweet. Bobby liked to think that she got on well with both of them.

She winced. There it was again. Her need to be liked. She

hated it, hated even acknowledging the desperate and pathetic nature of it, but as an intern, popularity was what it was all about. Bobby wasn't lazy but graduate trainee applications had so far led nowhere. Meanwhile she'd tried sales jobs with an estate agent and a recruitment agency but neither had lasted long. A 'recessionary slump' was the explanation in both instances. So an internship, *any* internship, in austere, credit-crunched, cash-strapped Britain was not to be sniffed at. A paid internship was something you did with a peg firmly clamped on your nose. And this one even had the promise of a job at the end of it. But jobs were rare and, in the spirit of the reality show competition that had infiltrated under the skin of Western society like a wriggly filariasis worm, Hipposync had decided to make it a contest.

She looked up from her screen and caught her rival looking at her.

Bobby smiled.

Pippa Elmsworthy smiled back and it was as if someone had suddenly lit a fire in the room. Pippa radiated deliciousness from every creamy, unblemished pore. Bobby had never seen limpid pools, but she was a hundred per cent certain they were an appropriate synonym for Pippa's baby blue eyes. Eyes that seemed possessed of a hypnotic power, judging by the way the postman had done an impression of an iced lollipop at midday in the Sahara when he'd brought a parcel in to be signed for that morning.

Even Mr Danmor had been seen to occasionally falter when Pippa had him in her sights. Though it had only happened the once, when Pippa managed to drop something behind the photocopier and had to lean over right next to where Mr Danmor was standing. To be fair to him, and bearing in mind he'd been able to read the maker's name on the suspenders holding up Ms Elmsworthy's stockings in that moment, he'd barely missed a beat. His raised eyebrows had morphed seamlessly into a little smile of recognition before transforming back into inquisitive politeness at the question Pippa had asked him prior to bending over. Bobby hoped fervently that smile meant he was wise to her games. Just as she hoped Miss Porter was, too.

Certainly from what she'd seen, the latter, who had her own set of laser irises, seemed impervious to the Elmsworthy charms. The trouble was that it wasn't only the eyes with Pippa, they were simply the icing on the strawberry blonde, toned of limb, all the right 'junk' suitably placed and firmly bolted on, cupcake. A package that added up to making it almost impossible not to notice the Pip, as Bobby had christened her (since 'the pip' was exactly what Ms Elmsworthy induced in Bobby whenever she was in the same room). It wasn't dislike Bobby felt, more a burgeoning awareness that they were polite rivals doing their utmost to be nice to one another while at the same time praying one of them would spill tea all over a *Principia Mathematica*, or something equally as irreplaceable. Bobby did not like herself for feeling that way, but she was honest enough to mentally admit it.

The click of the office door opening made both girls break off from their mutual smiles as in crept the stooped figure of Miss White-Tandy. In reality, it was more a slow crablike shuffle than a creep, slow being the predominant adjective. Miss WT—if she did have a first name, no one in the building seemed to know it—did everything slowly, largely because the circuits governing her motor function were well past their best before date. The Pip had decided that Miss WT was at least ninety, and Bobby wasn't going to argue.

'Gentleman with a book enquiry, if one of you would be so kind,' Miss WT announced with a slow vibrato that matched the repetitive articulations of her head.

'Thank you,' said Pippa.

Miss WT acknowledged the polite response with a slight nod and the pulling back of her lips, which, as expressions went, would have qualified equally as a smile or a grimace. She began to shuffle through a 180-degree turn and manoeuvred out of the room, closing the door behind her.

Bobby went back to her task. They'd agreed a rota for dealing with walk-ins, and it was most definitely, totally, absolutely, not Bobby's turn.

She heard the Pip get up, heard the clacking of heels on the wooden floor. It took her a moment before she realised the clacking was getting louder, not quieter, indicating that the Pip was approaching.

'Bobby,' the Pip breathed in a part-of-the-package husky voice, and leaned a hand on Bobby's desk. Said hand bore inexpensive, but classy jewellery and nail varnish to match the blue of the Pip's irises perfectly. 'I know it's my turn, I do. I really, really do. Only I'm in the middle of this really important thing for Miss Porter? It's a really long description of a Middoth thingy and it's been translated really badly? It's taken me ages to get halfway through it and if I stop now I'm frightened I'll lose my thread? Would you, just this once? It's the last time I ever ask you, I promise. I'll see the next three, I promise.'

Bobby turned her head slowly to look up into the Pip's exquisite, peachy face, forcing the muscles around her lips into a rictus smile.

'That's what you said last time and the time before.'

The limpid pools widened. It would be so easy to fall in and drown. 'I know. I know I'm pathetic. But I have this concentration thing? I was useless in school and the teachers had to give me extra time to do my exams?'

Bobby knew she should have organised her face into an expression of sympathy, but the narrowing of her eyes had more to do with an intense irritation at the way the Pip ended every single sentence on a questioning upswing.

'Surely, ten minutes won't—'

'But it will, it always does. I know you've helped me out loads over the last month. You've been sooo nice?'

The scream in Bobby's head, labelled 'sod off' and destined for her mouth, did a ninety-degree turn at her tonsils, bounced off the inside of her skull and was finally and ignominiously shouldered out of the way by a pullman of words that chugged its way up from the soft centre of her heart. She shut her eyes, counted to five and said, 'You are *so* going to have to see the next four, okay? No exceptions.'

Pippa smiled, and Bobby saw the limpid pools shimmer. She put her hand on Bobby's upper arm and squeezed in a gesture of gratitude. 'You're a treasure, Bobby.'

'Should be buried on a far-flung island in the middle of the ocean, you mean?' Bobby said, adding a jaunty tilt of her head in case she didn't get the joke.

The Pip continued to smile, but with no hint of registered humour. She repeated the squeeze before removing her hand from Bobby's arm and turning away.

Bobby sighed, saved her work on the PC and stood.

'How about I get us both a coffee while you see the customer?' the Pip suggested. 'I think I've got some yoghurty biccies, too. Think of it as our little reward for not turning into dust in this *desiccated old mausoleum.*' The last three words were delivered in a half-whisper meant clearly to imply that the two interns were definitely in 'it' together as co-conspirators.

Bobby watched, open-mouthed, as she clopped across to the door, too flabbergasted and infuriated by the girl's sheer, rhinoceros-hide gall to do anything but fume in silence and reflect how much she would have enjoyed seeing the Pip dropped in a couple of tons of 'it' from a great height at that moment.

CHAPTER FIVE

WALK-INS WERE SEEN in the interview room: a windowless box rendered passably welcoming by a desk inlaid with leather, some comfortable swivel chairs and a bookcase groaning under the weight of hardcovered tomes with catchy titles like *The Birds of America* by John James Audubon and *Cosmographia* by Claudius Ptolemaeus. Not a Grisham or a Sayers or a Tolkien in sight.

Bobby opened the door and saw a man wearing a safari jacket, jeans, and orthopaedic-class trainers rise from one of the comfortable chairs. Numerous layers of clothing under the jacket bore witness to the chilly weather outside. She stepped across the threshold and found herself peering into a pair of surprised-looking washed out eyes behind horn-rimmed glasses. Bobby immediately concluded he was American. The beginnings of a greyish beard lent his face a grubby appearance, which suggested lack of shaving facilities rather than the trendy stubble so many favoured these days in the vain hope it might make them look manly, but succeeded only in making them look like lazy, unshaven bums. Thick fingers swept spidery grey hair out of the pale eyes before offering a hand to Bobby. She took it and grimaced inwardly. It was, as she feared, slightly greasy.

'Name's Fitzgerald. Brandon Fitzgerald.' The accent confirmed her assessment in one drawl.

'Nice to meet you, Mr Fitzgerald,' Bobby said, taking in the empty cup of coffee on the desk and the way Brandon Fitzgerald clutched a battered backpack to his chest. 'I see that our receptionist has already offered you some refreshments.'

'Yes, she has. Is this some sort of exotic java blend? Flavours were really interesting.'

Bobby smiled. Miss WT's idea of coffee involved letting it steep for a minimum of four hours. Bobby often wondered if she'd learned her trade during a previous existence as a barista in the grand bazaar in Istanbul.

'Please, have a seat.'

Fitzgerald sat and Bobby took her place on the other side of the desk. She enjoyed sitting in this chair because with it came power. Not the 'I'm the boss and you're the underling' type of power. This was something else altogether. Something odd and rather wonderful emanating from the books on the shelves behind her. With her back to them she swore she could feel their scholarship flowing around her and through her, seeping into her body. It didn't hurt that the weight of all that knowledge possessed an extra oomph by dint of a combined value of several million pounds. This was Mr Porter's collection and as a consequence, Hipposync's inventory. Allowing them to sit in this room completely unattended spoke volumes of the confidence the company had in its clientele. The Pip, of course, thought they were completely insane to do so. Bobby suspected there was security of some sort, but it operated at a level invisible to her and everyone else. All she knew was that no one had ever tried to steal anything. But the Pip's reservations made her concentrate on Fitzgerald afresh. His clothes were rather scruffy. Just her luck if this was the client who would be the exception to the rule.

Bobby cleared her throat. 'Well, Mr Fitzgerald, what exactly is it we can do for you? Are you after anything in particular?'

Fitzgerald blinked. 'Wasn't easy to find this place. Been in England for a week, Oxford for two days.'

'Oh? I'm sorry to hear that,' Bobby said. 'We're a bit old fashioned. No website yet, even.' She proffered a smile and hoped that Fitzgerald didn't read the irony twinkling behind it. Calling

Hipposync Enterprises a bit old fashioned was like calling the Titanic a bit sunk.

'Fact is, I am selling, not buying,' Fitzgerald said.

'Ahh.' Bobby nodded. They'd covered this in one of the team talks. Miss Porter had explained that they were always in the market for a good book. 'So what exactly is it you're selling?'

At last, the tatty backpack was lifted away from Fitzgerald's chest, but he hesitated and his pale, expressionless eyes suddenly flashed.

Here it comes, Bobby thought.

'Say, you guys have Halloween at a different time to us? I mean you are in fancy dress, right?'

Bobby's smile, the one that showed no gum line and was framed by carefully applied aubergine lipstick, did not falter despite an inner seething that approached Gas Mark 7. She glanced down at her black lace ruffled blouse, black maxi skirt, and platform boots with silver clasps.

'No, Mr Fitzgerald, it is not Halloween and I am not in fancy dress.'

'No? Only with your hair half black and half white, with pink streaks like it is—'

'Not Halloween. And neither are my nails naturally dark purple, nor my upper eyelids naturally smoky grey. However this is Great Britain, and the last time I checked, it remains a free country. What you see, Mr Fitzgerald, is my chosen aesthetic. If it offends you, I would be happy to arrange for another member of staff—'

'No, no,' Fitzgerald said, backtracking. 'The thing is…'

Bobby lifted her eyebrows. A gesture that, when employed in such circumstances, was designed to induce mild discomfort in the critic. And the world was full of critics. They were as ubiquitous as insects and just as annoying. Fitzgerald, who would have easily passed for a woodlouse, looked like he wanted to crawl under the table.

'What is it you have for us, Mr Fitzgerald?' Bobby put him out of his misery.

This time the backpack made it all the way to his lap.

Sausage fingers unzipped a compartment and took out a square shape wrapped in green felt. He placed the parcel on the desk and peeled open the wrapping to reveal a slightly battered-looking book, its leather scuffed and worn. Slowly, Fitzgerald rotated the book and opened the cover so Bobby could read it.

Mary Shelley
Frankenstein or The Modern Prometheus

Bobby scanned the page breathlessly, looking for and finding the printer's details.

London: for Lackington, Hughes, Harding, Mavor, & Jones, 1818

'One of my favourites,' Bobby said, trying not to squeal.

'There's more,' Fitzgerald added in a dry, deep tone.

With trembling fingers, he carefully turned another page. There, in a bold handwriting, were the words:

To Lord Byron
From M. Shelley

'Ah,' Bobby said again, her frozen-on smile never slipping. 'That is interesting. And where exactly did you get this from, Mr Fitzgerald?'

Fitzgerald's eyes flicked up from the book and engaged Bobby's. A spark of challenge flickered within them. 'Found it in my grandfather's attic. We're finally thinking of selling his old place. I was sifting through junk and came across this at the bottom of a trunk, under a pile of crockery and old photos.'

'I see,' Bobby said. 'And may I ask why you chose to come to us as opposed to any of the other, bigger dealers?' Because there were bigger dealers. Lots of bigger dealers and many of them in the United States.

Fitzgerald's eyes blinked and stared, blinked and stared again behind the glasses. 'Well, my granddad, he was what you might call something of a rogue. As you can tell from my name, he was of Irish descent and known to be a little light fingered. One of the reasons he crossed the pond was to escape being thrown in jail. I don't want any Fitzgerald dirty laundry on display.'

Bobby imagined a rotating line of grubby underwear. 'Are you saying you suspect this might be stolen property?'

'No, I am not saying that. Let's just say that provenance is not going to be easy to come by. I heard Hipposync is very discreet.'

'Oh, we are, we are,' Bobby said, reassuringly. She pushed herself away from the desk. 'Would you excuse me for one moment? Can I get you another coffee?'

'Sure, uh…maybe some tea this time?'

Bobby stepped outside, closed the door and stood with her back to it, inhaling a couple of deep breaths through flared nostrils and fighting the urge to whoop. Though she had no idea how much such a book would be worth on the open market, an electric frisson of excitement rippled through her and told her that this was, indeed, a significant find.

She stuck her head through the door to reception and spoke to Miss WT. 'Could you supply Mr Fitzgerald with a cup of tea this time, Miss White Tandy?'

'Tea, dear? I think we could manage that,' came the warbled reply.

'Thanks.' Bobby wondered, fleetingly, if Fitzgerald knew what he was letting himself in for; if he thought the coffee was strong, Miss WT's tea could easily weather-proof wooden fencing. But it would take at least ten minutes at the rate Miss WT poured and stirred.

Bobby, her cheeks flushed, quick-stepped back to her office. The Pip greeted her, beaming.

'That didn't take too long,' she said. On the screen in front of her a kitten was attempting, and succeeding, to play 'Three Blind Mice' by padding up and down a piano keyboard.

'I see you're busy,' said Bobby.

'I just love kitten videos on YouTube,' Pippa gushed.

Bobby took two steps closer and stared at the screen and the thumbs up likes. 'You and a million other…fans, or so it seems. Who even posted this? Who's HBK_23 when he's at home?'

'How 'Bout them Kittens 16? Who knows? Don't you think it's cute, though?' Pippa pouted.

Bobby shook her head. 'Does about as much for me as cold custard.' She turned and went back to her desk. 'I need to look up what the punter's brought with him.'

'Anything interesting?' The Pip got up and joined Bobby at her workstation. She was holding a mug of steaming brown liquid in her left hand.

'Where's mine?' Bobby asked.

The Pip made a face. 'Only enough milk for one, I'm afraid? I didn't know how long you were going to be, so…'

Bobby shook her head. But the truth was, it didn't matter. The *Frankenstein* was much more important. And another coffee was only going to put more pressure on a bladder already three-quarters full from the day's mandatory litre of detoxifying water. Bobby typed in her search and watched as the screen filled with information. From behind her, she heard the Pip say, 'Wow.'

They were on Christaby's site. According to them, only five hundred copies of this edition were printed, and the last one with a signature had gone for £250,000. *What*, wondered Bobby, *would one dedicated to Lord Byron fetch?*

'I think I need to find Miss Porter,' Bobby said, as several dozen moths fluttered in her chest.

'She's out, they're both out. Urgent business, she told me. Not back for another half an hour at least?'

'Damn. Then I'm going to have to entertain Mr Fitzgerald until she gets back. I don't want this one wriggling off the hook.'

'She is going to love this,' the Pip said. And was that a slight quiver in her voice?

'Only if it turns out to be genuine. Right, I need the loo before I go back and sweet-talk our bibliophile.' She turned and hurried out, suppressing the urge the punch the air.

The staff loo was downstairs at the end of a very long corridor that took her into the back end of the building. Here were the offices of both the Porters, Mr Danmor, DC Farmer the company scribe, and stairs down to the basement. She opened the door at the end of the corridor and hurried down the steps, negotiating the wooden trunks taking up a lot of the space. The stencilled letters, DOF, marked several of these boxes. She'd received an oddly evasive reply from Mr Porter when she asked what DOF meant.

'DOF? Ah, now, that is a very interesting question and the very best person to answer that would be my niece.' He'd turned his twinklies towards Miss Porter.

She had not been anywhere near as evasive, yet Bobby had seen her fire-shot eyes dance away as she explained, 'Disused Old Furniture. Antiques and such like. We recycle it in those trunks. Transport them to a recycling unit.'

It was weird, but then again, Hipposync was weird central. And if Bobby Miracle was honest with herself, that was why she felt so at home here. Because there was weird, as in leaving a room and forgetting your keys only to walk back in two seconds later to find all the furniture suddenly stacked up in a passable impression of the Eiffel tower, and there was *weird*, as in the misplaced feeling of suddenly finding yourself somewhere you felt you always belonged because there, weird was the norm, not the exception. Not that Bobby considered herself at all weird. No, that was everyone else's problem, though it had a tendency to want to become Bobby's whenever she ventured out into the wide world. The fact was that very few places engendered a sense of belonging in Bobby, but Hipposync had that quality in spades. She'd promised herself she would do everything she could to make it stay that way and woodlouse Fitzgerald looked like he might be a first-class ticket.

There were two more doors in the basement, one with and one without a handle. The one with a handle was, mercifully, unoccupied. It was a cold, soulless little room. Aromatherapy oil did a lot to mask the smell of mushrooms and worse that pervaded the air. Bobby bit the bullet and made herself remember they were, after all, right next to the canal in Jericho.

The loo seat was black plastic and very cold. But Bobby wasn't there to make herself comfortable. Bladder empty, she washed her hands and examined her face in the mirror above the washbasin. She pulled her lips back from her teeth. Good, no smudges there. The aubergine lipstick, too, was intact and she let out a wry snort. Fancy dress indeed. She heard that and the

Halloween question at least three times a week and it truly did not bother her.

Well, not much anyway.

And yes, she was making a statement. Exactly like people with a dozen piercings, or with facial tattoos. It was a personal choice. And yes, it was a touch Goth, but corporate Bobby Goth was a million miles from university and teen Bobby Goth. She kept it smart and simple, always black or grey, velvet jackets, longish skirts or black trousers, offset perhaps with a mandarin collared silk blouse in scarlet or blue, but usually gunmetal. The only leather on show was a handbag or shoes, which sometimes were platform ankle boots with trousers, or kitten heel maryjanes with a dark skirt and tights. Very occasionally DMs when the mood took her. With her skin as pale as it was, the look really suited her and black was considered slenderising, which was as good an answer for the 'Why do you always wear it?' brigade as any. She thought of the Pip's fashion victim style and shuddered. Bobby Miracle would have looked ridiculous in fake tan with her midriff on display. So yes, she did really like Poe and everything Sherlock-related; she loved walking through Oxford's evocative dark streets; and Holywell cemetery, off Cross Street, was probably her favourite place in the world. But so what? It was quiet and serene, full of memories and history, like a plantation of statues. A place full of drunkenly leaning cross pattées, saltires and Celtic wheel heads. Even the music flowing through her head was of a type. Down here in the bowels of Hipposync, where they were so near to the canal, she could almost hear PJ Harvey singing 'Down by the Water'. And yes, it had driven her parents wild when she'd been a teenager. But she wasn't a kid anymore.

So why bother, as the Pip had so bluntly asked?

She bothered because it was who she was. In was in her DNA. End of. When she got up in the morning, contemplating dressing in any other way simply never, ever occurred to her. And yes she knew that it would result in people staring and asking questions, and wondering why it was she decided to look like a long-lost (but glamorous) cousin of the Munsters. But Mr Porter hadn't stared, nor Miss Porter, nor Mr Danmor, nor Miss WT. They had barely batted an eyelid and that was one of the things she really, really liked about Hipposync. They were all so non-judgemental. And if she handled Fitzgerald and his *Frankenstein* correctly, she might just get to stay.

Right, go on, get up there and charm him with everything you known about the good ol' US of A. Bobby saluted herself in the mirror and turned to leave, put her hand on the door handle, depressed it and pulled. But pulling was as far as she got because despite yanking hard, the door itself would not budge.

Cursing, she yanked harder. Was it possible the lock had jammed? But this was the door to the corridor. There was no lock. Bobby slapped the wood with her hand and yanked again on the handle, this time with both hands, all to no avail. What on earth was going on? After three more minutes of yanking, she started to yell.

'Hello? Hello? Can anyone hear me?'

She knew the answer before the words had truly escaped her lips. She was as far away from anyone who could hear as it was possible to be. With two solid doors and thirty feet of corridor between her and the slightly deaf Miss WT, she might as well have been in a different country.

Phone.

Bobby squeezed her eyes shut. She'd brought her handbag to the loo, but the phone lay on her desk, connected through a USB umbilical to her PC, where it was charging nicely. Disappointment and frustration twisted inside her. What about Mr Fitzgerald and his *Frankenstein* sitting in the interview room? He would think that she'd abandoned him.

Her groan of frustration turned into a tooth-grinding roar.
Why?

Why, of all the bloody times she'd been down here did this have to happen now?

Bobby's tooth-grinding roar turned into a scream of unbridled exasperation.

Inside her head an old pantomime song kept going around and around like a stuck record.

Oh dear what can the matter be
Three old ladies stuck in the lavatory

Except she substituted 'three old ladies' with 'Bobby the idiot'.

She could have wept.

But she didn't.

It wasn't something a Miracle did.

CHAPTER SIX

When the door finally opened, Bobby had been incarcerated for almost twenty-five minutes.

Miss WT shuffled in, her initial surprise giving way instantly to mild admonishment.

'There you are,' she warbled. 'We wondered where you'd got to. Tummy trouble? I can come back if you need some time for the air to clear. I may even have a candle—'

'The air is perfectly okay, thank you,' Bobby said with exaggerated calm. 'The door jammed.'

'Really? Well, I'd hurry back upstairs if I were you, dear. Miss Porter is looking for you.'

Bobby opened her mouth to speak, thought better of it, and sprinted out and up the stairs along the corridor to the interview room. She slowed to a quick walk a few yards from the door, took a deep breath and threw it open. 'I'm so sorr—' The apology froze unfinished. The room was empty. 'No, no, no,' she wailed.

'Bobby, is that you?' The Pip's disembodied voice drifted out from the direction of the office.

Bobby slammed her open palm down on the leather inlaid desk and squeezed her eyes shut for a count of three before storming out, complaining loudly as she walked. 'Can you believe it, I got locked in the bl—'

The rarely used, but heartfelt oath she was about to deliver died on her lips as she registered who was present in the office.

Pippa was not alone. She, Miss Porter, and Mr Danmor were sporting purple gloves and all three wore a flushed look of triumphant surprise. The sort of look seen occasionally on the faces of holidaymakers who book last minute deals fully expecting a half completed dungeon on the edge of a building site but who find, on getting out of the complimentary airport bus, that their £157-for-a-week-all-in has bagged them a penthouse apartment in Puerta Banús. Obviously the result of an administrative cock up, and obviously something they'd need to report…once the week was over. Said look was starkly evident on the Pip's face as she held up a book that looked the exact size, shape, and colour of Fitzgerald's *Frankenstein*.

'Bobby,' Mr Danmor said, 'where have you been? You've missed all the excitement.'

But Bobby didn't reply. Or rather couldn't reply. The bit of her brain that controlled speech had been hijacked by despair and confusion. All she could do was stare at the book in the Pip's hand and croak, 'Is that what I think it is?'

'Yes, it is. Isn't it fantastic?' The Pip's teeth gleamed.

'But…'

'When you didn't come back for, like, ages, I thought I'd better go and talk to Mr Fitzgerald? He wanted to discuss money and—'

'And,' Miss Porter took over, 'Pippa, here, brokered a cash deal.'

'Cash deal?' Bobby mumbled.

'£100,000,' Mr Danmor said, grinning.

'But it's worth—' Bobby began.

'Three times as much on the open market.' Mr Danmor nodded. 'It's a steal.'

Miss Porter sent him a warning look. 'What Mr Danmor is trying to say is that Mr Fitzgerald has gone away happy, and we are likely to make a significant profit.'

'But…but what about provenance?' Bobby asked. 'I was going to find you and ask what—'

'It's fine,' Miss Porter said, with a wave of her hand. 'We had it checked. Mr Fitzgerald's grandfather won it in a card game in London in 1904.'

'But, how do you know?'

Miss Porter's eyebrows went up a notch. 'You should be aware by now, Bobby, that we have some unique methods here.'

Bobby managed to nod. But knowing that Hipposync used unique methods did very little to explain them.

'Want to look?' the Pip asked.

'No,' Bobby said, a little too quickly, staring at the proffered book.

'You should,' Miss Porter said. 'It's a rare find. It has a dedication to—'

'Lord Byron, I know. I was *the one* who met Fitzgerald. I was going to sit with him until you got back.'

'Got back?' Miss Porter frowned. 'From where?'

Bobby turned to the Pip. 'You said they were out?'

'I thought they were. But you came back early, didn't you?' She turned her searchlight eyes on Mr Danmor.

'We did. But we've been back in the office for the last forty minutes.'

Bobby knew that she was breathing too quickly. When two fingers started to tingle, she reached for a chair and sat down. 'I was going to come and tell you, but I thought you were out, and then I went to the loo and…' Bobby's explanation spluttered out of her, but Mr Danmor's frown froze her words.

'If something like this comes through the door it's red alert time, Bobby. You have to find someone immediately. The loo can wait. Luckily, Pippa had the good sense to—'

'I went to the loo because I thought you weren't here,' Bobby explained. It sounded desperate and petulant even to her ears. 'Then the damned door jammed and I couldn't get out. I yelled and banged but no one could hear me.'

'Really? The door jammed? That's unusual.' Mr Danmor's lower lip came forward.

'I had Fitzgerald eating out of my hand. I—'

'Well, thankfully, no harm done,' Mr Danmor said. 'Thanks to Pippa.'

The Pip blushed disarmingly.

Bobby wanted to scream.

'Now, you'll have to excuse me as I have some other business to attend to,' Mr Danmor announced. 'Kylah, can I have a word?'

'I'll get someone to check the loo door for you, Bobby,' Miss Porter said as a parting shot. There must have been something in Bobby's face that twanged her sympathy string because she stepped back and put her hand on Bobby's arm. 'Put this one down to experience, okay?'

Experience my elbow, thought Bobby.

CHAPTER SEVEN

THE AFTERNOON WENT STEADILY DOWNHILL from there. The Pip finally made her a cup of tea with fresh milk—having volunteered to go out and buy some. Despite an unaccustomed spoonful of sugar, Bobby could only taste bitter disappointment in the warm brown liquid. She excused herself once to check out the loo, inspecting the door for any sign of interference and finding none. The door itself was solid with a single brushed steel handle. At the end of the corridor beyond were some stacked chairs. On impulse, Bobby took one and placed it so that the backrest lodged under the handle. The fit was almost perfect, jamming the handle and preventing the door from opening.

But finding such mundane and convenient means did not prove anything. And anyway who would want to do such a thing? Top of the list was the Pip, of course. But was that vapid mind capable of sabotage? And she would surely have heard the Pip's four-inch heels on the stairs, or, even barefoot, the scrape of the chair against the door. Then there was Miss WT. She seemed the most unlikely of all since she'd been left in reception making Fitzgerald tea, and the time it would have taken her to walk down the corridor could probably be measured in geological terms. So that only left Miss Porter and Mr Danmor. Bobby shook her head.

This was stupid.

Back at her desk, she fell into a despondent funk. She saw no sign of Miss Porter or Mr Danmor for the rest of the afternoon. Bobby left promptly at 5 pm, refusing the Pip's offer of a quick drink, wanting only to go home to lick her wounds.

A two-bedroom flat above a café on the Iffley road was what Bobby laughingly called her *résidence*, in a kitsch French accent. She shared it with a girl she'd known from school: a John Lewis management trainee currently on a five-week course in Bristol. So Bobby went home to the remnants of a day-old fish pie and a half bottle of sauvignon to brood. And brood she did.

She'd blown it at Hipposync. Fitzgerald's *Frankenstein* had been her one golden opportunity and it needed to be golden to compete with the goddess, Pip. The brooding became increasingly morose so that by the time the bottle was three-quarters empty, a plan of some sort had formed in her head. It stank of defeat and cheesy umbrage and the need to save face, but ignominy was a word that Bobby despised. She'd leave Hipposync and look for somewhere else. It would save them the trouble of booting her out. She'd say she had another offer.

And as ill thought out plans went it probably ranked up there with Lieutenant Colonel Custer turning down the offer of Gatling guns for the Battle of the Little Bighorn with a dismissive wave and, 'Nah, we'll be fine.'

What she needed was someone with whom to talk this through. Even more depressing was the stark realisation that there was no one. Of course there was the usual host of Insta friends, all of whom would comment if she posted her status as 'Downer after work cock-up' with pithy suggestions. But for six months she'd used the excuse of having no Wi-Fi at the flat to avoid trying to keep up with the social media froth. She did not miss in the slightest reading that someone was 'About to eat, yummee' or an emo 'Why me' rant from a member of the living dead. And telling the world about being locked in a loo qualified more for ROFLOLs than actual sympathy, of that there was no doubt. Of course she had parents who would have listened, but it was a habit that had simply not developed.

Of all the people she could think of who would be wise and come up with exactly the right tactic to deal with the situation, there was only one. But Lucille Miracle, Bobby's paternal grandmother, had long since passed. When she died, many of the emotional links Bobby had with home died, too. Her parents weren't unkind or stupid, but they were dispassionate and happy to delegate much of the early parenting skills that they did not possess to Lucille. Bobby would as likely telephone her mother and father for sympathy and advice as go to Somalia on a sailing holiday.

At midnight, with the sauvignon drained, Bobby Miracle went to bed.

CHAPTER EIGHT

A THREE-QUARTER MOON framed Holywell cemetery in silver and shadow; the air as still as frozen water, the trees winter bare. Bobby wandered along an icy path, the stars above reflecting in the glimmering dewdrops on the grass at her feet. She was hurrying, her bladder, as it had been that afternoon, full.

At last she came to an uncomfortable standstill. A crypt guarded on the one side by a lion, on the other by a great dog, stood before her. In its granite facade a door awaited her; the exact same loo door as had mysteriously jammed and locked her in that morning. Without hesitation, Bobby opened the door onto the Hipposync bathroom and flicked on the light. Black plastic loo seat in a cubicle, Brown and Durant toiletries, as expected.

Bobby checked her appearance in the mirror and saw that her eyeliner was thicker and her lips darker than she normally wore. A tap dripped in the sink and she instinctively reached out to turn it off. But when she looked back up into the mirror, she was not alone. There, staring intently out at her was Pippa Elmsworthy. Well, Pippa after an hour in a makeup chair on the set of *Saw 75*.

The fine hair on Bobby's bare arms brambled to attention as a cold shudder passed through her. She wheeled around, but the room behind her stood empty. Slowly, she turned back to the mirror.

Pippa, her hair matted, the skin around her eyes cracked and dark as smoke, the limpid pools themselves now terror-filled turbulent seas, continued to stare back.

Bobby heard the outer door click shut. She went to it and depressed the handle and found it locked once again. Across the room, in the mirror, Pippa shook her head as if in warning.

And then Bobby heard it. Something moving outside, rustling the frozen grass in whispering motion. There came the sound of a hundred chalks on a hundred blackboards, only she knew that this was not chalk: these were nails scraping against the panels of the crypt-loo door. As she watched, the surface began bulging inwards to take on the shape of a body. Bobby took several nervous steps back, her eyes fixed on the door.

When she glanced at the mirror, Pippa's eyes were wide and staring with an abject terror, her head still shaking. She looked terrified. And with good reason, because whatever prowled on the other side of the door was clearly trying to get in. It would be madness to try and open it now, to confront whatever was there. Bobby's eyes darted from Pippa to the door and back again. This time, the reflected girl opened her mouth in a silent, terrified scream.

The door groaned again and Bobby dragged her eyes back to it. Quickly, she scrambled into the cubicle, shut the door, and sat on the loo. She heard the door open with a creak. Heard the wind moan and the dragging noise of something approaching. Instinct drove her back and she half fell onto the seat.

And as she fell in the most ungainly manner, she kept going. , down through where the seat should have been, through the floor of the cemetery, a helter-skelter ride of flailing arms and twisting turns until, at last, she landed and jerked herself awake.

SOMEONE ELSE DREAMT, too. In another city, in another world—one usually hidden from human eyes. And yet even there the dreams had a very human theme.

Asher Lodge did not need unconsciousness to speak to the dead. An inherited skill, he was born with the power to switch that ability on or off. Of course, when it came to most of his relatives, he made sure that the switch was on for at least an hour every week, and especially on birthdays, Samhain, the Winter solstice and, for his Uncle Stan, the weekend of the Donnegaltee dog races.

Normally when he slept, his unconscious mind took no calls, except, it seemed on Thursday nights.

Tonight was Thursday night.

The scream began like the far off screech of a hunting bird glimpsed on the distant horizon: barely audible but high-pitched and keening, tugging at his dream awareness like a bothersome child. From there it grew into a steam engine whistle, insistent and loud until the crescendo howl of unimaginable pain and horror thrust him into full consciousness, panting and sweating, the echo of its stark terror reverberating inside his skull like a gong.

Asher sat up and quickly lit a candle. His pocket watch said 3.10 am. The darkest hour. He swept back his hair, letting his pulse slow to a canter. He would get up and read to rid himself of the horror he'd shared. Across the room, reflected in the light of the candle, two green eyes stared back at him. Borodin was a cat that shared the space of Asher's apartment. At least it had a cat's body, though Asher suspected that inside that body existed something else altogether. A mind that was part feline (judging from the way it could disassemble small animals), part circus acrobat (judging from the way it could clean parts of its body that should not, rightly, ever have a tongue anywhere near them unless it was someone else's and then only in certain niche circles), and part death row criminal (judging from the way it sat, sometimes for hours, staring out of the window at the world outside). Since trans-species relocation into animals was known to be an alternative form of punishment for the most severe forms of crime, and occasionally a great protective option for criminal trial witnesses who might never want to be found, Asher also suspected that the powers responsible might have been having a bit of a laugh when it came to Borodin. The only thing he could be completely sure of was that Borodin never let on.

'Bad dream,' Asher said, as the cat watched him pad to the bathroom. 'Go back to sleep.'

Asher felt bothered not only by the recurrent dream but also by the knowledge that this time it had been different. This time there had been two terrified, agonised voices. He tried not to think what that implied as he washed his hands. Fetching some water, he sat in a chair under a flickering lamp and read that day's newspaper, which he'd bought and not had time to look at. He felt a warm, furry body rub against his bare leg and reached down to scratch an upturned head.

'Maybe tomorrow we can ask Crouch if he knows anything, eh?'

Borodin purred in response.

CHAPTER NINE

FHIFAA HQ in New Thameswick occupied a corner block at the junction of Worming Street and Poultice Rd. Built of granite and marble in a baroque style, the building exuded power and impregnability, and felt damp and cold even on the hottest July day. Now, in early winter, Asher made sure he wore a heavy coat over his jacket. A coat he was not likely to remove until he got home that evening. Above the door, an ornate carving of a hawk sitting atop a tree depicted an organisation with keen eyes and myriad branches. Surrounding the emblem was a wreath upon which were carved the words:

Fae Human Intelligence & Felonious Activities Agency

Upstairs, Asher sat at a desk in a soulless room opposite a feckless colleague called Braithwaite, whose chief interests in life were sport, drinking, and women. This morning, Braithwaite nursed a hangover 'the size of a stripper's tip' and had a mouth like a 'satchel of cricket boxes'. A night out with some old schoolmates had turned into a 'beasting session'. And though Braithwaite didn't actually use his fingers to make quotation marks in the air, he might as well have. Because he obviously thought that way and spoke that way, emphasising each well-practised idiom and metaphor in a way that told Asher that such phrases were common currency amongst Braithwaite's set. A trite lexicon that had to be trotted out whenever that set were together to ensure they were all part of the same little club. The Crack of Doom where the 'beasting' took place was the sort of place where girls danced around a pole for a silver scruple, around the punter for two, and did quite a bit more for five. Where the drinks were spiked with so much cheap industrial alcohol that happy hour could very easily turn into four miserable days. More than five of their crassly named signature cocktail—a Lippetysklit—was the equivalent of a full frontal lobotomy in terms of irreparable neuronal damage.

An expensive education, though failing in its primary goals, had at least given Braithwaite a taste for hyperbole and an inability to say no to a good time. But this morning's hangover also meant that small talk was off the agenda, which, from Asher's perspective, deserved a silent round of applause. Not that he harboured an overt dislike for Braithwaite, it was simply that, when sober, he could be a tiresomely loquacious berk, always on the lookout for a way to lever himself up the promotional ladder using whoever was close by as the rungs.

Asher fired up his pongcluetor and unscrewed the top of the lemonade drive attached to its rear in readiness for beemail. Some people still preferred pigeons, but slowly and surely the world was coming to terms with new biocculocultech. Asher's in-tray was fuller than it needed to be and so he set to work, dealing with all the mundane tasks required of a department responsible for border intelligence and migration.

Across the desk, Braithwaite rested his head on his arms, groaning.

'My old Dad swore on a Thameswick Fry complete with two greasy eggs and black pudding as a morning after cure,' Asher said as he waited for the machine to boot up.

Two bloodshot eyes looked pleadingly up at him. 'Your father, my dear Lodge, is a better man than I.'

Asher thought about correcting Braithwaite's use of 'is', but decided against it and shrugged. Both Asher's parents and his one brother were dead, though he still spoke to them regularly, or at least used to, but Braithwaite did not need to know that. He'd deliberately avoided giving too much of himself away to his colleague since joining the department. Asher had a very strong survival instinct.

A bee buzzed into the lemonade pot and hovered over an elaborate arrangement of miniature platforms at the rear of the pongcluetor, where it did a little dance before heading out of the window. It was too cold for bees to still be around naturally; the beemail bees were specially bred for maritime climes somewhere in the far north. Asher waited while the elephant mites inside the white box did their thing. A geek once told him that a million elephant mites would soon be the memory standard in a modern pongcluetor. Asher remembered the time when all they had at their disposal was a pathetic 10 elephant mite Hamstrad. The only things slower than that were the phases of the moon.

A message appeared on the screen to an accompanying chime.

My office, 10 mins. Rathbone.

Asher blew out air, pushed away from his desk and paused only to ask Braithwaite if he wanted something from the canteen. Braithwaite declined the offer, at least the groan sounded like a no, and so Asher headed off, leaving Braithwaite to suffer alone.

Rathbone was the head of client services, Asher's line manager and a regular winner of the Officious Git of the Year Award with hardly any effort required on his part. His office sat at the top of two flights of foot-worn stone stairs at the end of a cheerless corridor in a senselessly gigantic room and, despite a big fire crackling in a hearth as big as a small house, freezing to boot. He was a short barrel of a man with a bald head fringed by wispy grey tufts. All he needed was a touch of white foundation, a red nose and size 38 boots, and he'd be a shoe-in for Bonko the Clown. His piglike eyes followed Lodge as he crossed the room.

'Ah, Inspector Lodge. Come and take a seat.'

Asher complied.

'Tea? Coffee?'

'Coffee, please.'

Rathbone spoke into a brass tube to order refreshments and then sat back, steepling his fingers in front of his pudgy face in an attempt at gravitas. An attempt, Asher concluded, that worked quite well so long as you removed 'gravit' from the equation and added an extra 's' to 'as'.

Finally, Rathbone spoke. 'I know that settling here has not been easy. I realise that compared to your work in investigative crime, the Department must seem very tame. Very tame, indeed.'

Asher shrugged. 'It's work.'

'It is.' Rathbone nodded sagely and kept it up for several seconds to emphasise his point. It made him look like a nodding china pug. 'Very important work, too. We must never underestimate how important.'

No danger with you reminding us every ten seconds. Asher frowned and hoped he hadn't voiced that thought aloud.

'And,' Rathbone continued, 'I take it that you're coping well after your…surgery?'

Asher winced but decided not to let it show, though he added a mental curse for good measure. Rathbone would not, could not, let it lie. 'It's fine, I'm fine.'

'Really?' Rathbone smiled. 'Psychosurgery is very traumatic. Many people take years to recover. And as you know, my door is always open if there is any problem.'

'Yes, you've told me. Many times.'

Rathbone's steepled fingers intertwined. 'It's just that we've had a complaint from the owner of an establishment called,' Rathbone peered down at a sheet of paper on his desk, 'They Think It's Soul Over.'

No matter how many times he heard it, the name still made Asher cringe. He expelled a little air and let his mouth shape a mirthless grin. 'Malachite is a toerag. I got a tipoff that he's meddling in black market transference—'

'That's as may be,' Rathbone said, interrupting carefully. 'And I'm sure that this Malachite deserves investigation. It's just that it's not the way we do things here at FHIFAA, Mr Lodge.' He leaned across the desk, attempting his best fatherly look and failing epically. Asher imagined a custard pie springing up from the blotter and splattering Rathbone's face to the accompaniment of a clown horn.

'We both know that necreddos are better suited to, how shall I put it, calmer jobs,' the section chief went on. 'Not one necreddo has done well in homicide, despite the fact that it would seem such a natural environment for them. I think that you were very wise to have your ablation surgery.'

'Partial ablation,' Asher corrected him.

'Partial ablation surgery,' Rathbone repeated with a nod to the correction. 'But still for the best.' He looked suddenly uncomfortable. 'After what happened to your poor brother—'

Asher bristled. 'That's water under the bridge.'

Rathbone flinched. He was at once a man in quicksand, clutching at reeds to pull himself out. He made a grab at paternal benevolence and hauled. 'If you get any information of wrongdoing, all you need do is walk up the steps and bring it to me. I will make certain that the correct people get to hear immediately.'

Asher nodded. This was the point at which he should tell Rathbone about his Thursday dreams. Let someone else take the weight. He looked at the flabby bureaucrat and knew that it was more likely he'd swallow a decomposed bat. Two, even.

'Now,' Rathbone said, sitting back and grinning.

Asher waited for the noise of whoopee cushion. It did not materialise.

'I need you to contact Vampire Services. We desperately need some statistics on the Sanguinite influx now that a treaty with Oneg has been signed and migration limits have been lifted. Rumours are rife of an invasion.' Rathbone said. 'Can't see it myself. Too cold here for them, I reckon.' He beamed. 'Though I have invested a few scruples in garlic shares.'

Asher forced a smile.

'So if I can have those figures by close of play today, I'd be very grateful.'

'I'll do my best,' Asher said, getting up.

'But you haven't had your coffee…'

'I'll get one downstairs. Drink it at my desk.'

'That's the spirit.' Rathbone offered up a smile loaded with relief. Asher waited for a kiddie car to come trundling in so that he could make an exit. Nothing happened.

Rathbone frowned. 'Anything else I can do for you?'

Say hello to Bonko for me was what Asher thought. 'No thanks,' was what he said.

CHAPTER TEN

Asher got back to his desk, pondering Rathbone's words and feeling as if the grey walls around him were about to collapse on his head. Despite being a clown, everything he'd said had the ring of truth to it. And yet, hearing it had been like standing barefoot on a bed of nails. Some necreddos were revered and highly paid members of society. Some carved a niche for themselves in the world of spiritualism, acting as go-betweens for the living and the dead; it was the natural path to take and was the one his mother chose. But Asher and his brother Ridger craved excitement. And there was nothing more exciting than the homicide squad. The psychic energy released from a murder was massive. A desperate, vomited expulsion of terror and pain and rage. Much like what Asher experienced in his nightmares involving the dying Bewildered crying out to him, but ten times stronger with his mind wedged open by the potions the enforcers' apothecaries cooked up. Advances in criminal psychophiltres had changed the landscape of homicide detection. But the necreddos were the vital cog. Without them, scanning the ether for the right signals remained a pipe dream.

But no one could have anticipated the huge cost to the user in those early days of the necrosquads. No one had foreseen that delving into the realms of the violently ruptured souls would open up the visitor to other, darker forces that existed in that betwixt and between zone. Ridger Lodge had paid the price. Fallen, or been thrown (even Ridger had not been sure), to his death from the tallest building in New Thameswick and Asher almost followed suit. He'd seen no way out after what happened in the Black Cat—

He stopped it there. No point revisiting that. Besides, the apothecaries had told him not to and they'd put in a few roadblocks to give him time to steer his thoughts away. He supposed, therefore, that the surgery had been successful.

These days there were better potions. Safer potions. But they'd come too late for Asher. His old bosses stepped in and slammed shut the gates before Asher had succumbed. Especially after the Black Cat. They deemed it too dangerous for him to try and so he'd been seconded to FHIFAA. But being seconded didn't stop him from taking an interest in things. Neither did it stop the nuisance calls from the recently dead Bewildered. And he still had loyal friends in homicide.

By the time he got back to his desk, Asher found a beemail from a hawkshaw shapeshifter by the name of Crouch.

Heads up, AL. Two snuffs of dubious origin. Mustard Wharf.

In the chair opposite, Braithwaite had gravitated from head down on folded arms to head back lolling in a chair. Asher pinned him with a look.

'Anyone asks, I'm off to see the migration lads.'

'Migration. Got it,' Braithwaite said, his face the colour of pond water. 'And are you? Going to migration, I mean?'

Asher tapped his nose. 'Best you don't ask. Can't tell them anything when they torture you, then, can you?'

'Ha, good one, Lodge.' Braithwaite tried a laugh but it morphed into a groan as the effort triggered another wave of head pain.

Asher's smile dripped schadenfreude all over his shirt.

Yuletide decorations adorned the streets. Bunting fluttered in the breeze and sprigs of white-berried mistletoe and holly bursting with red fruit hung from almost every door. On the corners, chestnuts roasted on braziers and the mulled cider vendors were dragging in punters with a two for one offer. Asher took a cab to the North Dock and found Mustard Wharf easily enough. He paused at the top of an alley running down towards the river at the side of a pub called the Zephyr. High tide lapped the bank below, the water brown and thick with silt and mud.

He made for a dark grey statue depicting a dashing seafarer looking out towards the river. The imagery was upright and heroic, the moustachioed face held erect, a sword in one hand, a flowing cape behind. The tableaux was spoiled only by the pigeon perched amiably on top of the statue's hat looking down at Asher, its head at a jaunty angle.

'Crouch,' Asher said by way of greeting.

The statue melted into a smaller animated version wearing proper clothes, a bowler hat, and a cane instead of the sword. The moustache remained. Crouch the hawkshaw was average by design; dusky skin, lightish brown hair and eyes that landed somewhere on the spectrum between blue black and hazel, depending on his mood. His granite manifestation came directly from his father, a gabbroic igneomagus who'd carved out a long career as a locum statue in the city's many museums. If ever they needed to clean a statue, they'd call on Old Man Crouch who would stand in, minus any given limb if necessary, until the real thing was returned. But being able to become a twelve-foot tall statue at any moment had its pros and cons, as far as the younger Crouch was concerned.

A sexier skill might have been the ability to transform into a wolf or a hunting bird, but the igneomagi had once been warriors and flesh did not stand up well to arrows and spears. So they'd forsaken all that for rock; igneous now meant exactly what it said on the tin. And although turning into granite might be seen as a very limited skill, Crouch's party piece, after several libations, involved inviting people to break bits of furniture over his transmogrified head and was always a crowd pleaser. Stake-outs were a doddle, being impervious to arrows was a big plus, but hammers could do some real damage. And as for the pigeons, their guano could give you a nasty burn if you weren't quick.

In the street, an unlikely-looking choir was trying to make a scruple or two from the revellers leaving the pub, most of them stoked up on mulled wine and good cheer. On closer inspection, Asher noted that the choir were dressed in bits of red cloth and each wore white curly wigs. They had bells on their arms and legs that jingled while they sang some short and (very) rude songs. The landlord of the Zephyr, armed with a nail-studded club, glowered in the doorway, listening.

'Rude Rolf the blue-hosed antelope, had a very woolly sock, and if you asked him nicely, he'd wrap the thing around his—'

'RIGHT!' yelled the landlord, wading in and scattering the choir.

'Where's your Yuletide cheer, Bert?' whined one of the red robed singers from a very safe distance.

'YAY!' Bert brandished the club above his head. 'There, that do for you? Now bugger off back to the arches before I start roasting your chestnuts on this open fire. You're upsetting my punters.'

The choir trudged away, muttering. When they'd gone twenty yards, they stopped, passed around a flagon of 'white fire' cider (*can be used as barbecue lighter fluid* was also written on the label) and stood in a huddle. Five seconds later, they all turned and chanted:

'He's sad, he's bad, we think he's effing mad!

Zephyr Bert, Zephyr Bert.'

'What's all that about?' Asher asked, as Bert, club raised, gave chase to the vagrant choir.

Crouch shook his head. 'They're dressed as the Yule Father. Bloody stupid, if you ask me. But he's all over New Thameswick. Yule Father, I ask you? It'll never catch on.'

'Tell me about the snuffs,' Asher asked.

'They've taken the bodies,' Crouch explained with resigned sigh. 'Just as well. One look at 'em would put you off your dinner for a week.'

'That bad?'

Crouch nodded. His skin bore an iridescent quality when angry: dancing lights over the darkness that roiled beneath the policeman's shape he currently projected. A shape that Asher was both familiar with and quite fond of.

'Torn to pieces, both of 'em. No sign of robbery. Nothing to rob, anyway. Both Bewildereds by the look of 'em. Dead about a week they reckon.'

Asher nodded. 'I'd say eight days.'

It was Crouch's turn to nod. 'That's what the taker said.'

'Whose case is it?'

'You're looking at him.'

'I see they're sparing no expense then.' Asher grinned.

'Quality over quantity, mate.'

'What about the current necreddos? They pick anything up?'

Crouch shook his head and sighed. 'That's the really weird thing. They heard nothing. But then the Bewildered generally don't shout—'

'Because they're not in the ledgers, yeah, I know.'

Crouch made his tired eyes into slits. 'And you're certain you heard them?'

'Certain. My take on this is that the surgery did something to me. Admittedly it shut me off from the rabble, but it looks like it's opened me up to the Bewildered.'

'Midden,' Crouch said.

'Exactly. Wouldn't be a problem, but since somebody has taken a liking to skewering a Bewildered every Thursday night…'

Crouch nodded again. 'That must be a real pain in the Derry Air.' He paused and looked at Asher. 'Trouble is that there are those in the Department that are saying good riddance. That maybe it's not such a bad thing.'

'It is bad. Of course it's bad. They may be weird, but they're still people, Crouch.'

'I know. Just not our people.'

'That stinks.'

Crouch held up both hands. 'I'm just saying.'

Asher nodded and gritted his teeth. He could hear the discussion in his head. Crouch would have a Rathbone equivalent more concerned with managing overtime and arrest rates than the death of people who had half an existence and whose contribution to society was precisely zero. And he could see Crouch listening to the speech and not saying anything but thinking that nothing ever happened without good cause, or worse, bad cause. And if you looked under enough rocks, something would be there looking back at you, wanting to turn you into its dinner. The Bewildered were currently on someone, or something's menu. The trouble was, if that someone or something got a taste for them, who knew where its appetite might lead next. One of the reasons he trusted Crouch was his nose for a bad smell when it drifted up out of the drains. It was what made him a good copper.

'Can you get me the lithos of the bodies once they're printed?' Asher asked.

Crouch said nothing. He stood there, chewing the inside of his lip.

'Is there a problem?' Asher spoke louder this time.

Crouch looked like he'd swallowed a fly. 'Look, Asher, should you be meddling with this stuff?'

'No, but what choice do I have? I hear them, Crouch. I can't *not* hear them. Unless we stop this, they're going to keep waking me up. Plus, it's getting worse. I heard them again last night. I reckon you're going to find more bodies over the next few days.'

Crouch frowned. Asher knew that was the clincher. Crouch would never stand idly by, knowing that a crime was going to be committed. He looked over his shoulder towards the river. 'Whoever did this wanted them to suffer.'

'And they do,' Asher said. 'I can hear them, remember?'

Crouch wrinkled his nose before sending the necreddo a final questioning look. 'We both know that if anyone finds out about this, you're in deep doings.'

Asher grinned. 'You too.'

Crouch shrugged.

Asher looked out over the brown water. 'I hear their pain, Crouch. And it isn't normal. Whatever is doing this rips them apart.'

'Save the funny stuff for later,' Crouch said. 'My aching ribs can't take any more.'

CHAPTER ELEVEN

BOBBY MIRACLE WOKE UP LATE. She eschewed breakfast but was delayed by traffic problems that extended her bus journey by a further ten frustrating minutes so that her watch read 9.16 am when she breathlessly opened the front door of Hipposync Enterprises. Miss WT looked up.

'Ah, Ms Miracle. Miss Porter would like to see you as soon as you get in.'

'I'm so sorry. Slept late,' Bobby panted. 'I had this really weird dream and then the bus got held up in traffic and—'

Miss WT blinked. She even did that slowly, like a chameleon eyeing up a tasty bug. 'She did say as soon as you got in.'

'Yes, of course. Sorry.'

Bobby hurried along the corridor, shrugging off her coat as she went. She threw her bag on her desk and saw that Pippa was already at work, cataloguing.

'Morning,' said Pippa. 'You okay, you're a bit flushed?'

'Bad night,' Bobby muttered.

'Oh dear. Would you like me to make you a coffee?'

Bobby resisted the urge to say, 'Like you made me yesterday?' and instead said, 'No, I've been summoned. Maybe when I get back?'

She had time to register Pippa's look of wary sympathy before hurrying back out and making for Miss Porter's office. It stood right at the end of the corridor next to Mr Porter's, and was light and modern with brushed steel furnishings and blond wood, the complete opposite of Mr Danmor's dark panelled library cave. Miss Porter's room smelt of fresh pine and mountain mist. But Bobby preferred the old wood and leather of Mr Danmor's. Bobby knocked and entered. Miss Porter got up from behind her desk and pulled a seat forward for her.

'Thanks for coming straight in—' Miss Porter began.

'I'm so sorry I'm late. There are three sets of traffic lights on the Iffley Road. I'm not making excuses but—'

'Don't worry. I didn't ask you here to talk about punctuality.' Miss Porter, dressed in her usual business garb of dark suit trousers and pristine white blouse, perched a hip on the edge of her desk and asked earnestly, 'How do you think things are going, Bobby?'

Bobby's stomach did a swallow dive. As opening gambits in any HR interview went, 'How do *you* think things are going' was never good. Like asking a turkey if it had had enough to eat over the last three months two days before Christmas. Mouth suddenly arid, Bobby said, 'Do you mean the internship?'

'Yes. It's been a month. I just felt we ought to have a little talk.'

Little talk. Bobby nodded. She knew what this was about. She'd been here before. Had T-shirts in all the colours of the rainbow. A wryly ironic smile crawled over her lips. She was on the Good Ship Screw-up and it was already half a mile offshore. 'I enjoy the work. I know that rare books make up only a small part of what you do here and I have to say that the secrecy aspect of things is a little irritating, but I can live with that.'

'Many of our clients want us to be very discreet,' Miss Porter said.

Bobby sighed. 'I know how it must've looked yesterday. We… *I* almost lost Fitzgerald as a client. But I swear I could not get out of the loo. I've no idea how it happened and I know how it sounds, but you have to believe me.'

'We're having the door checked today and I do believe you. Only an imbecile would throw away an opportunity like yesterday, and you don't strike me as an imbecile, Bobby. It's all a bit odd, I have to admit. But it's not Fitzgerald or the loo that I really wanted to talk to you about.'

Bobby nodded and let her gaze drop to her aubergine-coloured nails, black suede ankle boots, and spider web lace tights under a dark grey pleated silk and sheer mesh sweater dress. She'd cinched it this morning with a plum-coloured belt. Her wardrobe mantra consisted of 'black and grey with a splash of colour'. But there were all sorts of shades of black and grey and she did not think in those simple terms. Not when it came to dressing and definitely not when it came to the world at large. She looked back up into a pair of gold-flecked eyes that had not strayed from her face.

'I know,' Bobby said. 'And I understand that choosing to dress the way I do can sometimes be challenging for some people. But it's who I am. It's what I am.'

'Bobby, the way you choose to present yourself to the world is neither here nor there. I wouldn't care if you turned up in a shell suit and towelling headband—'

But having taken the explanatory leap, Bobby plunged on, head first into very deep water. 'And yes, I suppose I could take a leaf out of Pippa's book. I mean, it would make my life a lot easier if I wore tight jeans or a frilly dress, but I'd be cheating myself. It's a lifestyle choice. I like grey and black. It makes me feel…comfortable.'

'As I said, there's nothing wrong with black or grey—'

'And you don't need to actually say it. I mean, the way I look *is* something the people here could work around, I'm sure. But there are the customers to consider. And when you add that to messing up and turning up late, I suppose it's a no-brainer.'

A small pause developed in which Miss Porter seemed momentarily taken aback by the fact that Bobby had stopped berating herself. But she recovered quickly. 'I was going over your application form and wanted to ask you about your grandmother.'

A dull dread dragged at Bobby's insides and sent the colour scooting out of her face. She hadn't expected this. Not from Miss Porter, who had struck Bobby as someone who never aimed below the belt. And this was so far below the belt as to qualify as a knee-capping. Dredging up her family's history of mental illness as an excuse to get rid of her appeared a tad extreme to say the least. She'd messed up. Fine. But opening the cupboard door and laying out the Miracle skeleton struck Bobby as a bit uncalled for.

She drew back her shoulders. 'I knew, if I was honest with myself,' she said through compressed lips, 'the minute Pippa turned up. I don't begrudge it, you're either the chosen one or you aren't. So why don't I save us both a little time and just leave.'

'But your grandmother—'

'Was locked in an asylum when I was ten, yes I know. I would rather not discuss it, thank you. Look, I do like you and Mr Danmor and the books you have here are amazing. I think your Mr Porter is lovely and I would have liked to have said goodbye to him personally, but I see now that that's not going to happen.'

Miss Porter frowned, folded her arms across her chest, unfolded them and put a hand on each hip as she contemplated Bobby and tried, from the look on her face, to wrestle meaning out of what she'd just heard. There was more than a hint of incredulity in her voice when she finally said, 'Are you saying that you want to leave?'

Face burning, Bobby clung onto her dignity as best she could. 'I think it would be for the best, don't you?'

Miss Porter shrugged, the movement masking her exasperation. 'Very well. If you've made up your mind.' She held out her hand and Bobby stood and shook it. It felt final, and for some reason Bobby couldn't quite meet Miss Porter's gold-flecked eyes.

Rushing out, Bobby passed the Pip in the corridor and felt a hand on her arm. 'You okay? You look a bit…upset?'

'I'm fine,' Bobby lied.

'She wants to see me now.' Pippa made a face.

'Oh really? I wonder why.' Bobby kept her eyes wide and bright.

The Pip's limpid pools glowed. 'But what about you?'

'This is…not for me.' Bobby turned away.

Only when the clacking sound of the Pip's heels had left the room did she allow her shoulders to sag. Exhaling heavily, she logged off her PC and switched it off. Over on the other desk, the Pip's machine was trying to save its screen via a montage of drifting fluffy kittens. She heard voices echo along the corridor. Pippa giggling, Miss Porter's throaty laugh. She didn't want to be there when they got back. Did not want to have to congratulate Pippa and see those eyes light up again; did not like herself for feeling that way. She grabbed her coat, headed for the door and almost collided with Miss WT wobbling past with quite alarming speed, her stooped gait in turbo mode. When she reached Miss Porter's room, the elderly receptionist's voice sounded unusually strident.

'I'm so sorry to interrupt, ma'am, but we're picking up some very strange readings on the…' there was a brief pause, '*security surveillance console*. It's gone straight to orange.'

Miss Porter said, 'Funny you should say that because I've been having a really strange feeling all morning. Is Mr Danmor in the…' Now it was her turn to pause dramatically, '*blue room?*'

'Not yet,' answered Miss WT.

'Could you run and find him and tell him to meet me there, Pippa?'

Bobby grimaced. The Pip was already in the inner sanctum it seemed. Bobby ducked back in, waited until the running footsteps receded and stuck her head once more into the corridor to make sure it was empty. She saw no one as she hurried out to the front office, wanting, more than anything now, to be away from Hipposync and Pippa as quickly as she possibly could. A wave of disappointment and humiliation washed over her. She'd honestly hoped that here, of all places, she might have found a bit of acceptance. But it turned out to be like everywhere else where she'd come up against someone flouncy and trendy and… normal. What the hell was so great about normal anyway? Hot tears stung her eyes. She would miss old Mr Porter and doddery Miss WT.

Too late now. Boats had been burned, bridges demolished, fields of corn slashed and aflame.

Dabbing at her eyes to avoid smudging her mascara, Bobby headed for the door completely unaware of the fact that, as far as grabbing the wrong end of a stick went, she'd just become a podium finisher with the national anthem about to play.

Orange lights flashed as Bobby opened the latch on the front door of Hipposync. Fire drill? Oh well, it didn't matter now. A draft of chilly air slapped at her and she shivered, pulling her coat about her. All she wanted was to get away and forget. Chalk it up as just another missed opportunity.

On the threshold, she turned and looked back down the corridor, shrugged and stepped out, letting the door swing closed behind her. There were six inches of travel left in that swing when she remembered that her handbag was still on the desk in the office. Cursing, she turned and thrust her hand into the gap before the door closed. At that moment, the keening alarm stopped and the light in the corridor beyond the door turned red. Why a fire drill now of all times? Bloody ironic if it was, because Bobby's fingers, which were firmly gripping the door, felt suddenly icy cold. The door, too, seemed a lot heavier than she remembered it. As if a huge and powerful hand was trying to shut it.

But Bobby's keys were in her handbag. Along with her phone and her purse. Might as well have been her heart, her eyes, and her ears. She could go nowhere without them. Quickly she placed her other hand on the edge of the door, put the weight of her shoulder against it, and pushed. It slid open a few inches but then started to shut again. She looked up at the gap between the top of the door and the frame, expecting to see a giant spring-loaded closer. But there was nothing. It didn't make any sense, but sense wasn't going to help if she had no money for the bus. Groaning, Bobby used all her strength to push against the reluctant door and managed to gain a few more inches of traction.

Enough for her to slip her body inside.

The minute she slid past it, the door shut with a definite and resounding click of the mortice lock. She noticed a couple of things instantly. The corridor oozed silence, as if all the noise had been sucked out of it to leave a big, quiet hole, and her fingers still felt icy cold. When she examined them, those same fingers seemed to shimmer slightly.

'Pins and needles,' she muttered before turning and heading

for the office where she'd left her handbag. She passed the reception area where Miss WT was doing her usual excellent impression of a stick insect in fancy dress.

'Forgot my bag,' Bobby said, giving Miss WT a cursory wave and hurrying past. Miss WT did not respond. Bobby had taken five steps further down the corridor when the image of Miss WT finally registered with that bit of her brain that labelled things as 'weird, or not quite right.' She stopped and retraced her steps and leaned back to look through the open doorway at the receptionist. Miss WT was in the middle of picking up the telephone with one hand and pressing a number on the keypad with the other. Still.

'Miss WT?' Bobby's question met with no response. She stepped into the room and tiptoed forward, illogically concerned that too much loud noise might disturb whatever parlous state of fear Miss WT was in.

'Hello?' Bobby breathed. 'Are you okay?'

Miss WT's finger hovered over the number 5 on the keypad. Bobby waved a hand back and forth in front of her open, shining eyes. They did not blink. She leaned in to listen to the earpiece of the phone. No dialling tone. Miss WT's handbag sat on the edge of the desk. Bobby carefully rummaged inside and found what she hoped she might: a small silver compact. She snapped it open and held the mirrored surface in front of Miss WT's mouth and nose. Held it there for quite some time. But regardless of how long or how close she held it, it did not mist up. Miss WT was definitely not breathing.

Bobby slapped the compact shut, trying to quell the gnawing disquiet grinding away in her gut. This was weird. Very weird indeed. Still staring at the frozen Miss WT, she stepped back into the corridor and hurried around to her office. She threw open the door and saw that the Pip had turned a questioning face towards her.

'Thank God—' the words froze on Bobby's lips.

Yes, the Pip was looking at her, but her eyes, though open, weren't seeing and her face was completely blank. Bobby's mind scrambled for some sort of explanation and what it came up with sprang from an active imagination with a predilection for all things Whovian—the old type, not the new musical theatre type — and a soft spot for science fiction and fantasy. To Bobby's untrained but imaginative eye, both the Pip and Miss WT looked as if they were in a state of suspended animation.

She frowned as the thought crystalized. Because, though she liked nothing more than buying an armchair ticket for the Tardis, or losing herself in a fictional battle between vampires and werewolves, these were very guilty pleasures she shared with no one else. 'Suspended animation' fell heavily under the heading of weird or occult which were very much locked drawers in Bobby's mental cupboard. A cupboard steel lined and iron reinforced by her parents actively discouraging her from all forms of fanciful imaginings. All done with a gentle, intellectual bullying resulting in a rebellious appetite Bobby fed voraciously with books and films once she got to university and away from her parents' stultifying influence. It was an enigma that she often found difficult to reconcile. Her preoccupation with all things Goth, her clothing and music, art and literature, stemmed from an intangible attraction to the darker side of real life. Yes, she knew about fictitious vampires and the undead and all the rest of 'it' because 'it' was a part of modern pop culture and you either played along or missed out completely on the party. That didn't mean she believed in any of 'it'. If anything 'it' had convinced her that 'it' was nothing more than celluloid (or digital) smoke and mirrors. The sensible, boring parenting she'd endured had, rightly or wrongly, left a streak of common sense a mile wide in Bobby. The fact was that she believed in very little, other than herself—and even that belief had been sorely tested during her postgraduate search for gainful employment.

Yet here she was at 9.45 on a Friday morning, barely clinging onto her self-respect, having been forced to save face by resigning in order to avoid the embarrassment of being dismissed for tardiness and ineptitude. Well, mainly ineptitude. And now they had the gall to present her with something like…this.

Some people, at this point, might scream, or in any one of a hundred different ways, panic. Bobby Miracle, however, was not some people and hysteria was a country she had yet to visit. In truth, it wasn't even on her bucket list. Other people might have become highly irritated at the 'joke', but since irritation generally involved, in Bobby's world, the small and menial things in life, such as always leaving the top of the toothpaste unscrewed so that the first three millimetres of paste became as hard as carbon fibre, finding a whole building and its occupants frozen in time seemed a little over the top in the joke rankings.

'Blast,' she said. Which was about as bad as things got in the Miracle lexicon. When it came to oaths, she confined herself to 'b' words, which gave her a bit of scope, even if seven letters was her safe maximum. It did allow for 'balls' and the odd 'bloody'. Of course, there was the inevitable 's' and she'd once used an 'f' word after hearing it at school from a boy called Jordan when she was seven, but shocked the vicar so badly he'd poured a whole cup of hot tea into his lap. In contrast, the invective that exploded out of his mouth by return involved two 'b' words, an elongated 'f' and an 's'. His already red face supernova'd into scarlet while her mother watched, appalled by the whole incident. It did, however, provide the only opportunity ever, so far as Bobby could imagine, for anyone (in this case Mrs Miracle, Bobby's mother) to calmly say, once the air returned to a sober magnolia from the clerically induced blue it had become: 'More tea, vicar?'

She frowned, rid her mind of distracting reminiscences and sat on her own chair at her own desk, to think.

She fished out her mobile. Dead. She looked at her watch. Stopped.

Wonderful, she thought. *Absolutely blastedly spiffing*. She tried applying logic. This was like being an extra in *Tales of the Unexpected*, one who did not have the benefit of a script. But this was definitely not a film set and she was not an actress. Therefore it had to be 'real' in the sense that it was actually happening.

Bizarrely, Bobby found herself smiling. Her mother and father had prepared her for all sorts of things. How to manage her money, how to cope with university interviews, how to rebuff drunks at parties, but there'd never been a lesson on how to sort out an office plunged into a frozen time warp.

Maybe that's where they'd gone wrong.

CHAPTER TWELVE

WILLIAM AND MARY MIRACLE had lived in a rambling old farmhouse in Wiltshire with Bobby their only child. They avoided TV, fashion, and humour, and thought a day out at the British Lawnmower Museum fair game as a birthday treat.

Bobby's one escape from the round of cello lessons, homework, and the grind of the girls' school she attended, was a grandmother who lived in an annexe in the old house. In truth, it was Bobby and her parents who had taken over the majority of what was, in legal terms, her grandmother's house. Lucille Miracle, a sparkly eyed, charming and wonderful eccentric, illuminated the first ten years of Bobby's life with wonder and joy. She read books to her about children who lost their way in forests and were abducted by old women who attempted to turn them into Sunday roasts; had pictures of strange, lonely and abandoned places in curly-edged albums; and knew some very dubious rhymes. Sometimes, Lucille would take Bobby on trips to old, quiet places where they never met anyone. Sometimes they would go out at night just to stare at the stars. Lucille would dress in clothes her own grandmother had once owned and talk of strange people, of weird happenings, and tell little Roberta that there really weren't stranger things at sea and that there were places in the world where, if you scratched hard enough, you could see through to the other side. So long as you knew how to look. And knowing was key because there were things on the other side scratching, too. And you never wanted to be scratching the same spot at the same time. Bobby would listen, spellbound. And it was all done with a conspiratorial glint and a promise from Bobby that she would say nothing to her parents about any of it.

It was always to be their little secret.

Often, when she let herself think of it, Bobby realised that her grandmother had been that strange and wonderful amalgam of older sister, wise woman, and friend.

Lucille had a boyfriend, equally as exotic, by the name of Hubert Slayer, who would come over to the old house and take tea with Lucille. Sometimes, when they forgot that Bobby was there, she'd catch them talking in a strange language and holding hands. But one day when Bobby was ten years and two months old, everything changed.

She'd come home from school to find her mother and father waiting at the gate with anxious faces. But before they could even begin to explain, Bobby heard a distant screech that sounded like her grandmother. She'd been looking forward to seeing Lucille, who'd gone away with Hubert for a long weekend break. Hearing her yell made Bobby want to rush inside, but from the gate with her father's hand on her arm to stop her from entering, Bobby looked up to a second-floor window and saw Lucille's face, not full of fun, but full of pain and anguish, flailing her arms as if fighting off some demon that only she could see. The story, when she finally heard it from her father, was that Hubert and Lucille had visited an old friend in the country at a very isolated spot. Neighbours half a mile away reported hearing strange noises and seeing strange lights the night that Lucille and Hubert arrived. Those same neighbours were awakened before dawn by Lucille, tattered and bleeding, screaming and tearing at her hair in their garden. When the police arrived, Hubert was dead from a heart attack and the owner of the property was found miles away three days later, her feet bloody ribbons of flesh from running, but no longer bleeding because she'd been very dead. The coroner's report said that she had died from exhaustion.

Lucille was the only survivor.

In the weeks that followed they tried to cope with her in the house, but Bobby received strict orders to stay well away. It wasn't difficult. The Lucille that yelled and banged on the walls was not the Lucille she'd known and loved. Worse was the fact that whatever words she spoke, they were in a language that no one understood, though Bobby recognised the odd word from when Lucille and Hubert lapsed into secret conversation. And yet, on the rare occasions when Bobby did catch the odd glimpse, she was convinced that Lucille Miracle had been trying to tell her something. Once, when Bobby was playing in the garden, Lucille thrust up a bathroom window and started shouting at the frightened little girl. Shouting and gesticulating in a wild and incoherent way until the mental health nurse that the Miracles employed managed to pull her away and slam the window shut. It had been a frightening experience for Bobby. Even more frightening when the image of her grandmother wildly thrusting her arms above her head as if miming a dive and yelling the word, 'Rack! Rack!' over and over kept her awake for hours.

Within a month Lucille's long dark hair turned silver white and the nightlong screams combined with the destructively flailing arms led, after five weeks of misery, to an admission to a 'special' hospital. Bobby watched the ambulance take her grandmother away from the safe distance of an upstairs window. After that, Bobby's memory of Lucille was of a drugged, catatonic old woman wasting away for month after month in an airless room in a cheerless institution, finally succumbing and finding peace the week before Bobby turned fourteen.

When Bobby offered to help her father go through her grandmother's things after the funeral, he'd firmly, but politely refused with an unusually stern warning.

'Your grandmother was full of imagination and nonsense, Roberta. Bad things can come from such thoughts. She let her mind wander, let others lead her astray to places where no sensible woman had any right to be.' He'd grabbed Bobby then, grabbed her firmly and stared intently into her face. 'Promise me you'll stay away from all of this.' He had tears in his eyes when he spoke and his hands fluttered like birds towards the dream catchers and strange wax effigies that lined her grandmother's 'cabinet of wonders' living room.

So Bobby stayed away.

But that didn't stop her from remembering, nor from wanting to know. She pestered and pestered her parents, asking what really happened to her grandmother until finally, years later, she learned the truth. Certainly the version of it that her mother chose to believe. One rainy afternoon on her sixteenth birthday, her parents finally relented.

'The police found certain...items.' Mary Miracle choked back the tears. 'I think that your grandmother had been to help a friend rid her house of some kind of restless spirit.' She shook her head. 'All ridiculous nonsense. Silly meddling in things best left alone. And look where it got them. Seeing Hubert have a heart attack must have sent your grandmother mad.'

It might, Bobby thought. It wasn't much of an explanation, but it was something. But then her grandmother knew CPR and how to replace dislocated joints and all sorts of stuff. And that doubt was enough for Roberta Miracle to start wondering, to start developing a cold and deductive fascination with what the occult had done to her wonderful grandmother. Later, when she'd grown into them, she took to wearing Lucille Miracle's clothes, and with them came the growing interest in the aesthetic.

The darker side of life.

But more than anything she enjoyed the feeling of closeness that looking like her grandmother brought. A closeness that brought back memories of the Lucille that had loved her granddaughter, that Bobby missed so much, before the craziness and the white hair turned her into the scary mad lady who kept screaming like a jackdaw the words, 'Rack! Rack!'

BOBBY CAME BACK to herself with a start. She was still looking at her watch and it was still stopped. Blimey, she hadn't travelled that meandering memory lane in a long time and she did not remember it being such a bumpy road.

She went back to look at the still inanimate Pip. There was probably a very good explanation for all of this, though she could not for the life of her think what it might be. Instead, she chose the path of least resistance and decided to make it someone else's problem. She reached for her mobile, intending to phone for an ambulance and the police and then remembered it didn't work. Fine, she'd fetch them herself.

Without a backward glance Bobby walked back up the corridor, handbag in hand, and faced the front door. She put her hand on the mortice lock lever and the door disappeared instantly to be replaced by a very solid, very rough, brick wall. Bobby leapt back, her insides flipping over.

'This is not funny,' she said to no one in particular. But if this was some kind of elaborate practical joke at her expense, no one, least of all Bobby, was laughing. Rationalisation, exhausted already, found a precarious toehold and dug in. This was all some kind of technological windup, obviously. The whys and the wherefores were neither here nor there. Perhaps this was how Hipposync said goodbye to all their employees—interns included —with elaborately macabre pranks? Well, it wasn't going to work with Bobby Miracle. She was not in the mood.

Though she acknowledged the little rodent of panic scurrying round the hamster wheel of disquiet somewhere in her gut, she decided that knowledge was her best weapon. Well, knowledge and one of Mr Porter's very large steel ferruled umbrellas sitting in the hammered copper umbrella stand. She chose the one with the tip guarded by a rubber cover that she removed with a flourish. Thus armed, Bobby slowly tiptoed away into the depths of Hipposync Enterprises to see what she could find.

Ten minutes later, she remained disappointed. Whatever state Hipposync was in, it was one in which everything was frozen o'clock. Computers, people, everything. She could open doors and filing cabinets, even the fridge in the tearoom, but there was no electricity for the kettle and no water in the taps. When she tried pouring water out from a bottle of Slavabad Spring someone left in the fridge, though she could lift it out and unscrew the top, pouring it into a glass proved impossible. The water stayed resolutely in the bottle even with the thing held upside down. *Great*, she thought. Now she could add 'dehydration' and 'starvation' to 'bizarre', which already had subheadings including 'disbelief', 'confusion' and 'WTF'. She left Mr Danmor's office until the very last. Of course, there was a chance that Miss Porter had gone to meet Mr Danmor, but when she opened his office door, he was there alone, mannequinlike, his hand on a weird-looking sphere with a hand-shaped cavity etched into it. Danmor's mouth was open and it looked like he'd been speaking to someone when the freeze-frame weirdness kicked in.

Bobby walked into the room. Bookshelves containing novels and very old ledgers and artefacts lined the walls. One shelf in particular tweaked her curiosity. All the books were old and leather-bound with titles like *Postlapsarianism for the Uninitiated*, and *Thaumaturgy: A Primer*. Next to them was *A Short History of New Thameswick*, *The Fall and Rise of the Undead*, and *A Treaty on the First Troll War*.

Weird. But then Hipposync did publish some very strange stuff. Bobby crept around Mr Danmor, still not sure if the coma-like existence she was finding everyone in allowed for a degree of hearing and sight. She doubted it, but decided against making silly faces or attempting to moonwalk just in case. So as to not tread on anyone's sensibilities, she stepped behind him and peered around his arm at the contents of his desk.

Invoices and letters to collectors sat in a neat pile in a wire tray. But centre stage was a small notebook. Not all of it legible, but one word she could make out easily because it was heavily underlined.

Cuthbertson

Who was Cuthbertson and did he, or she, have anything to do with what was going on? She took a step back to look at Mr Danmor, glanced down again at what he'd written, and found herself wondering if he'd ever considered being a doctor. He certainly had the handwriting for it. She could read the word 'autopsy', and what looked like 'malign haunting', but the rest was just a scrawl. Hadn't Miss Porter asked Pippa to fetch Mr Danmor and tell him to meet her in the blue room?

Sounded like a very popular place. Perhaps it was time she took a look at it.

Now all she needed to do was work out where the hell it was.

CHAPTER THIRTEEN

Asher left the wharf at a little after 10.30. Traversing the city, he became increasingly aware of a wave of Yule Father-related revelry. Crouch's explanations seemed to have lifted the blinkers off his eyes. His carriage took him past the park in which someone had built a wooden shed, painted the roof white and hung white sheets around the entrance. A group of bored-looking imps dressed up in dungarees and floppy green-tasselled hats stood on the pavement next to a sign pointing to the shed. The sign read,

This way to the North Pole,
Meet the Yule Father in his grott

The 'o' at the end of 'grotto' had sagged and hung forlornly off the end of the sign. Despite this, a group of excited children tugging on the hands of wary-looking parents were queuing to get into the 'grott'. Through the doorway, Asher caught a glimpse of a seated corpulent man sporting a woolly beard and red tunic. The colour of the man's face matched his coat.

Asher tutted. He knew what this was. Just like the Bewildered somehow falling through the cracks between the Fae and the non-Fae worlds, something cultural had leaked through, too. But of course it was a two-way street, Asher was well aware of that.

Whole departments existed in FHIFAA full of ologists that monitored such things for their social impact. But sometimes you had to ask yourself if it was worth it. He was fairly certain that, at this precise moment, someone on the other side was looking at a garden full of pottery gnomes—scale models of what you would find scurrying about under any hedge in New Thameswick—and wondering exactly the same thing. Culture, and especially cross-dimensional cultural leak, was a very strange thing. Personally, he didn't mind since his interaction with non-Fae was essential to both his job and his personal life, but celebrating Christmas in a world with as many gods as there were stars in the firmament was taking it a bit far. But then there was the little matter of consumerism to consider. When you factored that in, non-Fae Youle Father red was the new stygian black.

Back at the office, Braithwaite seemed to have recovered. He was no longer the colour of a Yule Elf's hat and, judging by the three empty bottles of dog hair potion on the desk, he'd taken the cure.

'Any messages?' Asher asked, easing into his chair.

'Rathbone wants to see you.'

'Again? Has he been sniffing?'

'He did wander down.'

'You told him I was with Migration?'

'I forgot.' Braithwaite squirmed in his chair and made a face meant to portray cringing horror.

Asher leaned across and whispered, 'What do you mean, forgot?'

'I mean, I couldn't remember what you said. I had a whopper of a headache when you left, so when Rathbone asked I checked your beemail and…'

'What?' Asher whispered through gritted teeth.

'You didn't log off. Look, see your log's still on.' Braithwaite pointed to the Cherrywood key in the top of Asher's pong-cluetor.

'So he knows I went to see the constabulary?'

Braithwaite nodded.

'Marvellous,' Asher said.

'Sorry, Lodge.'

Asher shook his head, got up and headed towards the stairs.

A half-hearted 'sorry' from Braithwaite followed him. At the bottom of the stairs, Asher glanced back. Braithwaite was grinning. It took all sorts. Asher knew that well enough. His mother would tell him that cream always rose to the top, behind the clouds the sun still shone, and that everyone had a place in this world. Asher did his best to apply these metaphors and epithets, but so far the only place in the world he could think of for Braithwaite was under a rock with all the other things that crawled.

Rathbone was waiting, wearing a sad clown face.

'Ah, Mr Lodge. Take a seat.'

Asher sat. The expected whoopee cushion trump did not occur.

'I can explain—'

Rathbone lifted a quelling hand. Thankfully it did not contain a rubber chicken. 'Please let me finish. I am very disappointed. Not only have you failed to carry out your duties, but you have deliberately flaunted my instructions, ignored my advice and pursued activities that have nothing to do with our work here.'

'If you'd let me ex—'

Rathbone raised an eyebrow. 'You'll be pleased to know that Mr Braithwaite has been tasked with obtaining the figures you were meant to get. All in all, he is an exemplary worker and someone you would do well to emulate. Whenever I venture down to the department, he is always diligently working at his desk.'

Diligently nursing a hangover more like.

'This is not simply a question of me hanging onto the necrosquad's boot straps,' Asher said slowly.

Rathbone's sad clown face became even sadder. Asher imagined discordant heartstrings twanging somewhere. 'Asher—you don't mind if I call you Asher? If only I could believe that. You realise that this sort of behaviour requires that I place you on report?' He let the threat hang in the air like a hovering raptor. Asher suspected that he ought to say something. However, discretion trumped stupidity and he stayed silent, absorbing Rathbone's headmasterly look of admonishment and hoping that the bell for recess would ring soon.

'However,' Rathbone said eventually, having decided that enough time had passed in loaded silence for Asher to learn his lesson, 'it may well be that I have a way forward that will suit the both of us. This afternoon I received a call from security. Apparently we have a lockdown situation in DOF's British office.'

Asher frowned. 'Lockdown? That's pretty rare, isn't it?'

'Extremely. You will be aware that it kicks in when there is a significant breach, or precognitive risk of breach, in fimmigration security. We need someone to go over there and find out what is going on. I immediately thought of you. You have investigative experience and it will get you well away from here and any temptation you have to continue with your misguided dalliance with the necrosquad.'

'I can explain all if you'd give me a minute.'

'Not even ten seconds. Please report to the duty officer on the fourth floor. They are expecting you.' And though the words came out full of reasonable entreaty, his smile was one of smug challenge.

As a general principle Asher preferred to make things as awkward as possible for supercilious desk jockeys like Rathbone. After all, what was authority for if not to be challenged? But for once he decided discretion might be his best option, since his interest had been well and truly piqued by the prospect of looking into a genuine lockdown. Rathbone had couched it in terms of doing Asher a favour, when they both knew it was merely a way of getting a disturbed troublemaker out of the section head's hair. But that was okay. Explanation of Asher's concern for the Bewildered could wait.

As he left, he could have sworn he heard a kiddy-car horn honk somewhere.

CHAPTER FOURTEEN

Bobby found the blue room through a process of trial and error. Largely because the steps leading to it tried their best to stop her from ever getting there. It felt like being on some Escher stairs which continue to climb no matter where you stand on them. She missed the right turn on the landing three times and only suspected something was wrong by a change in the air pressure whenever she stood on it. As if there existed a lot more space than was obviously on show. When she turned through ninety degrees, there they were at last; another set of stairs leading down. Bobby gasped. Not only through surprise but because there, at the very bottom, stood Miss Porter, frozen solid like everyone else in the building. Beyond her stood a blue door.

Bobby walked softly towards the slim figure, manoeuvring carefully around her, staring at the glint in those stunning eyes. From her expression, Bobby could see she'd known something was amiss. But when Bobby reached up to touch Miss Porter's skin, it felt tepid and waxy. Armed with Mr Porter's big umbrella, Bobby walked softly towards the blue door. The handle was very cold to the touch, but it moved without resistance and the door opened without a sound. She stood on the threshold, disappointment vying with relief. She wasn't sure what she'd expected to find, but an empty room wasn't on the list. There were two other doors; both closed and situated next to each other on the far wall. The place was well named, too. Everything was an innocuous shade of pastel blue.

Bobby paused long enough to let her brain adjust before stepping in. She immediately felt the change in temperature, as if she'd crossed into another weather zone, or the chill cabinet aisle in a supermarket.

She looked back and saw nothing but the open door she'd come through and the corridor with Miss Porter inanimately guarding the way. She walked across to the first closed door, depressed the handle and pulled. It opened onto a shallow storage cupboard, shelves stacked high with stationery. When she did the same with the other door, it opened, to her surprise, onto a red brick wall.

'Great,' she said out loud, though she was certain no one was listening but her.

The way Miss Porter had whispered 'blue room' so dramatically to Miss WT, Bobby expected something a little more exotic. An inner sanctum, a security room stacked with high tech equipment—anything other than a room that hosted a store cupboard and a dummy exit and was painted blue. She had to admit that the door opening onto a wall puzzled her, yet compared with all the weirdness going on upstairs, it was small beer indeed, even if the carpenter who fitted that door must have given himself a hernia from laughing so much when he'd taken payment for the work.

Bobby looked around and shivered. Something about the blue in this room rankled and left her most disquieted. One of her university girlfriends had decorated her bedroom in the exact same shade of blue and had talked a load of feng shui about it being calming and soothing and instilling peace and quiet. But the shade of this room seemed to exude a zinging energy that made Bobby's molars ache. It was the hue of standing on the high platform before a bungee jump. The exact shade of the sky when sitting strapped into the front row seat of a rollercoaster with a reassuring name like Sphincter Challenger Max.

She went to the door leading to the corridor, closed it,

studied its shut surface and found no signs or instructions that might help. She looked around again. Four walls, three doors. Just a room painted blue. There was nothing at all to be worried about in here even if the blue screamed wrong in every way possible. Ah well, whatever it was Miss Porter had come down here to do, the world froze before she managed to do it. Bobby turned to leave. She was one step away from exiting when she heard the squeak of a depressed handle and saw, over her shoulder, the door in front of the brick wall begin to open.

Her heart stuttered in her chest and the rest of her internal organs felt as if they were running south through a sieve, yet even as her brain screamed at her to run, she knew she had two options. One was to leg it into the building, the other was to step behind the opening door and see what came through.

If she chose to run, she wouldn't know what awful thing had entered here and she'd be forced to find somewhere to hide and wait for that something to find her.

If, on the other hand, she hid behind the slowly opening door, at least she'd know her enemy.

Decision made, she moved quickly and flattened herself against the blue wall. Almost immediately, a shadow appeared on the floor in the doorway. But shadows needed light, and the last time she'd looked, brick walls did not give off any light.

The shadow solidified and stepped forward into the room. She looked down at a pair of thin legs clad in dark trousers over dark pointed shoes and the tail of a midnight blue velvet coat. A pale hand crept forward beyond the edge of the door and a figure stepped into the room. Bobby's eyes ran up a straight back to a head a few inches taller than hers with curling black hair around a glimpsed profile of a pale, angular face.

There are moments in life when instinct grabs hold of common sense, stuffs a sock into its reasonable, sensible, imploring mouth, and hurls it, wide-eyed and mumbling, out of the nearest window. Breathtakingly liberating when it happens, it is a moment that has to be lived with from then on, and, unless a convenient swimming pool below the window beckons, one that comes already loaded with doubt, self-recriminatory consequences, and a wish never to see the replay. Bobby was faced with one of those moments now. Stay hidden and hope for the best, or grasp the stinging plant and confront the intruder? Umbrella poised, Bobby stepped out from behind the door and lightly touched the metal tip against the man's neck.

'Stay exactly where you are,' she said.

The frock-coated figure froze and brought both hands up. He said something that sounded like one of those unpronounceable place names in Wales with four times as many consonants as vowels.

'Speak English,' Bobby demanded.

'What do you want?' said the man. If there was an accent it wasn't one she could place. If she'd been asked to guess it would be an amalgam of Scots and something else Celtic much further south and to the west.

'What I want,' Bobby said, 'is the explanation for why everyone has turned into a waxwork and how it is that you just appeared through a door that opens onto a brick wall.'

The man didn't move. 'Those are two questions,' he croaked.

'If it's difficult for you, answer one at a time.'

'I would, only you are pressing cold iron into my neck. By my calculations I have fifteen seconds before I pass…' He stumbled to his knees.

Alarmed, Bobby withdrew the ferrule a couple of inches.

'Thank you,' the man said after ten long seconds of stertorous breathing and almost as many gasps.

Lots and lots of large and heavy thoughts were galloping through Bobby's head. Her mental landscape resembled a scene from a documentary on wildebeest migration. But two ideas crystallised and galloped to the front. The first was that the man might not be alone. With her left foot she slammed the door shut behind her. The second followed hot on the heels of the first and was the sudden realisation that she was now alone with this man with nowhere to go. She was buoyed by the fact that somehow the bottom end of Mr Porter's umbrella seemed to cause him quite a lot of pain. Bobby flicked over to Page 2 of her *Zorro* script.

'On your knees,' she said.

'I am already on my knees,' he said.

'Okay, well then…on the floor, face down, hands behind your back.'

He complied.

CHAPTER FIFTEEN

She still wore her coat. It was dark, woollen, and belted. She pulled the belt free of the loops, knelt on the man's back, and tied it around his hands. When she finished she stood up and said, 'Right, get back up to your knees and face me.'

Somehow he managed to make the movement look almost elegant where it should have been embarrassingly awkward.

As he turned, she saw his face properly for the first time. The angular features would have lent him a pinched appearance were it not for the dark eyebrows, unfairly long eyelashes, and neat nose, which somehow softened everything into a very acceptable package. A three-day stubble surrounded a full mouth now drawn into a thin and angry line.

'Who do you work for?'

'Umm, excuse me,' Bobby said. 'Let's not forget who's holding the umbrella here.'

The man's eyes drifted from Bobby's face towards the umbrella tip. 'Iron shod.' He shook his head and let out a mirthless laugh. 'Ingenious.'

'Yes, well, the man I work for…used to work for…knows what he's doing even if no one else does. Anyway, my point is I think it's me who should be asking the questions. So, right, who exactly are you?'

The man hesitated for a moment then shrugged. 'Lodge, Asher Lodge. And you are?'

'Roberta Miracle.' It came out before she could stop herself. She hadn't wanted to give her name but his request, after volunteering his own, seemed reasonable. 'Where did you come from?'

'Look, Ms Miracle,' he shook his head, 'and I don't believe for one minute that's your real name. The ironic villain nom de plume thing doesn't do it for me.'

Bobby's eyes became slits. 'For your information it's an adulteration of an old Celtic name. Meurick. Nothing ironical about it at all.'

Asher tilted his head in what might have been an apology. 'Fine, Ms Miracle. Since you're the only one left in the building, I have to assume you are the cause of this…situation. If so, you need to know I've been sent by the authorities to apprehend you.'

'Nice to see you're on top of your game, then' Bobby said, letting her eyebrows climb a notch.

Asher winced. 'You came at me from behind.'

'Villains generally do.' She sent him a flinty expression. 'So you're some sort of policeman, is that it?'

'Sort of.'

'The Met? MI5?'

'I'm a FHIFAA agent here to check on a DOF lockdown—'

Bobby cut across his words with a guffaw. 'Why does a furniture recycling company need a football agent?'

'What?'

'DOF. Disused Old Furniture,' Bobby said.

Asher stared.

'DOF?'

'The Department of Fimmigration has nothing to do with furniture,' Asher said, very slowly.

'But—' Bobby flushed. She did not like being lied to.

'And they are not going to look kindly on this…attack.'

'With an umbrella, you mean?'

'An iron-tipped umbrella.'

'What's the big deal about iron?'

Asher did not reply to that one.

'Nice uniform, by the way,' Bobby said after a while. 'What branch is it? Sleepy Hollow tactical force?'

'They usually wear black and red.'

This time it was Bobby's turn to be struck dumb. She knew her jaw was open and it took a large amount of willpower to shut it again. 'Very funny. Even if you are a security bod it still doesn't explain how you just came through a brick wall,' Bobby said. 'Is it false?'

'No. You know it isn't.'

'How do I know?'

Asher held her gaze. 'Because if you have the skill set to remain functional in the middle of a trans-dimensional stasis field, you must know about permanent portways.'

Bobby stared at him, searching his eyes for any sign of a telltale titter. She found none and suddenly felt like Nemo being left on the draining board to flop about while someone changed his water.

She pulled herself together. 'Are you telling me you know Miss Porter and Mr Danmor?'

'Of course I do. They're DOF. I'm here on their behalf. What have you done with them?'

By way of explanation and still holding up the umbrella, Bobby walked across the room, opened the door that led to the rest of the building, and showed Asher Miss Porter's frozen form beyond. Asher scowled and tried to get up.

Bobby jabbed the umbrella towards him. 'Oh no you don't. How do I know it isn't you who did all this? Maybe you set off some kind of nerve gas or something and waited until everyone passed out, and now you're here to steal the books.'

'Books?' Asher looked confused.

'Yes, books. Rare books. Don't pretend you don't know what we do here at Hipposync.'

Asher's expression transformed from suspicion into dawning understanding without passing go. 'Wait a minute. Ernest Porter's on leave and Kylah employed two interns this summer. I thought Miracle was a misprint. And there was another one, an Elmslee.'

'Elmsworthy,' Bobby corrected him, still smarting from being called a misprint.

'I only had half an hour to read the file,' Asher said in apology.

Bobby peered at him. 'Are you trying to tell me you're on the same team as Miss Porter?'

'Yes, of course I am. I've been sent here to find out what's going on.'

The stampeding wildebeest in Bobby's head picked up speed. The drumming hooves were making her head hurt. He could be lying. Although he did look very concerned when he'd seen Miss Porter. But what on earth was all this Department of Fimmigration stuff anyway? She'd never heard of it. In fact it sounded made up and barely believable. But then, what had happened to her that morning hardly qualified as run-of-the-mill.

'Right,' she said, leaning against the wall and lowering the umbrella a touch. 'I'm giving you ten minutes to explain everything to me.'

'Explain everything?'

'FIFA for a start.'

'Fae Human Intelligence and Felonious Activity Agency.'

'That's not what F.I.F.A stands for.'

'Who said it did?'

Bobby scowled. 'Okay. What about Department of Fimmigration then? And trans-dimensional stasis field? And permanent portway? Frankly, they all sound like you made them up on the spot. But since I have no explanation for how Miss WT, the Pip, Miss Porter and Mr Danmor have all turned into frozen dummies, I'm prepared to give it a shot. So yes, everything in ten minutes.'

'Can I get off my knees? Old injury, you know.'

Bobby nodded and watched him struggle up and manoeuvre himself to sit with his back against the opposite wall.

'I'm listening,' she said.

And listen she did, with growing incredulity and horror that anyone could think her so naive and gullible to believe in Fae and fimmigration and lockdown states and other worlds and other beings.

'I can see you are not completely convinced,' Asher said after nine-and-a-half minutes of seeing an increasingly dark scowl develop on Bobby's face.

'You could say that,' she said.

'Then I suppose I'm going to have to prove it to you.'

'And how do you propose to do that?'

'I'll make a deal with you. I let you out of here and we go straight to the local police. You hand me over and, though it might take a couple of hours, eventually they'll get me through to the right department and I'll be set free. I could then take you somewhere to prove to you it's all true. Through a portway.'

Bobby considered this. Definitely not what she expected. She chewed the inside of her lip and thought. Going to the police was the clincher. Correction, getting out of here was the clincher. The blue room made her feel quite sick. Fresh air and an Oxford drizzle seemed like the best cure. Besides, outside there'd be people and witnesses and men in white coats to drag this lunatic away.

'What's to stop me forcing you to let me out of here this minute?'

'Nothing. But I would put up significant resistance and it would mean you'd have to hurt me quite badly with your iron. I don't think you want to do that.'

'Really?'

'And there's also the small point of you needing a valid explanation for all of this.'

'Don't flatter yourself. I was out of the door when all this happened. If I hadn't forgotten my handbag—'

'But you had. And all this has happened. And yes, if I got you out and you ran to the nearest cab and disappeared into the city you might never see me again. But you'll always be left wondering. Did this really happen? Did you make it up? If you did make it up, which part of your addled brain was responsible? Believe me, trying to forget something like this is not easy. However, if you co-operate and help me, I can arrange for the forgetting.'

Bobby laughed. It came out as a humourless bray. 'That's the best Rohypnol chat-up line I've ever heard. You're really selling yourself, you know that?'

'You know that isn't what I meant.'

'Do I? Look, Mr Ledge, or whatever your name really is, I don't know what's going on here. I have a sneaking suspicion there's a twenty-two-year-old TV producer who's going to come out of the woodwork at any moment and tell me I've been on some weird, cringe-making prank show. I'm surprised you're not a talking hamburger.'

'There is no TV producer, Rebecca. This is real.'

'The name's Roberta and I don't remember giving you permission to call me anything and this isn't real, we both know that.'

'It is real and I can prove it to you,' he said slowly and with exaggerated patience. 'Let me prove it to you.'

'Why? Why do you need to prove it to me?'

'Because, Ms Miracle, I think I am going to very much need your help. Lockdowns imply a major security breach and you are the only one left standing. If it's any consolation, I no longer believe you are responsible. But, like it or not, you're in this up to your neck.'

She had not expected that last bit. Up to your neck inevitably left you desperately needing to know exactly what it was you were up to your neck in. Deep water? Shark infested custard? Some sort of disgusting effluent? Judging from the way this stank she'd go for the latter. But this…this man didn't strike her as your common or garden thief. He seemed genuine and yet, if she accepted even one iota of his argument, it would mean accepting that at least part of what he was saying was true. That there were Fae and Departments of Fimmigration and…she felt the heat begin to rise from her sternum and up over her throat.

It was nonsense. All of it. There was no such thing as bloody Fae or sodding fimmigration. So why, then, did she feel this undeniable tingling in the core of her being? In some deep, dark crevice of her mind a bud of repressed longing, hidden for so long under the suffocating blanket of scepticism she'd worn like a shield for the best part of twenty years, was stirring into life. She knew who'd planted that bulb. Planted it and fed it in the rich, loamy soil of her granddaughter's imagination. Lucille Miracle had made it a game to secretly nurture and hide the roots away from the sensible eyes and ears of her parents for fear they might be plucked out like a weed. But her grandmother stopped feeding it and her father, suspecting the truth, had pointed out the monstrosity of what could grow from such wild and unnatural planting if you weren't very, very careful. And Bobby had seen and cried and buried that dried out bulb in the deep, dark crevice. Her father warned her, begged her to arm herself with common sense and wisdom and not yield to the temptation of the imagination. And she, as a good daughter, had complied. And yet, somewhere deep in her heart, Bobby refused to give up her grandmother's legacy completely. That was why she still wore Lucille's clothes. Wore them and rationalised it under an aesthetic that was easy to swallow because it conformed with a pop culture trope to which she could easily adapt.

Suddenly, the irony of it was so acute it felt like she might break in two.

Corporate Goth Bobby. Who was she trying to kid?

Well, if her grandmother were here now, in this room with Lodge the unfunny comedian, what would she have done or said? Would she have tilted back her head and rolled her mad eyes and screamed, 'Rack! Rack!'

'Hello?' said Asher, 'anyone home?'

Bobby came back to herself, her mouth a razor cut in her face. 'So, how do we get out, Mr Lodge?' she said.

'The same way I came in.'

'Through a brick wall?'

'It is the only way. There is no other door. And the name is Asher, by the way.'

'If my grandmother could only see me now.' Bobby shook her head. 'You first. We find a policeman, right?'

'Right.'

'And if we get out of this and I find it's a wind-up, I'll be putting this umbrella tip somewhere the sun never shines and ramming it in so hard it'll take a team of surgeons a whole day to remove it.'

'That is the worst iron ferruled umbrella chat-up line I've ever heard,' Asher said, his face a poker.

She held the umbrella out like a sword. 'Not the slightest bit funny. Especially when I expect you'll want me to untie you?'

'That will not be necessary. The portway has flesh recognition.' He stood facing Bobby with his back to the door, crouching slightly to get his hands to the handle. She heard the faint mechanical click and saw the door open, letting cold, grey Oxford light in.

'Hmm,' said Asher. 'I do believe it has started to rain.'

'Just as well I've got the umbrella then,' Bobby said and pointed it menacingly towards him.

CHAPTER SIXTEEN

ASHER JERKED backwards and out into the daylight. Bobby followed. They emerged into the car park of the café next door that backed onto the old canal boatyard. Over her shoulder, Bobby caught a stab of silver light outlining the doorway before it zipped shut to leave nothing but Hipposync's brick wall.

'See?' Asher said. 'Now do you believe me?'

'Policeman,' she said curtly, trying to hide the consternation she felt inside. The door had disappeared. How could the door simply disappear like that?

'Why don't you telephonically contact one?'

'Telephonically contact one? What, dial 999? I could, but then you might have bugged my phone so that whatever I ring goes to some number you've set up and a joke police car will turn up here in five minutes. No, let's not telephonically contact anyone; let's perambulate directionally instead. We're bound to come across one sooner or later.' She sent him a sideways glance but he was either oblivious to, or deliberately chose to ignore, her mockery.

They headed east. Up Walton Crescent and Little Clarendon Street towards St Giles and the tourists and students and shops. The streets were wet with rain, the sky pewter, the air damp and unseasonably warm under a soggy blanket of yet another Atlantic low. Bobby walked at Asher's side, happy his hands were still bound; a fact which made him look like an off duty policeman with muscle memory syndrome.

'Am I to assume you weren't in the building when the lockdown kicked in?' ASHER ASKED.

'As I said, I was on the way out. I just managed to squeeze back in as the front door was closing. It made my hand go funny.' She looked again at her fingers. The weird shimmer was less but still evident.

'Hmm,' Asher said. 'That should not have happened. Tell me exactly what took place prior to your leaving.'

There wasn't that much to tell, or so she thought. But by the time she'd regurgitated the day before, starting with Fitzgerald and the *Frankenstein*, they'd walked half a mile. He stopped her only when she got to the bit where she got locked in the loo. He made her tell that bit twice. At first she refused, but he was insistent.

'And the explanation for you being unable to open the door?'

'There wasn't one. Miss Porter said she'd be looking into it.'

Asher pursed his lips but had the good taste to resist the obvious scatological quip. 'Go on.'

So she did, right up to the point where she finally found the blue room and he appeared through the brick wall. By the time she'd finished they were on St Giles and heading towards the city centre. They'd gone forty yards when Bobby spotted two special constables walking towards them.

'Right, here we go.'

'I think now you ought to untie me,' Asher said.

They moved to the edge of the pavement and Bobby undid the belt around his hands. She watched as Asher massaged his wrists. 'Let me do the talking,' he said.

The wildebeest in Bobby's head, alert but quietly grazing up to that point, were spooked into another ground-trembling gallop. Why was this man, clearly a thief or worse and dressed like someone from a steampunk band (she'd bet he had a hat with a feather in it somewhere), not running from her and the police like he ought to be? She'd brought him here so that when she untied him, besides the police, there'd be too many people around for him to try anything weird. But now the idiot was actually walking towards the officers with his hand up, beckoning.

'Officers, might I have a word?'

Bobby watched in frozen horror while an ugly thought pushed its way through the mud of her confusion and mushroomed into grey, dirt-flecked clarity. Could it possibly be that Lodge…Asher was telling the truth here? If he was, then…Her mind went into pause mode while a little egg-timer rotated behind her retinas as she tried to assimilate the fact that, as well as being lumbered with a bloke from a Conan Doyle story, she was being forced to consider, very much against her will, the twisted Holmesian cliché of having eliminated the impossible to be left with something even more improbable as an answer.

The police officers watched Asher's approach with that wary expression typical of law enforcement employees used to seeing the worst examples of humanity prostrate and yelling obscenities at them outside kebab shops in any given city centre on any given Friday night between the hours of midnight and 4 am.

'Hello officer,' said Asher, and flashed them his badge. 'My name is Asher Lodge and I'm a first tier investigative agent with FHIFAA.'

Bobby watched the exchange from a few paces back. As expected, the police's response was less than effusive.

'Had a late night have we, sir?' asked the female constable, frowning at the badge.

'Not at all,' Asher said. 'However, I have a witness to a lockdown situation and she requires proof of my credentials.'

'Does she now?' The male officer sent a sceptical glance in Bobby's direction.

'Yes. Can you communicate through radiofrequency transmission that I request a formal identification check.'

Bobby watched the two officers exchange glances. No words were spoken. They were a partnership and they understood one another very well. And though Bobby didn't know either of them, she read those glances as if they'd been chalked up on a blackboard in foot high letters. In any language you cared to choose, they said, 'Drugs or mental illness, what do you reckon? I'll have a quid on it being miaow miaow.'

Without really knowing why, other than the fact that she harboured a soft spot for stray dogs and homeless people, Bobby stepped forward, put on her sunniest smile, and grabbed Asher's arm.

'Sorry. He's in character. The University of the Undead Conference? It's on today at the Randolph. He's a bit excited, aren't you, luv?'

'Great,' sighed the female officer. 'Does that mean we're likely to come across a lot more jokers like him today?'

'Very likely,' said Bobby. She gave Asher's arm a squeeze. 'Come on, before they throw you in jail for dressing like a complete prat.' She pulled him away. He resisted, but she pulled harder. 'Don't look back,' she ordered out of the corner of her mouth.

'But—'

'It's obvious they haven't heard of FHIFAA. Or rather they have and it doesn't mean what you think it does. Either way, they think you're a loony.'

'Someone who worships the moon?'

'Exactly that.'

When they were a safe distance away she risked an over the shoulder glance. The police had moved on and were talking to a man sitting on a bench and singing 'Delilah' loudly, surrounded by a dozen cans of cider.

'Right. You're safe.'

'But I have not been able to satisfy your request for provenance.'

'It's okay. We'll do without the provenance. I believe you. At least I believe you think you are who you are.'

'So involving the police will not be necessary?'

'No. Let's call it quits. This is where I go my way and you go yours. Back to Hipposync if you want to. Whereas I require a blueberry muffin the size of Belgium and a double shot mochaccino.' She turned away.

Asher gripped her arm. 'But I need your help.'

Bobby looked down at his hand and then up into his face. 'You need someone's help all right, but it's not mine. And technically, that's assault.'

Asher did not relinquish his grip. 'But we made a bargain. You said that if we went to the police, you'd help me.'

'Yes, I know. But then we didn't really establish your bona fides with said police, did we?'

'You did not allow me much opportunity.'

He was earnest, this one. She had to give him that. 'No, I didn't. That's because they were about to ring for an ambulance. The kind with nice, soft padded walls.'

'So you must let me prove my bona fides another way,' Asher said.

'You really need to put some work in on those chat-up lines,' Bobby replied, shaking her head and staring pointedly at his restraining hand and then back into his face. He resisted, his eyes very dark and very intense. He seemed to be thinking furiously.

'I have it. It will take only a few minutes. I promise you will not be harmed.'

'If you think you're taking me to some dark alley—'

'Choose a restaurant near here. One that is closed but that you are familiar with.' He let her arm go.

'A shut restaurant?' she said and knew her eyebrows were reaching for her hairline. Humour him, she thought. What does five more minutes of ultra weirdness matter in a day already only three stops short of bizarre central?

'Okay. Well, there's Boudins. Slightly French with a hint of Tangiers. It's back on Little Clarendon Street.'

He turned and retraced his steps. Bobby watched him and then, much to her own surprise, followed, muttering, 'I must be stark raving mad.'

Boudins had a double frontage with 'Specials' written on the glass either side of the door. It was still only a little after ten in the morning and the place was firmly shut, its stools and chairs upturned on the handful of tables inside.

'Try the door,' Asher said.

Bobby did. It rattled a little but did not budge.

'You are happy it is locked?'

'Yes,' she said, slightly irritated that he needed to state the obvious and vaguely aware his delivery reminded her very much of a street magician. The kind who could put your phone into a beer bottle or make you find your dead father's name on a playing card stuck to the bumper of a refuse truck parked in the next street.

'However, it is a restaurant and so people watching will think nothing of us walking in.'

'Don't tell me you have the key?'

'No, but I have this.' He stepped forward and took a small round object from his pocket with a flourish. It looked smooth and highly polished, a deep green mottled colour with streaks of white, yellow, and purple. One side of it was flattened.

'A door knob?' she asked.

'We call it an Aperio. It allows ingress to anywhere that has a door, so long as you are familiar with the destination, or can picture it clearly in your head.'

Bobby watched Asher deftly place the Aperio onto the frame on the hinged side of the Boudins' front door, twist, and push. The door opened silently.

'After you,' he said.

'But this is breaking and entering,' she protested, once her jaw regained the ability to shut.

'We are entering, yes, but we have broken nothing. Besides, Boudins is not our destination.'

'What are you talking about?'

Asher stepped through and held the door open for her. 'All I'm doing is keeping my end of the bargain. Please, follow me.'

Bobby hesitated.

'At least half a dozen people will see you entering this place with me. And there is closed circuit televisual coverage.'

He was right. There was indeed CCTV coverage all over the street, so it wasn't exactly an abduction. Shaking her head, but still clutching her umbrella, Bobby followed him through the door.

CHAPTER SEVENTEEN

THE SMELL HIT HER FIRST. The pungent aroma of manure catching in her throat. But then she looked around and what she saw caused her breath to seize. She wasn't in Boudins. She was outdoors, on the steps of an austere-looking building of grey stone, in front of two massive black studded doors set between two Doric pillars. Above the doors, carved into the stone, were a hawk, a tree, and the letters *FHIFAA*. At least they became FHIFAA as she focused on them, since a first glance revealed nothing but three indecipherable runic glyphs.

But she had only a fleeting second to wonder whether that had in fact happened because her eyes did not linger on the building. They were being dragged from one incredible sight to another. Everything was completely different from anything she had ever seen. She drank it all in. And like a good pinot noir, it was making her feel instantly light headed. Or was that the smell? As she studied the streets, the source of the pungent aroma became instantly obvious. Piles of 'source' sat steaming in the road some fifty feet away from where she stood. That same source was being replenished quite frequently from the backsides of the many horses trotting noisily up and down the street, pulling buggies or two-wheeled cabs. Others pulled large wagons laden with canvas-covered lumps, which, she assumed, were goods.

Not one of the vehicles was manned.

The air felt bitter, much colder than Oxford, and the sky was the flat and still grey that presaged snow. The noise differed, too. The clatter of hooves on the road mingling with the constant yells and cries from street vendors scattered over the pavement next to barrows and braziers. Ropes spanned the street from tall poles, each strung with holly and mistletoe. Hanging from every other pole were lit lanterns flickering with real flames, even though it was still daylight.

And then there were the people. People and other… non-people. The people, i.e. the ones that looked like her and Asher, all wore retro clothes with a capital R; the men in long coats and the women in long dresses and high-collared blouses with heavy capes. Clothes not dissimilar to those she sometimes wore for work. If she wanted a label it would have been neo-Victorian. Certainly it put Asher's dress sense into context. Compared to some of the people on the street, his garb was pretty sober. But very quickly, Bobby's eyes were drawn to the others, the non-people, mingling on the pavement with everyone else.

A large and shapeless brown hill in a striped robe sauntered along wearing a trilby. It waved to Asher, who waved back.

'How's it going, Asher?' said the hill, or rather rumbled the hill, since what Bobby heard was more a kind of growl with the odd word in it.

'Not too bad, Binkhorst. You?'

'Audit at the bank. Workin' me to the bone. I've lost half a ton in a week.'

'You'll survive,' Asher said.

The hill snorted. It sounded like a small volcano clearing its throat.

Asher turned back from this exchange and caught Bobby staring. 'What?'

'What? What do you mean what? That…*thing* is what!'

'Binkhorst?' Asher said jauntily. 'Accountant mate of mine. He's a troll. Likes the horses, does Binks.'

'What, betting on them or sandwiched in a bun?'

'There is no need to be offensive,' Asher said.

'Isn't there? Where the hell are we, Asher?'

'New Thameswick.'

'And where exactly is that?'

'It's here. It always has been here. Right under your nose.'

Bobby sighed. 'No, from the smell of the place I think I would have noticed. Please, no riddles.'

'We're standing just inside the restaurant in your world. So if you squinted your eyes and peered in a certain way whilst you were there you might see this place now that I have a door open. But the fact is, none of your lot can see it unless the tenth gate is open.'

'Tenth gate? There you go again. You may be fluent in gibberish but I flunked the entrance exam. How come I'm seeing things? Who's opened my gate?'

'Coming through using an Aperio or via a portway activates it automatically.'

'There it is again: 'Coming through'. Coming through what to where? Are you saying that we've somehow travelled into another kind of world?'

'The Fae world. *My* world. And congratulations, by the way. Not many people get to visit here alive. Generally you need to be either one of us or apply for a Visa. And the major qualification for that is death.'

For a moment she was genuinely lost for words. When she eventually found some she could only glare and mumble, 'Umm, thanks for sharing.'

'FHIFAA agents have special dispensation for guests, or prisoners.'

'Which am I?'

Asher ignored her.

Bobby tilted her head and smiled. It did not look convincing. 'It's a film set, isn't it? You've set me up, haven't you?'

Asher shook his head. 'This is real. If it was a film set, do you think we'd employ Pogue Lempit over there?' He pointed towards a small man with no teeth, whose facial features would have made the front page of *Gargoyle's Health* any day of the week.

Bobby almost gagged, but managed to whisper, 'That poor man. Was it an accident?'

'His mother preferred the term 'unplanned'. Does a roaring trade in scaring children who refuse to behave.'

Pogue caught Asher looking at him, raised his hand and smiled. Bobby felt her stomach begin to turn.

'Is he human?'

'No. Of course not. He's a Carpathstahn Hill Wight.'

'And all the other…creatures, they're not people in fancy dress then?'

'No. Everyone here is Fae, or Fae-related.'

Bobby shook her head. 'But that's just…made up nonsense, isn't it?'

Asher shrugged. 'What are your eyes and ears and nose telling you?'

'But I don't believe in this stuff. Superstition, fairies, monsters —I mean, come on. I wasn't born yest—'

'If you don't believe it, how come you dress like a witch?'

That one stopped her mid-rant. 'Like a *what?*' She let out a guffaw. 'I've been called a lot of things. Goth Bitch, Dollgotha, Frankendyke, but never Witch.'

'Well, here you could be arrested for impersonating one.' Asher gave a vague wave of his hand. 'Regardless of what you believe or don't, this is reality for us.'

'And you work here?' Bobby pointed to the building behind.

Asher nodded.

'Are we going in?'

Asher shrugged. 'Or we could get some coffee. You said you wanted some. Have a favourite bean?'

'Well, it's not 'been taken for a ride'—'

His glare cut her off.

'Okay. Sumatran Mandheling. When I can afford it.'

'Right. Then I'll make that my bonus bona fides.'

Asher stood on the pavement and whistled. A large two-wheeled Hansom cab pulled up, pulled by a large black horse with a white star on its forehead. He said simply, 'The original coffee shop,' and held his hand out to help Bobby on.

'Tell me why there is no driver?'

'The horses know where to go. This one's called Gary, by the way.'

'Right.'

Gary whinnied a greeting.

'Very intelligent beings, Fae horses. Related to centaurs. One week in four they have two legs. Most of them learn The Knowledge that way. You see them riding around on bikes with bits of maps on the handlebars.'

'I don't believe you.'

Asher shrugged.

Bobby didn't say much after that. Too busy taking in the sights. They were travelling to what must have been the financial district. Signs for usurers, loans and pawnbrokers vied with banks with unlikely names like Joubert, Sedgwick and Tansle, Ghoul and Co, The Soul Exchange, and The Royal Bank of Shetland. She pointed to a large Gothic mansion flying a black and white flag. It bore an uncanny resemblance to the Sagrada Familia.

'What's that?'

'That is the Le Fey Academy. Where they train witches.'

Bobby stared. It was ornate and art nouveau mysterious as well as being altogether beautiful. Eventually, they turned into some more elaborately decorated streets with much larger stores.

'This is Mercantile Parade. You can get almost anything you want here. Anything you can't get here is definitely available in the bazaar. That's Herods.' Asher pointed out a six-storey building with green and gold awnings. 'Most famous shop in New Thameswick. Has everything you can buy anywhere else for twice the price. Mainly so you can have one of their little bags to show you've been there.'

They drove along wide avenues flanked by grand stone buildings for a good ten minutes before Gary took a small side street lined by shops of such a weird and wonderful nature Bobby could only stare in silent wonder. Finally, they pulled up in front of a four-storey building, the ground floor of which had been given over to a single establishment. A huge hourglass filled with red sand stood above the door. Below it in gold lettering were the words:

The Original Coffee Shop

'Hmm,' Bobby said as she studied the ornate facade. 'Not exactly Starbucks.'

Asher opened the door and they stepped inside. Not much of a coffee shop by Bobby's standards, or by anyone else's come to that. There were no tables or chairs, no smell of coffee and no one drinking anything at all. Behind a tall counter stood a man dressed in a high-collared white shirt, black tie and an apron with 'The Original Coffee Shop' written upon it. Scattered over the counter were jars full of biscotti, amaretti, flapjacks, and smoked cupcakes. On their own under a glass cake stand dome, were other sweets with unlikely labels such as snail porridge truffles, silicone cakes, and a variety of very dark scrabbly things with blue-black carapaces that were still moving.

'Can I help you?' asked the barista.

'We'd like some Sumatran coffee, please.' Asher turned to Bobby. 'Latte? Cappuccino?'

'Cappuccino would be great,' Bobby said.

'Here or take out?'

'Here, please.'

'Name you'd like to be known as?'

Asher gave their names and Bobby watched as the barista wrote down the order and stuck two pieces of paper onto some coffee cups. Then he turned and disappeared behind a curtain.

'Why can't we watch him make it?' Bobby whispered, adding a suspicious frown for good measure.

'Because he doesn't.'

'Then who—' The barista came back and smiled at them both.

'It'll be number six. Enjoy.'

Bobby looked around. 'Number six? Where are the other five?'

Asher smiled. 'This way.' He stepped towards the wall. Bobby noticed ornate and brightly coloured drapes with numbers above them. Asher moved to the far right toward the number six, pulled back the drapes and revealed a wooden door.

'Ready?' he said and pushed it open. Bobby walked through into a different room. The place was half empty and an air-conditioned breeze wafted down from a rotating ceiling fan. There was seating for no more than fifteen on stools and a padded bench at four tables. Outside, the day appeared very different through the large windows. Bright and breezy as opposed to the greyness they'd left. But the biggest difference was in the way the room smelled. The aroma of roasted coffee hung in the air like a wonderful pair of welcoming arms. A diminutive Asian man beamed at them from behind a counter supporting a gleaming array of silver equipment. They moved to a table and sat. A minute later, the Asian man called, 'Asher, two cappuccinos?'

Asher raised a hand and the man brought over two fresh cups. Bobby, still frowning, took a sip. The taste exploded in her mouth. She took another sip and studied Asher over the rim of her cup as he, too, sipped the beverage.

'This is fantastic,' she said. 'This is the best coffee I've ever…What is this place?'

'For us, it's still The Original Coffee Shop. But for the indigenous population,' he pointed to the small menu folded in the centre of the table. 'It's The Roast, Tharmin City Office complex, Jakarta.'

The cup, once again halfway to Bobby's lips for a third sip, stopped in mid-air. 'Jakarta is in Indonesia,' she said in a low voice that hovered on the edge of a sardonic laugh.

Asher nodded. A movement without the bat of an eyelid anywhere near it.

A long moment of reciprocal blinking ended when Asher added, 'Go outside if you don't believe me. Does that look like New Thameswick in December?'

Bobby looked. It was definitely not like pungent, cold New Thameswick, nor Oxford, come to think of it. She stood and walked to the door, opened it and felt the caress of hot, humid air wash over her. She stepped out onto the pavement full of people dressed for subtropical weather—the men all small and dark-haired, the women tiny and pretty in summer dresses—and drew stares like a schoolboy drew…things schoolboys drew, usually, in Bobby's limited experience as a schoolgirl: a lurid combination of the cylindrical and spherical. The street buzzed with sound and was gridlocked with cars; the majority recognisable Japanese or Korean.

She was trembling when she got back inside. So much so she had to hold her cup in both hands.

'I don't understand.'

'Door number six in the original coffee shop is a Portway. We travel by peregrination through portals. All highly regulated. For example, The Original Coffee Shop will have bought a license for a Portway into this place and it kicks in whenever the barista deploys certain prearranged portal access codes. We appear here as members of the indigenous population.'

'And how does he do that?'

'It's…complicated. I can lend you a book if you like. With commercialism has come organisation. Some clever people have tried making Fae power into a system, to make it safer and a bit more, um, reproducible. I don't mean alchemy, though they are often looked on as pioneers. Big companies have got involved and it's spawned industry. Take transport, for example. The biggest one here is Trans-Con. Organised portways generally work well, like us being able to travel here. Though occasionally they don't and we might have ended up sitting on a boulder on Saturn.'

'But how? How does it work?'

'Ah, it's a combination of learning how to bend the universe around your will and having the ability to do that. And as for power, it's simply there, out in the world. Best way to describe it is as a kind of dark energy—energy your scientists think is responsible for expanding the universe. Only we think of it in terms of energy threads and what we do is knit those threads together to make a wearable jumper. Sometimes it ends up as a wonky beanie hat; sometimes it's a fifty thousand-scruple designer coat. Trans-Con use lots of clever people who've been to university to work together in their open plan knitting office. But really anyone can try and use it. Though usually, to do it properly means five years of study to become a wizard. Or it could mean simply shaking a particular stick at something in a special way because your great-great-granddad did it once and turned a troll into a rock. It can be a bit random like that. Trans-

Con takes the random out of the equation. But there are pockets of dark energy hidden in things that jump out at you when you least expect it. Artefacts and such.'

'It sounds messy,' Bobby said. 'Sounds out of control, like anyone could get hold of something powerful and become a real nuisance.'

'That happens everywhere.'

'Really?' Bobby said, with a sceptical smile.

'Perhaps you'd care to explain methamphetamine or Chernobyl?'

'Ah,' she frowned. As analogies went, it was a tough one. Her trembling was worse now, as were her turbulent thoughts.

'So, do I pass the test?' Asher asked.

'I don't know what to think.'

'Don't think, just accept. We need to go back to Oxford. All I ask is that you help me do my job.'

Bobby hesitated. As with all people faced with the inexplicable, the choice was stark. Logic told her all this was impossible, that she was dreaming, that this was an elaborate hoax. If it was, they must have a budget the size of China. And, more importantly, why on earth would anyone want to spend that much money, go to such incredible lengths just to hoodwink her? She took another sip. The coffee worked its own magic. This truly was the most fantastic thing she'd ever tasted. For a moment she wondered if he'd put something in it, but then she threw that thought out. He'd had lots of opportunity already to do weird stuff, properly weird stuff.

Jakarta!

No, the coffee's wonder was all in the taste. They obviously roasted their own beans here and it made a difference. It also, much to her surprise, made up her mind.

'Okay, I'll go with you. But only if you promise to bring me back here again once Miss Porter and Mr Danmor are back to normal?'

'Deal.' Asher smiled and held out his hand. Bobby shook it, all the while wondering what it was she was letting herself in for. But then, she argued, what else did the unemployed Bobby Miracle have to do for the rest of the day?

CHAPTER EIGHTEEN

'Why do we have to go back if we've got your opening thingy?' Bobby asked as Gary guided them back through the streets towards the FHIFAA building. 'Won't any doorway do?'

'Theoretically, yes,' Asher answered. 'But going back through the same Portway uses up less power and the department is on an austerity drive.'

Bobby stayed silent for a couple of minutes. There were so many things she could have asked, but one thing niggled like a hair under a contact lens. She turned abruptly to Asher. 'What did you mean when you said I dressed like a witch?'

'You do.'

'I do not have a pointy hat.'

Asher made a great show of looking up at her bare head and shook his head. 'When was the last time you saw a witch wearing a pointy hat?'

'Halloween?' There was a pause while she waited for him to stop laughing before Bobby asked, 'And what's so funny about that?'

Asher sighed. 'Okay.' He leaned forward toward Gary's rear end. 'Take us to South Milton Street.'

The cab changed direction and took a sharp left. The streets were busy with shoppers here. It was difficult to know which was more colourful: the flags and bunting in the shop windows, or the fifty-seven varieties of being staring into them. Four hundred yards later, the cab pulled up in front of some very large premises with silver and black frontage and the words 'Coven Garden' emblazoned in what looked like burnished diamonds above a black awning.

Asher got out and spoke to Gary. 'We'll be five minutes. I'm just showing the lady what goes on here.' Gary whinnied. Asher turned to Bobby. 'Come on. See for yourself.'

For the third time that morning, Asher pushed open a door and let Bobby go first. Inside, the floor space was divided into sections, very much like a department store. Signs hung from the ceiling: 'Hexes', 'Love Potions', 'Cures', 'Curses'. Each section was manned, or rather womanned, by several very attractive salespeople, all female. But the one striking thing about each and every one of them was the way they were dressed. Bobby would have been happy to accept any item of clothing that these women were wearing as part of her own wardrobe.

'What is this place?' Bobby whispered.

'Exactly what it looks like. It's a witching house. Where you come if you want something special for your friends, or your enemies.'

'But…'

A girl approached. She wore her white hair held in an elaborate arrangement of black combs, though her eyebrows were jet black and shaped. Her face was also white, with dark blue lipstick and matching eye shadow. Around a forehead tattooed with delicate entwining lines she wore a circlet of gemstones. A dark green velvet strapless dress fitted tightly around the bodice with long flared sleeves. It ended in a scalloped hem over gossamer tights and black pumps. Over one breast she wore a badge. It said:

> My body is my instrument.
> Owner adjustments only.

'Would madam care to try some Extract of Heather tincture? Three scruples an ounce. Guaranteed to add a little luck to your day.' There was a brogue in there somewhere. It made her voice tinkle.

'Really?'

'Your hand, please.'

Bobby held out her hand and the girl turned it over and squeezed a single droplet of tincture on it. There were rings on every one of the girl's fingers. The tincture tingled and smelled of thyme and spearmint.

'Thank you,' Bobby said.

The girl smiled before glancing at Asher. Her gaze lingered there appraisingly and a touch disdainfully, before drifting back again to Bobby. By the time it arrived at her, the smile had returned. 'By the way, I love your shirt.'

Bobby grinned. When she'd gone, she whispered to Asher, 'Oh dear, if looks could kill, eh? Do you know her?'

'Never seen her before. And don't joke. Some looks can kill in here.'

Bobby giggled. It petered out when she saw Asher's uncomfortable expression. He leaned in to explain and dropped his voice. 'Not many men come in here. If they do it's generally for a lip balm so they can get a Coven Garden bag with rope handles and even then only if there's a trusted friend outside to keep an eye on you. Breathe the wrong way and a waft of one of their aerosol potions could send you straight home to propose to your milkman.'

'Ha ha, very funny.'

'Nothing funny about it at all. Did you not see the sign on the way in, 'Leave your WVXY at the door'?'

'WVXY?'

'WV is World View, XY is borrowed from your world. Something to do with getenics?'

'Genetics,' Bobby corrected him.

'Well anyway, in a post-persecution world, not everyone has accepted the witch's role in society…yet. Especially those that liked the smell of burning flesh. Witches are still trying to change attitudes. The trouble is that their own attitude tends to get in the way.'

'What about yours?'

'I believe witches deserve the same respect as wizards, that they've been objectified for far too long by society, and that anyone who wants to write a poem about the power of cauldrons should be allowed to do so. I also believe that they should dress however they want. It's an acknowledgement of their freedom to express themselves and it is not up to anyone to be judgemental.'

Bobby checked his face for any sign of a grin. It was a blank sheet. 'Wow, did they teach you all that stuff at school?'

Asher dropped his voice again. 'There are also listening ports all over this store.' He straightened and added in a normal indoor voice, 'They reserve the right to evict anyone who is witchist. At school, witch studies are now compulsory and considered educational, though some of the teachers are a bit earnest. Mine was something of a…character. She expected you to stand up and wave when she entered a room for a start. But it's difficult to concentrate when your teacher hosts a nesting woodpecker in her hair and wears camouflage pyjama bottoms and no shoes. You can see what I meant about the way you dress, can you not? It's almost like you're one of the staff here.'

'Well, yes. I agree there's a certain similarity. But I'm no witch.'

'Maybe not. But you're no Goth weirdo here either, Roberta.'

Bobby frowned. It was a good point. And, damn it all, she liked the way he said her name. Lots of rolling Rs in there that had no right to do what they did to her smile centre.

Outside, Gary stood waiting. Asher was about to step up when Bobby's eyes were drawn to something fluttering above his head. She stepped back just in time to avoid a healthy dollop of pigeon guano, which landed on the exact spot she'd been standing on ten seconds before. The heather tincture obviously worked.

Asher reached up and grabbed the carrier pigeon, who didn't seem in the slightest perturbed by the manhandling. He unclipped a message from its leg and read it. Bobby watched his features harden.

'Problems?'

'Yes. It looks like I'm going to have to stay here for a while.

I'll take you back to FHIFAA and get you back to Hipposync. I won't be long—'

'I'm not going back to that place alone. Seeing Miss WT paralysed with a droplet of drool running down the side of her mouth is enough to give anyone the creeps.'

'Everyone there is in the stasis field—'

'Except me. I'll stay here if you don't mind. I can do some shopping—'

'You wouldn't last five minutes before someone would have you volunteering blood for the vampire shelter or recruiting you to some zombie cult or other.'

'Thanks,' Bobby said, offended. 'I'm a veteran of Oxford Street Boxing Day sales, I'll have you know.'

'Besides, you're not meant to be here. You need a licence for free passage. You can only really go where I go.'

'Charming. In that case I'll have to come with you, won't I?'

'This is not a jaunt. I'll be on official FHIFAA business.' Asher hesitated before adding, 'Sort of.'

'Get me a deputy's badge then,' Bobby said, irked.

Asher gave her a look that would have flailed a furry animal. 'This is not a Spaghetti Heston.'

'You mean Western,' Bobby corrected him.

'Whatever,' Asher said. After feeding the pigeon some seed from a waistcoat pocket, he let it go and it disappeared into the grey sky. Asher climbed into the cab and said to Gary, 'Trenches Road.'

CHAPTER NINETEEN

AFTER FIVE MINUTES of trundling through heavy traffic, they'd left the commercial area behind and Bobby noted they were in a far less salubrious part of the city. The grand stone buildings and wide avenues gave way to wooden houses with sagging roofs, blackened oak frames with lime rendered panels and bent and crooked eaves. A mist had appeared and through it, silhouetted against the sky, were even more crooked chimneys that leaned precariously as they spewed smoke skywards. The road was barely wide enough for two-way traffic and the upper levels of the houses leaned towards the middle of the road. Bobby could lift a hand up and touch the bottom of the second storeys quite easily.

They travelled ever deeper into this murky, cramped claustrophobic area. When Bobby managed to catch a glimpse of the locals huddling in doorways, her glance met hooded eyes under suspicious brows.

'Nice area,' Bobby said.

'Loaded with history,' Asher nodded.

'Loaded with filth more like,' Bobby made a face.

'There are worse spots.'

'Where? On the moon?'

'Just because it isn't to your taste—'

'More biological hazard awareness than taste, I'd say. Why don't the authorities smarten this place up?'

'Smarten it up? What for? This is Blatt. It's a major tourist attraction.'

Bobby's sceptical snort made Asher suddenly bristle. She pointed at a dog lying slumped in the gutter on the side of the road, its tongue lolling, one dead eye staring at the sky. Asher shouted at Gary to stop and hailed one of the ladies of the area, who tottered out on high-heeled lace up boots from a doorway. She wore a bodice of some kind and a skirt so scalloped at the front, the ratio of flesh to clothing would have made even a wrecking ball blush.

'Hello deary, after a good time are you? Three scruples for my individual attention, five if that witch wants in on it, six if she wants to use a broom—'

'I am not a witch,' Bobby said through gritted teeth.

'Why are you dressed up as one then?'

Asher sighed. 'We're not after any of your…services today, thank you. It's about the dog. Is it really dead? If it is, why hasn't someone cleared it away?'

'Who, Snowy?'

Bobby looked across at the dog. It was jet black.

'Yes,' Asher said.

The woman raised a curved thumb and middle finger to her painted mouth and let out a piercing whistle. The dog lifted its black head, looked at the woman, wagged its tail twice and then flopped back down again.

'No, he's in character, is Snowy.' She leaned in so that the window of the Hansom cab framed her face. Under the streaks of mud and grime, her features were almost attractive. She would have been even more almost attractive if her teeth hadn't all been black and stumpy. She dropped her voice conspiratorially. 'Used to be an actor, apparently. You know, previous life. Funny name he had, something like Laurence Olbus or Obliviate.'

'Obliviate?' Bobby asked.

'Yeah, acted in plays and wossname.'

Something went ping in Bobby's head. 'You mean Olivier?'

'Yeah, that's the one.' The woman made a face. 'Excuse me, having trouble with me teeth.'

To Bobby's horror and disgust, the woman lifted a finger and began poking at the black stumps in her mouth. A second later, a complete upper denture fell forward into the woman's hand to reveal a row of wholesome, clean, white teeth beneath. Her voice changed, too. Having realised there was no sale here she suddenly became less estuary and a lot more Henley on Thameswick. 'Sorry, poppy seed under my top set.' She flicked at the gap between an incisor and a canine.

'So, you're saying the dog is acting?' Bobby asked when her tongue recovered from having been turned to cardboard by:

1) Even the faintest possibility a black dog called Snowy playing dead in the gutter had anything at all to do with a world famous deceased actor, and

2) Wondering why this woman wore rotten dentures.

'Of course. Aren't we all?' She winked at them both.

Faced with this simple admission, groaning as it was under the weight of all kinds of interesting philosophical baggage, and delivered with a twinkly-eyed challenge, even Asher seemed momentarily nonplussed.

'Thanks,' he said after a long moment, 'for clearing that up.'

'Don't thank me. Thank Snowy. He comes out with all sorts of remarkable ideas, does our Snowy. What did he say last week? All the world's a cage, and all the men and women in it are…in jail. He's a laugh a minute.' She lowered her eyes; Bobby noticed that the stye in one of them was stuck on. 'He's even thinking of starting an evening class. Says he has a method. Sure I can't tempt you with a two-scruple special?' She slipped her stumps back over her teeth and dropped effortlessly back into her role. 'Might be eligible for a discount? Or the witch could do somethin' with a pointy hat—'

'No, no thanks,' Asher turned to the horse. 'On you go, Gary.'

They lumbered off, Gary quickly accelerating to a trot.

When she'd assimilated as much of the information about

Snowy and the 'actor' that her brain would allow without frying itself, Bobby said, 'That woman has a perfect set of teeth.'

'Yes,' Asher said.

'And Snowy is an acting coach.'

'Uh-huh.'

'So, is this,' she waved her hand around at the Dickensian streets, 'all a sham?'

'Not all of it. Just most of it. They're simply catering for people's expectations, that's all. The Nippontuck come here in droves. They fully expect a bit of poverty and chimney sweeps and the like.'

'But…'

'It's called the Glamour. One of the many things I see I shall have to explain to you.'

'I'm listening.'

And explain Asher did. About the fact that with little literature or cinema, people—and all the other creatures—wanted to have experiences. Fiction for want of a better word, up close and personal. That was why they had places like Blatt. Some people could do it through charms and spells; others needed papier mâché and balsa wood. But it added up to the same thing, by and large. It was all about giving people what they wanted and letting them have it in a way that pleased their senses, if only for a very short while.

'So it's an adult theme park, basically?'

'In a manner of speaking. There are other places in many other cities and countries, but not, perhaps, as elaborate as here in New Thameswick.'

'But what makes your lot tick?'

'Ah, good question.'

Asher tried to explain about the allure of gold, a metal inert and inured to thaumaturgy, and how his lot were highly attracted to it. As a result, lots of Fae wanted to get across to Bobby's world to try and earn, or steal, their fortune. But not many people wanted to come the other way since in his world, wonder-working or thaumaturgy or magic, he explained, was pretty much an innate skill. So those that did come across either came as reincarnated animals, like Snowy, or as mistakes, like the mysterious Bewildered. He also explained about Hipposync and that Mr Porter was a very senior official in the DOF and that Matt Danmor and Kylah Porter were Fae agents.

'So how come I don't see wights like Pogue Lempit on the streets of my Oxford?'

'Because of the Glamour. Fae would never present themselves as their real manifestations in your world. They tried it once and it all ended badly, though the historical version you have is riddled with inaccuracies. I mean Hobbiton isn't, and never was, in New Zealand. The one thing I'd say about your lot is that they are persistent when it comes to eradicating anything they consider to be unwelcome or a threat. So, in 711, the strongest and wisest set down some rules. Fae are not allowed to appear as themselves in the non-Fae world. If they do, they are deported. Nor are Fae allowed to use wonderworking that can harm non-Fae. Obviously, they do and so we have to have ways of monitoring all that. Hence the DOF.'

'So, what sort of government do you have here?'

'A bad one, like everywhere else. We tried making sure no politician could stand for government for more than one term, to avoid short term policies designed purely to ensure re-election.'

'That sounds good.'

'Yes. Unfortunately, no politician has, as yet, lasted the full term. They get very animated during question time in parliament and usually end up hexing each other into other dimensions. It is a fundamental right to be able to bear wands in the parliament building. At the moment, there are only seventy-three out of a possible two hundred members sitting. And they've survived because they are all related in some way or another and are under threat from their parents to behave.'

'What about the prime minister?'

'Well, there is one, but he's advised by the grand wizard who really runs the show and has done for about a hundred years. Nice chap by the name of Ogden Hamage. He's known as Magister Hamage. Does a good job, too. Happens to be the head of the university, so keeps all the other wizards in check, as well.'

'Army?'

'Small, for border skirmishes mainly.'

'Police?'

'Oh, yes. Lots of them. The clever ones are hawkshaws, the ones that are good with coshes are constables, and the ones that like fava beans and Chianti are custody sergeants.'

'But if people can do wonderworking, why is there crime?'

'There's something you need to understand about our lot. Caprice is what we're all about. Trickery is a way of life. You lot have altruism; our lot have mischief and fraud. It's what makes most of our people tick.'

They trundled down dark alleys and narrow streets until finally they emerged onto an embankment where a large patch of scrubby brown grass sat incongruously between the houses, stretching towards the river.

'This is it. The trenches.'

'Trenches? Was there a battle fought here?'

'Not exactly. But there was once a barracks here and this patch of land used to be the site of the latrines.' Even as he spoke, a whiff of something extremely unpleasant—even more unpleasant than the horse manure— reached Bobby, borne on the cold breeze. 'This spot hasn't been developed because no one wants to build here. It's too risky. Under our feet is fifty years' worth of—'

'I get it,' Bobby said.

'Well, be careful what you touch or you really will get it. And it has no known cure.'

'So why are we in this awful place?'

'*That* is why.' Asher pointed towards a man coming towards them, walking gingerly across the grass, his eyes fixed on his feet, a blue kerchief held to his nose.

'Why is he walking like that?'

'Sinkholes.'

'You can have an operation for that where I come from.'

Asher sent her a sideways glance. 'Sinkholes in the ground. You don't want to fall in one of them. Last bloke who did lost both legs.'

'Oh dear, infection?'

'No. Eaten. Things live in the stuff buried here. They're

called zleepers and they're mightily aggrieved that we've dumped fifty years' worth of human waste on their heads.'

Bobby said nothing. It all sounded very unlikely, but then she'd just seen a department store run by witches and a black dog called Snowy who was also a classical actor. She would have pinched herself if her fingers weren't so cold. Instead, she watched the man approach until he was close enough for Asher to make some introductions.

'Roberta, this is Hawkshaw Crouch.'

'How do you do.' Bobby held out her hand.

Crouch smiled but did not reciprocate. 'Nice try. We had a witch in my class at school. Shook hands with her once and ended up in a pond with my mate Jasper. It's bloody cold being a newt, I can tell you.'

'She is not a witch,' Asher explained.

'Then why's she dressed like one?'

'Because…it's a long story.'

Crouch nodded. 'Nice to meet you, Roberta, but no hand-holding, thanks.'

'It's Bobby. My friends call me Bobby.' She spoke to Crouch but it was aimed at the two of them.

'So, what's up?' Asher demanded, bringing an abrupt end to the niceties.

'This Bewildered thing. We've been keeping an eye out, at your request. This is one of the places they meet up. Not bothered much here.'

'I wonder why?' Bobby said, wiping her eyes. The breeze had strengthened and with it a stench of such wondrous awfulness she'd stopped breathing through her nose altogether.

'Exactly,' Crouch said, wincing. 'Anyway, one of our boys spotted a couple of loiterers. One of them is a Crotapian blob, and the other a lowlife dealing in post-mortem parking—'

'Malachite,' Asher said, making it sound like a solid manifestation of the reek that pervaded the air.

'You know him?' Crouch frowned.

'Unfortunately, yes. Is he here?'

'Yeah. No cause for arrest yet, but he's being questioned. We've commandeered a room at the Shoveler's Arms. They've got rubbish beer but the rooms have anti-stench charms, so it'll do me. Come on. Let's get out of this miasma. Follow me.'

They followed Crouch as he zigzagged his way over the open ground and the marked path. Bobby could make out furrows on either side. Presumably these were where the trenches had been dug. But she noticed that the grass did not grow any greener between the lines.

CHAPTER TWENTY

The Shoveler's Arms had a beer garden that backed onto the river. Blackened palings made up the rear wall and a gate guarded some very rickety steps leading down to the muddy riverbank itself. Asher and Bobby followed Crouch through a side door into a dark and dingy interior filled with oily smoke from a crackling fire. Groups of unshaven, whispering men sat hunched in corners over tankards of foaming beer. Most of the drinkers seemed also to have pipes from which strangely coloured smoke spiralled up. Like a fuel-flooded lawnmower, the low murmur of conversation sputtered into silence as the three visitors entered. The atmosphere felt about as welcoming as a dentist's waiting room.

Several pairs of eyes, some even on the same face, followed them as they walked through the smoky room.

'Want something to drink?' Crouch asked.

Bobby glanced at the cloudy beverages on the tables, toyed momentarily with asking for a spritzer and then dismissed that thought as one would any airy fantasy.

'They do a good Boatman's Peculiar.'

'I'm sure they do. But not for me,' Bobby said.

'Nor me,' Asher said. 'Where's Malachite?'

'Suit yourself. He's in the back.'

They negotiated the haphazardly arranged tables and found

a door at the rear. Beyond it was a small room with a view of the river through a window at its rear. But it wasn't the river that drew Bobby's eye. The ugliest statue she'd ever seen stood looking out towards the water. When it moved an arm and took a bite out of something red and dangly in its hand, she let out a small scream.

'What is that?'

'A Crotapian.'

'But, it's alive?'

'That's debatable,' Crouch said.

Inside the room, Malachite sat on a chair. His expression had negotiated a bend beyond surly and was now on the straits of miserable. Two large men wearing black topcoats with silver armbands sat slightly behind and on either side. They both nodded to Asher and their eyes slid in Bobby's direction with a look combining weariness and grudging respect in equal measure.

'This is Roberta Miracle,' Crouch said. 'She's with Inspector Lodge.'

'What's this?' Malachite said, his eyes sharpening as Bobby stepped clear of Asher.

'Visitors,' Crouch said, cheerily. 'Heard you were the cabaret and decided to stop by.'

'Hello, Malachite,' Asher said.

'Hinspector Lodge…Am I glad to see you. This is all a complete misunderstanding!'

Bobby searched for a word to describe his tone. Wheedling emerged at the top of a derogatory list.

'Really?' Asher said. 'As in, 'I know nothing about the Bewildered, and yet here I am caught in a Bewildered haunt looking for them kind of misunderstanding'?'

'That's hexactly the point,' Malachite said. 'As I was trying to hexplain to Mr Crouch 'ere, after you called to see me, I decided to see what I could do to 'elp, you know, find stuff out?'

'So you are here being Malachite The Exemplary Citizen, are you?'

Malachite ignored the sardonic tone and grasped onto this suggestion with desperate enthusiasm. 'Hexactly. I made some enquiries and found that the Bewildered 'ad certain…meeting places.'

'So you thought you'd come along and find out what you could,' Crouch said. 'If only the rest of New Thameswick had the same sense of civic duty.'

'Thank you, Hinspector Lodge. So, if we've finished 'ere—'

Crouch banged his open hand down on the table. Bobby jumped. But not half as high as Malachite. 'Shut up, you gonad. You're as community minded as a sewer rat. Tell us why you were down here?'

'Ask Hinspector Lodge. 'E'll tell you—'

'I don't believe your story for one minute, Malachite.' Asher pierced the blinking man with a stare. 'What are you doing here?'

'Workin' for you, Hinspector. Doin' my level best.'

'Excuse me,' Bobby said. 'What are Bewildered?'

Everyone in the room turned towards her.

'I'll tell you later,' Asher said in a low voice.

'I was asking him.' She pointed at Malachite.

Malachite's eyes focused instantly on Bobby's finger. His hands went up either side of his chest. 'Woah, woah, wait a minute. Using witchery is bad news. This is cruelty, this is. This is violatin' my Fae rights, this is.'

'I am not a witch,' Bobby said, calmly.

'Yeah, right,' Crouch whispered theatrically, having seen the fear in Malachite's face and, being a good copper, capitalising upon it.

'Hinspector Lodge?' Malachite eyes flicked between Bobby's finger and Asher's face and back again half a dozen times in as many seconds. 'This is mental torture, this is. I swear I've done nothin' wrong.'

'Okay, then tell us what you found out?'

'Nothin'. I mean, I didn't get a chance. I'd 'eard they'd come and meet down here. Drawn by the smell or the river. Stealth hoperation.'

Bobby watched as Asher's, and then Crouch's eyes flicked up to the blob in the garden who, she had to agree, looked about as stealthy as a supertanker in the Panama Canal.

'Honest, Hinspector. I came down to the trenches, that's all. See if I could find anything out. Mr Crouch has got me all wrong.'

'I bet he has.'

'I'd love to be wrong about you, Malachite, I really would,' Crouch said. 'We'll be watching you very closely from now on. Very closely indeed.'

'Only fair, Mr Crouch, only fair. So can I go?' He threw Bobby a worried glance.

'I suppose so. And take your mountain with you.'

Malachite scraped his chair on the stone floor in his hurry to get up. Bobby watched him leave.

Crouch shook his head. 'His story stinks worse than the trenches.'

'Agreed,' Asher said, 'but he's done nothing wrong.'

'He's using up good air,' Crouch said. 'That's grounds for arrest in my book.'

'Can you watch him?' Asher asked.

'Yeah. We'll keep an eye open. Right,' Crouch beckoned to the two constables. 'Come on you two. Let's get out of this cesspit.' He turned to Bobby. 'Nice to meet you, Roberta.' He still did not offer his hand.

CHAPTER TWENTY-ONE

IN THE DARKEST and dingiest corner of the Shoveler's Arms, a man watched Malachite leave. On the table in front of him, his beer remained untouched. He'd bought it only to allay suspicion. Such foul concoctions merely addled the brain and were poisons he had long since sworn to eschew along with pleasures of the flesh and Wednesdays. On Wednesdays, he and the other pure of faith buried themselves under five feet of earth. They would sleep, away from distraction and light and sound and water and sustenance, then awaken and dig themselves out to be reborn, once more, into the world. Born in the sin of bitter disappointment at learning that the world remained the same. One day, they would emerge and it would be a very different world. A world where their lord and master would once again proffer favour to the faithful. Then, and only then, would they be allowed the pleasures so long denied to them. Their self-induced living death defined them and they'd called themselves the Widicombs (Wednesdays I die and I come back).

When he lay buried under the ground, the man would fantasise about the darkest of pleasures and how they would be taken. Fantasise with such ferocity that those periods of living death swiftly became rituals of intense desire. All in His name. And soon, His name would be known again and spoken in fear and trepidation like it had been, once before. The man let his hand stray to the amulet on his wrist. On it was written a name in a language known only to a chosen few. A name so sorely mistreated...Of course, he would not think it, let alone speak it here in this rat's nest. He would wait until the time came to scream it out into the world. Then everyone would know it again.

His reflection on the fate the world was about to suffer was broken by more noise. The hawkshaws were making an exit. They had interviewed Malachite. The man smiled to himself, unconcerned. Malachite was a liability. His usefulness was all that was keeping him alive. The man smiled again. Malachite knew it. That was why he'd employed that Crotapian monstrosity of a bodyguard. It would do him no good; the Widicombs would not tolerate his incompetence. Perhaps Malachite, once his usefulness expired, was set to become the first Widinotcomb.

Two other people were leaving the pub now. A man with the distinctive look of a necreddo and a witch. The hawkshaws were obviously employing new tactics, not that it would do them any good. Steps were in hand and there was nothing anyone could do in this world to prevent the chaos that would follow. The man smiled again. It was Tuesday. He would deal with the meddlers and he would meet the other Widicombs tomorrow and discuss all he'd witnessed before burying himself in the earth and letting himself dream of things to come. But first, time to get rid of fresh vermin.

He got up and stalked to the rear of the pub and the door that led out into the garden and the steps leading down to the river.

———

Bobby and Asher hurried back the way they came. It was easy to see the stones set in the earth that marked the path back across the open ground. Bobby had a sackful of questions, but she didn't ask them. Not here. It was not a place to linger. They hurried, heads down, keeping the river on their left. They were halfway back to the lane where the cab dropped them off when she saw a figure emerge from over the palings onto the path thirty yards ahead.

Asher came to an abrupt halt. He swivelled his head and Bobby followed his gaze. A second figure clambered over the black wood thirty yards behind them. Asher flicked his eyes to the south, to the open ground and the houses two hundred yards beyond. He gave a little shake of his head as he discounted the option.

'What's going on?' Bobby asked.

'An ambush, it seems,' Asher said. 'Can you run?'

She looked down at her platform DMs. 'I don't exactly have the footwear for it, but I suppose I could jog a bit.'

'Then jog a bit quickly and follow me. Stay on the path. Our only option is to keep going.'

'But that bloke is blocking our way, isn't he?'

'It would seem so. Come on.'

Asher set off again, more quickly this time. Their sudden spurt of speed galvanised the black-cloaked figure behind them, but the one in front did not move. She could see how this might work. She guessed they'd planned to pincer her and Asher but their sprint meant that they'd get to the figure ahead before the one behind got to them. Asher was no fool.

They closed the gap quickly, Bobby fighting against the weight of her footwear. If there was any doubt as to intent, it evaporated within ten seconds as the figure in front took out two daggers from a belt around his waist. But that did not slow Asher down.

'I will preoccupy this filth, you must keep running. Do not look back.'

'But there are two of them!'

'Do *not* look back.'

There was no time for any more discussion; Asher sprinted forward, seizing the advantage as the figure lunged at him. He sidestepped and went in under the man's arm, pushed up with his hand and a dagger flew up and out into the grass. Bobby ducked past and ran as hard as she could in her heavy boots, catching a glimpse of a pale, unshaven face with deep, sunken, hateful eyes exaggerated by dark rings of black makeup, and a lurid scar right in the centre of the forehead—almost like a reversed Z-shape crossed by curving arms.

Bobby realised at this point that Asher looked like he'd been trained to cope. Whereas she definitely had the wrong footwear. She couldn't run normally, heel to toe, or she'd go flying and it was proving difficult to stick to the path. She knew when she'd strayed off it because she experienced a shooting feeling up her leg whenever her foot hit the furrow of the trench. A weird kind of hollow beat followed by a little surge like the tingle you felt when you put your tongue on the terminals of a battery. She heard a yell behind her and risked a backwards glance. The second assassin—no idea where that word came from but it seemed to suit—skirted around Asher and the man he was grappling with and sprinted after her. There seemed no chance of making it if she kept to the path. Breathing heavily now, she noticed a gap in the bordering wall where some bricks had fallen in. Not much of a gap but if she made straight for it, it would be the shortest arm of a triangle. She could hear her pursuer now, hear his rapid footfalls, and hear the effort of his breathing. She knew what Asher had said about the trenches and the path but another glance behind her told her it was the shortcut or nothing.

'Sugar,' Bobby said to no one in particular and branched off towards the gap in the wall. The scrub consisted of lots of tussocks and the going wasn't easy but, she rationalised, if it wasn't easy for her, it would not be for him. She ran five, ten, fifteen yards. Another twenty or so to go. She might just make it. And then something wrapped itself around her knees, swiftly, clamping her lower legs together so the momentum of her forward movement sent her toppling. She fell, jarring her wrists, the rough, scorched grass cracking coldly against her cheeks, the breath hurtling out of her chest in a grunting wheeze. She tried to get up but her legs were locked together. She struggled onto her back and saw, through eyes wet with cold and fear, what she at first thought was a snake around her calves. But this snake had three heads of dark polished stone. From somewhere deep in her memory she dredged up the term bolas, a throwing tool used to capture game. She'd seen films of gauchos using them to catch prey, but it was a passing reflection because a shadow suddenly loomed above her. She squinted up into a face half silhouetted against the grey day. This one was a clone of Asher's opponent. The same pale, unshaven face, the same dark rings around the pitiless eyes, and dyslexic Z-shaped scar etched into his forehead.

Unable to help herself, Bobby scooted back, her hands against the damp earth once again feeling that strange electric charge.

'What do you want?' Bobby said.

'Quiet, witch. Accept your fate in the name of Gazorch the Pantocrator, Demon Lord.' The assassin reached to his belt and took out a blade. It was of dull metal, with a pistol grip handle. Wicked, practical; a tool of this man's trade. Meanwhile Bobby gained five yards by shuffling backwards and tried desperately to loosen the rope from her legs. Her struggles seemed to please her hunter. He smiled to reveal sharply filed teeth, some with metal tips.

From fifty yards away, she heard Asher call her name. It came out as an anguished cry. 'Roberta!'

The smile on the assassin's face slid away. With a grunt he lunged towards her, wanting to finish the job, but as lunges went, this one was pretty ineffective. He half stumbled, his upper half mainly, and fell forward, as if his legs were trapped. Bobby's eyes dropped to the man's feet. They were indeed trapped. Clasped by a pair of white, mud-coated, long-nailed hands. Within seconds the pair became two and then four as whatever clasped him was joined by others that clawed their way up towards ankles and then knees. The assassin lunged, and tried to kick out, but his legs were caught in vicelike grips. Bobby watched in fascinated horror as the ground beneath him suddenly turned a rich black colour and the air filled with a terrible, nauseating stench as something dark and red brown seeped up in a circle, turning the solid earth into a blood coloured mud hole.

She threw a glance over the assassin's shoulder. A figure lay on the ground where Asher had been fighting. Dark clad, motionless. Asher, meanwhile, sprinted towards them on the path. Instinctively, Bobby called to him.

'Don't come over here! Stay on the path. Stay on the path!'

Asher hesitated and slowed down, staring across.

The assassin's eyes became desperate ovals of terror. His hands, holding the dagger, slashed and beat at his captors, but no blood flowed where the lethal weapon struck.

Bobby didn't linger. Quickly she unwrapped the bolas and struggled to her feet. The assassin stood sunk to his knees in the filthy pool. Slashing wildly at the hands, he managed to get one foot free. That was enough for Bobby, who ran towards Asher and the path, risking only one final glance as they reached the edge of the trenches. It did not look like the assassin stood a chance, judging by the number of pale white hands that now had him in their deadly grip. Bobby shuddered and turned away.

Five minutes later, breathless and bruised and with Asher sporting a neatly sliced cut above his eye, they were sitting in Gary's cab and heading back to FHIFAA.

'Who were those men?' Bobby demanded.

Asher shook his head. 'Thieves or assassins. Though they bore the marks of a sect, did you see?'

'You mean the weird scars and the filed teeth?' Bobby shivered. 'Did they just happen to be there or were we targeted?'

'I do not know, Roberta.'

'Mine said something about a Gazorch. That I should accept my fate in the name of Gazorch the Pantocrator…a demon lord, I think he said.'

Asher's eyes narrowed. 'You're sure he said that name?'

'I'm hardly likely to forget it, am I?'

Asher frowned. Eventually he said, 'It is the name of a demon. One that has a very bad reputation. It may be that his followers prey on those foolish enough to walk across the trenches.'

'Charming.' Bobby shook her head. Her legs were trembling from the adrenaline. Her boots were muddy; the platforms caked in foul-smelling clods. She retrieved a tissue from her bag and started cleaning them. When she looked up, she caught Asher looking at her. 'What?'

'You strayed off the path,' Asher said.

'Have you been talking to my mother?'

'It is not something to make light of.'

Bobby frowned at the rebuke. 'I didn't have any choice.'

'You saw what happened to the assassin,' Asher said.

'Yeah, and what exactly *did* happen to him?'

'Indeed,' Asher said. He kept staring at her.

'Don't say 'indeed' like that. As if there's some great hidden meaning in it. Spit it out. What are you trying to say?'

'It is merely highly intriguing that the assassin was attacked by the zleepers, the denizens of the trenches, and yet you were not. An observation, that is all.'

Bobby frowned. 'Well, maybe I was saved by falling on my backside. Maybe my running woke them up and he was unlucky enough to be the one standing when they came to call.'

'Indeed.'

'There it is again. What else could it be?'

'I do not know.'

'Exactly. So, what about this Malachite bloke and the Bewildered? Let's have it. I need something to take my mind off those hands coming up out of the mud, if it was mud. It smelled more like—'

'As I said. The trenches have a reputation.'

'So, come on, why are you so interested in this Bewildered thing, then?'

'They are people: the Bewildered.'

'Why are they called that?'

'Because…because they are.'

'Thank God that's been cleared up,' Bobby said, irked.

'It's complicated. I should not be discussing it with you whilst the case is under investigation.'

'So, by the same convoluted reasoning, I should not be talking to you about the case you are investigating in Oxford then either, should I?'

'You are a part of that case.'

'Don't be such a bloody stick in the…whatever it was those zleepers were floating in.'

'Look,' Asher said through gritted teeth, 'some things are best not discussed. Our priority is to get back to Oxford and sort out the problem there. I presume you are now happy with my bona fides.'

Bobby shrugged.

'What else can I do to prove I am what I say I am?'

'Tell me about the Bewildered.'

'No.'

'What are you scared of?'

They were pulling up outside FHIFAA with its pillars and huge black doors. Asher tossed some coins into a leather bag around Gary's neck and he trotted off.

'Help me sort out the lockdown and I'll tell you about the Bewildered, I promise.'

Bobby smiled. 'So, by my tally, it's another cup of coffee at The Roast and an explanation for the Bewildered. I still think I'm selling myself cheap.'

They argued as they walked up the stone steps to the large double doors. Three steps from the top the door opened and a man appeared.

'Did I hear something about selling yourself cheap?' There was a tutting noise and then, 'Lodge,' the man said, 'shame on you.'

'Braithwaite,' Asher said in a way that implied disgust.

'Where've you been?' The man's eyes slid toward Bobby. His face lit up. The illuminated message read 'Letch'. 'No, no need to answer. I can see for myself. Well, hello,' he smiled and then glanced at Asher again. 'I didn't know you were seeing a witch. Had no idea you were into that side of things.'

'I am not seeing anyone. Ms Miracle is assisting me in my investigation.'

'Oh, right,' Braithwaite said, while his eyes transmitted, *I bet she is.*

'Off early, Braithwaite?' Asher asked.

'Just come up for a breath of fresh air. Maybe I'll wander over to the Wigg and Gavell for a quick…coffee.'

Asher took a step up but Braithwaite didn't move anything other than his lips into a synthetic smile. 'So you're helping Asher with his enquiries then, eh? How about you help me with mine when you've finished with him. Won't take long, or so I've heard.' He grinned at Bobby. 'Here's my beemail.' He handed her a gilt edged card.

'Braithwaite, get out of the way,' Asher muttered.

'Why? Forms to fill in for the constabulary have we, Lodge? I heard you'd been seconded to some security gaffe. How's that going?' He didn't quite snigger but he might as well have.

'Well,' Asher said.

'Really?' Braithwaite said. 'Once a copper always a copper, eh?'

Bobby saw Asher's fists ball. She'd been good at maths in school. So adding the two and two of this little exchange took no effort whatsoever. She slid her arm out of Braithwaite's grasp.

'The last person that did that to me without permission spent a fortnight making frogspawn.'

Braithwaite flinched. 'There's no need to get uppity. Just passing the time of day.'

'I'm afraid we are not at liberty to discuss this case with you, Mr,' Bobby peered at the card, '…Braithwaite. And there's a spelling mistake here. Where it says Executive. There's a T, a W an A and a T missing.' She turned to Asher. 'We ought to get a move on. Magister Hamage's office is not going to be happy if we're late. We're simply wasting time here.'

'Magister Hamage?' Braithwaite asked in a tight voice. Bobby thought she saw a flicker of panic in the man's eyes. 'What's the Magister's office got to do with this? I thought this was some low-key cock-up they'd sent you to clean up.'

'If only,' Bobby said, blowing out air and shaking her head.

'But Rathbone said—'

'What did Rathbone say, Braithwaite?' Asher pounced on the slip.

'That it was just procedural guff. Something to keep you occupied. Nice easy job for someone coming back from a breakd…' His eyes flicked to Bobby. 'How come I wasn't let in on this?'

'Better ask Rathbone,' Bobby said and turned to Asher. 'Now, can we please get on?'

'With pleasure,' Asher said and pushed Braithwaite aside. He wore a grin as he jammed the Aperio onto the hinge side of the door and opened it.

Looking back over her shoulder, Bobby almost felt a pang of sympathy for Braithwaite. She didn't like to see grown men cry.

CHAPTER TWENTY-TWO

The first thing that struck Bobby when she stepped through into the blue room was how cold it felt. It had not been warm in New Thameswick, but here, inside Hipposync, the cold was deeper and somehow denser than she remembered. Asher followed right behind her.

'What is it?' he asked, sensing her hesitation.

'Temperature,' Bobby said through chattering lips. 'It's freezing.'

Asher nodded without a smile. 'Dark wonderworking. Thaumaturgy sucks the energy out of the atmosphere around it.'

His delivery was worryingly matter of fact and suddenly Bobby's gung-ho enthusiasm faltered. New Thameswick had been seductively weird, but now, back in Oxford, hearing the words 'dark wonderworking' and 'thaumaturgy' brought unpleasant reality back with a shivery bang. And she couldn't think of anything worse than one of those.

'That doesn't sound g…good,' she stuttered.

'It does not. Now, I suggest you retrace your steps and I will follow.'

Bobby led him through the door to where Miss Porter stood. She watched Asher shake his head.

'I despise lockdowns. Though I understand this is a reversible state, it still makes me shudder to see people I know well so close to death.'

'Is she?' Bobby's eyes widened. 'Close to death, I mean?'

'If left for long enough, eventually her systems would not be able to recover.'

Bobby stared at the mannequin in front of her who always seemed so alive and sure of herself when she wasn't a waxwork. 'How long have you two known each other?'

'Kylah was an instructor during my basic training. She ran the human affairs class.'

'Does that mean she's one of you?' Bobby couldn't keep the surprise out of her voice.

'Of course she is,' Asher answered.

'And Mr Danmor?'

'He's a…special case. A kind of co-opted agent.'

'So he is human?'

'He's a lucky man.'

'Miss Porter is quite special,' Bobby agreed.

Asher looked up. He appeared to be on the verge of laughter. 'There is that. But I meant it literally. He is a very lucky man. Or to put it another way, he is able to manipulate the chaotic action of fate and turn it to his advantage.'

'Hasn't had much luck with this little lot though, has he.'

'No. They must have been taken completely by surprise.' Asher examined Miss Porter very carefully, took a small blackberry-sized marble from his waistcoat pocket and held it to her ear. It glowed orange. 'All is well,' he said.

Bobby led the way up to Mr Danmor's office. There, Asher repeated his trick with the marble and Bobby showed him the note with 'Cuthbertson' written it. Asher studied Danmor's stance and pointed to the communicator. 'He was obviously reading in his report when the lockdown kicked in. We barely got any of it.'

'So you didn't get malign haunting or autopsy?' Bobby said, looking at the note.

'No, just the name. Cuthbertson.'

'Who is Cuthbertson?'

'I don't know. But it's someone important, that's clear.' Asher looked pensive. 'Tell me what happened when the lockdown kicked in?'

'As I said, I was halfway out of the door.'

'Can you show me?'

Bobby took him to the front door. Or where the front door used to be because now there was nothing but brick wall. Asher attached the Aperio and the door reappeared, though he made no attempt to open it.

'I'd gone outside and remembered I'd left my bag on the table in the office. I had to keep the door from closing and, once I was back in here, it shut and the brick wall appeared.' She walked down the corridor. 'I looked in at the front desk and Miss WT was as she is now.' Surprisingly the little gobbet of drool still glistened just below the corner of the receptionist's mouth.

Asher nodded and once again took his pebble and held it to the frozen Miss WT's ear. It glowed bright blue.

Alarmed, Bobby asked, 'Is Miss WT okay? Your Stone Age tricorder just glowed a different colour!'

'Yes, but that's what you'd expect from a Sith Fand.'

After quite a long few seconds in which silence took an arrow from its quiver and placed it on its bow, Bobby said, 'You did just said Sixth Fan, didn't you?'

'No, I said *Sith Fand*. Miss White Tandy is really a member of the Special Elf Service.'

If it was a cue for laughter, unfortunately the bit of Bobby's brain that might have found it funny had long since left the theatre and was at home, triple bolting the door.

'So Miss WT is not human?' She resisted, with great difficulty, substituting 'WT' with 'WTF'.

'No.'

'But…why…I mean…'

'You're curious as to why she has chosen to project this particular manifestation of the human form?'

'Barely a human form. More a heavily sedated crab form.'

'I suspect it is to minimise attention. It seems to have worked well.'

'But she's ancient and hardly able to move!'

'Yet it was she who was aware that the lockdown was kicking in and sent us the signal.'

'Miss WT?'

'Indeed. The question is and remains, why?'

It was then Bobby remembered the last remaining member of the team. Her hand flew to her mouth. 'Talking of barely human, we'd better look in on Pippa. I completely forgot about her.'

She hurried around to the intern's office. Pippa looked very pale. She yelled, 'Asher, come and put your marble to her ear!'

What she heard in reply might have been a cough, or just as easily some stifled laughter.

'It isn't funny,' Bobby said when he entered the room, wearing his best straight face.

'I know,' he said, but kept his eyes averted. The marble turned a sickly yellow, its glow very faint.

'That doesn't look good,' Bobby said.

'No. It's not designed for humans but even so…'

'I definitely don't like 'even so'. Can't we do something?'

'Break the lockdown. That would be the ideal scenario.'

Bobby sent her eyes towards the ceiling and feigned a count of ten. 'How, exactly, do we do that?'

'Find out what caused it in the first place,' Asher said.

'But that could take ages!'

'I know.' Asher looked away, thinking hard. 'There is another way. We could get her out of this environment. If you and I physically remove her, we could get her to an alms house—'

'A what?'

'Alms house. Somewhere you'd find an apothecary.'

'An apothecary?'

'Repeating everything I say in question form does not help.'

'It doesn't?'

Asher gave her a flinty stare. 'I mean somewhere she might find medical help.'

'A hospital?'

'Yes, that. A hospital.'

'Then let's do it.' Bobby went to Pippa. Though she didn't fall under the label 'friend' in Bobby's emotional filing cabinet, the Pip did not deserve to die frozen in suspended animation like this. She and Asher tried to carefully manoeuvre a rigid-limbed Pippa out from under the desk and failed. It proved easier to leave her sitting in the chair and carry both of them into the corridor and through to the blue room.

'So, I should call an ambulance?' Bobby asked. Asher looked at her blankly. 'Silly question. Right, let me out, I'll call and then we'll take her out while the ambulance is on its way. Maybe I ought to go to the hospital with her? I should call someone who knows her...Next of kin perhaps?' She began rummaging in the Pip's bag.

'No,' Asher shook his head. 'Let the apothecary do that. Feign ignorance. I need you here.'

She thought about protesting but didn't. Her curiosity had most definitely been piqued by all that had happened and she wanted to see this through.

Asher used the Aperio to open the door again. Bobby exited to the car park and phoned 999. Then she and Asher carried the frozen Pippa outside on her chair where Bobby draped her in a coat. The minute they got outside, Pippa started to moan and move her limbs, much to Bobby's relief.

'Hi,' Bobby said. 'How are you feeling?'

'Where am I?' a sick-looking Pip asked.

'The car park behind Hipposync. You fell and hit your head, remember?'

'Who's Hipposync?'

'Right,' Bobby said with a fixed smile. This was both bad and good. Bad for Pippa in terms of her amnesia, but good from the point of view of having to explain her predicament to the authorities.

'I have a splitting headache.' The Pip massaged her temples and then leaned over. 'I think I'm going to throw up.'

'The ambulance is on its way. I'm sure they'll give you something for it.'

She looked up into Bobby's face. 'Do I know you?'

Bobby smiled.

CHAPTER TWENTY-THREE

THE STORY she gave to the sceptical paramedic involved having found Pippa collapsed in the car park. The paramedic wanted to know if Pippa had ever had an epileptic fit. Bobby had no answers but was relieved when the paramedic fished out Pippa's phone and an envelope with her name and address. Fending off a momentary pang of guilt, Bobby silently blessed the NHS and let Pippa become someone else's responsibility. Moments later, she was on the way to the Radcliffe wearing an oxygen mask and looking a much better colour than she had a few moments before.

Asher was waiting inside.

'Why don't we repeat that trick with Miss Porter and Mr Danmor?'

'They're in stasis for their own protection. Something bad was happening, or about to happen. What we really need to do is find out exactly what.'

'Okay. How?'

Asher seemed to hesitate, but then said, 'I have not yet thanked you for your ruse with Braithwaite. He has a challenging personality.'

'You mean he's a prat?'

'That is a term I am not overly familiar with, but I think it is a very apt description nevertheless.' Asher smiled and then added, 'You seem capable of handling such people.'

'I've had lots of practice.' Bobby seized on the rare opportunity of Asher opening up—if the absence of his trademark flinty stare could be classed as opening up—to probe a little deeper. 'What did he mean when he said you were coming back from a break?'

'He meant breakdown. Braithwaite has the knack of twisting things so that they appear in the worst light. Or perhaps in the best light for him.' Asher turned away.

'So…you didn't have a breakdown?'

'I underwent surgery,' Asher answered. 'Psychosurgery.'

Bobby's mouth crinkled under a frown.

'It does not involve knives,' Asher said by way of reassurance.

'It still sounds unpleasant.'

'It is.' A small silence followed, pierced finally by Asher. 'I decided to have it when my brother killed himself.'

Bobby blinked. The room sounded suddenly very quiet around her.

'We're both necreddos,' Asher explained. 'Born able to speak to the dead. We both volunteered to be part of an experimental necrosquad: essential cogs in the constabulary's plans to cut down crime by interviewing the recently departed. And by that I mean murder victims. Unfortunately, what we were not able to predict was the associated and damaging psychic fallout. The recently murdered are a highly unstable group that exudes contaminating manta waves. There was inadequate shielding.'

'I'm sorry to hear about your brother.'

Asher nodded. 'He is sadly missed. However, he has found a peace of sorts.'

'So is that why you're so protective of the Bewildered?'

Asher nodded. 'The surgery is supposed to have restored filters which were removed while I was with the necrosquad through certain imbibed elixirs. I was ordered to refrain from communicating with the dead for the next six months. It is disconcerting to find that the Bewildered can bypass those filters with ease. Therefore, in part, my interest is purely selfish.'

'Oh, I wouldn't call it that. Like you say, they need a voice.

Especially if those men who attacked us have anything to do with their murder. And if you want my opinion, the Bewildered could do a lot worse than have you on their side.'

Asher nodded, accepting the compliment. 'But we have a different set of problems here to deal with.'

'Agreed. So what now?'

He strode away down the corridor with Bobby in pursuit. 'We follow what leads we have. It's obvious that Matt and Kylah were working on a case. The only clue we have is Cuthbertson. Perhaps we ought to find out exactly what they've been doing.'

'But how? Everything is frozen.'

'Including the pongcluetor?'

'Including the…pongcluetor, yes.' Bobby nodded. Mr Porter had used that word. She'd thought it a spoonerism, but now that Asher used it too she realised just how much about this place she did not know.

'But we are not,' Asher said over his shoulder. 'Come, Bobby. We have work to do.'

He didn't see the way she smiled at the way he'd said her name.

CHAPTER TWENTY-FOUR

ASHER WENT BACK to Danmor's office and picked up the notebook once more. Bobby followed him, barraging him with questions.

'So Miss Porter and Mr Danmor have been helping the police?'

'Yes, but that in itself is nothing new. The DOF are often called upon to help in situations here where the inexplicable plays a part.'

'No wonder they were always off in 'meetings'.' She paused and then added, 'But they weren't just 'meetings', were they?'

'No. They were bringing their expertise to bear.'

Hardly the detailed answer she craved, but it would do. 'A kind of paranormal consultancy.' Bobby grinned, and despite herself added, 'All a little bit sexy if you ask me. Sort of the Holmes and Watson of the bizarre.'

'You read too many books.'

'You can never read too many books. But how come we've never heard of such things? I mean, these days nothing gets past the press. Phone hacking, rifling through your bins, CCTV, side sampling your body waste using a straw down the sewer—'

'Where did you hear that?'

'From the part of my brain labelled *X-Files*. My point is, how come they've never been spotted bringing their expertise to bear? You'd have thought the press would be all over it. I can see the headlines now. *Hipposync Heroes Halt Haunting Horror.*'

'By being very careful and the selective use of amnesia charms.' Asher didn't look at her, but his preceding sigh said it all.

Bobby shook her head. 'I had no idea.'

Asher nodded.

'So do you think this Cuthbertson may have something to do with what's happened here?'

'Perhaps. There will be reports of all recent cooperative investigations,' he replied, distractedly. 'But I do not recall reading of a Cuthbertson.'

'Well, like I said, we'll get nothing from the computers.'

'I could attempt a memory charm. Unfortunately I have no idea how well it will work in situations whereby Matt's brain is in stasis. It might do more harm than good. However, I see little alternative. It does take quite some preparation. I will need to gain access to Kylah's consumables.' He turned to a locked cupboard and held up his marble. It glowed red for a few seconds followed by a discernible click.

'That's a very cool marble,' Bobby said. 'Your equivalent of a sonic screwdriver, I take it?'

'There is no such thing as a sonic screwdriver,' Asher muttered.

'Not true. I have a TV remote in that very shape—'

Asher silenced her with a look that would have done Medusa proud. He tried the cupboard and it opened without resistance. He peered inside and began to rummage. 'I need some sacridian chalk, some Holyhead salt, some powdered scarab wing—'

The sound of a well-oiled filing cabinet drawer opening interrupted Asher mid-flow.

'Or, we could maybe check to see if they've made copies of any reports. Like this one entitled *Malign Hauntings 2016-20?*' Bobby said with what might have passed for a smirk.

Asher turned around. Taciturn never quite works when your face has the look of someone in imminent danger of collapse from contact with a feather.

Bobby opened the file on the desk and Asher joined her to read it without comment.

'I see two other names here: Veronica Loosemore and Marie Evans,' Asher said after a while.

'Yes, both victims of possible malign haunting according to Mr Danmor. The first, the Loosemore woman, took place some time ago—nine weeks to be exact. Marie Evans a week later.'

'We need to speak to the relatives in both cases. See if we can ascertain what Kylah and Matt were after. And I am sure they would not mind if you dispensed with the formalities, by the way. You can call them Matt and Kylah. Now, where did the victims live?'

Bobby ran her finger down the paper. 'Marie Evans lived in Cardiff; Mrs Loosemore lived on the outskirts of London. She had two daughters. Both live in Woolwich.'

'I am familiar with London, but not all of it. Are you familiar with that area?'

'Not really. But I've been to the loo in Paddington a few times?'

'The loo?'

'Water closet?'

Asher looked at her blankly.

'The sort with a door…' Bobby let the suggestion hang.

'Ah yes, I see. For the Aperio.'

Bobby nodded. 'That's if I can use it, of course. We can get to Woolwich from there quite easily. You ever travelled by tube?'

'I once hid in a tea chest for four days, but I have never considered toothpaste packaging a viable mode of transport.'

Bobby narrowed her eyes. 'Let me know when you're being funny, will you? I'm having a hard time telling with you.'

'Maintain the effort,' Asher said with the hint of a smile. 'It will be worth it in the long run.'

———

Asher let Bobby use the Aperio by having her remember the loo door in Paddington station. From there, they took the Bakerloo line to Oxford Circus and then the Central to Bank.

From there it was the Docklands Light Railway to Woolwich Arsenal. Veronica Loosemore's daughters had not moved very far from where they were brought up. When Bobby phoned the number they'd found on the report, she introduced herself as someone following up with 'Met Support Services' and left it at that. It was Linda Hopwood, the youngest daughter, who greeted them at the door of a neat Victorian terraced house on Rippon road. Asher showed her his badge and Bobby suspected Linda would see what she wanted to see written there. Linda had the drawn features of a lifelong smoker and the chesty wheeze to match. Her sister, Yvonne, was fuller, more youthful-looking, though Bobby knew from the file that she was the elder of the two by three years. Asher turned down an offer of tea and, when they were seated in a comfortable and clean sitting room, explained how they were tying up loose ends on the enquiry and asked the sisters to tell them again, briefly, what had taken place.

'She never really recovered from my dad leavin',' Linda Hopwood said with a tight smile. 'I was thirteen; Von fifteen. Walked out to get some Sunday papers and never came back.'

'It almost killed our mum,' Yvonne added. 'If it weren't for 'avin' to look after us, she would've given up, I'm sure.'

'Did you not hear anything from your father after that?' Asher asked.

'Nothin'. Not a peep,' Linda said. Her hands were fidgeting in her lap. Bobby guessed they missed holding a cigarette.

'So your mother brought you both up on her own from then on?' Bobby asked. She got a stern look from Asher in return, but she wasn't going to simply sit there while these two women told their tragic story. Besides, Asher was coming over about as sympathetic as a tax inspector with piles.

'It was hard, I won't lie to you. Mum was fantastic. Worked at the shirt factory by day and cleaned the social club on Sat'-days. We never went without food nor clothes on our backs.'

'And she kept on living in the same house?' Bobby asked.

'Yeah. We looked after 'er. She wanted to stay independent, though she 'ad problems with her eyes and her knees.'

'So, can you tell us what happened in,' Asher consulted the report, 'March of this year?'

'She started not sleepin'. Kept tellin' us she was 'earin' voices. Kept tellin' us she thought our dad was tryin' to speak to 'er.'

'Your father?'

'Yeah. That was the start of it. It went downhill from there. She got bad really quickly. Wouldn't go to bed. Wouldn't sleep. Kept sayin' he was there waitin' for her and that he was mad. Really angry.'

Yvonne nodded. 'Course we thought it was dementia. We had her stay with us, but even then she'd wake screamin' in the middle of the night. And then we got her seen by the 'ospital. They gave her medicine and it did 'elp for a while.'

'Knocked her out more like,' Linda said. 'Turned her into a bit of a zombie, poor thing. But at least she weren't dreamin' those 'orrible dreams that kept wakin' her up.' She let out a sigh. 'All she wanted was to go back to 'er own 'ouse. She could be determined, our mum. Then on March 15th…'

'It was me that found 'er.' Yvonne took over, the sisters' eyes meeting briefly. 'We'd call around in turn, check everythin' was okay. Except that mornin' it wasn't. The place was a shambles, and I mean a real shambles. Everythin' that could have been smashed was smashed. Everythin'. I've never seen anythin' like it. And mum was…' she paused, taking a breath, looking again to Linda for support.

'Mum was in bed, under the covers. Von called me and I was 'ere in a flash. When we took the covers off, her face—it was awful. I still wake up and see her poor little face.'

'She must have been in real pain because her face was all twisted and…' Yvonne faltered and found a tissue. Her sister gave her a quick hug and continued.

'But they didn't find anythin' at the autopsy. Said it might 'ave been an 'eart attack but that it was over real quick.'

'Must have been awful for you both,' Bobby said softly.

Both women nodded. 'I just wish she 'adn't been alone that night, that's all. But she was so stubborn. Determined to stay in that 'ouse with all its awful memories,' Yvonne said.

'I think she stayed there because she was hopin' one day my dad would come home,' Linda mused. 'Fat chance of that, weren't there.'

Asher didn't say anything. They thanked the women and left quickly. This time, Asher used an office door in the DLR station to get them back to Hipposync.

'That was harrowing,' Bobby said as they headed back to Danmor's office. 'Those poor women.'

'Indeed.' Asher's expression was impenetrable.

Bobby sent him a look. She was getting to know that 'indeed'. It was his shield. Behind it hid all sorts of thinking that he wasn't prepare to share.

'Are you game for Marie Evans' husband?' Asher asked.

Bobby nodded. She happened to know Cardiff thanks to an old university friend who lived on the edge of Roath Park. This time the Aperio took them to a changing room in a department store in the heart of the city. They found a taxi rank and within minutes were on their way to Cherry Lane in a leafy suburb called Lisvane, full of modern detached boxes. Bobby called ahead and, using the same ruse, spoke to Gerald Evans, the husband of the deceased, to make sure he was home. On the drive outside the house sat a highly polished Jaguar next to a neat garden bordered by a dwarf box hedge. Gerald was obviously a proud man. But an attractive young woman in her mid-twenties opened the door. She introduced herself as Nikki Samuels, the Evans' next-door neighbour. They were shown into a sitting room where a man dressed in a shirt, tie, and blazer met them with a firm handshake.

Gerald sported the build and rearranged facial features of an ex-rugby player, but he spoke softly and without smiling. The house was immaculate and clean but with a distinct absence of photographs on any surface. Bobby did not need to remind herself that he had lost his wife only a few weeks ago—this house oozed grief from every corner.

'I realise this is a difficult time for you, sir,' Asher said, 'we were hoping that—'

'Have you found her?' Gerald's eyes were full of pleading.

'Found who?'

'Paula. My daughter. That's why you're here, isn't it? Either to tell me you've found her or that she's dead?' He half stumbled and his neighbour jerked forward to help him sit. Gerald was not elderly, probably in his early sixties, but he suddenly looked very old. Nikki exchanged a surreptitious glance with Asher, who shook his head quizzically.

'We're here to tell you neither of those things, Mr Evans. Due to unforeseen circumstances, we've been brought in to provide a fresh pair of eyes. Sometimes that helps. I realise that this must be hard for you, but it would be immensely useful if you would run through everything once again.'

Nikki looked momentarily angry, but then she nodded. 'It is hard for him. You can see that. But then you have your jobs to do, I suppose. I'll make us some tea, shall I?'

Haltingly, Gerald Evans told Asher and Bobby about the dreadful circumstances of his wife's sudden demise. Marie had become increasingly confused over the preceding years. Unable to remember things, forgetful of recent events: all the classic signs of early Alzheimer's compounded by a dysphasic stroke six months before. But the family rallied around. Gerald, fiercely loyal, steadfastly refused to admit his wife into a care home, and his daughter had supported him with once-weekly night duty to allow her father some respite. But Marie's erratic behaviour accelerated dramatically a month before she died. At certain times of the night, she'd become a howling, screaming, inconsolable being. A situation made all the worse by her inability to communicate her fears due to the stroke. They'd resorted, with the help of GPs and community mental health nurses, to having a special bed installed and strapping her down so as to avoid her harming herself as much as anything. A decision informed by the fate of Marie's twin sister, who'd also suffered from Alzheimer's and who had tragically disappeared from a nursing home three years before. Throughout these 'banshee' periods, as Gerald described them, the only coherent thing Marie would babble was 'Twister.'

'Twister?' Asher repeated.

'Yes,' Nikki said, appearing in the kitchen doorway. 'I heard her myself. On several occasions. Couldn't help it, since we live next door. It was always when she got agitated.'

'Can I ask if there was any pattern to this agitation? Any particular time it tended to occur?'

'Funny you should ask because when it happened, when it was bad enough to wake me up, it was always between three and four in the morning.'

'Was she agitated on the night she died?'

Gerald's eyes fell to his lap. Nikki put a hand on his shoulder as he spoke in a halting voice. 'We don't know…My daughter, Paula…she was with her. So we have no idea of knowing.'

There was something left unsaid here. A big hole that Bobby was conscious they might fall into if they weren't careful.

'So who was it that found Mrs Evans?'

'Gerald did,' Nikki answered. 'He was over at Paula's. One night a week he'd go over there to sleep while Paula stayed with her mother. Gerald came home and found the house a mess. Well, you should know, your lot took enough pictures. Every single thing that could be broken was broken. At first we all thought it was burglars, but then he went upstairs. Marie was… was dead. Gerald called me and then I called the police. It was a real mess.'

'Did you take photos of the house?' Bobby asked.

'Yes.'

'Can we see?'

'But you must have hundreds…'

'But you were first on the scene. Sometimes tiny things can get disturbed,' Asher said.

Nikki fetched her phone. The images were stark in exposing the destruction wreaked on the house. There was a lot of glass.

'Whoever did this was sick. They took every single photo Gerald had and smashed the glass and tore up the pictures.'

'Nothing was stolen?'

Nikki shook her head.

To everyone's surprise, Gerald said, 'Nothing except my daughter.'

A heavy silence ballooned in the wake of his words.

'What exactly do you mean by that, Mr Evans?' Asher asked.

'I mean that she's gone. Disappeared.' His voice was strident, full of anguish. 'She wasn't here when I found Marie. No sign of her. But I don't need to tell you that. I thought you'd come here today with news…' He broke down into a sob.

Asher didn't react other than to lean forward. 'Why do you think she was taken, Mr Evans?'

Evans brow's furrowed. 'Why do you think? Why would she disappear unless…unless someone took her. There's a lunatic out there who attacked my wife and scared her to death and who destroyed my house and took my daughter. So why have you not found him yet, eh? Why?'

'We will, Mr Evans. I promise you we will,' Asher said.

Bobby was amazed to hear the sincerity in his voice.

Nikki brought in the tea. It helped.

Asher asked some more questions but there was little else to learn. Ten minutes later, Nikki was seeing them to the door.

Asher hesitated, 'Did you see Mrs Evans? After her death, I mean?'

The young woman nodded and folded her arms tightly, as if trying to fend off the memory. 'It's not something I'm going to forget in a hurry. Her face was distorted horribly. Whatever happened must have been terrible. If it is burglars, I hope they catch them and string them up.'

'And are the police searching for Paula?'

Nikki's face took on a resigned expression. 'No. Paula rang me once a few days after she disappeared. She sounded really odd. She said she couldn't face things after what had happened. Told me to give her dad her love and said she needed to go away for a bit. There have been a couple of emails, too. But she hasn't spoken to her dad. I told the police. Showed them the emails. They say it isn't a police matter because she's been in contact. They can't make her come back. But it's so not like her. And Gerald is having none of it. He thinks she's been taken.'

'Thanks for your help,' Asher said and turned away. He walked down the path and out onto the street.

'Where are we going?' Bobby asked, joining him.

'We passed a park a few hundred yards away. It would not do any harm to walk a while.'

Bobby shrugged. The day had opened up slightly, brightening to a milky white from the leaden grey of the last few days. Asher didn't dawdle and constantly cocked his head as if he was listening. After several minutes of this, Bobby decided to break the silence.

'So,' she asked, 'what are your thoughts?'

'There is little doubt that some kind of malign force is abroad. Why Veronica Loosemore and Marie Evans have been targeted is, as yet, not known to me.' Asher paused to look up at the trees as a parliament of crows erupted raucously into the air.

'Do you think this is tied up with the lockdown at Hipposync?'

'Possibly. If Matt or Kylah got close enough to threaten such an entity, it might have targeted Hipposync.'

'How powerful do you think this thing is, then?'

Asher glanced behind and then up at the sky again. He sniffed the air and Bobby was aware of a faint smell, like stagnant water or old compost on the wind. And it was warm, that smell. On a December day out in the open, Bobby felt a gust of something hot and fetid brush her cheek. She put her hand up to her face as if to wipe it away.

'You feel it too. That is not good. In answer to your question, very powerful. I do not think it is wise to linger here any longer.'

'But we're on a street in Cardiff. There are cars and people and…'

Her words trickled away because suddenly there were no cars or people. Something pale moved in the trees on the edge of the park. A figure, its face turned upwards as if it were calling, its features insubstantial.

They were nearing the park entrance now. Just inside the gate stood a building, nothing more than a hut for storing the groundsman's equipment.

'Quickly,' Asher said. 'We head for that door.'

'But why—'

From behind them came a sudden roar. Asher started moving and Bobby felt her arm being grabbed. She half turned and what she saw turned her insides into an icy mush that froze her limbs. A hole had opened in the roadway, a pit out of which the smell emanated. Only now it was a hundred times worse, eye-wateringly so. Bobby shook her head, hoping to clear the vision. The road was still there and the houses and the pavement, but only a part of her and Asher were. Another part of them was somewhere else, a place where a stinking pit existed and out of which a huge, knobbly, and clawed three-fingered hand emerged. Bobby gawped as it gripped the road and began pulling whatever the arm belonged to, upwards.

'Do not look, Roberta. Run!' Asher yelled.

CHAPTER TWENTY-FIVE

He yanked at her arm and she turned to find the reality of the road they were crossing getting fainter and fainter. But Asher was not one for giving up. He fumbled in a pocket, took out what looked like a golf ball, and threw it towards the park and the hut. A silver thread unwound to leave a glittering line in the air as the ball flew forwards. Behind her, Bobby heard the rasping sound of something hard and leathery slithering over tarmac. It screamed at her to look around, but instinct told her it would risk her sanity if she did. Though the hut sat a mere few yards away, the thrown ball travelled three times the distance before it finally struck its target. Once it did, Asher's grip tightened on Bobby's arm and she saw him reach up with his other hand and grab at the silver thread. They were jerked forward, their feet barely touching the ground, through the gate, up to the solid wall of the concrete hut.

To their left, Bobby saw the pale figure in the trees and heard a hiss of displeasure. The stench was truly awful now. It seeped into her brain, urging her to look around at the thing that was coming for them. Asher was at the door, the Aperio in his hand. Bobby felt a waft of warm, stinking breath on her neck and then they were through with a snap into the blue room at Hipposync.

Asher slammed the door shut and Bobby heard a thud, like something very large slamming its weight against a solid surface.

'What the hell…was that?' she gasped.

Asher shook his head. 'This is not simply a malign spirit. This is something else. Something very bad indeed.'

Bobby's heart was hammering, her mouth as dry as cat litter. 'What was that thing I saw?'

'Something that does not exist in this world or mine. It cannot.'

'But I saw it. I heard it. I felt its breath.'

'We were taken to its world. Such displacement requires immense power. No wonder the lockdown kicked in.'

'But if it could do that to us in broad daylight, just think what it could do at 3.30 am to two poor old confused women!'

'I would rather not,' Asher said.

'Do you think it killed Cuthbertson too? And what about Paula Evans?'

Asher nodded. 'I would normally have suggested visiting the site of the third victim, Cuthbertson, but I no longer think it wise.'

'The pale figure in the woods—'

'Summoned the trogre, yes.'

'A what?' Bobby squinted at him. As made up names went, it was pretty pathetic.

'Trogre. An unhappy marriage of mountain troll and jungle ogre. They live wild and are best left to their own devices. Their scent is unmistakable.'

She stared at him. 'But it is a smell you recognised?'

He nodded. 'We're examined in that sort of thing. Part of our training.'

'Must have been a really fun practical. So the thing in the woods knew we were visiting the Evanses. It must have followed us.'

Asher nodded again. 'Whatever it is, it is now aware of us. But we are safe here.'

The adrenaline slowly leeched from Bobby's system but in its wake it left a terrible trembling. Asher saw it and came to her. She felt his hands on her upper arms. 'Sit down. It will be easier. This shock will pass quickly. The troll exudes a poison that can send living creatures mad. Do not think yourself weak. It is so repulsive that animals will run until their hearts burst.'

All too easy to believe. She felt drained and weak. The one compensation was that Asher sat close to her, concern etched on his face, those eyelashes like shop front awnings, his strong hands reassuringly on her shoulders.

Bobby sat with her back against the wall and shut her eyes to try and blank out Asher so that all her trampolining thoughts could settle. Unfortunately, they left her with the highly unpleasant knowledge that one of the linking factors between Evans and Loosemore was the way they looked in death. And, having seen at first hand the sort of beyond-anyone's-wildest-nightmares monstrosities merely visiting the relatives could conjure up, she could understand why. It made her feel a little sick. She opened her eyes but kept them away from Asher as decorum demanded and searched the room by way of distraction, finally alighting on something glittering faintly on the wall opposite.

'What's that?' she asked, pointing.

Asher stood up, his eyes suddenly keen. 'It is a message. Someone has been here.' He took a small silver box from his coat pocket, snapped it open and removed a pinch of powder, which he threw against the wall. Instantly, words, handwritten and large, flared into legibility.

Development in Bewildered case.
Malachite and his Crotapian dead.
One-legged assassin in custody.

Crouch.

'How did that get there?'

'Crouch probably delivered it himself and left it there because he couldn't find me. I must go back.'

'What?'

'I must report back. There is a malign force at large. I am certain of that now. '

'You think it was what killed Mrs Loosemore and Mrs Evans and maybe even Cuthbertson? Not the trogre?'

'I think it is possible.'

'But why?'

Asher shrugged. 'Hence my need to return. We have people who can find these things out.'

Bobby caught the lie as his eyes slid away. 'And of course, there are the Bewildered. Is it normal for someone like you to be working two cases at once?'

Asher frowned. His lack of response confirmed Bobby's conviction that there was quite a lot more going on here than he was ever likely to let on.

'Thought not.' She sucked in air through her nose as another wave of nausea washed over her.

'Here, I have some salts that will dissipate the trogre's stench.' He reached into an inside pocket and took out a small bottle, removed the glass stopper, and held it out to her. She sniffed gingerly. It smelled of baking bread and rich Christmas spice. Things that made her think warm, convivial thoughts in which the trogre was pushed firmly out of the door and left outside in the rain. A weird contentment stole over her and she watched in disappointment as Asher returned the little bottle to his coat, reached for the Aperio and moved back towards the door. 'I can't explain now.'

'Don't worry. We'll have lots of time while we sit in one of those driverless cabs as it trundles along the streets,' Bobby said with a sigh.

Asher opened the door. Bobby caught a faint whiff of fresh horse manure as she tried to push herself upright against the wall to follow. Tried and failed as her legs, suddenly rubber where they should have been flesh and bone, failed to comply. Asher watched her with a pained expression.

'It's okay. I'll be fine,' she said, trying to quell a trembling leg.

'Not while you're with me, you won't. Already you have been exposed to two attempts on your life. Sorry, Bobby. You need to stay here.'

'Here? No! No way—'

Asher was already halfway through the door. 'I'm sorry. But it is too dangerous for you to accompany me. You will be much safer here in Hipposync. I promise I will not be long. There are malign forces abroad both in New Thameswick and in this world, and this is the safest place for you.'

Bobby tried to find her legs, but they still would not follow instructions and folded beneath her as she hurled her body forward, reaching for the door edge. 'But you promised to tell me about—'

The door shut with a bang and she was left sprawled across the floor, alone in the blue room.

'—the bloody Bewildered. You promised, you complete and absolute shit!'

She banged her fist against the floor. Frustration added to the real trauma of a few minutes before threatened to overwhelm her, but she wouldn't give in to it. She used her anger as a weapon.

He'd promised.

So what now? Sit quietly until he turned up? How could she, knowing there was some weird supernatural entity out there, frightening people to death? Him and his bloody Bewildered. Gradually, she felt solid life return to her lower limbs. It took a good ten minutes during which she managed to conjure up several very inventive ways to repay Asher when she next saw him. Eventually, and under the blind, but curiously watchful eye of Miss Por—Kylah, whose frozen face she could clearly see through the open doorway on the other side of the room, Bobby regained her feet and her composure. After five minutes of pacing to ensure her legs were back to normal, Bobby walked out and stood in front of her boss.

'So, *Kylah*, what exactly would you do in this situation, eh? You with all your secrets. All your specialist training and sacridian salt and all those invocations and magic dust and knowledge and scary old books—'

She stopped there, her own words clicking like tumblers in a lock inside her head. After three blinks, Bobby started to smile.

'Thank you, Kylah,' she said and hurried up the stairs.

CHAPTER TWENTY-SIX

Asher hurried through FHIFAA's front doors, went directly up the worn stone steps to Rathbone's office and knocked. There was the customary delay, one that Asher suspected was merely an ego driven power play meant to keep the knocker on edge. Highly ironic when you came to think about it, because Asher could not have been more on edge had he been standing on the rim of Mount Etna's crater looking down into the fiery lava at its heart. Finally he heard Rathbone call, 'Come in,' and opened the door.

'Ah, Mr Lodge, back at last. What news do you have?'

Asher ignored the sarcasm and quickly and concisely, with no mention of Roberta Miracle, explained his findings. Rathbone listened, fingers steepled.

'A malign entity…you're sure?'

'Something that can conjure up a displacement field to a trogre nest leaves little room for suspicion.'

'Indeed, but we both know that the power required for such an event is considerable. It will, by now, be very weak. I think it's safe to say, almost spent.'

'Ordinarily I would agree,' Asher said, 'but the malign hauntings have taken place over two months. That means it has *survived* for that long. There are three possible deaths linked to this thing that we know of. It must be replenishing itself some—'

Rathbone let out a scoffing snort. 'Come, come, Mr Lodge. That, I think, is a bit of an exaggeration.'

'A trogre coming at you in the middle of a suburban street is no exaggeration…' Asher left a sizeable gap before adding, '…*sir.*' He could feel himself getting irked.

'Very well, let us examine the implications. If this is not a rogue entity, are you suggesting demonic intent? We both know that in order for such an occurrence to manifest it would require hive support. Millions of minds would need to believe, Mr Lodge. We monitor such things closely here, as you well know. And as for over there, well the Vatican seems to have that side of things pretty well sewn up. Last time I was in contact with Cardinal Segundo, the church was not in the habit of conjuring trogres.'

No, they don't need to, mused Asher. The church had enough monsters of its own. Just ask any choirboy encouraged to stay behind to help tidy the cassocks.

'I saw what I saw,' he insisted.

'Indeed,' Rathbone said in a way that suggested Asher's imagination needed a holiday. 'And we therefore have a rogue entity as an explanation for the lockdown and I can now get the paperwork started for reversal. We'll get them back up and running within twenty-four hours.'

Asher shook his head. 'I would not recommend that. First we need to send in a Search and Destroy squad—'

Rathbone sucked air in between his teeth. 'If there are any more deaths, I will get our friends in S&D involved, but we don't want to be spending scruples unnecessarily now, do we?'

If there are any more deaths. Ever the bureaucrat, Rathbone. 'I hardly think that the relatives of those people who died would consider it unnecessary, sir. Added to that is the fact that a human witness, Paula Evans, has gone missing apparently of her own volition. But I cannot discount the possibility that whatever is responsible has abducted this woman. Until this is fully investigated, the lockdown should still stand. As the investigating officer, my recommendations are that we deploy more manpower.' Asher's eyes drilled into Rathbone's impassive face.

'Really? Then perhaps your report will also include a paragraph or two explaining why it is that I have received word that one of my officers, who should have been tracking down malign entities in Oxford, managed to kill an opportunistic thief in the trenches?'

The silence that followed weighed almost a ton.

'That was no thief and neither was he opportunistic. It was a planned assassination attempt,' Asher said. 'Those so called 'thieves' were sectarian killers. They had ritualistic tattoos etched onto their foreheads. They did not want us interfering—'

'Ah,' Rathbone latched onto the word. '*Interfering*. In an investigation run by your old friends in the constabulary, am I right?'

Asher sighed. When he spoke, his words sounded hollow even in his own ears. 'Malign haunting could account for at least one of the deaths that Agents Danmor and Porter were investigating as part of DOF business. We have a spate of Bewildered murders here. Both events began at approximately the same time. We should not dismiss such—'

'A coincidence?' Rathbone said, rolling out the words so that it lay between them like a coiled snake. 'Those miserable souls? Have you ever thought of taking up writing, Mr Lodge? I believe that as an outlet for…an overactive imagination, it might be of some help to you.'

'Those miserable souls you talk about don't deserve to be murdered.' Asher became very still.

'Perhaps not. Yet there are those who consider the Bewildered might be better off dead since their unfortunate sojourn in this world of ours cannot be pleasant. You will remember a judicial review set up to consider euthanasia as the kindest answer. That at least suggested a solution of sorts.'

'As in a 'final solution', you mean?'

'Exactly.' Rathbone beamed.

'Done much in the way of human historical studies, Mr Rathbone? Only I think you'll find that someone over there has already tried that, in some shape or form, and it never ends well.' The smile on Asher's face felt like it had been painted on with glue that had dried and stiffened. And then he remembered.

How could he have forgotten? His reference to human history had murky parallels here in the Fae world. There had been a movement, even a formal committee, to consider the culling of the Bewildered and it had won a lot of support. New Thameswick held a referendum and the cullers lost by the narrowest of margins. Lots of law enforcement officers had been for the motion and Asher knew why. The Bewildered were a bloody nuisance. *No Better Than Rats* was the slogan. A light flickered on in a cupboard of Asher's mind. That was where he remembered seeing Rathbone's cheery clown face; on debating platforms canvassing for the kill squads. He hadn't liked his supercilious smile then and he didn't like it any better now. Thankfully, the *people* didn't like Rathbone's 'solution' either and the cullers had lost.

The *people*, as opposed to the powers that be, felt that the Bewildered did not deserve the purgatory they found themselves in. And no matter how much of a nuisance they were, they did not deserve to die.

Asher respected that. Respected the *people* who thought that way and woe betide anyone who tried to make them think in any other, though he suspected that Rathbone and his kind thought they simply needed guidance. Asher, for one, would be at the front of the barricades with the rest of the *people* if guidance ever came charging down the street on a horse, brandishing a sabre.

Rathbone's gaze slid away. 'You report to me, Mr Lodge, and I have now heard your preliminary findings and am prepared to act upon them as I see fit. Thank you for your diligence and I look forward to reading the full report in due course. But perhaps it, like your hysterical recommendations, ought to take second place to the task in hand.'

'What about the missing woman?'

Rathbone gave an irritated wave of his hand. 'That is a problem for the authorities over there, not us. That is why we have the DOF. You need to concentrate on your own work here.'

'What exactly do you want me to do?' Asher asked after a pause.

'The task you are getting paid to do here at FHIFAA, Mr

Lodge. I require the figures for migrant flows between Maplinland and Shin. By 4 pm, if you please.' Rathbone's grin was like a newborn baby's bum: inviting a sharp slap to elicit a cry. Asher, however, stayed remarkably calm. Seeing the horror in the faces of those relatives who'd found the corpses of Veronica Loosemore and Marie Evans had already made his mind up.

'No.'

'Excuse me?' Rathbone sat back in mock surprise. 'Are you refusing a direct order?'

'You have clerks who can do that. I do not think that it is an appropriate use of my training or skills. I have received word that there has been a further development in this case, which I believe to be of material relevance to us and the constabulary.'

'The constabulary. I see. Well now, Mr Lodge. In this department, *I* decide what is relevant.'

'Yes, you do. And that is why I can no longer be here.'

'Resigning, Mr Lodge?' Rathbone's grin looked manic.

'Don't worry, I'll put it in writing.' Asher pushed back and stood up so abruptly it made Rathbone flinch. 'This case has layers that go much deeper than you are willing to admit to. It is my professional opinion that unless we deal with the threat appropriately, many more people will die both here and in the human world. And the Bewildered are still people, Mr Rathbone, like it or not. My recommendation is that you do not release the lockdown until a Search and Destroy unit is sent to hunt down whatever it is that has terrorised and possibly contributed to the deaths of three humans, and might still have Paula Evans in captivity. This is clearly a fimmigration breach.'

'And you, Mr Lodge, will face immediate disciplinary action for unsanctioned absence from the workplace.'

'Then that is how it must be.' Asher got up and turned away. He'd walked three steps when he said over his shoulder, 'I don't mind working in a circus, but not when clowns are running it.'

'I could arrange for you to have some help, you know,' Rathbone said to his departing back. 'It's no shame to require counselling. After all, one in three of us will experience some kind of breakdown in the course of our working lives. Goes with the territory.' The pause that followed allowed Asher to reach the door before Rathbone added, 'I believe it is as high as one in two for necreddos.'

Asher hesitated but did not turn around. If he did, it was likely that someone might get badly hurt. He didn't think it would be him.

CHAPTER TWENTY-SEVEN

MALACHITE'S APARTMENT cowered in the basement of a four-storey terraced house with huge windows, a cream painted exterior and black lacquered doors and railings. It didn't look the sort of place where people could be killed, nor did it look like the sort of place Malachite should have been able to afford. The uniformed constable guarding the street entrance nodded to Asher and stood aside to let him in. Downstairs, the front door was open and the first thing that struck Asher was the smell. Thaumaturgy of whatever type left vestigia and generally you could tell if it was good or bad by the aroma. Producing flowers out of thin air at a kids' birthday party usually brought with it a scent of sweet pea, and all you had to pray for was that the heavy-set girl in pigtails didn't have any allergies. But Malachite's apartment stank like the blocked toilet in an unventilated charnel house. It spoke, to Asher, of dark deeds indeed.

'Someone heard screaming and called for a constable. By the time they got here, it was all over,' Crouch said, as he led the way through a small living room into what had once been a kitchen with wooden units and yellow walls, and was now replaced by a black and ochre abstract entitled *Blood Spatter Explosion*.

'They've taken Malachite and his Crotapian away, you'll be glad to hear,' Crouch said.

Asher raised a questioning eyebrow. 'Must have been a hole in the sac.'

Crouch read his expression and answered, 'Yeah. Needed five bags. They were both lollipops.'

Asher raised another eyebrow.

'Came to a sticky end,' Crouch continued with a shrug. 'Looks like someone used a decimator curse.'

Asher whistled softly. Decimator curses were not only murderous and therefore illegal in their own right, they'd been banned by every right-minded society under the Megalouf Convention. Whoever did all this had obviously not been troubled by flouting societal rules. Even those involving death and destruction.

'But there's more fun to be found out the back.' Crouch now walked on the mats put down by the CIC. The acronym stood for Curse Investigation and Clearance but everyone pronounced it with hard c's and adding the suffix -ers made it a better sounding slang noun; kickers. They would be back tomorrow to sift through the vestigia and physical evidence after the dust had settled. Asher followed into a room that should have been a pantry but had been transformed, presumably by Malachite, into a shrine. The various letters and runes scrawled on the wall seemed to writhe when Asher looked at them. They were powerful and, he guessed, illegal too. 'They've tried to cover things up, but we managed to get the Kickers to peel away the worst of the camo. This is what we found.' Crouch flicked off the lamps. On the far wall, above a small table covered in a variety of animal skulls, a shape glowed a lurid yellow. A reversed Z-shape crossed by curving arms.

'I've seen that before,' Asher said immediately.

'Yes, you have. We think it's the same as the one carved into the forehead of the dirt bag that attacked you near the trenches.'

'Think? Can't you check?'

Crouch shook his head. 'Gone quicker than you can say 'zleeper buffet'.'

'Then how…'

'We got the other one. The one your girlfriend managed to fend off. Though how she did I'll never know, 'cos he's a vicious git, even with one leg—the zleepers got his other one. He's got the mark on his forehead, too.'

'What does it mean?'

'They're Widicombs. Followers of Gazorch the Pantocrator.'

'Hasn't he been banned?'

Crouch nodded. 'For all eternity, yes. But that doesn't stop some lunatic faction from worshipping him now, does it?'

'Gazorch the Pantocrator,' whispered Asher to himself. 'But if Malachite was one of the faithful, why kill him?'

'Maybe because he was attracting too much attention? I don't know. And, of course, since he's been decimated and his soul cast to the wind, even you can't ask him, can you?'

Asher shook his head. One of the reasons the decimator curse was banned was that it left no means of contacting the deceased. 'So Malachite was a Gazorch freak. What has that got to do with the Bewildered and us being attacked on the trenches?'

'I was hoping you'd have some ideas yourself,' Crouch said.

'Well, I don't. Other than the vaguest hunch. There are no fumes without a flame, Crouch. But since it's now a demonic crime, we need to ask for some help, I think.'

'Please tell me you're not suggesting what I think you are?' Crouch groaned.

'Who else do we know? Besides, all that stuff between Duana and me is way in the past.'

'Yeah, right.'

'Well, do you have any better ideas?'

'No. But is all this okay with wossisname, Rathbone?'

'Oh yes, I've squared everything off with him.'

Crouch gave Asher an old-fashioned look. 'I don't like the sound of that one bit.'

'Let me worry about Rathbone. Look, we have only days before the next lot of Bewildered killings. And there will be more, I know it.'

'Funny you should say that, 'cos my sources tell me that there's been a distinct lack of Bewildered sightings over the last few days. It looks like they've dropped out of sight.'

'Then we ought to move.'

'But, Duana, I mean, can't we just stick bamboo spikes under our nails and be done with it?'

'Very funny, Crouch. Come on, we're wasting time.' Asher turned away and walked out of the house. He stood on the street and waited for a police cab to arrive.

'How's that foxy witch girlfriend of yours doing?' Crouch asked, joining Asher at the kerb and keeping his gaze straight ahead.

'Two points I'd like you to take note of. The first is that she is not my girlfriend and the second is that she is not a witch.'

'Weird way of showing it,' Crouch said.

Asher wanted to ask him if he meant the girlfriend bit or the witch bit, but he would only be fanning the flames. The last thing he needed at that moment was to be reminded of Bobby Miracle. The truth was he was having a hard time trying to forget. He kept seeing her face. Those dark lips surrounded by her half black and half white hair with the wild pink streaks. Those smoky grey lids above eyes that were so unflinching...It made his quiet moments quite distracting. So much so that he found himself defending her.

'She's a Goth. It's an aesthetic.'

'I prefer tincture of opium,' Crouch said.

Asher kept quiet, tried to ignore Crouch's smirk and the burning desire he suddenly had to clip the shapeshifter around the ear with his open palm.

CHAPTER TWENTY-EIGHT

BOBBY WENT DIRECTLY to Matt's room. His report on the deaths still sat on the desk but she ignored them and turned her attention to the bookshelves. Quickly, she grabbed a couple of likely volumes, a sheet of paper from the tray in the printer, and a pen. Thus armed, she sat at the desk and pulled one of the titles towards her. She sensed there were answers in the ink on these pages. The trick was knowing where and what to look up. But first of all she needed some definitions. Since Asher refused to explain the Bewildered, she studied the indexes and looked it up in a DOF lexicon of commonly used terms.

BEWILDERED: Human individuals who stray or inadvertently fall through Fae portways inevitably do so accidentally and, since most of those unfortunates that pass through do not have the tenth gate of awareness, their appreciation of the Fae world is that of a vague and shadowy place glimpsed as if through a dense veil. Though physical items are visible, Fae animals and beings remain insubstantial and spectrelike. In most cases, such existences result in severe cases of mental suffering for the individual, who is compelled to roam the landscape, existing on scraps of food and water, often hearing noises or voices but unable to visualise their source. The common term for this state is 'the Bewilderment'. Such entities are termed 'the Bewildered.'

In another book, this one called *Necromancer's Almanac*, the entry for the Bewildered made for even more disturbing reading.

At death, there is at last some release for the Bewildered. Their souls return to the human world, but it is not an easy passage, given that they have to cross the Abaddonian Plane. The Bewildered have spirits so damaged by their separation from the human world that their desire to establish contact with their families often manifests as poltergeist activity. In transit, and because of their prolonged journey across the void separating the worlds, they risk exposure to the Damned, those souls cursed to exist for eternity in oblivion. Reported cases of the Damned latching onto the Bewildered's souls are documented. These interlopers will seek to possess the body of the next living creature they comes across. Such parasitic hauntings can result in the worst form of poltergeist activity and are of an extremely violent nature. They are self-limiting as the interloper often causes the death of the living creature it tries to possess through sheer terror...

Then she looked up 'malign haunting'. There were several entries in more than one book, but the most complete and useful one she found was in *Thaumaturgy: A Primer*.

Malign Haunting:

The unwelcome presence of an unquiet non-physical entity intent on harm. Frequently, malign hauntings occur as a result of the death of a person who has been separated from the victim suffering the haunting for extended periods. Untimely or violent death is thought to cause great trauma to an unrested soul and this often results in the spirit revisiting living relatives either to warn, or to simply re-establish connections in the form of aggressive poltergeist activity. Unfortunately, the overenthusiastic nature of this attempt causes great distress to the victim. Often, where the living person is frail or ill or old, such visitations prove fatal due to the associated shock and awe associated with them. The more lurid descriptions of this aggressive activity have resulted in such paranormal experiences being given the name, 'malign hauntings', though this term should only apply to specific circumstances (see Premeditated Malign Haunting) associated with Bewilderment. By their very nature, such hauntings are usually self-limiting since the spirit has only a short time prior to transcending.

Premeditated Malign Haunting:
Here, a malevolent spirit deliberately targets living victims for vengeful, or other nefarious reasons. Often there is little to distinguish between the effect of premeditated and non-premeditated malign hauntings unless the precipitating entity is found and interrogated.

That certainly explained the horrifying stories Bobby had heard from both the Loosemores and the Evanses. She zeroed in on a few choice words and phrases. She still didn't quite know what 'true premeditated malign hauntings' entailed but it sounded about as welcome as trench foot. Not that she knew what trench foot really was either, but she knew she'd never order it on a menu. Yet it was the phrase 'separated from the person suffering the haunting for extended periods' that intrigued her for a reason that she could not yet quite fathom. So she wrote it down on her piece of paper, sat back and studied what she'd written.

From what she could understand, the poor Bewildered were fighting a losing battle whatever happened. At death, their desperation to return could, in itself, manifest as poltergeist activity. Enough to frighten their vulnerable relatives. Literally scare them to death. But worse was the fact that the Bewildered carried a separate risk; that of having parasitic entities possess them during their troubled journey between existences. And anything capable of that sort of activity never featured high on anyone's list of top ten children's entertainers. Her notes grew denser as the frozen silence inside Hipposync grew heavier. There were other words she'd looked up. Words such as 'necreddo', which told her more about how Asher could communicate with the dead. No wonder he hadn't wanted to brag about that. But then she turned her attention to the books on witchcraft; specifically one entitled *The Witche's Vade Mecum*. She told herself it was purely educational, given the persistent way everyone in New Thameswick assumed she was a witch by the way she dressed, but there was more than a little anticipation in her fingers when she opened the pages.

It took her four hours to speed read the book and as she did so, she got the weirdest impression that it was like drinking a big glass of water and seeing the level fall as she gulped, knowing that it was being absorbed by her thirsty body. The difference being that *The Witche's Vade Mecum* filled up her head and not her stomach. Her brain could not begin to understand nor even pronounce all the words, but as she read, a regular flash like predicative text went off in her head with each turn of the page. Maybe the thing was programmed to do just that. A type of assisted reading? And it all made perfect sense, too. There were a few incantations and spells, but mostly it was about seeing the truth for what it really was and encouraging people and things to realise that. Informed persuasion was what came across, helped by hard knowledge of which herbs did what best, which days of the week were best suited for various activities, and how to make poultices out of, well, almost anything.

When she finished and finally closed the book, she felt as if she'd just consumed a nutritious meal. Replete and somehow aware of the fact that it had done her a lot of good. She turned her attention back to her notes with renewed enthusiasm, reread them, and read them again. Something bothered her. An idea, as yet unformed, that simply wouldn't go away. It was something to do with witchery, or Asher being a necreddo or his preoccupation with the Bewildered, or the horrible deaths they'd investigated, of that there was no doubt. There was a thread here, a linking bit of string trying desperately to somehow tie things together.

She did the trick that her old professor taught her to do when proofreading an essay. The idea was to read it backwards, not as in right to left, but starting with the last paragraph. Forced dissociation meant the brain wasn't tricked by the context into jumping forward. She read again her paragraph on the Bewildered and how they could, very easily, become confused and terrified 'malign' spirits on their own. Was that it? Was the thing that she and Asher saw in the woods one of the Bewildered? Something to think about, yes, but the niggle remained. She scanned the notes again. The Bewildered's souls returned to their point of origin at death. Seeking, it seemed, an anchor point.

Most commonly a person, their nearest living relative and…of course! *That* was it. *That* was the common thread.

Veronica Loosemore's husband walked out on her when the children were young, like hundreds of other feckless fathers. But what if he hadn't walked out? What if he'd slipped through one of the cracked portways between the worlds and become one of the Bewildered? What if he'd died and come back to try and desperately re-establish a connection with his wife, only to have her die of fright? But how did that work with the Evanses? Mr Evans was still alive. So that theory couldn't apply…wait a minute. What was it the neighbour'd said about Mrs Evans? She'd kept saying something…what was it? Mister…blister…twister, yes, twister. But to a dysphasic brain, twister might well be the word that came out when the aim was actually something else altogether. Strokes could do that to you. Make you say words that sounded the same, but were a thousand miles away from the right meaning. If twister was not what Mrs Evans meant, perhaps it was indeed mister or blister or even…sister.

Bobby sat up. Light bulbs seldom, if ever, went on above her head, but she would have bet good money that one just had. Mrs Evans' twin sister suffered from Alzheimer's and disappeared from a nursing home a few years before. That in itself was not suspicious. That sort of thing happened. People wandered off, especially confused people, she knew they did. God, left unsupervised towards the end, her grandmother would have run headlong through a river in full flood. But what if Mrs Evans' twin sister also slipped between the cracks and died over 'there'? Bobby shuddered at the thought. Difficult to fathom how terrifying it must have been for someone, already abandoned by understanding and clarity, wandering lost and alone in the shadowy world of the Fae. It didn't bear thinking about. But at death, her soul would have rushed back to her nearest and dearest. And in this instance DNA took top trumps. This time it had not been a husband or a daughter, but a twin *sister*.

Bobby clutched the desk, her fingers white with concentration. There was a pattern here. A definite pattern. Now she needed to find out if any of Cuthbertson's relatives had gone missing. If they had, she'd found a solid link. A link to the Bewildered that would also partly explain Asher's compunction to investigate them, not that he'd bothered to share any of that knowledge with her.

But she couldn't just go to Cuthbertson's, even though the address was plain as day in the report. She was locked in Hipposync like a naughty child with no way out now that Asher had taken the Aperio. *He* would argue that it was for her own safety. But if she could only take a quick look inside Cuthbertson's house—the old man lived alone, she'd read that—she might be able to get somewhere. She felt suddenly and utterly convinced of its importance. She pushed back from the desk and growled in frustration. No good. She was stuck here with no way of communicating and no way of getting out. Her eyes drifted over the computer workstation, the filing cabinet, Kylah's cupboard, Matt standing at his desk. If only she had an Aperio like Asher, she could do it all in a…

Her eyes flicked back to Kylah's cupboard. Asher had unlocked it that morning. The question was, had he taken the trouble to relock it?

Bobby got up and walked across to the cupboard; a triangular corner affair made of dark oak with its door firmly closed. She lifted her fingers to the knob but let them drop again. This wasn't her cupboard. She shouldn't even be thinking about this. But it was a genuine emergency, wasn't it? She lifted her hand a second time, closed her fingers on the knob and pulled. The door opened with only the slightest creak. Inside were two shelves stacked with all kinds of things with interesting names that, having read the *Vade Mecum*, she knew the properties of. There was a range of black daggers, or *athames*, as they were referred to in the Wicca world. She counted seven. There were also a handful of daggers with different coloured handles, some elaborate metal and bone cups, stone rings and few other ornate artefacts. Did this mean that Kylah dabbled? But if she didn't, why would she need so many of these items? Unless they weren't hers. In a flash of insight, Bobby realised she was looking at the Hipposync equivalent of a school classroom's 'naughty cupboard'. These weren't Kylah's; these were items that Kylah, or Matt, had confiscated. It was the only explanation.

Next to the Wicca accoutrements were lots of neatly labelled bottles and muslin bags full of stuff that smelled of lavender or sage, or, very mysteriously, of blue skies or running streams or wet dog. On the very bottom sat a neatly arrayed collection of labelled black velvet bags. On a whim, she picked a few up and studied their names. She read Wolf's Bane, Demon's Bane, Pox Powder and one very intriguing one called Intractable Itch. More interesting, even, were the manufacturer's names. Bindle's Emporium, Wormwood Wytches, Pockdoor & Scamble. But the one that really caught her eye came from the Offa's Coven; labelled, Crone with the Wind, which, according to the description, was an extraction grenade allowing the user to summon up sudden breezes to waft away 'bad smells, enemies or other annoying elements' and instigate instant evacuation. She took a few of these potions and elixirs back to the desk and studied them. Wolf's Bane, she found out, was useful for training your dog not to mess the floor as well as an anti-lycanthropy potion. Pox Powder did exactly what it said on the muslin bag only in reverse; gave you a rash that would keep you off work for those, all too necessary, sick days. She tested the smells, but, sensibly, refrained from tasting anything.

But there were no answers here for her problem. She went back to the cupboard and continued searching. Finally, following five minutes of good rummaging, behind a collection of even more bottles and bags on the bottom shelf, she found a green and purple mottled knob. It looked the exact same shape as Asher's Aperio. She picked it up. It felt warm in her hand. A tingle of excitement rippled through her. No reason to assume that this thing would work, but it was worth a try, surely.

Now for the difficult bit.

Though she'd never been to Cuthbertson's house, there were photographs in the file. These photographs included one of a garden shed and the front door, as well as every room in the house. Asher had said you needed knowledge of your destination or at least be able to visualise it. Well, this was a good time to find out if that last bit was true. If she fixed her mind on the shed door and it opened, at least she'd be in Cuthbertson's garden. From there she could work out her next move. She put on her coat, placed the Aperio to the hinge side of the office door, and, holding up the image of the shed, shut her eyes, turned the knob and pushed.

CHAPTER TWENTY-NINE

EVEN BEFORE SHE opened her eyes she knew it had worked. Either that or someone had just spilled lawnmower oil in the corridor at Hipposync.

The shed's interior was late-afternoon December cold. Apart from the engine oil smell, the only things bothering Bobby were the thick swathes of ancient cobwebs in the corners filling the gap between the roof and corner posts. Spiders were not her favourite insect but she could cope with the odd one. Though judging from the thickness of the webs here, this shed could be hiding some very odd ones indeed. The one window looked out into the garden, not the view Bobby wanted. She would have preferred a peek at the house just to make sure no one was there, but it was not to be. She tried the shed door.

Locked.

She replaced the Aperio on the hinge side of the shed door and washed it open. Luckily, it swung in a way that let her see the back of the house and she eased it open a couple of inches. It was now dark enough to merit lights but none glowed in the Cuthbertson residence.

She took a deep breath, pushed the door fully open, and walked out onto the small patio, which marked the beginning of a neat, well tended garden. The irony of it did not escape her; dressed in her usual attire she probably was enough of a sight emerging from a locked shed to petrify the neighbours' cat, if not the neighbour. Still, needs must. The far end of the garden looked bare and dug over for vegetables. Between it and where she stood was a neat lawn. But she did not dwell and ran over the story she'd prepared in case anyone was in. She'd pretend to be part of the council's new bereavement service (*suitably dressed, ha ha Bobby, you are so very droll*) to follow up on anyone who required any help. Pretty thin and lame but the best she could come up with at short notice. And though Cuthbertson had no living relatives, bureaucracy was forever making mistakes like that. As to why she'd chosen the back door, she'd claim that despite knocking at the front, she'd got no answer. She quickly glanced around. The garden had high enough walls so as to avoid any prying neighbours. So far so good.

'Here goes,' she said in a low voice, stepped forward and knocked. She repeated the exercise twice more until she confirmed no one was home, placed the Aperio on the door and opened it. She stepped through into a kitchen that yelled seventies at her in orange and brown wallpaper and units. Folded on a towel rail under the sink was a pair of yellow rubber gloves. Mindful of not leaving fingerprints, she snapped them on, stepped forward and, hesitantly, let out a, 'Hello? Hello?''

No one answered. She heard only a faint click, as if the vibrations of her voice had disturbed an old piece of timber in the house. But it settled again very quickly into a post 'hello' silence. Satisfied that she was alone, Bobby walked slowly into the living room. Patterned carpet, a tiled fireplace, and a small plasma screen TV as the only nod to modernism in the room. A single, well-dented armchair covered in purple velour looked like it had been Cuthbertson's seat of choice. Bobby's eyes danced around the room and landed on the fireplace.

There were three photographs on the mantelpiece. A group of elderly men holding up vegetables at a fete, a black and white photo of the crew of a wartime bomber, and one of a dog. Folded flat next to these lay a bi-leafed wooden photo frame showing, on one side, a couple on their wedding day, and on the other, the same couple behind a cake upon which was written 'Golden Wedding'. Bobby studied the older, black and white wedding photo. The man looked slim and smart in RAF uniform, the woman neat and small and pretty in a wedding dress. Bobby removed the photo. On the rear, handwritten in fading ink, were the words: *December 26th 1948, Harry and Rose Cuthbertson*. She studied the second image; this one had a printed sticker on the rear. *H and R Cuthbertson Golden Wedding, Christmas 1998*.

A lifetime of loyalty in two snaps. But why not on display like the others? Bobby let her eyes cruise the room again. A gate leg table stood neatly folded up against the wall with two wheelback chairs tucked beneath it. Next to the fireplace stood a cabinet with sliding glass doors at the top. A veritable zoo of small glass and china animals stood patiently behind the glass. The bottom half of the cabinet had two drawers. She'd begin with that.

The light was definitely fading now and she did not have much time if she was going to rely on daylight and not risk putting any lights on, always assuming that the electricity had not been turned off. She pulled open the top cupboard and frowned at the layers of flotsam. Glasses cases, sets of screwdrivers, electric plugs and the debris of eighty years of existence. She tried the drawer beneath. This looked more promising since one side was crammed full of envelopes. But they were mainly bills and invitations to make hospital appointments. She learned that Harry Cuthbertson suffered from macula degeneration and arthritis. But fifteen minutes later and none the wiser regarding Rose Cuthbertson, she shut the drawer.

Nothing for it but upstairs. It was as she left the room that she heard the noise. Nothing much, merely a faint rustling somewhere in the chimney breast accompanied by a sudden downdraft of air that blew a few desiccated leaves onto the rug. It was an open coal fire, judging from the remnants left in the grate. Bobby surmised that the weather must be changing. Snow had been mentioned in one of the forecasts she'd heard. Certainly felt cold enough for snow at the Cuthbertson residence.

She hurried up the stairs. The first floor consisted of two bedrooms and a bathroom. She went for the main bedroom, which contained a double bed, a wardrobe, another fireplace and, at the bottom of the bed, a wooden trunk. She opened the wardrobe. Inside were two suits, three blazers, and a motley selection of trousers, all in brown or grey. In the drawers beneath were several clean but worn shirts and next to those, underpants and socks.

Bobby turned then to the trunk. She lifted the lid and saw, to her surprise, that it was packed with women's clothes. Not many, but a selection of dresses, varying in size from ten to eighteen and varying in terms of fashion as well, with the polka-dot Lindy Bop the oldest and smallest. Beneath all of those lay the wedding dress Bobby had seen in the photo downstairs and beneath the wedding dress, a blue cardboard folder. She lifted it out and put it on the bed and flicked open the cover. On the top were birth certificates and a marriage certificate, a variety of utility bills, some lottery tickets and then, in a separate and much thinner folder, Bobby struck gold. She lifted out the buff envelope upon which, in a spidery hand, someone —she assumed it was Cuthbertson—had written the word, 'Rose'.

She heard the scrabbling noise again. This time she was sure that it came from the chimney and again, a puff of wind blew down a little black cloud of soot.

Nesting crows?

She looked out of the bedroom window. The street outside was quiet, a couple of kids on bikes finding their way home from school the only sign of life. But definitely and welcomingly a sign of normal life. Satisfied, Bobby turned back and opened the envelope. There were clippings from local newspapers and photocopies of letters, mostly written by Cuthbertson, all pertaining to the same dreadful, tragic event. Bobby picked up a clipping and read it quickly. Rose Cuthbertson had gone on a shopping trip to the local Morrisons in July 2011. The store provided the transport and it was, by all accounts, part of Mrs Cuthbertson's routine every Tuesday. But on the third Tuesday of that month, she failed to return from her trip. The consequent police operation made the local and national press, but after six months and no trace found, the search was abandoned. A letter from the Chief Constable of Mercia police formally ended the enquiry thus:

It is unfortunately the case that a small percentage of missing persons remain missing, and their whereabouts and circumstances are never resolved. We do not like to admit defeat and you can remain assured that if any further information regarding Mrs Cuthbertson comes to light, we will pursue it with vigour.

A note designed to crush the spirit if ever she'd read one. Bobby could barely imagine how poor old Mr Cuthbertson would have felt on receiving such news. It must have been a devastating blow.

Yet she couldn't help but feel an incongruous surge of triumph. This was it. This was the link. Cuthbertson, like Loosemore and Evans, had lost someone close. And Bobby would put money on the fact that the lost had probably slipped across to become one of Asher's Bewildered.

Another gust rattled the chimney, this time loud enough to cause Bobby to frown. Something wasn't right here. She had nothing against gusts but…Glancing out of the window into the street, Bobby let her eyes drift upwards. Cuthbertson was not the only coal user in this street. Three doors up on the opposite side, a chimney oozed grey smoke and it drifted straight up with no hint of any breeze blowing it away.

The chimney rattled again. This time so violently that it made Bobby start. What was this? A bird, a squirrel? She did not like squirrels. She'd read about them getting into people's houses. Rats with bushy tails that's all they w—

Her thoughts were cut off by another rattle, which this time grew into a steady rumble like that of a train approaching a station. And it was an express, not a lumbering goods train. Senses heightened, Bobby located the source as definitely coming from the fireplace and it had nothing to do with squirrels, because inside the rushing onslaught of noise Bobby could hear something. Something discordant, like a hundred voices running backwards in a howling wind. And then all the light in the room dimmed but the fireplace itself got darker and rounder, and something grey and quick leapt out of it and into the wardrobe, despite its closed doors.

An intense coldness descended on the room now. Bobby

could feel it on her face, like the dank air from some deep cave. Outside the streetlights came on, but they did not seem capable of penetrating the bedroom, which remained a shadowy grey. Bobby knew what she needed to do. She needed to get to the bedroom door, fit the Aperio and leave. Take the file with her and just get out. She took a step and froze. In front of her, right next to the door, the wardrobe started to shake. It shook so wildly the legs started to creep sideways in a mad vibrational shuffle. Something was knocking violently inside it, driving it sideways, pushing it towards the bedroom door. Either it had come alive or Cuthbertson had inadvertently left the gate to Narnia open when he'd gone. The noise was now so loud that Bobby felt sure someone would hear. Even so, she decided that it might not be a bad thing to call for help. She yelled, but the noise from her voice got lost in the murk so that it sounded faint and thick, as if she'd screamed into a woollen scarf.

Not good. Definitely not good.

And then the wardrobe stopped moving. The sudden silence left her ears ringing and it was then that Bobby realised her exit was completely blocked. Panic, like a scurrying mouse in a room full of cats, broke free from its hiding place and gripped her in its chaotic fingers. Despite the cold, droplets of sweat began to run down the inside of Bobby's blouse. It smelled of sour, sharp fear. She turned to the window behind her and tried the handle but it was locked. She waved hard at the boys on their bicycles but they took no notice. She rapped on the glass, yelling at the top of her voice to no avail. Then, still with her back towards the room and with her heart pummelling her ribs, Bobby finally heard the noise that caused her stomach to lurch and all the saliva in her mouth to evaporate like ice in a desert. A strange, small, squeaking noise; the kind that is made when an un-oiled mechanism resists turning, just like a rusty lock on an old wardrobe door.

CHAPTER THIRTY

THE BUREAU of Demonology was housed in a Gothic mansion on a hill to the West of New Thameswick, in an area known as Bootown. Most of the staff lived and worked within a square mile since rent in that area was relatively inexpensive. The only part of the city where housing was cheaper was in Pegville, where they harvested methane gas from the city's biological waste, both human and animal. At least in Bootown you could actually light a flame without fear of blowing the roof off, even if the sort of vermin you were likely to come across had eight legs and spikes on their backs and were the size of basketballs (though the official line on the plague of krets was that they had very definitely been eradicated and the novice responsible for their invocation had moved to a different department). Small consolation to the residents who often found them nesting in toilets; a finding that had the curiously paradoxical effect of making the finder want to vacate the room at the same time as oiling the wheels of the gastroenterological reason for being in said room in the first place. The result was often a hasty, but inevitably messy, retreat.

'I hate this place,' Crouch said, as they approached the sentries guarding the drawbridge.

'It's simply another government department,' Asher said.

Crouch sent him a sceptical glare.

'They undertake enormously important work,' Asher persisted.

'Yeah, right, but why can't they do it in a cave under a mountain somewhere, not in the middle of the city?'

'You wouldn't be saying that if we were attacked by demons.'

Crouch bristled. 'I would and I will, because this place was the cause of the last three attacks.'

'Indeed. But they were contained. And it has left us much better prepared, you have to admit.'

'I'm admitting nothing.'

They went through the usual triple security checks and fifteen minutes later were in a cavernous entrance hall. Asher didn't need to ask the way. He'd been here many times. Duana Llewyn had her own laboratory on the third floor. Asher was about to knock when Crouch grabbed his arm.

'She does know we're coming, right?'

'I sent a beemail, remember. What are you so worried about?'

'Her, mainly.'

'Don't exaggerate,' Asher said and knocked.

They both heard a tinkling female voice say, 'Come in,' and Asher opened the door. Standing with her hands clasped in front of her demurely, was a pale, gauntly attractive woman with dirty blonde shoulder-length hair. Her grey blue eyes looked almost silver in the flat light spilling in through a quartered window. Surrounding her, almost like a royal court, were retorts, crucibles, open books, pestles and mortars, cauldrons and hats. Above, hanging haphazardly from the ceiling, were cages containing a selection of owls and crows, most of whom were also looking at Crouch and Asher with the same slightly amused and expectant expression.

'Duana,' Asher said and stepped forward. The moment he did, something huge and dark swopped down from the ceiling with a banshee scream. Whatever it was, it fell upon Asher with a face that was mainly mouth and teeth with three black eyes, and outstretched, overlarge hands with clawlike fingers. Asher shut his eyes and let the thing flow through him, which it did with surprising speed. From behind, he heard Crouch let out an oath that was more than half a scream. When Asher opened his eyes again, there was a small smile on Duana's face, which was the closest she ever came to confirming that she'd enjoyed herself.

'Hello, Duana,' Asher said.

'Hello, Asher Lodge,' Duana replied.

'What the fecund—' Crouch wailed.

'Hello, Crouch,' Duana interrupted the hawkshaw's angry tirade. 'Did you like my discouragement geist? He is new and I wanted to test his effectiveness.'

'Bloody thing went right through me,' Crouch spluttered.

'From the look of you I would say your lunch is set to follow.' Duana tilted her head and added without a morsel of humour, 'Note to self: there might be some mileage in secondarily using the geist as a defibrillator.'

Asher looked around to see a pale Crouch leaning weakly against the wall, shaking his head. His eyes were sweeping the room, waiting for the next of Duana's surprises.

The lady herself walked forward with an upright gait and her usual closed mouth smile, put two hands stiffly on Asher's upper arms and held her face at an angle for him to kiss her cheek. As demonstrations of affection went in the Duana Llewyn canon, it was pretty spectacular. She waved at Crouch, who waved back and shook his head some more.

Duana stood back and inspected Asher at arm's length, tilted her head in a trademark gesture once more and said, 'You have lost weight. I heard about the surgery. I surmise that your departure from the necrosquad left you spiritually deflated and you are only now recovering.'

'It's nice to see you too, Duana,' Asher smiled. He was very fond of this woman who was frighteningly bright, incapable of lying, fiercely loyal, totally absorbed in her work and demanding yet pleasingly generous in bed. When it came to affection and warmth, however, she was an iguana, albeit a very attractive one with a propensity for low cut blouses and tight-fitting skirts. Crouch made the common mistake of thinking her a sociopath, but had the sense not to say it out loud within a two-mile radius. Duana Llewyn's hearing was excellent.

'Do you have to scare the crap out of us every time?' Crouch said, still miffed.

'No,' Duana said. 'But I have so few visitors now that the university has stopped sending students—'

'I wonder why,' muttered Crouch.

'—I decided to capitalise on your visit. An effective use of circumstance, I feel.'

'Oh yeah,' Crouch said. 'Very effective. Absolutely.'

'Good, I am glad you agree.'

Crouch looked like he wanted to say something else but sensibly held back. Asher smiled. Any and all attempts at sardonic humour were completely lost on Duana.

'It's been a while,' Asher said.

'Five months, four days and…' Duana glanced at the eight clocks on her wall, '…two-and-a-quarter hours.'

'Right,' Asher said with a smile.

'But you have not come here to renew our lapsed relationship, I think. You would not have brought Hawkshaw Crouch if that was your intent.'

'Don't mind me,' Crouch said.

'Duana, we're here for help.'

The demonmaster's face perked up. 'So, this is a professional visit. Then I am intrigued.'

Crouch joined Asher and they cleared some books, a stuffed vulture, a half-eaten sandwich and a battered hat from two stools while Duana took up her preferred spot, silhouetted against the window, face serene as she lent her attention to what Asher had to say about the Bewildered and Malachite. When he'd finished, she tilted her head.

CHAPTER THIRTY-ONE

'GAZORCH THE PANTOCRATOR, as you know, is a demon lord of the entrance gate, predominantly eminent in the 8th century until he was cast out during the 5th insurrection. A few acolytes in equatorial Scram kept the faith, but the cannibal resurgences of 2012 and 2016 brought him once more to the fore when his followers succeeded in raising the summoner demon, Habihemhock—himself the avowed servant of Gazorch. Don't forget that Gazorch, like all quasi-deities, requires a world made ready before he will deign to manifest. Habihemhock's job is to do all the preparation. But getting as far as raising Habihemhock is an extremely dangerous manoeuvre in itself. In 2016 it resulted in major damage to seventeen houses and the death of two hundred people, including the host that Habihemhock had infested. A Special Elf Service squad led by Captain Porter infiltrated the cabal's nest and the reverse invocation was a textbook operation performed in extremely hostile circumstances. I was involved with the protective counter charms. Gazorchites were banished under stringent demonic anti-resurgence curses. The sentence was necessarily severe and included the burying of the sect summoning amulet under a mile of ocean and the secretion of his ceremonial tractate in the catacombs of Bilharzovia, thus rendering their discovery nigh on impossible. Of course, neither are required if enough acolytes adopt the faith, and to safeguard that a stipulated covenant was put in place. A sequilltan acolytes need to profess their adulation for Gazorch before any possibility of a manifestation. This was the maximum sentence and particularly harsh but deserved, since he is a murderous monster. Unfortunately, we also lost track of Habihemhock some time ago, but we know that he was cast adrift without a vessel.'

'Vessel?' Crouch asked.

'Corporeal manifestation. A body, for want of a better word,' Duana explained. 'He was exorcised into limbo. And long may it stay that way.'

'You won a medal if I remember rightly,' Crouch said.

'So did Kylah Porter. Youngest ever to win the DBM. Many were recognised for their work that night.'

'So what do you make of this stuff?' Asher threw down an impograph of the crime scene.

Duana held it up to the light. She did not take long to answer. 'These Widicombs are Gazorchites, there is no doubt. Decimator curses, or a variant of—which is what this crime scene demonstrates—were much favoured by Gazorch's followers.'

Asher frowned. 'But why destroy Malachite if he was one of their own?'

'Perhaps he became a threat to them?' Duana mused.

'Exactly,' Crouch said.

'I would propose the more interesting question though, is why was Malachite, of all people, co-opted in the first instance.' Duana turned to look out of the window. 'It will not come as a surprise to you to learn that we have known a Gazorch cell has been operating here in New Thameswick for some time. Our agents have been monitoring it. The cell was run by a man called Stohb. But he was murdered by his own men some months ago.'

'Malachite is a hearse chaser,' Crouch said. 'All he does is peddle post-mortem stay overs.'

'True,' Duana said. 'His area of expertise was soul transition.'

'We know he was a link to the Bewildered,' Asher said.

Crouch nodded. 'He was observed sniffing round their gathering places.'

'But what's a Gazorch sect got to do with the Bewildered? And, where have they all gone?' Asher asked.

Duana picked up a stuffed dormouse and sniffed it. 'The obvious answer is sacrifice. Gazorch is known for his bloodlust. This may be some dark or untried method of raising Habihemhock. Sacrificing the Bewildered, the least missed members of society, would make sense in that instance. It is also possible that these murders have ramifications in the human world that the Widicombs could not foresee.'

Crouch's dusky features darkened further as little bolts of angry light danced over his skin. 'Three humans have died already according to Asher, and Gods know how many Bewildered. That's one hell of an attrition rate.'

Asher's expression hardened. 'We have to stop them.'

'But how? We don't know who they are or where they are,' Crouch grumbled.

'Perhaps if you try communicating with the Bewildered to find out how they are coerced?' Duana suggested.

'Oh yeah, no worries, great idea.' Crouch glowered. 'Trouble is, I don't actually speak howling-at-the-moon.'

'You don't have to,' Asher said, smiling. 'There is a saying, if you want to catch a wolf, dress yourself as a lamb.' He got up and walked over and kissed Duana on the cheek. 'Thanks, Duana. Always a pleasure.'

She frowned. 'You do not need to thank me for exchanging knowledge.'

'One of my foibles,' Asher said. He grabbed Crouch and made for the door.

'I am still available for physical intercourse Tuesdays between 7 and 9 pm.' Duana's matter of fact statement froze Crouch midstride.

Asher turned and smiled. 'Thanks, Duana. I'll bear that in mind.'

'Thursdays I have congress with Sallinger and Sundays with Drucilla. But Tuesdays—'

Asher held up a hand. 'I'll get back to you on that.'

Crouch piped up in a weak and desperate voice, 'I'm free on Tuesdays if he isn't.'

This time, Asher really did clip him one round the ear.

CHAPTER THIRTY-TWO

Bobby stood in Cuthbertson's bedroom, mesmerised by the slow turning of the cupboard latch. She was next to the window with the street light behind, but already dense shadows, darker than night, were slithering out of every corner, creeping inexorably towards the centre of the room. To her left, an aluminium telescopic pole stood propped against the wall with a red, yellow, and blue microfibre brush at its end. Whoever had been in to rid the bedroom of cobwebs had left it there. She reached across and grabbed it. As weapons went, it felt pretty insubstantial. But it was, still, a weapon…of sorts.

The temperature in the room plummeted. She'd spent enough time reading the books in Matt's library to know that this was not good. She could even hear Asher in her head saying, 'Thaumaturgy sucks energy from the atmosphere', and this well and truly sucked. It was definitely not the sharp sting of a December dusk that surrounded her, but the bone chilling clammy dampness of a Christmas graveyard. She turned once more to the window and slapped the glass.

No one looked up.

No one noticed.

She heard the cupboard door fly open and snapped her head around. Her eyes fixed on nothing, but nevertheless it sent fresh chills coursing through her. A black space was all her eyes saw, but it appeared much larger and deeper than it should have been. Bobby's chest was heaving. She'd seen all the films. She was expecting at the very least a massive spider, or a girl with hair hanging down in front of her face, or a ballooning figure with distorted features towering over her imperiously. But there was none of that. At least not at first. In the gloom, Bobby strained to see, but it was her ears that told her what was happening. A sound, like dripping liquid, reached her. She peered through the darkness to see something thick and black running over the edge of the cupboard floor onto the wooden boards of the bedroom. The liquid pooled there, dark and viscous and glistening. Bobby waited, her heart drumming madly in her chest, its soft thudding the only noise in a room from which all other sound had been dredged. The same could not be said for the aroma. The stink took her stomach, spun it through 360 degrees, stripped it of any and all of its dignity and made it sit there, burbling threateningly while its silent companion, her nose, endured the assault.

Bobby's eyes started to water.

From out of the cupboard the black liquid continued to run, except now the pool began, as a show of strength, to defy gravity and grow upwards, its diameter fixed, building into a column of viscous fluid. From out of its vertical surface small protuberances danced in the air, like the wafting tentacles of an anemone on a black coral reef.

Bobby dragged her eyes away and glanced out of the window. It was almost totally dark outside. If only she had a light of some kind to signal with. She patted her pockets, but there was nothing except keys, dark glasses, and something soft and lumpy that felt very much like a handkerchief.

The silence cracked with a hiss that grew like the harbinger wind of an oncoming storm soughing through a field of dead corn. Bobby had never experienced such an event, let alone heard anything sough, but her imagination wasn't messing around here and the simpler metaphor of 'like steam from a kettle' seemed woefully inadequate. She swivelled and heard her own breath ooze out of her lips at what she saw. In seconds, the column had grown into a dark, quivering, vaguely human shape blossoming up from the dark pool. It had no face but where there should have been features was instead an oval shape that writhed and wriggled. Bobby realised that she was looking at a solid ball of black flies. Nice bile-in-the-back-of-the-throat touch, that. Below the neck, appendages flowed outwards, reaching blindly for the walls and ceiling and, she knew, for her. As manifestations of horrifying apparitions went, this thing certainly looked like it knew what it was doing.

Bobby stepped back, brushing up against the windowsill as she considered the thing. Disgusting, horrible and clearly supernatural, of that she was certain. But she was also aware that while the script called for her to be quaking with fear or waving goodbye to her reason as it sailed away into the sunset, neither of those things was happening. She was repulsed, yes. Horrified, definitely. Fearful of coming to harm, obviously. But was she losing her ability to function through abject fear?

No.

Not even when the thing opened its mouth to scream—well, not scream exactly: it was more a howling, wailing ululation.

Not even when the flailing tentacles stiffened with intent.

And that surprised her.

She knew with sickening certainty that the thing, though blind, knew where she stood. Suddenly it pulled itself up and hunched forwards, looking very much like it was preparing to launch.

Instinct has little to do with wisdom when it kicks in. Part of Bobby wanted to hurl herself backwards at the window behind her, smash through it and escape, regardless of the likely outcome of a shattered skull or fractured vertebrae. A limb-breaking topple into the garden seemed better than staying in the bedroom with this monstrosity, true. But another part of her, the one that made her defiantly present herself to the world in a way that asked questions of convention, wasn't having any of that. Instinct grabbed the lightweight aluminium brush in both hands and swung it in a wide arc across the room at the thing.

She expected solid resistance. What she had not expected was for the handle to actually sink into the black flailing shape. It felt as if she'd plunged into a solid lump of treacle before a charge of power ran up the length of the pole into her arms and made her let go. Weirdly, the pole stayed pointing out into the room, impaled somehow just below the figure's buzzing head. The figure screamed with rage and started vibrating wildly, tentacles organising themselves into fingers that pawed at the handle until it clattered to the floor, ripped out by the thing's pseudopodia.

A renewed anger gripped the figure and it opened its dreadful mouth and screamed furiously, the tentacles rippling apart once more.

If ever there was a moment for Bobby to clamber up the wall, screaming and hearing the tenuous thread that kept her mind anchored to her soul snap, this was it. But it didn't happen. And the reason, pre-washed and ready to eat like an overpriced supermarket salad, popped into her head and was digested to yield instant understanding of how this moment of confrontation between Bobby Miracle and the unspeakably unknown encapsulated the yin and yang of her mental makeup.

Being a Goth meant she'd always been first in line for the university film club showings of the latest paranormal-scream-Halloween-schlock blockbuster. It was expected of her. But while her pale, dark-clad fellows sank lower in their seats, cringing, pupils dilated, bleating and grunting at each new manufactured shock, Bobby would watch unscathed and unmoved. Her spine was too stiffened by the imparted wisdom she'd absorbed throughout her formative years. Lucille Miracle believed everything had a reason, even if that reason could not easily be explained, and she had drummed that lesson into Bobby with tender insistence. Whilst Bobby's father insisted the supernatural was fodder for the weak-minded. Mixed messages of the most extreme type, but curiously not that incompatible. As a consequence, it took a great deal to scare Bobby Miracle. Films didn't come close—even cemeteries and the dark left her unmoved. Only books occasionally gave her a delicious shudder. But even then they needed to be the subtle and clever type, suggesting hidden pockets of dread and the creeping atmospheric horror experienced by solitary academics in isolated hotel rooms in Suffolk…

Bobby knew the thing across the room had malevolent intent and that staying put and doing nothing was not an option. Realisation drove her to urgently reassess her surroundings.

Window? Too hard.

Door? Blocked access.

Ceiling? Too high.

Floor? Too solid.

Bed? There was always the bed. She could get under it and…do what exactly? Hide, like a four year old? That was ridiculous. What she really needed was a *Star Trek* communicator. If ever there was a moment for Scotty to beam her up, this was it.

Her hands went again to her pockets. Keys, dark glasses and…her fingers sensed the curiously soft lump once again. Material, definitely. But she didn't do handkerchiefs so…Her fingers reached in and pulled out the velvet bag from Kylah's cupboard. A frown creased her forehead. She had no recollection of putting it in there. She stared at it in the gloom, her fingers fumbling at the drawstring while the black tentacles crept ever closer. Was there something in it that could help? She upended the bag and emptied its contents onto her hand. Disappointment flooded through her. All it contained was a white linen handkerchief covered with weird drawings and four small stones carefully strung by a meshwork of thread to each corner. What was she meant to do with this? Blow her nose?

Crap. Nothing but a new age trinket. A doily sporting a hand drawn rune that probably said 'hearth and home' in some weird Wiccan language. All about as useful as a china chisel. Cursing silently, she balled it up and threw it in utter frustration in the direction of the monster opposite.

And that was when all hell—for want of a better idiom which, under the circumstances, would have been a bit of an ask —broke loose.

The handkerchief, an extraction grenade also known as Crone with the Wind, did not plummet to the floor as it should have. Instead, it hung in the air three feet from Bobby, straightened itself out into a square, and started to spin. A movement that brought with it a rapidly-building wind that tented the handkerchief forward, toward the malevolent figure. Within seconds it wasn't a mere wind, but a miniature gale of almost hurricane force which finally hurled the handkerchief forward where it struck the apparition, forcing it backwards towards the cupboard, and smashing them both, with a clatter, against the wall. The tentacles were suddenly plastered flat, the stench blown away and from somewhere Bobby's nostrils twitched with the smell of…was that coconut oil?

She was vaguely aware of a bright light behind her beyond the window but her eyes were glued to the tentacled thing. She wanted to yell in triumphant delight, but almost as suddenly as the wind had risen, it started to weaken. The apparition fought to disengage itself from the cupboard and strained forward, tentacles peeling off the wall with sickly snaps.

Ah well, thought Bobby, at least I didn't go down without a fight.

'Right, you swine, come and get me!' she yelled and reached for the brush a second time. But her hand never found the handle as something, something strong and powerful, grabbed her around the waist and yanked her backwards through the window into a blinding light.

CHAPTER THIRTY-THREE

DESPITE LEANING a little too far towards the jaunty pun angle when it came to naming it, the people who'd designed the thaumaturgy behind the Crone with the Wind extraction grenade had put a lot of thought into its mode of action. And they'd thought of almost everything. So when, twenty seconds later, a breathless Bobby snapped upright and opened her eyes expecting to see her worst nightmare, but saw instead a deserted beach of bleached white sand and the gently waving fronds of palm trees, it took her a bit by surprise. She blinked in the glare of a blazing tropical sun, did a quick 360-degree pirouette, and was delighted and astonished to see no sign of whatever it was that had come out of the wardrobe. It took a moment to assimilate all that, too, because her 360-degree pirouette revealed nothing but sand, sea, a small outcrop of rocks and then more sea. No buildings, people, fast-food outlets or cars. Nothing but…a desert island.

'Idyllic' as an adjective is probably overused. Idyllic beaches in brochures, depicted by photographs taken at dawn on a midsummer morning when the coast is deserted, tend not to reflect the New Year's day Oxford Street sales conditions that will ensue at noon on any given August day. But this beach *was* idyllic. So idyllic that even the rule of natural history ensuring that razor shells stick out at flesh-lacerating, strategically optimal intervals (usually where the terrain is ideal for sandcastle building) did not apply. So idyllic that not even the faux wormcasts that turn out to be surreptitiously interred dog turds were not in existence. So idyllic that even the seaweed didn't stink.

Strictly speaking it needn't have been a desert island, but the wonderworkers who'd created the spell understood that anyone needing it required something that was the dead opposite of the sphincter-popping situation that demanded its deployment. In Bobby's case, this meant light where there had been darkness, warmth where there was cold, and clean sea air instead of stench. Gasping, Bobby looked about her, bemused and suddenly quite hot. But mostly and exultantly, relieved. She had no idea what had come out of that wardrobe and would be very content if she never found out.

There was a moment's incredulous self-aware humiliation when she realised she'd attacked a malevolent force with a broom, but then the sound of waves lapping on the shore kicked in and the thought dissolved. As narrow escapes went, this one had the diameter of a gnat's whisker. Bobby kicked off her shoes and let the warm sand spread up between her toes; an antidote to arcane terror as good as anything Offa's Coven could have come up with. She took a deep breath and walked towards the azure sea along an impossibly golden shoreline.

There was something very spiritual about having one's feet washed by warm, clear blue salt water. After several minutes of its soothing balm, Bobby noticed something on the sand near the outcrop of rocks and, for a moment, peered at it in disbelief. It looked like a beach bag. No, not simply a beach bag, but the beach bag her mother used on the Miracles' infrequent seaside trips when Bobby was young, and long before her decision to hide from the sun had become a part of her makeup. For now, the warmth of the sand, the sea, and the sun were a salve for her traumatised soul. Bobby approached the bag slowly, looking around to see to whom it might belong. But there was no one in sight and no other footprints on the beach. Feeling more than a little guilty, Bobby opened up the bag. Inside were sunglasses, a hat, a bottle of iced water and Factor 25 sun cream. The people behind Crone with the Wind were good, she had to admit. Bobby donned the hat, took a drink of water, sat with her back against a rock, and pondered her position.

Judging by the sun, the palm trees, and the colour and temperature of the water, this was not anywhere in Great Britain she'd ever come across or seen in a brochure. She'd also escaped the clutches of something pretty nasty in Cuthbertson's house, something that had clearly not wanted her to get away with the knowledge she'd gained. A shadowy memory of how the thing had manifested stirred in her mind and made her glance around at the deserted beach. It stayed deserted, yet Bobby couldn't help wondering how a frail mind in a frail body such as Cuthbertson's or Loosemore's had coped with such a dreadful entity, or something like it, even for one minute.

Not well, she surmised.

Bobby did sometimes wonder about death. Occupational hazard when some of your favourite places were graveyards. Bobby had never bought in to the heaven and hell thing, but now, after Hipposync and New Thameswick and especially after Cuthbertson's house, there was a pressing need to come to terms with the fact that there was something beyond the here and now out there waiting for her. Waiting for everyone, or so it seemed. Another awfully big adventure? Or, if Cuthbertson's monster was anything to go by, horror and torment. Like most things, she suspected, there was probably a middle ground, and she reminded herself to ask Asher about that if and when she ever saw him again.

Thinking about Asher made her frown. She grabbed a fistful of white sand and let it run through her fingers. Asher had left her at Hipposync and gone off to solve his mystery, arguing that it was not safe for her to accompany him. She might never forgive him for that, the patronising sod. But not forgiving him meant at the very least being able to communicate that fact to him. And how, exactly, was she supposed to do that given her current situation on a desert island in the middle of…somewhere. Unless, of course, this was all a figment of her imagination? Unless the thing in Cuthbertson's wardrobe had been so horrible as to have succeeded in sending her mind on an all expenses paid trip to la-la land, which meant that at any moment now she might snap out of this and confront the thing all over again.

But if that *wasn't* the case and she really *was* on a desert island, having escaped the clutches of the thing in the wardrobe, what next? Bobby had not read the small print on the velvet bag. In fact she hadn't read the large print either. Pretty stupid, all things considered. The giggle, when it came, started from somewhere at the back of her throat and sent an expulsion of air upwards so that it erupted out through her mouth in a bad impression of a horse braying, spattering her chest with spittle. That triggered a full-blown guffaw at her own ridiculousness that, in turn, sent her into a paroxysm of eye-watering laughter. After three minutes of it, Bobby realised she really ought to stop, but thinking about the morning's events merely brought on more gales of laughter, doubling her up on the sand and eliciting panting groans from the pain in her belly.

What was it exactly she had not read?

The small print on an extraction grenade she'd inadvertently filched from the cupboard of an agent for the Department of Fimmigration—a border agency for another world that existed in parallel with her own.

You could not make it up.

Gradually, the laughter waned, though the odd giggle still bubbled up. Difficult to imagine a more ridiculous scenario, but she began to realise that her laughter was a safety valve for what was really bothering her. The fact she was *actually* here and that everything had *actually* happened and that she, Bobby Miracle, had to accept the fact that it was all *true*. And once she did that…she put her hand out to feel the rock behind her just in case the world tilted a bit more than it already had at that moment. Because once she did accept all of that—accepted it and didn't dismiss it as all part of some weird and wonderful hallucinogenic trip induced by the nerve gas pumped through Hipposync, or a stray mushroom of the wrong type that had somehow slipped into her scrambled eggs that morning—then it changed *everything*. And not simply the fact of finding a vital clue in what was happening in terms of the malign haunting. Accepting the sand under her fingers, the sound of the waves in her ears, and the hat that she wore on her head were real were game changers.

Everything said to her by her practical, dowdy, no-nonsense mother and her caring, sad, pragmatic father about her grandmother had, therefore, been *lies*. And everything her grandmother had whispered to her with those laughing eyes had been nothing but the *truth*.

The implication of it scared Bobby's brain. All this time she'd cast her grandmother as a slightly batty but wise eccentric. But if what happened that morning—what was still happening—was anything to go by, knowing about the healing power of leaves and the right twig to use to find water, or going to a friend's house to sort out a restless spirit seemed pretty damn normal all of a sudden.

Bobby's mind flooded with unanswerable questions tempered only by a huge and deep sadness. She had not been able to, nor allowed to, communicate and spend time with her grandmother during those last few very difficult years. And yet, in the shade of the rocky outcrop, Bobby now saw the tenderness mingling with the horrible frustration in Lucille Miracle's eyes in those rare moments when her mind was not away with the fair—

She stopped herself there. That idiom was off the menu. It could mean something else altogether now.

Ah well. No point thinking too much about any of it because there was no going back. And, nice though this Robinson Crusoe lark was, now she'd accepted the situation there were things that needed to be done. So, she ought to try and get back to Oxford, or New Thameswick even, to let Asher know what she'd found out. There was no knowing how long this desert island might last and she needed to find a way off it as soon as possible.

The question was, how?

Bobby walked up and down the beach, looking for all the things anyone might under the circumstances. Abandoned canoes, inflatables, shipwrecked wood she could bind together with vines to make a raft. But there was nothing. No sign of any previous habitation. It took her fifteen minutes to walk around the entire circumference and all to no avail. She was hot, her dark clothes sticky against her skin. She reached into the beach bag for another sip of water and saw that the fluid had replenished itself. So at least there was some sort of contingency here in terms of survival. She suspected, with annoying insight, that there was probably something very simple she should or could do. A few choice words, an incantation that would dissolve the spell, if that was what it was. But she had not taken any notice of the instructions.

'Come on, Bobby, *think*.'

She looked at the beach bag and ran her hand around the brim of her hat. She was only a spoonful of sugar away from being Mary Bloody Pop— the sardonic thought fizzed like a firework in her head. Of course! What on earth was the matter with her? She picked up her coat from where she'd left in on the sand in the shadow of the outcrop and reached into the pocket.

The Aperio bulged there, tantalisingly promising a way out. But the fist of triumph she made lost power halfway into the air. To use the Aperio, she needed a door. And as far as she could see, there was no door anywhere near.

'Brilliant,' she said, bitterly. Once again, her thoughts strayed unbidden to her grandmother who would, she felt sure, have known exactly what to do in this situation. 'Come on, Lucille, help me out here,' she said.

It started as a small change in the ever-lapping waves. A dark mound where there should have been smooth sea. Bobby watched it, at first with concern and then with growing intrigue as the mound gradually became elevated from the water and slowly inched its way up the beach, the way she'd seen turtles do on nature documentaries. With almost agonising slowness, it flippered its way onto the sand and arced slowly towards where she stood, immobile. After several minutes of observation, Bobby decided to investigate. She walked across the warm shore until she was within fifteen metres of the shambling animal. The turtle looked up at her and stopped. Reptile and human regarded one another until Bobby said, 'I hope you aren't lunch.'

Whether it was the sound of her voice that acted as the trigger or not was difficult to say, but the turtle began to shimmer and dissolve into a whirling sandstorm, which darkened and then lightened again as Bobby stood, bottle of water held up as a makeshift weapon, given what had already happened. But when the sand fell away, Bobby was not at all prepared for what she saw standing unmistakably before her. When the shimmering ethereal figure spoke, the bottle dropped from Bobby's hand like a hot potato.

'Hello, Roberta.' The same voice. The same soft sing-song accent.

Bobby's trembling hands flew to her face. 'Gran?'

Lucille Miracle smiled. 'Yes, Roberta, it's me.'

Bobby fell to her knees in front of this wonderful spectre, the epitome of her grandmother before she'd become that lost, wild *thing* locked in the asylum. 'But how…'

'You summoned me, Roberta.'

'Did I? But how can you be…and the turtle…I mean…'

'Useful vessels, turtles. Not difficult to catch. And metaphysical transport isn't that easy to come by around here, I'll have you know.'

'But this is a dream, right?'

'No, not a dream. I'm here just like you are. Though where 'here' is might not be easy to show on a map.'

'But Gran, you're…you.'

'I was always me, Roberta. Even after the attack, I was me. But I was trapped by somethin' terrible that wanted to kill me. But I wouldn't let it. So long as I breathed, it couldn't do anythin'. Nasty piece of work too, always lookin' for new ways to cause pain. But then demons isn't known for their community spirit—'

'Demon? Wa…who…wait a minute. What are you saying? What demon? You were ill. I saw you.'

'What you saw was only the brittle shell. But I was deep inside, with him. I got a hold of one leg and I wouldn't let go, no matter what. And there was no way out, not until good old death came to visit, bless him.'

Bobby reached out a hand, but her fingers passed right through her ethereal grandmother's form. She seemed ageless, old, and young at the same time, but with eyes full of fierce pride. 'I am so sorry, Gran. I didn't know. I would have tried harder.'

Lucille shook her head. 'That was what the bugger wanted. It was better your mother and father did as they did.'

'They didn't know, though, did they?'

'Perhaps. Perhaps not. Even if they suspected, they wouldn't let themselves believe. Somethin' your father denied all his life.'

Bobby's head gave a little shake; as if she wanted to agitate the words into some sort of order she could understand. 'Denied? Denied what?'

Still Lucille's eyes shone. 'That I was what I was. He could have come into the fold, and though I tried I could see his little heart wasn't in it. And when you came along he wanted more than anythin' to protect you, too. And how could I blame him for wantin' that? If I'd had time I might have persuaded him to let me teach you more than you already knew but…'

Quite a lot going on in that sentence. Stuff that was making Bobby's brain sizzle in a way that had nothing to do with the heat. She decided to break things down.

'Whoa. What were you teaching me exactly?'

'The old ways.'

Bobby shook her head again, still not quite sure what the implication was here. 'But you just said 'teach me more than I already knew'. That's the point.' She waved an arm around ineffectually. 'I really don't know anything.'

'Don't you, Roberta? Could have fooled me. Haven't you just defied a Sambolith?'

Bobby blinked 'A Sambolith? Is that what that…thing was?'

Lucille nodded. 'And a very unpleasant one, too. Ripe as a badger's ar—'

'—But that was pure luck,' Bobby protested, remembering how flowery a turn of phrase her grandmother used to have.

'Was it? Funny thing, pure luck. Most people never experience it and even when they do, they ignore it. So let's say it was pure luck that made you pick up that particular charm from that particular cupboard and absentmindedly put it in your pocket even though you don't remember doin' it. And that it was pure luck you remembered it was in your pocket. And pure luck you used it to curse the thing that wanted to turn your flesh into splodge. That's quite a lot of pure luck there. More than *most* people have in a lifetime, I'd say.'

'But of course it was luck. What else could it be?'

'Did I ever tell you about the cunning folk, Roberta?'

'I don't think so.'

'Hmm, maybe that was one of the things your dad and I agreed upon. Shame, could have saved you a lot of trouble if I had.'

'So tell me now,' Bobby urged.

Lucille turned her head up and sniffed the air. 'Not enough time.'

'Please, Gran.'

Lucille Miracle smiled and shook her head. 'It's just knowin' when to listen and when to act mostly. Tellin' silly people what they should already know. But doin' it with a flourish and a little bit of alchemy and not so's you rob them blind. Oh, and listenin' to your old granny while she passes on The Knowin'. I didn't have time to pass it all on to you, and I've always regretted that. But now I reckon maybe I didn't need to. I reckon you already have it, Roberta Miracle. So listen to your heart, my girl. Part of your head already does. Look at the way you dress for a start. You just need to open them valves a little wider to let real understandin' in. Listen and learn.'

Bobby looked aghast. 'No, no, no. This is where you fade away after giving me a woolly message, isn't it? I need instructions, Gran, not wisdom.'

'Very overrated, instructions. But then you're young, so perhaps you need a bit of both.' Lucille stood, pensive and patient, as if she was waiting for something.

After several long seconds of painful brain-racking, Bobby pleaded again, 'Please, Gran. At least give me a clue.'

Lucille's smile did not waver. 'What is it you have in your coat?'

'The Aperio, you mean?'

'I do.'

'But it's useless without a door. There isn't any door. I've looked everywhere.'

'Not everywhere, Roberta.'

'What does *that* mean?' she wailed.

'It means that *this* is the part where I give the woolly message and fade away.'

'No, not yet, Gran, please…'

But already the image was fading, twisting, the sand rising up like a whirlwind only to settle back into the shape of a turtle that turned and started hauling itself back towards the sea.

Bobby got up off her knees and followed it, tears of frustration and grief at something lost, then found, and now about to be lost again streaming down her face.

'Gran!' she wailed. But the turtle did not stop or turn around. 'Great,' Bobby yelled to the sky as the turtle entered the blue waters. 'Don't bother next time. It just makes things WORSE. Stranding me here on a BLASTED desert island, not giving me time to talk to my grandmother properly, giving me something that can open doors when there aren't any ISN'T FUNNY. And neither is FACTOR EFFING 25 sun cream—I need at least Factor 30. And especially NOT FUNNY is telling me to listen to my heart. That's not advice, that's an agony aunt's PLATITUDE. You're as bad as bloody ASHER. I trusted him and look where it's got me. I mean, what the hell does he know? Him and his cronies think that because I dress like this, I'm a BLOODY WITCH—'

She felt it and heard it simultaneously. A click, like a handle being depressed, and something heavy moving on creaky hinges.

Bobby frowned and then sucked in air as she visualised, with a millisecond to spare, where she might want to go to as the door of acceptance inside her head finally swung open and the Aperio did its thing.

CHAPTER THIRTY-FOUR

It wasn't difficult for Asher and Crouch to disguise themselves as a couple of Bewildered. They found some tattered and filthy rags in a second-hand emporium, asked a couple of constables to trample all over them with dirty boots, greased their own hair down to make it look like they hadn't washed for several months, and made themselves as scruffy as possible. They could have walked into any minicab office in any city in the UK and been offered a job there and then. Instead, they waited in the back room of a pub called The Empty Vessel a couple of streets away from the trenches until some of the true Bewildered turned up. It took three hours, but a whistle from one of the constables told them that some had been spotted.

No one was quite sure why these troubled souls were so attracted to the trenches. One theory suggested that the reek could permeate through the fog of their half-blind existence. Another was that the river somehow called to them in an elemental way. Whatever the reason, their herd mentality seemed to kick in so that they found some comfort in being close to others of their kind. The small group of three—two women and a boy—found cowering and feeling their way along, was the first group that had been spotted for almost two days. The most curious thing of all was that the Bewildered did not attract the attention of the zleepers and could wander freely over the furrowed ground. This gave them some immunity from the attention of anyone wishing to do them harm. But once they strayed, or were enticed, off the trenches and closer to the river, they became fair game for whomever, or whatever, was taking them.

Crouch and Asher crept out from the back of the pub and hurried through the back streets. The gloom of an overcast December afternoon cloaked their passage. No one stopped them. No one took a great deal of notice. When they got to the same gap through which Bobby and Asher had escaped the clutches of their would-be assassins, they stepped out onto the blighted ground, being careful to stick to the path, and made their way towards the point where the three true Bewildered were congregating. It brought them right next to where the pilings guarded them from the river.

They were, of course, wraiths to the three ahead of them and therefore it was easy not to attract attention, but since the Bewildered groups tended to stay close together, Asher and Crouch crept nearer so as to make it appear that they were as one. A different odour, not unlike that wafting up from the front door of Bishop's Cheese Emporium on Cow Street in July, mingled with the country smell of slurry and hung around the three Bewildered like a miasmic cloak.

In terms of emulating their behaviour, there was a lot of shuffling and mumbling and stuttering utterances, with which Asher struggled, but Crouch had no difficulty at all, since it mimicked quite accurately his physical state on most Friday nights after an evening in The Empty Vessel. They shambled for over an hour, shuffling up and down the area next to the pilings, listening to the confused and incoherent whispers from the wretches they were following. Yet the words also gave a poignant clue as to lives previously lived. Lives disrupted when the interdimensional seas parted to suck them through into the shadow world they now occupied.

'—No, Betty, no, in the oven, in the oven—'

'—All I want is a ticket, not a suitcase—'

'—I'm a size ten, I tell you—'

Asher and Crouch whispered, too, safe in the knowledge that the Bewildered would only hear them as voices in the ether.

'How long are we giving this, then?' Crouch asked. 'It's freezing here, they stink and I could murder a sausage on a stick. They do a nice spiced venison andouille at The Empty Vessel. Go lovely with a couple of roast parsnips.'

'We have only been here an hour. Of course, you could pretend to be a gargoyle and perch yourself on a pole to watch.'

Crouch whined. 'That won't change the fact that it'll be pitch dark soon and all the sausages will be gone.'

'Shut up, Crouch…wait, what is that?' Asher pointed towards a faint glow on the other side of the pilings that grew brighter as they stared. Along with the glow came the aroma of something warm and pleasingly pungent.

'Roasted caramabs,' whispered Crouch excitedly. 'I'd know that perfume anywhere.'

Indeed, as the glow got brighter, the smell got stronger. Strong enough to mask the competing reeks from the trenches and the Bewildered. And it was a smell that the latter clearly registered, too, because they clustered forward towards where the glow strengthened.

'What should we do?' Crouch said.

'First you need to wipe the saliva from your chin. Then we follow our hungry friends—cautiously.'

The Bewildered were now congregated around a single point at the pilings and Asher crept a little closer. The glimmer suddenly became the light from a lantern held high. Beneath it emerged a shadowy hooded figure, who immediately began handing out small parcels of food.

'It's like feeding time at the zoo,' Crouch whispered.

'Get closer. Pretend you want some,' Asher said.

Crouch did not need telling twice. Asher watched as he approached the figure and snatched a small parcel that he brought back to where Asher sat hunched.

'Mmm, delicious,' Crouch said with his mouth full. '—usty bread and 'oasted 'aramab.'

'You do realised that the food might have been poisoned or drugged,' Asher observed.

Crouch stopped chewing, thought for a moment, looked at the food and then continued eating. 'Bastards,' he said, before taking another bite.

But Asher's attention had been drawn to the figure with the lantern as he bent to haul up a set of steps and lay them over the pilings. Slowly the glow started to sink down the way it came up. The Bewildered, completely seduced by the food, immediately began clambering over to follow their magnanimous benefactor.

'Come on,' Asher said. 'We follow.'

Negotiating the makeshift steps, they climbed down the wooden ladder, which didn't end where it should have—on the muddy floor of the riverbank. Instead it kept descending down through the earth, the glow of the lantern and the smell of food beckoning to the shambling Bewildered and, for a whole different set of reasons, to Asher and Crouch following on behind. As Asher passed through the hole where there should have been sticky mud, he noticed the way that the edge shimmered with a dull silvery sheen and realised that this was not an entrance made out of iron with hinges and a handle. This was, for want of a better word, wonderworking. Asher knew that once they were ensconced, this hole in the ground would disappear and the river bottom would return to its natural state. And as with all wonderworking, it came with mixed blessings. On the one hand, it at least meant that wherever they were going would not instantly fill with water once the tide came in and covered them in four feet of Thameswick brown sludge. On the other hand, it was going to be bloody difficult for anyone to find them. He hoped that the constables they'd left on observation duty had not succumbed to the charms of The Empty Vessel and had marked where they'd descended.

Asher's foot finally reached the bottom of the ladder and stepped off onto hard packed earth. Up ahead, through the bobbing and sniffing heads of the caramab-entranced Bewildered, Asher could see torches flickering in sconces on the stone walls. The hooded man carrying the lantern walked on and the Bewildered dutifully followed. The caves were dry and after a few yards the torchlit walls revealed all sorts of things drawn and carved on the rocky canvas. Most of the graffiti involved highly unpleasant depictions of humans, presumably blasphemers, who were coming to very sticky ends in a variety of unspeakable ways. The carvings and paintings looked ancient, but there were signs of others having been here, wherever here was, and Asher had a feeling that its current position under the river might not be a permanent arrangement. The clues for that were to be found in the discarded food wrappers and the odd scrawled autograph, such as *Hieronymus was here, 1474*.

The tunnel soon became a cavern and Asher realised that it was much warmer down here. At least two fires burned in iron braziers with steam rising from boiling cauldrons above them. In the middle of the vast space were two large stone circles. In one of these a wooden cage stood, its door held open by a pulley and a rope. In the middle of the cage a makeshift banquet awaited, consisting of platters of steaming caramab meat and chunks of bread. The Bewildered did not need any further invitation. In one final mad rush they scrambled into the cage and began devouring the food. Asher found himself jostled by Crouch, who'd joined the surge.

'What are you—' Asher hissed.

'Trying not to arouse suspicion,' Crouch said. 'I'm in character. Plus I'm starving.'

There was a kind of twisted logic in this and, despite knowing they were obviously walking into a trap, Asher followed. The wooden door slid into place with a clatter as soon as they were all inside. Asher quickly noticed another two Bewildered slumbering on matted straw at the far end of the cage. Either drugged or satiated by the food, he surmised. He pretended to grab some bread but didn't eat it, instead watching their mysterious guide put down his lantern and shrug off his hood. Instantly, another half dozen figures emerged from the shadows and lit more torches. This revealed a plethora of crossbows, swords and other assorted weaponry leaning against the cavern walls and was proof, if any more was needed, that this was no charity shelter.

There was no mistaking this lot now, not with the painted black rims around their eyes, the shaved heads, and the forehead tattoos. This was the same Widicomb Gazorch sect that had attacked him and Bobby on the trenches the day before.

Asher moved close to the bars, away from the chomping and slavering noises of frenzied eating—some of the loudest of which came from Crouch, who seemed incapable of not groaning his admiration as he held a piece of dripping caramab up in front of a face transformed in gourmet delight. Asher cupped his ear and tuned in to the Gazorchites' conversation. It helped that they were not trying to mute their voices; why should they since the Bewildered heard nothing but whispers in the dark.

But Asher heard. Heard and understood.

'Five this time then, is it?' said one, smaller and slighter than the rest, a ratty smile revealing his pointed teeth.

'Five,' said the one who'd brought them in. Asher decided to call him 'Bait' for obvious reasons. 'Added to the two already in the cage, makes…uh…'

'Seven, you spletch,' said Ratty. 'There's going to be a lot of squealing.'

'Where's our voyager?' Bait asked.

'Cobain? In the pantry, getting tanked.'

Bait cursed. 'I told him to take it easy. He'll need all his wits about him to piggyback.'

'Last wish and all that. Said he wanted caramab vindaloo and three pints of mead. Seemed reasonable.'

'He'd better not be drunk or I'll kill him.'

Not one of the Widicombs spoke for a while. They looked at one another in mild confusion until Ratty piped up, 'Uh, isn't that the idea?'

'Yes, but insubordination requires punishment.'

'Seems a bit pointless when we're going to slit his throat in ten minutes.'

Another Widicomb stepped forward. 'Not the point. We'll kill five in one go. That means he's got five chances here. Five wild horses to ride on. We don't want him falling off because he's bladdered.'

'Come off it, Poldirk. This'll be the sixth time we've tried this and none of them has worked.'

The other sect members all nodded and muttered.

'That's not true and you know it.' Poldirk drew himself up. 'Stohb managed it. You saw the message on the wall.'

'I saw *a* message on *a* wall. But anyone could have written 'The zealot has landed' in fiery letters. I definitely didn't recognise the handwriting.'

'Yeah, well, what about when his head appeared in that yellow smoke that belched out from the fire afterwards? That was definitely Stohb,' Poldirk argued.

'Sounded like him,' Ratty said, 'but it was very smoky and them red eyes of his gave me the willies.'

'Shut up. You bin sippin' too much mead.'

'Yeah? Well, Cobain isn't convinced. And it's a Friday. We normally do this on a Thursday.'

'Oh, I see. Suddenly everyone's a critic. Anyway, we were too busy sorting out Malachite last night. Change is as good as a rest, I say.'

'Come off it, Poldirk. There's been no other message from Stohb and we've lost another five of our mates. Cobain thinks he's being slaughtered for nothing and—'

Asher felt the earth shudder under his feet and a distant roar like thunder echoed through the chamber.

'Yeah, keep it up you lot,' said Poldirk. Though he couldn't see in the gloom, Asher imagined the man wearing a nasty grin. 'Gazorch the Pantocrator is listening, you know. Let's not forget why we're here. To do the master's bidding. Our next task is to kill five Bewildered and allow our valiant charioteer to get to the other side, riding one of their souls.'

'You rang?' slurred a portly man, who emerged into the torchlight. He immediately put his fist, thumb inwards, against the bottom end of his sternum and belched.

'Are you bladdered, Cobain?' Poldirk asked.

'As a skunk,' said Cobain.

Poldirk shook his head. 'Right, come on, let's get on with it.'

'But I haven't had me pud,' protested Cobain.

Poldirk drew a dagger. 'Sod your pudding. Get into that circle. Bilger, you do the prep.'

A large Gazorchite stepped forward, ushering Cobain into

the smaller of the two stone circles, where he began to draw a chalk pentagram.

'Come on, Kirtzinger, you get the cattle. The two from last week and three from today's crop.'

Ratty, whose real name was obviously Kirtzinger, shuffled forward towards the wooden cages. Asher watched as he undid the lock on the gate and moved in, fearless of any reprisal. The man walked right past Asher and Crouch and kicked the two slumbering Bewildered awake, dragging them shouting and screaming out into the larger of the stone circles. Then he turned and came back for more.

'Make sure he picks you,' Asher whispered to Crouch.

Crouch, his mouth still full, nodded.

They both manoeuvred themselves directly into Kirtzinger's path and, together with the boy that came in with them, were pulled into the large circle. Once there, a couple of Gazorchites quickly looped a rope around all five of them so that they became a single huddle of humanity. Asher was on the far side of Crouch, separated from him by two Bewildered. Up close, their stench was truly awful. But not as bad as their pitiful confused wailing.

'What now, Asher?' Crouch managed to whisper through the noise.

'We wait and see,' Asher said.

'As plans go, I've heard better ones,' Crouch hissed.

But Asher was only half listening. Poldirk had moved around to a lectern. He stuck a thick candle into a holder and put both hands onto a very thick black book, commencing an incantation. Meanwhile, Kirtzinger threw the end of the rope looped around the Bewildered up through a pulley and Asher felt it tighten around him.

Poldirk's chanting sounded like a First Nation Indian had forgotten the words to 'Delilah' but had decided to carry on with his own version anyway. There were moans, there were whoops, there was shrill soprano and deep profundo.

This caused another bout of wailing from the three Bewildered in the huddle and made them shuffle around so that Asher lost sight of Poldirk for a moment. But he could still hear him and the words remained unfamiliar and weirdly guttural, without much break between them. Cobain looked a lot less chipper than a few moments before, since he was now on his knees with Bilger behind him, resting a very large butcher's knife on Cobain's trembling shoulder. Meanwhile, four other Widicombs joined Kirtzinger on the outside of the circle of victims. They too had knives in their hands.

The light in the cavern had changed. The flickering yellow of the torches was becoming a rich red, as Poldirk's incantations grew louder. Asher caught a glimpse of the book he read from. Smoke drifted up from its open pages.

'This is not good, Asher,' whispered Crouch urgently.

Asher didn't say anything. Crouch was right. But they'd needed to see, needed to understand this murderous plot. The reason that the number of Bewildered being slaughtered increased weekly was obviously simple, though diabolical, maths. The more the Gazorchites killed, the greater the chance of their 'volunteer' piggybacking to the other side, wherever that meant. And clearly Stohb—their leader, according to Duana—had succeeded. All valuable intel, but about as useful as a cardboard bucket if they couldn't let anyone else know.

Kirtzinger and the others outside the circle held up their weapons.

'They're going to stick us like pigs,' hissed Crouch. Lights began to dance over the shapeshifter's skin.

'Agreed. So it's time we did something about it, don't you think?'

Crouch shot him a look of horror. 'Asher, no. They said six months rest at least before you contact the de—'

'We don't have six months. We have six seconds.'

Asher took a deep breath in through his nostrils, shut his eyes, and bent his head down so that the tips of his middle and index finger met his forehead. This was the first time since his surgery that he'd attempted to contact the dead. And, though it had been second nature to him a few months before, just like a downhill skier after a knee operation, he had no idea how it would feel. They'd told him he might need help with rehab but he'd steered well away from that. They'd also warned him that the problem might not have resolved completely. There was always the chance that since opening up the channels towards those unfortunates who'd suffered violent deaths, he might still be susceptible to their destructive psyches. In truth, he had not yet dared flex this inherited psychic muscle, fearing the worst, hiding behind everyone's well-meaning concern about his readiness. The Bewildered's agonised Thursday night pleading had not helped that fear. But now he had no choice.

CHAPTER THIRTY-FIVE

Asher let himself drift down, falling through the dark layers like a drowning man. It took no effort at all, simply came to him as naturally as a whale slipping into the ocean's depths. But the waters Asher navigated were not full of plankton. His seas were the deeps of the dead and it had been a while. But the wizards in the alm's house knew their stuff. He heard no screams, no clamour of agonies. He knew, in an instant, that the damage done by the drugs used in the necrosquad had been repaired and he was back in control and swimming in familiar waters.

All he ever needed was a name. Once he had that, he could delve down through the currents, drawn as if by an invisible thread guiding his passage to a point where the murky waters were lit by a single light. And when Asher called, they never said no. They all had their story to tell and were inevitably keen to share it, especially so with a relative. So much left unsaid, no matter how much time death took to visit. Murder victims always wanted to scream and shout loudest. Of all the dead, they had the biggest stories. But in this case, the name belonged to Marta Kirtzinger. This woman had not died a violent death, and was just happy to chat. Even more happy to take up Asher's special offer when he suggested it.

Because necreddos didn't only talk to the dead. They could also act as taxi drivers.

There were other names he visited. Bilger, Poldirk, Cobain and one more, added in a flash of desperate inspiration—a Mrs Llewyn, for which he hoped he'd be forgiven. It would have been useful to have found out the names of the other Gazorchites, but four would have to do. He came back to himself just as the first of the awakened spirits of the dead appeared. And, right on queue, it was Mrs Kirtzinger. Everyone, even the Bewildered, could see her. A small, round-shouldered woman with her grandson's slightly weaselly features. She manifested right behind him on the circle, took one look at him and let forth a tirade.

'Wayne! What are you doing? How many times have I told you not to play with knives? You know if the constables find you carrying one of those, it's two years in Haringey for you, my lad, and you know what that place is like. You'll be some lifer's plaything before you can say you're already spoken for.'

Kirtzinger dropped the knife. Perhaps it was the surprise of hearing his grandmother's voice so strident and loud in his ear, or the fact that when he dared turn his head, she was standing there, her wispy hair moving in an unseen breeze, her accusatory knobbly finger pointing right at him. It didn't matter though, because five seconds after he dropped the knife, a similar thing happened to the content of his bladder. Other voices joined Mrs Kirtzinger's, all equally as critical at finding their offspring dressed up for a Halloween party and sporting lethal weapons.

'—Simeon Bilger, you let that other boy go, you big bully—'

'—Are you playing with fire again, Chadwick Poldirk—'

'—Marion Cobain, how many times have I told you about dropping food on your vest—'

That was the thing about grandmothers. They may have passed on, but to them, their grandchildren would always be their grandchildren, and they had a knack of picking up on all of those bad habits. And there was nothing more guaranteed to reduce a grown Gazorchite to a lump of quivering jelly than having a dead relative bellowing in his ears. And 'Marion'? Come on.

Kirtzinger screamed. Bilger staggered back, wiping a big chunk out of his pentagram as he did so. Cobain rolled up into a ball and started sucking his thumb while Poldirk merely stood there, shaking, smoke still rising from his book. The other three Widicombs stood watching, paralysed, with looks of stunned astonishment on their faces.

Asher decided they needed a bit of direction and so shouted out, 'The incantation, it's calling up the dead!'

If they were surprised to hear a voice coming from the huddle of Bewildered, they did not let on. Instead, the spirits turned towards the lectern and Poldirk.

'Do you think you could get Wayne to free us, Mrs Kirtzinger?' Asher asked.

The apparition looked up at him and tutted. 'Of course, dear. Wayne, you untie these nice people straight away.'

'But Gran—'

'Don't you but Gran me!' Mrs Kirtzinger raised her voice. Unfortunately, it also raised her haunting aura, which made her head grow twice as big and her eyes bulge alarmingly.

'Okay, okay, please Gran, I'll do it.'

'And be quick about it.'

Kirtzinger's trembling fingers reached for the knife and he sliced through the rope. The bundle of prisoners fell out like a bunch of tied flowers. Crouch and Asher, however, did not wait.

'There,' Asher said. 'That way.' He pointed to another passage across the cavern. They ran to the poorly lit tunnel whose floor seemed slick with water, glistening in the guttering torchlight. The way twisted and turned and Asher had the sinking feeling they were running deeper into trouble rather than away from it.

'How long will the ghosts hold them?'

'Without me there as the conduit, no more than a few seconds.'

'So are we looking for somewhere to hide? Because I don't know if you've noticed, but the smell in here is ripe and getting worse.'

Crouch was right. Asher had noticed and the smell was dreadful. The sweet, sickly smell of something very rotten indeed.

'I suggest we go another hundred yards and then see if we can at least set up some resistance.'

'Agreed,' said Crouch grimly. 'We'll find somewhere narrow. Somewhere we can ambush them and pick a few of the bastards off—' His words died on his lips. They'd reached a bend but as they rounded it, the far wall disappeared into a void. They both skidded to a halt. Not that there was any danger of them falling over the edge. The terrible smell acted like a barrier to bring them both up sharp.

'There's something down there,' Crouch said, inching towards the poorly lit rim of a precipice. 'Gods, that stench!'

'Dark vestigia. I think we need to see,' Asher said. He took a small box from his pocket, took out a piece of what looked like grey coal, blew on it and watched it glow into a orange ball of light. He threw it over the edge and it drifted slowly down. Ten seconds later, they saw something that would make Asher regret his actions for many years to come. In the lurid orange glow of his gloflare, the stacked bodies of dozens of people lay, tossed aside like so many bits of discarded meat.

'It's a slaughterhouse,' Asher said, biting back the threatening bile.

Crouch had less self-control and leaned weakly against the wall to let the still warm caramab splatter onto the floor. 'Bastards,' he whispered when he could. 'Filthy, murdering bastards.'

Asher wasn't going to argue the toss. From somewhere back in the tunnel, they heard a shout.

'We can't stay here,' Asher said. 'Come on.'

But their flight from the sickening dumping ground did not last long. The floor suddenly curved away on an upwards slope. They went no further forwards than thirty yards to a very dead end.

'It's too wide here,' Crouch said. 'They'll pick us off with arrows.'

'I do not hold with hiding in the darkness. I suggest we go back and confront them.'

'Okay,' Crouch said, and Asher heard the acceptance in his voice. 'Come to think of it, this was a bloody stupid idea.'

'And yet stupid ideas are no longer stupid if they are done by good people for good reasons.'

'I hope there's room for that on my gravestone,' Crouch said in a dry rumble.

They'd retraced their steps past the noisome burial chamber to where the tunnel narrowed again and straightened. It was impossible to judge distance in the semi-darkness, but Asher thought he could see a dull orange glow approaching. 'What arms do you have?' Asher asked.

'A couple of constabulary issue daggers, a knuckle duster, and a cosh hidden in my socks. You?'

'Nothing.'

'Right, here's a dagger and a duster.' He handed them to Asher. 'I'll go first. At the narrowest point I'll change into something suitably obstructive and block the passage. It'll buy you a little time. At least until they break me apart with hammers.'

'Crouch, you're a good man. I am glad you came with me.'

'No problem. Just remember to remind me never to do it again.'

Both men smiled for a fraction of a second and shook hands before turning towards the Gazorchites who, by now, were rounding the bend some forty yards away. The vanguard saw Asher and Crouch and let out a cry of triumph and hatred. Something struck the wall to the left of Asher's head.

'Crossbows,' Crouch muttered. 'Keep low.'

Hunched, the two men started forward at a run. They'd gone ten yards when the tunnel in front of them lit up with silver light. A globe appeared and grew at incredible speed so as to fill the whole passage, expanding and encompassing it so that the tunnel became a sphere, which elongated and widened into a large bricklined corridor. Within ten seconds, it had engulfed them. Asher fell to his knees, hand up against the brightness. He heard shouts, several screams, and then more shouts of the, 'Keep your hands where we can see them, you scum,' type.

Harmonious chords to a copper's ears.

A bit of him wanted to shout, 'We're on your side,' but Asher had been in enough situations where the lines between friend and foe were so thin as to be virtually unrecognizable to know better. But he also knew constabulary speak when he heard it. And so, with huge relief, he put his hands up above his head willingly, squinting against the blinding light. Almost immediately he felt a hand on his arm pushing it back down, and heard a calm, direct female voice saying, 'There is no need for a FHIFAA inspector to yield, Asher.' A shapely silhouette stepped out of the light and Asher turned his head away from the glare to see Duana Llewyn standing in front of three heavily armed men. 'And the same applies to you, Inspector Crouch.'

Asher dropped his hands and grinned. 'You got my message, then?'

'It was good to see my grandmother again.' Duana arched one eyebrow. 'We were able to clear up a misunderstanding about a lost earring.'

'Glad to be of service,' Asher said. He stood and ran a hand over the brick wall. 'This is new.'

'It's a field gaol. We can now bring our environment to the criminals. Get them secure before we leave. Much less mess and paperwork. You're familiar with krudian quantum displacement theory?'

'I've read a bit about it,' Asher nodded. Out of the corner of his eye, he saw Crouch frown in suspicion.

Duana took Asher's tacit acknowledgement as carte blanche to explain. 'Using the Chong-Montgomery formula, we are now able to manipulate spatial environments so as to allow them to exist in two different places at the same time. A superposition, so long as they are connected by thaumaturgical consistency.'

'There were thirty-seven words in that sentence and I understood about eight of them,' Crouch muttered. 'Apart from sounding like a load of krudian physics, what is thaumaturgical consistency exactly?'

Duana pointed to a small piece of rope tied to a bracket on the wall.

'A bit of old rope?' Crouch asked fearfully.

'It is actually a manifestation of a complex alchemical and arithmechanical construct which is invisible under normal circumstances, but in order to allow ease of use, has been physically reconstructed as a rope. Or, as we prefer to call it in krudian terms, string.'

'So this whole thing, this…gaol inside a cave under New Thameswick is held together by string?'

'Crudely put, but in effect, yes.'

'What if it breaks?'

'We will evaporate,' Duana said, cheerfully. But her attention was already drifting to the caves beyond the end of the brick corridor. She walked towards the dark space and shone a torch onto the walls. 'This is an interesting architectural construct. It is ancient and, I suspect, contains many interesting details.'

'And some pretty diabolical ones,' Crouch said.

'Ah yes, please elucidate.'

Asher and Crouch filled Duana and the demon squad officers in on events. Asher declined the offer of showing them exactly where the burial chamber was. He didn't need to. They could all smell it. When Duana came back from inspecting it, she looked tight-lipped and as angry as he had ever seen her. 'These are unprecedented crimes,' she said.

'Yes, and carried out against the most helpless and vulnerable. Isn't it about time we tried to help the Bewildered?' Asher said.

Duana tilted her head. 'It needs to be brought to the attention of someone who can help. Someone in authority.'

'Can you do that?'

'I will try.'

Crouch recovered quickly, now that the danger of imminent death had gone, though he kept glancing up at the rope tied to a bracket. 'So—and correct me if I'm wrong—all those people were killed to try and get one of Gazorch's misguided Widicombs to piggyback on their dead souls over to the other side? I don't see the point.'

'They may see humans as an untapped resource,' Asher explained.

'As sacrifices?' Crouch said, looking confused.

'Possibly. Then again…'

'But surely—' Crouch's protestations were cut short by Duana.

'There are many millions of gullible people in the human world, Inspector Crouch,' she said.

'You're not suggesting humans might follow him, are you? I mean, Gazorch's filth. Who would want to follow him?'

'You would be surprised and, I fear disappointed, Crouch. I gather you are not familiar with the history of human culture?'

'Nah. Got enough problems looking after this lot.'

'Then you will not have heard of the Church of Dyfagmeld which came to prominence in the last century. It has almost a million human members.'

'Is Dyfagmeld a god?' Crouch asked.

'No, an acronym for Disown Your Family And Give Me Every Last Dollar. It is very successful and preys on the need in many humans to have faith in something. Quite often said faith involves the promise of purgatory, humiliation, and self-sacrifice in the absence of critical thinking. In such a culture, you night see how support for a demon who can offer all the pleasures of the flesh for a down payment of a couple of souls might win favour.'

'So Stohb might be over there doing just that,' Asher said. 'Promising people all sorts of things in the name of faith?'

'Yes. But he will be at a very early phase of proselytization,' Duana replied. 'It should be no trouble to flush him out.'

'Great. So everyone's a winner,' Crouch looked at his watch, 'and it's still only nine o'clock. The Empty Vessel should be in full swing. Fancy joining me for a pint of Mountain Drool, Asher?'

'I need to get back to Oxford. There's work—'

'There will be no work until the morning. Though Rathbone attempted to initiate the reversal, it was vetoed by us as a result of your discovery here.'

'I won't exactly be flavour of the month at FHIFAA, then.'

Duana tilted her head. 'Is that a cause for concern?'

Asher smiled. 'Not really.'

'Then I suggest you join Inspector Crouch for a celebratory drink. And you should take solace from the fact that you will not be bothered by calls from the Bewildered tonight.'

Asher nodded. He hugged Duana, who reciprocated by tapping him gently on the back, then made for a door in the room's brick wall. Crouch though, was hanging back.

'What's wrong?' Asher said.

Crouch turned to Duana. 'I don't suppose Tuesday nights are still, um, *open*, if you'll pardon the expression?'

Duana tilted her head. 'Give me your beemail address. If there is no one more attractive available, I might call you.'

'Result,' said Crouch, pulling a fist down out of the air. 'Right, come on, Asher. It's your round and they'd better not be out of venison sausages.'

CHAPTER THIRTY-SIX

Bobby stood, frozen, in an all too familiar room. There'd been no sensation of physical movement, of having to cross a threshold. This time the Aperio, or perhaps it was an onward leg of Crone with the Wind, had simply taken her there. She knew exactly where she was because she'd spent countless hours in that room, even slept in the large bed with its old-fashioned candlewick bedspread, cosy and tucked in under a blanket of warmth and love with a lavender posy in a muslin bag on the pillow. Tears welled and ran silently down her cheeks. Tears of longing and grief and of shame.

This was her grandmother's room in her parent's house. Or rather, her grandmother's room in her grandmother's house, because the property had originally been Lucille Miracle's and it was she who had bequeathed the place to her son and his family. Bobby sat on the bed, overwhelmed by a sense of poignancy. It was not exactly how she remembered it because her mother had taken down her grandmother's prints and removed her trinkets, using the argument that to keep them all would make a valuable guest bedroom maudlin. Both she and her father knew how flawed that argument was in that the Miracles' lifestyle was not one peppered with weekend visitors. But in a way Bobby had appreciated the need to move on and removing all traces of Lucille from this room had been a process, of sorts, that helped heal the ordeal of those last years of her descent into madness. Or, as she now knew, her *apparent* descent. Yet, when the walls changed from warm rose to buttercup yellow it had been the final, grief-ridden act for Bobby. Now, sitting on her grandmother's bed, she realised she had not been in this room for ten years. She got up and went to the door and tried the handle. It was locked, as she knew it would be. Her parents kept it that way, as if locking it eliminated any chance of inadvertently opening it and facing an unpalatable past full of unpleasant reminders.

Bobby glanced at her watch. A quarter to midnight, but just after noon on the beach she'd moments before left. The bedside lamp glowed and she wondered for a moment who had turned it on, but then dismissed it as an irrelevance. Having the bedside lamp lit in a locked room was nothing compared to what had happened to her that day. Nevertheless, though the chance was small, she did not want to attract any attention from anyone outside who might casually pass and wonder why a light was on in a locked room. Bobby crossed to the window. Outside, a black winter night spat rain at the glass. She saw her own reflection looking back at her and was surprised she didn't look any different. She certainly felt different. Aware and awake and…alive.

She drew the curtains and turned to face the bed. Her parents would be in their own beds by now, just a few yards away. She knew their routine, was always amused by it on her increasingly infrequent visits that had somehow shrunk to the dutiful minimum of Christmas and birthdays. Whenever she stayed, if it was planned, her mother would prepare far too much food and her father would gently press her for details of her unending quest for work, and after half a day she'd feel the press of boredom in the dull old house slowly stifling her. But now was different. The same house, still the same parents, but this room was not a part of that. This was her grandmother's room. A grandmother she'd loved to bits and who had been taken from her by a cruel…a cruel what, Bobby?

The challenging thought came with its own voice. One that she used to hear a lot when she was in school and already beginning to withdraw from the pack. A carping, mocking voice always ready to turn the screw.

Go on, say it. Listen to how it sounds.
Demon?

She could hear the voice gearing up to hurl a volley of sceptical abuse. The kind that held her back from so many things for so many years.

But Bobby reached out and touched the old pink candlewick bedspread and the voice let out a strangled scream and ran for the hills.

Yeah, thought Bobby fiercely, hurling a challenge at its retreating back, *I'm here, in my grandmother's room, at her invitation. Go on: mock that, why don't you? Explain that, why don't you?*

The silence that followed was the most wonderful noise Bobby had never heard.

She stepped across to the bed and lay on it. Though an echo of the sadness she felt for her grandmother's suffering pulled at her, the memory of their meeting on the beach was wonderfully fresh. And with that meeting had come solace. From what her grandmother had told her, there genuinely wasn't anything anyone could have done to help Lucille Miracle. Not then. And she could not, and would not, blame her helpless, straight-laced, ordinary parents for it anymore. How could she?

She flopped back and stared at the ceiling. There were so many things to think about. Asher, Cuthbertson, the Sambolith, the beach. And now here. Why had she been brought here?

On impulse, Bobby sat up and went to the old dresser with its speckled mirror. There was little on its surface except a lacquered jewellery box containing some scuffed green glass earrings. The dresser had drawers. Bobby went through all of them and they were all equally empty.

She returned to the bed and sat on it once more. The mattress felt very comfortable, and the feel of her fingers on the old bedspread brought back memories of innocent times. Her eyes drifted around the room and the ornate plaster coving running around the edge of the ceiling. Her grandmother used to explain how the pattern was called dentil egg and dart and once Bobby had learned that, the ceiling took on a whole new existence, as if it was the repository for some magic bird. As a child she'd lain in this exact same spot a hundred times and counted the number of 'eggs'.

Her eyes drifted again. Wistfully, she acknowledged that not much else was left. The old lamp stand had gone, replaced by the ugly metallic bedside light, but as a token, her mother's fanciful wish for a guest bedroom meant she'd kept Lucille's old magazine rack. Once it had been full of books of mythology Bobby and her grandmother read together. Now it held nothing but a couple of forlorn magazines about country living that must have been a dozen or more years old. Bobby got up and reached for them, thumbed through them, giggled at the fashions and tossed them aside. The rack squatted square and heavy, made of brass and some sort of wood given a finish to look like a tortoiseshell. Basically a box on four brass feet and a brass rail. She'd loved that box. It smelled of old wood and…Bobby sat up.

Tortoise shell and turtles? Could it possibly be?

She was quickly learning not to accept anything as coincidence.

Bobby picked up the rack and put it on the bed. Chocolate dark inside, the wood was rough and relatively unfinished compared to the warm, smooth rich facing. She used her phone as a torch. There was nothing to see, nothing to feel except the smallest of ridges on the inside of the base about halfway along, right at the point where the base met the upright wall of the box. It could be a nail that had worked loose, except its head felt oddly smooth and not metallic. But no matter how hard Bobby tried to prise it out, it wouldn't budge.

She sat back. What was she doing? This was just a little burr the carpenter had been unable to dislodge, wasn't it? And yet, she couldn't help but believe something had brought her there for a reason and the magazine rack was the only thing left that linked her and her grandmother. She quashed her misgivings and, in desperation, took the rack to the dresser and put in on its shorter end, squatted on the floor and peered in. She could just about see the excrescence. It was the same colour as the rest of the wood, but elevated and smooth, more like a knob that anything el—

She sat back to let her mind stop whirling. The thing looked like the knob of a door. What was the point of having a door in the bottom of a magazine rack? Especially one that wouldn't open. It didn't make any sense at all. Unless…

Her grandmother had said for her to use the Aperio and she had, mentally. But what if she'd also meant literally?

Quickly, Bobby reached for the Aperio and put it into the bottom of the rack on the side opposite the little projection. It stuck. Always a good sign. She turned the Aperio and pushed. Nothing happened. Cursing, she pulled at it to remove it and instead, saw the base of the rack open. Quivering with anticipation, she lifted up the small trap door. Beyond, in yet another gasp-inducing realisation, was a space as big as the rack itself. Nestling in the bottom were two objects. One a white envelope, the other a necklace. With trembling fingers, Bobby removed them both. The necklace was made of tiny black oval beads and carried three small charms, which she recognised immediately as a double-edged ceremonial knife used in witchcraft and known as an athame; a white-handled ritualistic Wiccan knife known as a bolline; and a stone ring, much like she'd found in Kylah's cupboard.

But how did she know this stuff?

Bobby realised to her amazement that she'd mentally referenced *The Witche's Vade Mecum*; a text now firmly lodged in her memory banks though she'd only read it the once and at speed.

Shrugging, she carefully laid the necklace on the dressing table and reached for the envelope. In a moment of teary recognition, Bobby read her own name written there.

For the attention of Roberta Miracle

She took the envelope, arose on unsteady legs and sat, once more, on the bed. She knew this was Lucille's handwriting instantly and hesitated. More revelations? Shaking her head, she opened the envelope. Inside on lined blue paper was a handwritten note, dated 2nd October 2012.

CHAPTER THIRTY-SEVEN

My darling Bobby,

Since you are reading this, I know that you have found my little hidey-hole and that it is very likely that you are no longer the child I said goodbye to when you left for school this morning. I wish I could be there to see you as you are now, but I know that if you are reading this, it is not to be. I had plans to teach you so much, you clever, clever girl. But my duty comes before family, though none of us who chose the path ever expect to be called to confront the challenge that awaits me this day. I do not know what will happen, but I do know that our enemy is strong and very powerful and that we must do everything that we can to stop him.

To that end I am leaving you my necklace. If I lose the battle today, the necklace would be lost forever if I did not place it here. If I win, I will hand it to you myself when the time comes and this letter will long have been cast into the fire. Something tells me I must prepare for the worst.

Be strong. Be proud of your heritage. Accept the way and know that I will always be there for you in your hour of need.

Your loving grandmother,
Lucille
Gwrach

BOBBY READ the note a dozen times, the first five times through eyes blurred with tears. When they finally dried, she tried to make sense of it all. Lucille had gone to help a friend, or so her father had said. From the tone of this note it seemed much more than that. But it was the word at the end that stumped her. She turned to her phone and searched for it. When she finally got to a definition, it confirmed everything.

Gwrach was from Britain's oldest language that was still spoken in Wales. In modern Welsh, it meant witch. But in medieval days, it meant much more: the elder female, the wise mother, the cunning woman.

Cunning.

And then an image of Lucille being taken away, screaming at her, uttering a guttural shout that had frightened the girl Bobby had been danced across her memory. She'd heard it as 'Rack, Rack', but now suddenly realised Lucille had been telling her something else altogether, uttering her defiance or maybe telling her granddaughter the truth. And as she heard it again, the Rack transformed into Rach, with the soft aspirated ending that she'd transmuted into the more commonly heard hardness of a C and a K. She even knew how the word was spelled now.

Gwrach.

Bobby put the note down and picked up the necklace. The charms were small and intricate, the beads of some ebony mineral. Without hesitation, she put it around her neck. It somehow felt like the right thing to do. She lay back down on the bed and closed her eyes, seeing sparks of understanding fly like a New Year's Eve firework display. But for once, she felt at peace with herself. There was going to be much to do, she knew that, and it would need to start with tomorrow and explaining to her parents why she was at their house, because she'd need a shower before going back to Oxford. The sparks faded and fatigue rushed in. Bobby Miracle drifted off to sleep in her grandmother's bed, armed with the knowledge that she was not the same person who had left for work that morning.

And never would be again.

CHAPTER THIRTY-EIGHT

ASHER WAITED **in the foyer** of the Bureau of Demonology for Crouch. He was already fifteen minutes late. Finally a carriage drew up and Crouch got out.

Very carefully.

His dusky skin had taken on a khaki hue and he clutched his stomach like someone recovering from major abdominal surgery. But Crouch's attempt at rearranging his intestinal configuration had nothing to do with a surgeon's knife and everything to do with a few too many venison sausages and nine pints of Mountain Drool.

'Good morning,' Asher said.

'It was noticed that you left early,' Crouch said, lifting up his dark glasses to reveal eyes that were more red than white.

'I left at midnight.'

'Before we started on the lava shots?'

Asher nodded.

'Before Madame Stopit and her Python?'

Asher nodded again. 'Entertaining, was she?'

'She obviously has no gag reflex.' Crouch winced at the memory. 'And I suppose you missed the complimentary curry, too?'

Asher nodded. 'Luckily, yes. Coffee?'

'No, not yet,' Crouch said, turning a tad paler. 'Look, do we have to meet Duana now?'

'She has offered to cook us breakfast.'

'Oh, Gods.'

Asher smiled and they walked through security.

Crouch winced as they patted him down. 'So why didn't you stay? Everyone was asking after you.'

'Really? I am surprised anyone could speak.'

'Yeah, but…'

'If you want the truth, I had too much on my mind.'

'What? We cracked the case. We're heroes, you and me.'

'Perhaps. However, I am still not satisfied that all aspects have been completely explained.'

'Really? You could have fooled me.'

Asher said nothing. He didn't believe in kicking a man while he was down.

Duana had laid on a breakfast of devilled kidneys, smoked haddock, and eggs in all forms. 'Mmm, this looks delicious,' Asher said.

Crouch went and stood at the other end of the room. Green didn't suit him.

'You do not want breakfast?' Duana asked.

Crouch shook his head.

'Are you ill?'

'Already eaten,' Crouch mumbled.

'You are lying. Wearing dark glasses indoors is a sign of photophobia. I surmise that you are hungover. I have a potion for that. Its main ingredient is uncooked spleen of pike added to raw egg and—'

'Now you're being cruel,' Asher muttered, as Crouch put a hand out to the wall for support.

Duana smiled. At least that's how Asher interpreted the faint twitch at the corner of her mouth.

'I do have a potion. It is odourless and colourless,' she whispered to Asher.

'I'm sure Crouch would be very grateful.'

She fetched a glass-stoppered bottle and poured a small measure into a beaker that she handed to Crouch. 'Drink this.'

'If I end up as a frog or a stoat…'

'Drink it.'

Crouch did. Within three minutes his complexion changed from pond slime to his normal dusky grey. Five minutes later he was wolfing down a huge plate of breakfast.

'Right, so, what's the damage, Duana?' Crouch asked.

The demonmaster watched him with the kind of frowning distaste more usually found on the faces of spectators outside the bars of a lion enclosure at feeding time. 'From what we've learned from our RASTA probes—'

Crouch held up his knife and stuck out his lower jaw by way of pausing Duana. 'Don't forget I'm just a simple copper.'

Duana raised one eyebrow as if to imply he should know better, but acquiesced to his request. 'RASTA,' she repeated, 'Reverse Analysis of Thaumaturgical Activity. We can confirm that the Gazorchites were in the process of simultaneous murder and sacrifice, attempting to allow Cobain to cleave to one of the Bewildered's spirits as it navigated through Abaddon. From your report on what you overheard, the man Stohb appears to have succeeded in a similar endeavour. All other attempts have failed.'

'So this Stohb is possibly the cause of the lockdown at Hipposync?' Crouch asked.

Duana nodded. 'If he was able to cleave to a Bewildered spirit and pass over, he will be able to haunt any inanimate object. If said object found its way into Hipposync Enterprises—'

'It would have triggered the alarm and the lockdown.' Asher buttered some toast, and took a bite.

'All this just to start the Church of Gazorch the Pantocrator,' Crouch tutted.

Duana nodded again. 'And not the first time. Quite apart from the thwarted attempt in 2016, in which I played a small part, there was one a few years earlier that we almost missed. Thankfully, some of our co-opted human observers picked it up and acted swiftly, though it cost two of them their lives.'

'Bastard doesn't stop trying, does he,' Crouch said.

'No. But now we know Stohb is at large, we can deploy Search and Destroy squads quickly. In fact, we already have.'

'Tell Rathbone that,' Asher said.

'Mr Rathbone has no jurisdiction here.' Duana held Asher's gaze.

'So you think this Stohb is responsible for all the Muncher deaths the DOF were investigating, too?' Crouch asked.

'Very difficult to know. The reported deaths could be simply due to the spate of Bewildered activity. Their returning spirits would adopt marked and aggressive poltergeist behaviour. And all cases involved frail individuals, do not forget,' Duana explained.

'Or they could all be down to Stohb trying to muscle in,' Asher muttered.

Duana shook her head. 'Though all three cases appear bad enough to qualify as a malign haunting, Stohb could only have attempted cleaving with one soul. Therefore only one of the deaths would constitute true premeditated malign haunting involving Stohb. However, the old and sick are far less likely to survive an attempted possession. One can only assume that he was disappointed in his efforts and resorted to an inanimate object in which to hide.'

'What about the missing woman, Paula Evans?' Asher asked. 'Any theories?'

Duana shrugged. 'It may be simply that she was so traumatised by witnessing poltergeist activity that she has become disturbed and gone into hiding.'

'You don't think Stohb has her?'

Duana inclined her head. 'We cannot, of course, rule that out. But if Stohb possessed her and she triggered the lockdown, her presence would have been obvious. Yet, there is no record of anyone unaccounted for having been to Hipposync on the day of the triggered lockdown. Therefore our inanimate object theory seems much more likely.'

Asher nodded grimly. 'The easiest thing to do would be to send a squad to Oxford and each malign haunting site. See if they can flush Stohb out.'

'Happily, they are already at work,' Duana nodded.

'These eggs are brilliant,' Crouch said, spooning up a third helping and breaking the sombre moment.

'I am so glad. Especially since you appear to have spilled most of them down your shirt,' Duana said.

Asher stood up. 'Duana, I must go. I know we managed to delay Rathbone, but the lockdown reversal in Oxford is set for ten. I need to be there.'

Duana nodded. 'The S&D squads should have completed their work by now.'

'Mind if I stay and finish me breakfast?' Crouch said.

'Only on one condition. That you allow me to try out my new intruder geist. I have made some modifications.'

'Go on, then. But you'd better have some tissue paper handy.'

'By the way, did our prisoners tell you anything else?' Asher asked at the door.

'No,' Duana said. 'They were all dead by the time we got them into custody.'

'What?'

'Suicide charms. They all chose to die before incurring the wrath of Gazorch the Pantocrator.'

'You don't happen to have any more butter, Duana, do you?' Crouch asked.

Asher left them to it and went to the door, applied the Aperio and, at 9.40 AM, stepped across into the blue room at Hipposync Enterprises.

IN THE END, extracting herself from her parents' house was quite straightforward for Bobby. She let herself out with the Aperio and knocked on the front door of the house at 7.30 am once she'd seen the kitchen light go on. She explained away her presence by her attendance at a party nearby, which went on far too late. She'd slept over, got an early taxi to the house and now wanted a shower and some breakfast. It only became slightly awkward when her dad insisted on driving her to the station at nine forty-five. But there was little point arguing. Lying was a complicated business. Once inside the station, she went to the loo and used the Aperio on the cubicle door, thinking blue room thoughts. She stepped in and almost collided with Asher, who had obviously arrived but a few seconds before her. The look on his face was priceless.

'Where did you come from?' Asher asked. 'How did you get out?'

'Nice to see you, too, Asher,' Bobby said.

'I thought I made it clear that you were to stay here.' Asher glared at her.

Bobby folded her arms across her chest. 'Yes, you did. But you also waltzed away without any explanation. So what was I supposed to think? For all I knew you might have buzzed off for good.'

'I told you, there were things I had to do—'

'Same here. So I borrowed Kylah's Aperio.'

Asher became very still and quiet.

'You can close your mouth whenever you want,' Bobby said.

'Do you have any concept of the word 'security'?'

Bobby sighed. 'We can do this two ways. Either you can play the affronted headmaster to my naughty schoolgirl, or we can both be mature and swap stories, because I have lots of information I think you'll want to hear.'

'Information? What kind of information?'

'About Cuthbertson mainly. At least about whatever I met in Cuthbertson's house.'

'You have been to Cuthbertson's house?' breathed Asher.

'Do you want to sit down? You look a little shaky.'

'Have you any idea—'

'Oh, and I've been on a desert island and to my grandmother's bedroom. I've had a lot of time to think—'

Asher began to wave his hands in front of his face to stop her. 'Enough. I cannot listen to this now.' He looked at his watch and glanced up at Kylah just a few feet away. 'They are about to begin the reversal. We must stay in here until it is done.'

'What's so special about this room, anyway?'

'It is insulated. It exists outside of the protective field covering the rest of the building. We would not be able to use the Aperio anywhere else and it makes things much easier for visitors who have security clearance. It's like a neutral zone.'

'Will there be bangs and whistles?'

'No,' Asher said, irritably. 'Though, you may want to suck on a boiled sweet.'

'Now there's an offer I don't get every day.'

CHAPTER THIRTY-NINE

Asher ignored her and fished out a wrapped chocolate lime from his pocket. He offered it to her. Bobby eyed it suspiciously.

'How do I know this won't hex me into a coma or send my legs to sleep again?'

'Because it is merely a boiled sweet. Here, look,' Asher unwrapped his own and put it in his mouth.

Bobby shrugged and did the same. It tasted delicious. Asher was now staring at his watch. 'Ten seconds,' he said.

Bobby waited.

'Five, four, three, two, one.'

It felt like being shot to the top of a mountain and back down again in the world's speediest cable car. There was no pain, but Bobby's ears popped and a noise like a faraway train approaching very fast came with it. A wave of light passed over them both and then came the noise. The hum of electricity and a filing cabinet drawer slamming shut somewhere and suddenly the door opened and Bobby stared at the surprised face and gold-flecked eyes of Kylah Porter. Her gaze flicked between Bobby and Asher before she said, 'Ah.'

Five minutes later the place swarmed with BOD agents doing a security sweep. Asher, Bobby, and Kylah convened in Matt's office at Asher's insistence and drank hot coffee courtesy of Miss WT. They took turns with their explanations. Matt and Kylah went first. Initially, they were wary of discussing DOF business in front of Bobby, but Asher shrugged off their concern.

'She is embroiled in this case and has been from the beginning.'

So Kylah filled them in on what she and Matt knew, and about their visit to the Cuthbertson place.

When they'd finished, Asher asked, 'Could it be you brought something back with you?'

'It's possible,' Kylah said, 'Though we had no sign of any activity when we were there.'

'Well, there's something definitely there now,' Bobby said.

Everyone looked at her.

Asher broke the stalemate. 'First I need to fill you in on what we think has been happening.' He told them about finding Bobby alone in Hipposync, about his parallel investigation involving the Bewildered and of how they now believed that at least one of the malign hauntings was tied up with Stohb, who had very probably stolen across and remained at large.

'You think Stohb triggered the lockdown?' Kylah asked. 'But isn't he just a sect lackey?'

Asher sighed and said, 'Still the most likely suspect I'd say. Something certainly set the alarms off. If it's still here, we'll find it.'

'What do you mean *if* it's still here?' Matt asked. 'Isn't that the whole point of the lockdown?'

'It is, but there are…extenuating circumstances.'

They all waited for Asher to explain.

'Normally, any intrusion by unregistered Fae or contaminated objects into this building triggers a lockdown. However, this one took place exactly as Ms Miracle left the building. Not knowing anything about it, she forced her way back in before total closure was achieved.'

'Are you saying I let the thing out?' Bobby asked, suddenly finding it very difficult to swallow.

Asher shrugged. 'If the sweep comes up negative, then very probably, yes. Let's say Stohb somehow managed to haunt an inanimate object of Kylah's or Matt's on their visit to Cuthbertson's and got in here. He would stay hidden and undetected under a shield charm until he showed himself, or tried to possess someone or something else. Once he did that, even for a fraction of a second, he would be detected and the lockdown would kick in, making it impossible for him to get out. Your unusual exit and re-entry is the only explanation.'

Kylah frowned. 'I thought that once triggered, neither of those things were possible. How is it you managed to overcome the safeguards?'

Bobby shrugged. Perhaps she ought to let Lucille Miracle explain. 'All I know is that I was halfway out of the building when—'

There was a knock on the door and Asher got up to exchange a few word with a BOD agent. When he turned back to the room, his face was grim.

'There is no sign of anything. The building is clean.'

'But—' Bobby protested.

'No one is blaming you, Bobby,' Kylah said, yet it was there in those eyes. The sort of look air-sea rescuers wore when they picked up the idiot in the pedalo who'd fallen asleep and drifted out to sea in a Force Eight wind. All those resources wasted on a feckless twit. Bobby felt the bubble of confidence she'd floated on since finding her grandmother's note and necklace deflating at a rate of knots. Who was she kidding here? She'd wanted to tell them all about it, what she'd learned in the library about hauntings and the Bewildered, her fight with the thing at Cuthbertson's, her grandmother's legacy. But suddenly it all sounded puerile. These people were professionals and she was nothing but an intern with an imagination and a penchant for drab dark clothes, who'd borrowed something arcane and gone on a mind-bending trip with the wonderful Lucille Miracle.

Or had she? Could whatever it was that Asher had charmed her with to paralyse her legs have also sent her on a mental away day with the fairies?

There was another knock on the door. Kylah opened it and there was Miss WT with a beaming Pippa in tow.

'Miss Elmsworthy is here.'

'Hi everyone. Sorry I'm late?' The Pip glowed.

'Don't apologise, we're all a little late this morning.'

'You're better, I see,' Matt said.

Pippa beamed. 'Yes. The hospital said it was a virus? They gave me some fluids and I was fine after a few hours. I'm a hundred per cent now thank you.'

Kylah stepped forward. 'Pippa, can you give us a few minutes? I'll be with you shortly. '

'Sure,' Pippa said. She looked at Bobby and wiggled a few fingers. 'Morning, Bobs,' she said and with a flick of her hair, turned away.

Bobby felt like throwing something, preferably a dense paperweight, and immediately hated herself for even thinking it. Kylah was smiling, but her eyes stayed very serious.

'Let's go to my office.'

Bobby shrugged and followed, leaving Asher and Matt deep in conversation.

Kylah ushered Bobby in and closed the door. 'Okay, I realise this is all a bit fraught, but since we have the real possibility of a rogue entity on the loose, I'd like to get things squared away here so that we can get on with helping the BOD with their work.'

Bobby sat, worrying at her fingers.

Kylah perched on the edge of her desk. 'Obviously, I am aware that you have been very helpful in sorting out this little mess.'

'Asher…Inspector Lodge thinks I caused most of it. Tried to lock me in here in case I made things worse.'

'He did all of that to protect you. He could have taken you back to New Thameswick and had you thrown into an isolation cell. Obviously he trusts you. But you were not to know. In fact, you were not to know anything at all. Of course that has all changed, but at the same time, nothing has changed.'

Bobby weighed up the words and they were heavy with candour. She wanted to blame Asher for her predicament but anger had obscured the truth of it. Asher *had* trusted her and she had betrayed that trust. There was no longer a smile on the captain's lovely face as she pressed on.

'What I mean to say is that we have to now pick up from

where we left off several days ago. It is always difficult after a lockdown, but there we have it.'

'I know.' Bobby said, trying to quell the sick feeling she had inside.

'We had already made the decision regarding you and Pippa. Though, according to Asher, you have proven yourself to be highly resourceful, you have to realise I have already given my word and I can not go back on that.'

Perish the thought.

'No, of course not,' Bobby said.

'There is also the fact that you are now aware of many things you should be ignorant of and I am afraid that we cannot allow that to continue.'

'What do you mean?'

'I mean we will need to make a small adjustment to your memory. The last twenty-four hours will be eradicated from your brain. It will be as if nothing had happened. It is the law.'

'I met my dead grandmother. I thought she was mad but—'

Kylah shut her eyes momentarily and let her shoulders sag. 'Bobby, it's probably best not to discuss anything or dwell on the last few days.'

'I see,' Bobby said. A part of her was screaming. The part that had found her grandmother and understood why she was like she was. But another part of her knew how walking away from Hipposync with such knowledge might make things a hundred times worse. What would she do? She couldn't tell anyone. She had no idea of how to be a witch. So maybe it was best to forget the whole sorry mess. Besides, she still had her grandmother's note and the necklace, and while she wouldn't remember how she got them, they would, at least, allow her to re-establish one lost relationship. Although she'd probably think it was all a mad woman's writing without the context of her memory of Cuthbertson and the beach...

'It's the law, Bobby,' Kylah repeated gently.

Bobby nodded. She stood up and felt the bulge in her coat pocket bang against her thigh. 'Oh, I borrowed this,' she said and handed back the Aperio.

Kylah took it. There was genuine regret in her expression when she said, 'I suggest you make sure you leave nothing behind this time. Shall we meet in five minutes in the blue room? That way we can get you to wherever it is you want to go with the least fuss.'

CHAPTER FORTY

BOBBY WENT BACK to the office and straight to her desk. She picked up a couple of ballpoints and the voodoo coffin desk tidy that she'd somehow missed last time. Pippa watched her in silence for several seconds.

'I haven't had a chance to say thank you,' Pippa said in a small voice.

Bobby looked up. 'For what?'

'For what? That bloke…Asher, is it? He said you'd arranged the ambulance for me.'

'Oh, that. You'd have done the same. Sorry I couldn't come with you, it's just that—'

'Did I just sort of…pass out?'

'Sort of,' Bobby nodded. Her eyes flicked to the screen in front of Pippa. It was paused on her favourite kitten video. 'I wasn't sure what best to do, so I dialled 999 and…is that the same video you showed me before?'

'Yes.' Pippa developed a soppy grin, clicked on the play button and the white kitten began walking along a keyboard, playing 'Three Blind Mice' with its paws.

'That's CGI, it must be.' Bobby couldn't hide the cynicism in her voice.

'That's the amazing thing, though? It isn't CGI. It's real and it's gone viral. Isn't it soooo cute?' The kitten played three bars with catlike grace.

And we know it isn't CGI because the clever geeks who made the video said so, right? At least it's distracting enough to get us away from discussing your illness, though.

'Yeah. Very…cute,' Bobby said, noting that one million, nine hundred and ninety-eight thousand people who'd liked the video certainly thought so, even if she didn't.

But if Pippa wanted to believe it was a feline Mozart, that was up to her. If Pippa didn't mind that Bobby had abandoned her to the NHS because she was off chasing ghosts, so be it, too. Inside her head, all Bobby wanted to do was scream. She stepped on the urge, turned back to her desk, took one last look to make sure she'd forgotten nothing, sighed, and pivoted one last time to face Pippa. She held out her hand. They shook.

'I'll miss you?' Pippa said.

'Me too. Good luck with this.' Bobby turned away, hating herself for hoping that Pippa might crash and burn in the first week.

She went next to the kitchen and retrieved her three-quarters-full jar of dry roasted coffee. Seeing it reminded her of The Roast in Tharmin City and it was with that bitter reminder of promises broken that she put it into her coat pocket where, until a few moments before, the Aperio had sat. Leaving the kitchen, she popped her head around the door of Miss WT's office. The old lady smiled at her. The knowledge that she was not all she appeared to be passed briefly through Bobby's head before she shrugged it off.

'I'll be off, then.'

'Take care, dear.' She looked up and smiled. Bobby had never seen lips move so slowly. 'Take care.'

Bobby rather hoped not to have to see Asher, but it was turning into one of those mornings when what she wanted didn't seem to matter at all. He was loitering on the stairs that led to the blue room, the stairs that you walked right past unless you knew what you were looking for. He looked unhappy and sombre and, damn him, pretty much the best thing she'd stumbled across in…well, ever.

'Sorry,' he said as she walked down the steps. It took her completely by surprise.

'You ran out on me,' she said, wanting more than anything at that moment to let him know that he wasn't forgiven.

'It was for your own safety,' he said.

'Of course. I'd forgotten. I'm a woman and in cases of extreme danger we're rendered completely helpless by the tendency we have for our fallopian tubes to drop down and tangle around our legs.'

'You know that has nothing to do with it. This is a serious business. People have been killed.'

'Okay, then what about the second cup of coffee you promised me? Or has that been put to one side for my own good, too?'

Asher sighed. 'I had not forgotten that, Bobby, but other things have taken priority and for that I apologise. What with investigating the Muncher deaths and being captured by the Widicombs. And not forgetting becoming an honorary Bewildered. They have it particularly tough, you know.'

She listened for a sardonic tone, but heard none.

Damn. He had the knack of taking the South Westerly out of your spinnaker, did Asher. But Bobby was in no mood for forgiveness. 'If it's that tough for them, you should think about helping them permanently. Maybe setting up a charity of some kind.'

'If you mean by charity sharing a bone with your dog even though you are hungry, in New Thameswick it's far more likely that the bone would be boiled, made into thin soup, given a catchy name like Broth-Er-Lee-Love and then sold back to the dog for profit.'

'That's not an excuse.'

Asher's shoulders slumped. 'It isn't, I know…' He hesitated, as if building up to something pre-prepared.

Bobby blinked.

'There is something truly remarkable about you, Bobby,' Asher said. 'You do not scare easily and you say things as you see them. I only wish—'

He didn't finish. Kylah appeared at the top of the stairs. 'Ah, Bobby. Ready?'

Bobby looked at Asher, who suddenly looked about ten years old and lost for words. She shrugged and turned to Kylah. 'Yes.'

As she followed Kylah down the stairs, from behind she heard Asher ask, 'There is no other way, is there?'

They both turned to look back up at him. 'We've been through this,' Kylah replied. 'It's the law, Asher.'

He nodded.

'What will you do now?' Bobby asked.

'Go back. Look for a job. Maybe start a charity.' Asher didn't smile.

Bobby turned away. She didn't want him to see her eyes glistening. She was relieved and disappointed in equal measure when he didn't try to stop her.

Kylah opened the door to the blue room. 'This won't take a moment and I promise you it's completely painless.'

'So, I won't remember anything or anyone?'

'No. But it is 100% selective. It'll be as if you'd never heard of Hipposync and related events, but everything else will be untouched.'

Bobby walked through the door. Asher stood behind her in the corridor, watching. The urge to turn around was almost overwhelming and she had to work hard to stop the trembling in her legs. When Kylah finally closed the door, a hole opened up in Bobby's chest big enough for her to fall into. She closed her eyes, bit her lip, and breathed through her nose. It seemed the best way to slow the emotional log flume that threatened to cause a flood at any moment.

'We're all really grateful, Bobby. I want you to know that,' Kylah said. Bobby opened her eyes. The fimmigration agent removed a headband bearing an opalescent stone from a small leather satchel. 'And yes, I realise that this may appear to be a very odd way of showing it but this,' she held up the pentrievant, 'is the best way to deal with these things. I only wish it could be different.'

Bobby nodded, tight lipped, and watched as Kylah came

close and attached her Aperio to the opposite door. 'Tell me where it is you want to go.'

A lot has been written about coffee and its role in thinking. Most of it by people between the ages of twenty-two and thirty with a lot of time on their hands and jobs in Southern California. Most of it is about as edifying and useless as the grounds left in the filter basket. Sartre was a coffee drinker, though how he managed to fit a cup in between all the other things he rammed down his throat, up his nose and in his veins, was anyone's guess. If a sip of sweet coffee led to Jean Paul coming up with 'Hell is other people', surely a cappuccino could help Bobby sort out her head and help her believe that Asher was only a dream, because she already knew that hell *was* other people, or at least other people's wardrobes. So, Bobby reasoned, if a cup of joe was good enough for JPS, that giant of philosophy and believer in lost causes, it was as good a beverage as any to start her new life with.

'I was promised a cup of coffee this morning,' she said in a quivering voice, 'so how about Has Beans on Mortimer Street? Know it?'

'I do,' said Kylah.

Bobby walked towards the door and stood facing it. Kylah opened it a fraction, then walked behind Bobby and attached the headband.

'Thank you for your help,' Kylah said.

Bobby felt the slightest tingle and…stepped through the front door of Has Beans. For one terrifying, disorientating moment, she stood wondering who she was and what she was doing there. Then she smelled the coffee and a cup seemed suddenly like a very good idea.

CHAPTER FORTY-ONE

Asher waited outside while Kylah did her voodoo on Bobby.

It was all for the best, wasn't it?

People could make themselves believe almost anything. Like believing that swallowing tapeworm eggs was all for the best when it came to dieting. It did the job all right and had the added advantage of making you sick at the very thought of it. What better way to start a weight loss programme than throwing up?

And suddenly Asher did feel sick.

Okay, so she hadn't listened to him and put herself in danger and used all sorts of initiative, which, in his book, was a commodity worth bottling. She'd even used Kylah's Aperio, and that took some guts. And, she knew how to dress. Black didn't have to be dour; it could be elegant and practical. He'd seen the way the witches at Coven Garden looked at her. As if she was some kind of exotic bird. And she'd been funny and feisty and…

The door to the blue room opened and Kylah stepped out.

Too late. All far too late.

'All yours,' Kylah said. Her eyes seemed a little red.

'Did it proceed without incident?'

'It did.' Kylah's eyes became slits. 'Do I detect a twinge of regret in those steely eyes, Asher? Did this one melt that iron heart of yours a little?'

'She was headstrong,' he said, hating himself for saying it.

'That's not what I asked you.'

'No, it isn't. And the truth is that I did find her companionable and…yes, attractive.'

Kylah's face softened. 'Thanks for sorting things out.'

Asher shrugged. 'We dispatched S&D squads to all three Muncher locations. Let's see what they come up with.'

Kylah hugged him and he was grateful for it. They were, after all, old friends.

Because he genuinely couldn't think of anywhere else to go, Asher went back through the blue room to FHIFAA headquarters. The idea of clearing out his desk seemed like a good one. He realised that there might be disciplinary action. There would certainly be a demotion if not a sacking. *Well*, he thought, *I'll save them all the bloody trouble*.

Braithwaite sat at his desk, reading a file. On seeing Asher, he threw the file down and the magazine inside it fell onto the floor to reveal the sort of glossy publication normally found wrapped in brown paper on the very top shelf of a newsagent's. From the glance Lodge had of the page on display, Braithwaite's tastes were niche to say the least.

'I didn't think that was possible without a block and tackle,' he said, pointedly.

'This is research,' Braithwaite countered, colouring visibly.

'For what? A Marquis de Sod fondue party?'

Braithwaite quickly picked up the magazine and tucked it into the file. 'You're a fine one to talk, gallivanting with witches.'

'She is not a witch. And there's been no gallivanting.'

'No?' Braithwaite smirked. 'That's not the way it looks to me. Besides, if she isn't a witch then she's human, which is twice as bad. Talk about me having pervy tastes. I wouldn't go near one of them for 100 scruples.'

Asher thought about the term 'one of them', and about the mindset of anyone who'd actually use such a phrase about people of whom he had no knowledge. 'One of them' had placed herself in mortal danger to actually preserve the lifestyle of twits like Braithwaite. The incongruity of it, after what he'd been through, lit a fuse in Lodge's head that fizzed and sizzled down both arms and into his fists. He walked around the desk. Braithwaite stood up in abrupt alarm, the smug smile on his greasy lips frozen and heading for the hills.

Asher picked up the file and removed the magazine, tore a page out, scrunched it up, grabbed Braithwaite's testicles roughly in one hand and yanked him to tip toes. There followed a moment of bulging eyes and silent screaming which Asher took great advantage of by pushing the crumpled paper into his colleague's open mouth.

'Eat it,' he said.

'Lodge,' sputtered Braithwaite.

'Eat it, or I'll roll up your 'research' and stuff it whole down your throat.'

'You're a psycho, you know that?' Braithwaite said, though it sounded more like 'Fo uh fyco, u wow wat.'

Asher nodded. 'Common knowledge. Now eat it, and three more like it, you slimy, arrogant, supercilious turd.'

'Why?' wailed Braithwaite.

'Because the person you're insulting, though more than capable, isn't here to make you do it herself.'

Asher perched on the edge of the desk while Braithwaite slowly, painfully, chewed and swallowed four pages of the magazine.

'Excellent,' Asher said when he'd finished. 'Now, remember the taste of that when you next decide to be a complete twat, as Roberta Miracle so aptly described you.'

He didn't look at Braithwaite after that. He took a clean sheet of paper from the pile on his desk, dipped his pen in ink and wrote out his resignation. When he finished he folded the letter carefully and put it in his pocket. His pongcluetor pinged and he opened a beemail from the BOD, read it, and let a slow smile slide over his lips.

Asher knew that in any complex investigation it is very easy to wander up the wrong alley, and he'd been up enough of those in his time. As in any jigsaw puzzle, especially the really complicated ones involving lots of water or sky, where each of the 1,500 pieces are differentiated only by a seagull's lip, or a dollop of white froth capping a wave, it is so easy to convince yourself that a particular piece must fit *there* because it's the blue of the ocean. Of course that bit *looks* like a smidgen of ocean, but unless you adopt a different perspective, it remains impossible to see that the umbrella on the terrace of the hotel in the top left hand corner has the exact same colour blue. And in any crime, as in a jigsaw puzzle, assumptions can be very dangerous things. Assumptions always need to be interrogated in a scruffy room with no windows, two bolted down chairs and a table. Sometimes they even need a good kick up the backside (with the video camera turned off) in order for them to confess that, yes, they have a tendency to be inaccurate.

Asher pondered the assumptions they'd made in the Bewildered case as he made his way up to Rathbone's office and found them wanting.

Judging by the number of half-empty cups and plates covered with biscuit crumbs littered around the room, Rathbone had hosted a busy meeting that morning. However, there were only two people left when Lodge entered: Rathbone and, much to Asher's delight, Duana Llewyn. Rathbone's clown hair was dishevelled, his tie loose, and his face flushed and covered in a thin film of sweat. Asher surmised that this meeting had not gone well for FHIFAA's chief of operations.

'Ah, Lod…Asher, come and have a seat.'

Asher was not in the mood for playing ball. 'No, thank you. I'd rather stand.'

'Very well. I gather that…uh…congratulations are in order.'

Asher smiled. Rathbone's ability to make congratulations sound as agreeable as a pile of regurgitated dog food took a lot of practice.

'Thank you, Mr Rathbone.'

'Though I should point out that I remain very much unable to accept the manner in which it was accomplished—'

'That manner being the one in which I warned you that there were Bewildered-related matters connected to the case and that we needed to send in at least one S&D squad?'

Rathbone loosened his tie further. He looked like a man trying to swallow a spider, and not the type slathered in peanut sauce and sold in the marketplace by Thai Me Down Bundit, whose funnel web in soy sauce was to die for. Frequently.

'Quite,' Rathbone said, or rather squeezed out of his clamped together teeth. 'You are to be commended for your actions, I might add.'

'That's very kind of you, Mr Rathbone.'

'Nothing to do with me…' Rathbone muttered a little too quickly. He paused, squeezed his eyes shut and then opened them again. 'I am also to offer you a promotion and—'

'Stop, you're embarrassing me,' Asher said, reflecting on the telling bits of throwaway phrases such as, 'Nothing to do with me' and 'I am also to offer' and enjoying himself immensely as a result. 'Besides, I said I was resigning. Here, as promised, is the letter.'

Rathbone's eyes lit up like hilltop beacons on Yule Night. 'This is ah…unexpected news indeed, uh…Asher. However, if you are sure?'

'No doubt whatsoever.'

Rathbone snatched the letter out of Asher's hands and filed it carefully under a heavy paperweight in case it tried to escape, without reading it.

'So, will you be taking a holiday?' he asked, suddenly the epitome of a rattlesnake full of bonhomie.

'No, I've been offered another post.'

'May I ask where?'

Asher let his eyes drift over to Duana, who tilted her head and said, 'We are setting up a new rapid response team at the BOD. We've never had a necreddo before. I think it's time we did.'

Rathbone swallowed. His Adam's apple looked like a second twitching nose. After a while, he cleared his throat. 'Well, may I wish you both the best of luck.'

In Asher's head, he thought he could hear the faint whizzing noise of an incoming custard pie with Rathbone's name written all over it.

CHAPTER FORTY-TWO

Bobby Miracle bought herself a double shot cappuccino. She had no idea what the matter was but there were fuzzy bits in her memory where there should have been detail. She remembered losing out on the job at Hipposync and then, on a whim, she remembered going down to see her parents. And now, here she was, job hunting again and feeling a very strong urge for coffee. She liked coffee, but rarely felt this terrible craving for it. Choosing a quiet corner, she took the cup over to a spare seat and sat.

Ten-thirty in the morning and Has Beans was half full. As Bobby leant forward to put her bag between her feet, she heard something jangle against the flesh of her throat. She put her hand on the unfamiliar shape. Had she put on a new necklace? She tried peering down her nose at it but it was too short to see through the gaps in her blouse. This wasn't normal. Had she been out last night and drunk too much? It didn't feel like it. There was a distinct absence of hangover pain, though the fuzziness might easily be explained by alcohol. She did feel tired though, as if she hadn't got enough sleep. Sighing, she lifted the large white cup and took a sip.

It was good and strong and suddenly she was thinking about a place in Indonesia where they served Sumatran Mandheling in brown cups. It was a vivid thought. An imagined thought, too, because she'd never been to Indonesia, so it could not have been a memory. But she could even remember the name of the shop, The Roast, and the address and…she shook her head. This wasn't right. She looked around in slight panic. No one was staring and yet she suddenly felt weirdly exposed. An old fear stuck its head out from behind a wardrobe in her head (why wardrobe?). One that had been stuffed there and forgotten for many years, since her grandmother fell ill.

Madness ran in her family.

She'd watched her grandmother go doolally and it had been a frightening experience for a ten year old. Even more frightening when, in dark moments, Bobby wondered whether such things could be passed on. And, like opening a bottle of fizzy pop vigorously shaken on a long journey, the fear bubbled up and spilled over. Was this how it happened? Were these the first signs? Did her grandmother wake up one morning and find gaps in her memory that she couldn't explain? Have vivid thoughts about coffee shops in far-flung countries that she'd never been to?

With trembling hands, Bobby took another sip of coffee. This time there was no denying the effect it had. Something was happening inside her head. Another jolt of vivid imagery. A carriage with a driverless horse called Gary. A dog lying in the gutter, playing dead. If felt like someone had opened a ten-gallon carboy of disjointed snapshots and sounds, and started pouring its glugging contents into Bobby's head.

It must be the coffee. Yes, that was it. Somebody had spiked her coffee. She looked up at the barista. He was a cheerful, slim twenty-something with a goatee, who'd taken in her garb and asked if she was in a play. But he'd smiled at her and drawn a happy face in her froth. Plus, he wasn't looking over to see what effect his coffee was having. Nobody was. And yet…she was torn between throwing the coffee away and taking another sip. The images popping into her head were so alive. So real.

It must be the coffee.

Put it down, girl.

But there was something compelling about these thoughts. If only they could fall into some sort of order.

No more coffee, Roberta.

Her hand shook so badly now that she could barely hold the cup and it rattled as she tried returning it to the saucer.

Okay, okay, one more sip.

She needed both hands to clasp the cup firmly enough to get it to her lips.

This time, as the liquid hit her throat, a stab of pain like the worst brain freeze she'd ever experienced shot through the front of her head. And then…clarity.

Bobby Miracle, in defiance of all that was krudian, *remembered.*

She remembered her grandmother. She remembered the Bewildered, Hipposync, Cuthbertson's house, the desert island and…Asher Lodge. A man who had tried to protect her from demons and from herself. A man who dressed like a seventies rock star and acted and talked like someone Conan Doyle had dreamed up. A man, she now realised, who at their last goodbye had not wanted her to leave…

'Shit!'

The word splurged out and drew a few stares. But this was Oxford and most people had heard a lot worse. Suddenly Bobby's mind resembled a cinema screen with four films playing at once. You could only watch one properly, but you were aware that another three were vying for your attention. She took another sip and the detail came flooding in. It was like layers of colour being applied by a fancy printer, the images building, red on blue and then yellow and green and then texture and sound. She finished the coffee and bought another cup, and by the time she was at the bottom of the second it was all there.

Everything that had happened.

And with it came a dollop of confusion and a harsh realisation that it should not be.

So why? How?

Logic fought its way through the layers of startling imagery. She knew about the pentrievant. Knew what Kylah had said. So why was she remembering when she'd been prepared for total amnesia? She looked down at the handbag between her knees and once again felt the jangle at her throat.

Her grandmother's necklace.

Her grandmother's letter.

Quickly Bobby reached into her bag for the envelope she now remembered finding and read it once again.

Since you are reading this, I know that you have found my little hidey-hole and that it is very likely that you are no longer the child I said goodbye to when you left for school this morning. I wish I could be there to see you as you are now, but I know that if you are reading this, it is not to be. I had plans to teach you so much, you clever, clever girl. But my duty comes before family, though none of us who chose the path ever expect to be called to confront the challenge that awaits me this day. I do not know what will happen, but I do know that our enemy is strong and very powerful and that we must do everything that we can to stop him.

To that end I am leaving you my necklace. If I lose the battle today, the necklace would be lost forever if I did not place it here. If I win, I will hand it to you myself when the time comes and this letter will long have been cast into the fire. Something tells me I must prepare for the worst.

Be strong. Be proud of your heritage. Accept the way and know that I will always be there for you in your hour of need.

It was obvious, really. She hadn't told Kylah or Asher about finding her grandmother's letter or the necklace. Somehow the chance simply hadn't presented itself. But it was the one thing that was different about the Bobby Miracle who now sat in Has Beans and the Bobby Miracle who'd gone to work yesterday. Though she had no proof, she was convinced that the necklace had somehow protected her from whatever it was Kylah Porter and the pentrievant had tried to do. And knowing that she had some inherent cunning might explain how she'd managed to evade the lockdown in the first instance. With that knowledge came the realisation that she therefore knew an awful lot about some things she ought not to know about at all.

Bobby rewound the mental video in her head and replayed it at half speed so she could pore over the details. Then she took out her tablet and googled 'Hipposync' and 'New Thameswick', and came up blank for both. A fact in itself that was highly unusual.

Next she typed in 'Asher Lodge' and found a slew of properties, a couple of management agencies, and very few people. Certainly no necreddos. There were a few 'White Tandy's, but none that fit the description of the receptionist at Hipposync. And then of course there was Pippa. Good old Pippa, whom Bobby had saved from lockdown suspended animation and who loved kitten videos. Without knowing she was doing it, Bobby started surfing YouTube, watching one white ball of fluff torment a bemused Labrador whose paws alone were twice as big as the feline. Following that, she watched a kitten that sat up in bed, a kitten that miaowed 'I love you' and finally Pippa's pièce de résistance: a kitten playing 'Three Blind Mice' on the piano.

Incredibly, 1,999,278 people had already watched and liked that video, with the number growing with each refresh of the URL. Bobby let her eyes stray to the 'artist' and read *HBK_23*. Obviously someone with far too much time on his or her hands.

As the kitten magically played the notes, she wondered what things might have been like if she'd left Pippa in the lockdown, simply allowed her life to ebb away. Very different, for sure. She crushed the thought with a grimace. Pippa would be dead and being fond of kitten videos was not punishable by death, as far as Bobby knew. However, the same might not apply to HBK_23, who'd made the damned thing. The video continued to play with the sound off, so Bobby dug out some earphones from the depths of her handbag and plugged them in. Grudgingly, she had to admit that it was, in all truth, quite remarkable. Either someone had managed to train the kitten to play 'Three Blind Mice' or this was masterful computerized wizardry. Bobby knew the latter had to be it; you couldn't train cats to play music. That was like training a fish to ride a bicycle or a dog to recite Shakespeahhh—

The thought struck Bobby like a sucker punch. A great roundhouse of comprehension that hit with such force it made her fillings rattle. Was it possible? Was it possible that this was the answer to all of it?

Pippa.

When you thought about it, really thought about it, mixed it all together like the ingredients of a Christmas cake and then licked your fingers, the flavour it came up with was staring-you-in-the-face *trouble*.

Bobby sat up and typed furiously at her keyboard. She found the article on the *Cardiff Echo* website. From that she managed to find an address and from that it was easy enough to find the number. She dialled and got through to Mr Evans, husband of malign haunting victim Marie Evans, reintroducing herself as Asher's assistant from Support Services.

'There are still a few details I need, Mr Evans,' she explained, trying to make her voice sound calm. 'About your missing daughter.'

'Have you found her?' Desperation cracked Mr Evans' voice.

'Not yet. Tell me, do you know if your daughter had a Facebook page?' She waited, praying that Evans was not one of his generation who dismissed social media out of hand.

'Yes, she did…Paula's good at all that. Works in IT at the college. She bought me a computer a few years ago,' he said wistfully, 'made sure I knew how to use it. I'm one of her Facebook friends.'

'That's fantastic. And did Paula have another name? It'll make it easier to search for her.'

'Yes. Ann. Paula Ann, after Marie's mother.' Evans paused. 'Do you think we'll ever see Paula again?'

'I wouldn't give up hope just yet, Mr Evans.'

'Thanks for that. Thanks for being nice.'

And there it was. That was *exactly* the trouble.

Cosy, pleasant, and nice. Simple words with a whole load of baggage in the subtext. It was so easy to think that people were good or nice if they spoke kindly or had photogenic profiles. Hollywood had been doing that since movies began. How much more satisfying was it when the ugly bad guy got his just desserts? The heroine had to be pure of heart if she looked like *that*, didn't she? And, boy it was hard to accept the opposite point of view.

But Mary Shelley knew the truth of it even if she was looking at it through the opposite end of the telescope.

Ugly and despicable shells might contain something warm and emotionally intelligent. More importantly, what's shiny and beautiful on the outside does not mean it's the same under the wrapping. You only had to look at a polecat to understand that.

She typed in the name Paula Evans and watched as hundreds of contacts appeared just as she feared they would. Paula Evans was a common name. But when she added Ann, the results contracted to a mere handful. She zeroed in on one with the right address but with an avatar as a profile picture and waited with a hammering heart while the page loaded. Twenty seconds later she was on her feet, stuffing her tablet into her bag, and running out of the door at full pelt towards Hipposync.

CHAPTER FORTY-THREE

CRIME, **even Fae crime,** requires an open mind in order to gain insight. It is easy to understand that a hungry thief steals bread from Cruster's the baker because he needs to eat. It is not so easy to understand how murderous zealots can herd a group of people into a building or a cave and systematically slaughter them in the name of faith. It was the coward's argument, the curse of justification. And justification came in many forms. The least understandable might be doctrine or the written word of a religion, the more understandable was the need for progress. The scientists who worked for years on trying to make napalm more sticky by measuring how quickly it ran down a piece of glass undoubtedly considered their work tremendously worthwhile. And in terms of the wider field of fixotropic material research it probably was. And yet...

Evil was *very* good at finding ways to hide in mindless routine and banal rationalisation. Occasionally you simply had to see things, or be shown things, from a slightly different angle for the light to shine on those very dark places, and someone was about to ignite a hundred candela illumination for Asher Lodge.

———

'You're not a Rathbone fan,' Duana said as she and Asher walked down the stairs of FHIFAA HQ.

'Is the Venerable Mistanga a Klatchian?'

There was only the slightest hesitation before she answered, 'Yes.'

Asher sent her a wry smile.

'You have no second thoughts about working for us, Asher?' Duana turned her frosty blue gaze up at the ornately carved and painted ceiling depicting frolicking putti playing hide and seek between cotton clouds. 'We do not have the budget or the manpower of FHIFAA, you understand that?'

Asher shrugged. 'So long as it gets me out of sitting in an office.'

'I can guarantee that. I take it you enjoyed investigating the lockdown?'

'Enjoy isn't exactly the word I'd use. I'd feel happier if I could be sure we'd resolved it completely. It's left me with a very uneasy feeling of a job half done. Still no word from the S&D squads?'

Duana shook her head. 'They have found no trace as yet.'

'Loose ends.' Asher shook his head in response. 'I hate loose ends.'

They'd reached the foyer and Duana's heels made a click-clack noise on the marble floor. The security men were all staring and practising how to look away sharpish whenever Duana threw them a challenging glance, which was about once every four steps. 'At least you can be assured of no further attacks on the Bewildered.'

'Yes, but we still have not isolated the trigger. I wish we could have talked for longer with the intern, but I could not interfere in DOF business.'

Duana must have picked up on something in Asher's tone. 'Does the intern have a name?'

'Roberta,' Asher said. 'But her friends call her Bobby.'

'So, in that irritatingly formal way you have, I suppose you called her Roberta?'

Asher ignored her. 'She said she'd found some important

things out but Kylah was keen to have her reversed to ignorance as soon as possible.'

'It is a requirement.'

They paused in front of the large front doors. 'The Gazorchites are not going to give up though, are they?'

'No,' Duana said. 'He promises unending pleasure when he returns.'

'What, like as many massages as you can stand at Madame Sprig's in Splatt?' Asher grinned. 'Remember she ran a lottery with that as a prize a couple of years ago.'

Duana nodded, eyebrows arched. 'Yes. The winner remains in an induced coma. The blisters are very slow to heal.'

They lapsed into a contemplative silence, which ended when Asher said, 'I'm curious. I know you were involved in thwarting the last attempt at getting Gazorch back into the world, but didn't you say that the time before that a successful repelling took place from the human side? Presumably by non-Fae?'

Duana nodded. 'An astonishing feat under the circumstances. Many non-Fae have natural ability but have no real knowledge of how to use such skill. A little like the Yugol foot jugglers one sees in circuses over here. They simply use their talents for entertainment, whereas an equivalent skill in the human world can earn one very large amounts of gold for being able to kick an inflated ball into a net. I think they call it succour. Regardless of the detail, you appreciate the principle.

'Luckily, the non-Fae agents that carried out the operation on the Gazorch case were of the highest calibre. One of our soothsayers picked up on plans by an illegal coven to attempt a summoning. There were strong parallels with the 2016 episode in which I was involved. The coven got as far as raising Habihemhock, the summoner demon. The NF agents interrupted the ceremony and managed to perform an exorcism. They drove him from his host successfully, but at high cost. One of the agents was killed, another became insane, but Habihemhock was trapped by the third.'

'Sounds horrible. Did the third agent manage an entrapment spell?'

'She did not. Her plan was a very simple one. She allowed the monster in.'

'What?'

'It's an old method and very effective. She invited possession and as a consequence, the possessing spirit was forced to share the host as opposed to ruling it entirely. Something as malign as Habihemhock would be too powerful to suppress completely, but if the host is strong enough, it is possible to contain it. An enormous effort of will is required and it is a constant battle, day and night. To an outside observer it would seem like the host had become completely insane.'

'And we thought we'd had it tough. Who was the agent?'

'You don't know?' Duana's tone was incredulous. 'There is a statue to her in Calumnity Park. I'm surprised you've never seen it. Come on, it's on our way.'

The day was brisk and bright and Asher was glad to be able to walk. Duana had the great gift of abhorring small talk; one of the many things Asher liked about her. The park was only two blocks away and on this quiet morning populated by only a few people walking dogs or flying foxes on pieces of string. The large statue stood in the middle, high up on a square stone plinth. Asher realised he must have seen it and never registered its meaning. It was big, three people in weathered bronze triumphant over a squirming demon. At the head of the trio stood a woman with determination in her expression and power in her stance. The sculptor had captured her age perfectly and this was a woman in the autumn of her years but still handsome and almost regal. In one hand she held the wand of power and in the other the orb of justice. Asher looked up at a strong and proud face that was tantalisingly familiar. He let his eyes fall to the plaque.

Valour Personified: On the night of October 2nd, 2012

> three soldiers of truth fought and
> overcame a force set to threaten peace
> in the worlds of men and Fae.
> May their names be spoken with pride

when good deeds are needed.
Catrin Caster, Hubert Slayer, and Lucille Miracle.

Asher started. He stepped closer and read the plaque again. No, it couldn't be. He looked up into the face and felt his pulse quicken. 'She *is* a bloody witch,' he whispered.

From behind him, he heard Duana say, 'Of course she is.'

'I'm not talking about Lucille Miracle. I'm talking about her granddaughter.'

'Asher, you look quite flushed. Are you well?'

'No, I am most definitely not well. If anything, I think I ought to bite my own foot off as punishment.' He looked up at the sky as if for inspiration, but all he saw was a familiar pale blue canvass dotted with scudding clouds, the December sun low in the south. And tomorrow would be the same with only slight modifications. If he chose to, he could come back to this very spot and stare at the sky again. How those robbed of their freedom must despise not being able to do the same. Asher started pacing, running both hands through his hair as he forced himself to think.

'Asher, do you require an apothecary?' Duana enquired with concern.

He looked at her, as if seeing her for the first time. 'No, I need a kick up the backside with a size twelve steel toe cap.'

'Why?'

'Because of assumptions.'

'Assumptions?'

'Yes. Those convenient little things that help us solve problems without hard evidence. Much beloved of dreamers and idiots. Put me down for the latter. I think we have underestimated our enemy, Duana. And I have done someone a great injustice. Someone who deserves better.'

'Is this someone of the female persuasion to whom you are attracted?'

Asher's instinct was to guffaw. But Duana could see through all of that and her question slid through his bluff shield like a knife. 'I…yes. Is it that obvious?'

'You have demonstrated many of the signs of distraction and

preoccupation common in those suffering a sense of loss and longing.'

'You make me sound like a lost dog.'

Duana raised an eyebrow. 'The comparison may be a valid one. And yet dogs are open in expressing their moods, whereas you are not making a lot of sense.'

'Idiots tend not to. Duana, I want you to go back to your office and await my call. Be ready with that rapid response team.'

'Why? Where are you going?'

'To Oxford. Time I tied up all those loose ends.'

———

MATT WAITED in his office for Kylah to return. It had taken him a little longer to recover from the lockdown, but then, as Kylah was always pointing out, being 90% human was bound to leave its mark. He'd spent the time sorting out the room after Roberta Miracle had rearranged his bookshelves. Shame about her. He really liked the girl. But locking yourself in the loo when a paying customer was waiting did not bode well for business. The thought of all that money—or the prospect of losing it—must have got to her. That was the thing. You could never tell with people. He'd had her down as capable and competent, albeit with a stubbornly individualistic streak. It would have been nice to have another human around who knew about the arts and books, too. Someone he could chat to about the weather or the price of eggs or what film she'd seen recently. He'd tried taking Kylah to the cinema, but wielding a lightsaber under the aegis of the Force could not compare with fighting the undead army of Xanaitigua the Processor (likes using whirring blades), which she'd been doing that very afternoon before trying to settle down for two hours in the posh seats at the Odeon.

However, Pippa, God bless her, had survived lockdown and come through with flying colours. She'd handled the Fitzgerald situation like a pro and though not quite having the spark that Bobby Miracle had, it was still a relief to have someone about the place besides Fae.

The door opened and Matt's significant other walked in. Five two, olive-skinned and with that deadly combination of dark, lustrous hair and blue-gold-flecked eyes, Kylah always made him catch his breath.

'I brought Pippa along with me for the formalities,' she said.

The girl in question breezed in behind Kylah, sent an exaggeratedly excited rictus smile in Matt's direction and waved. 'Hi.'

'Hi Pippa. Right, got the contract ready here,' he said, pulling out a folder and laying it on the table. 'You've already had a copy, I think. So unless there's anything in particular you wanted to ask us, it's simply a matter of signing. That is, if you still want the job?'

'Of course I want the job,' Pippa gushed, her smile a hot coal on a cold winter's night.

She took the pen Matt held out and signed.

'Okay,' Kylah said when it was done. 'Provisional contract with non-disclosure clause signed, subject to the usual employment checks of course.' She beamed. 'I suppose there's nothing left to do but to give you the official tour.'

Pippa frowned. 'What you mean, the official tour?'

'There are parts of this building you need to know about, now you're an actual employee.'

Matt saw her suspicious smile and explained, 'Occasionally we might need you to do the odd thing…and by that I mean very odd thing. It might seem a little strange so it's only fair that we show you the other side of our operation.'

'Ooh. Very mysterious.' Pippa giggled.

Matt smiled. He and Kylah had discussed this at length. They both agreed on needing some help running the office and while Kylah had been keen to employ someone from the Fae side of things, Matt had argued that, since most of their legitimate customers were human, it would be best not to frighten them off within the first five minutes. Reluctantly, Kylah had agreed with the casting vote coming from her uncle, whom Matt bribed with a packet of HobNobs.

Even so, Hipposync was a garrison for the DOF and it would be only a matter of time before Pippa was exposed to its workings. She needed to be primed. And the first thing would be to show her the hidden library and its access. It was no accident Hipposync was located in Oxford. All that learning and scholarship made for an invaluable resource. But it was a two-way street. And so Mr Porter had come up with the idea of the hidden library; a place where the esoteric texts Hipposync stored were made available to a select few human scholars who could access the books without knocking on the front door.

They showed Pippa the four exits, front door, filing room skylight with telescopic ladder in case of fire, the tunnel under the canal which emerged forty feet up Doublet Road through a manhole, and finally the blue room.

'So this is for people who want to access the library discreetly,' Matt explained before adding, 'amongst other things.'

'Why would they want to do that? Discreetly I mean?'

'Quite often the kind of people who want to pore over late mediaeval texts tend to keep odd hours. This room isn't subject to the usual safeguards. Anyone using this entrance out of hours is directed to the library and nowhere else. So that alarms aren't triggered when they decide to look up recruitment techniques for the third crusade as written by Giraldus Cambrensis at two o'clock in the morning.'

'Why two o'clock?'

'This is Oxford we're talking about, remember.'

'How many people have access?' Pippa asked.

'No more than twenty or so,' Matt said. 'Select few. Highly vetted, you know.'

'And they come in through this door?' Pippa walked forward into the room and stood in front of a door in the far wall. 'Bit chilly in here, isn't it?'

Matt and Kylah followed. 'Yes. Catches the wind, does this corner of the building.'

Pippa studied the door in the wall. 'I'm trying to visualise where this door is from the outside,' she said.

Matt chuckled. 'You'll hardly notice it. In fact you might walk around the building half a dozen times and not even see it. Well disguised.'

Pippa beamed. 'I like secrets,' she said, and stepped past them back towards the door to the corridor before turning to face the room. 'So, let me get this straight: they come in through that door from the outside. Do they have a key?'

'No, there's a biometric keypad. All they have to do is remember to bring their eyes and a thumbprint.'

'And then they walk straight through into the building and through the door behind me. That's never locked, I assume?'

'No,' Kylah said.

'No,' said Pippa, still smiling brightly. 'I don't suppose you'd want to. I mean, who'd want to be trapped in here? In this room with its *special status*.'

Matt frowned. She'd delivered 'special status' with exceptionally heavy emphasis. Of course the room did have special status, even if it was not in the way he'd explained it. Still, it was extremely perspicacious of bright-eyed Pippa to have worked that out.

'No,' he agreed. 'You don't want to be locked in here…Even worse than being locked in the loo.' His quip brought a tinkling laugh from Pippa and a questioning frown from Kylah.

Pippa's phone chirped a message tone. She glanced down and back up at Matt with a grin. A contented grin of the sort one got after finally finishing decorating a bedroom, or completing an essay, or when your favourite kitten video finally gets over two million hits.

'Right,' Kylah said, 'We'd better show you the library itself—
'

There was a loud click as the inner door locked. The temperature in the room fell by ten degrees in five seconds.

'You have no idea how long I've been waiting for this moment,' Pippa said. Her chin dropped and she peered at Kylah with eyes as sunny as a January day in Edinburgh.

Matt looked at Kylah and saw her eyes harden. His glance rebounded towards Pippa, who'd reached up to the top of the doorframe and pulled down a small triangular-shaped piece of dull glass. Kylah lunged towards her but before she'd made six inches, the bauble flared a brilliant scarlet and Kylah and Matt were thrown against the wall, the air hissing out of their lungs from the impact. Kylah struggled to free her arms from whatever invisible force was pinning them. Matt's were already pinioned.

Faint wavy tendrils of light began emanating from the bauble in Pippa's hands and radiating towards the DOF agents' wrists and legs. One tendril with a snake's head slithered forward and bit into the flesh of Matt's arm. His head lolled forward in unconsciousness.

'He can't think when he's asleep,' said Pippa with a delicious smile, before she started to shudder. Fire danced around her hair and through it the real shape of the thing possessing her shone. A hunched shape with a shaved head that glistened, except for a dark scar that bore the mark of Gazorch the Pantocrator.

The voice that now emerged was nothing like the tinkling tones of Pippa Elmsworthy. This one was male and dripping with hatred. 'Many years pass, Kylah Porter. Memories might fade, yet the seed of vengeance grows into a strong tree that will not bend in the wind. I have not bent. My master remains resolute in his prison of emptiness. And here I am as his emissary to wreak pain and misery on this world that dared defy us. What sweeter death will open the damn of chaos than yours? The heroine crushed. The rightful master reinstated. And all because of a pretty face.' Pippa stepped forward and let the pulsing bauble go so that it floated in the very centre of the room. 'And so convenient of you to provide the ideal environment to allow me to carry out my task. You two and I finally alone in the one room in this carefully guarded building where access to all things good and bad is allowed. And yes, I triggered the lockdown so that I could secrete the convocant here where it would elicit no further alarm. I'm sure He,' she fell to her knees, head bowed, arms upstretched in supplication, 'will be grateful.'

'You'll never breach the covenant!' cried Kylah.

What had once been Pippa smiled. It was not a pleasant thing to see. 'Won't I? Tell me, Kylah Porter, do you like kitten videos?' She began to hum the invocation.

CHAPTER FORTY-FOUR

Bobby rang the doorbell for Hipposync Enterprises. Rang it again and then slapped the wood hard.

'Come on, come on,' she whispered through gritted teeth. She hoped Miss WT hadn't gone to the loo. She was looking at a ten-minute walk if that was the case. She slapped at the door once more.

'All right,' warbled a shaky voice from inside. 'I hear you.'

Bobby shifted her weight from one foot to the other impatiently while several bolts were pulled back and a latch lifted. Miss WT stared out from behind the security chain.

'May I help you?'

'Yes. You may. Miss WT, it's me. Bobby.'

'Bobby?'

'Please, can we drop the charade? The memory thing didn't work. You must let me in. I have to speak to Kylah.'

'I am sorry, Miss Porter is busy. Perhaps if I could take your number?'

An iota of doubt flashed across Bobby's mind. Was she going mad? Was she haranguing this poor old lady because she'd hallucinated a past existence over a cup of coffee in Has Beans? No, of course it was true. All of it.

'This is a genuine emergency. Please, we both know I was here just a few minutes ago.'

'If I could have your name?'

'Please. I'm begging you. This is urgent. I have to speak to her.'

'I'm afraid we're closed at the moment. Staff training. If I could add your—'

'What does it take for a Sith Fand to bloody LISTEN?'

Miss WT's wobbly face stopped wobbling. Something dark flickered behind her rheumy eyes.

'It's about Pippa and the lockdown and—'

With sudden swiftness Miss WT pulled back two security bolts and opened the door. Bobby stepped over the threshold, acknowledging the fact that it was the first time she'd come through this door properly for some time. Bobby had taken one step down the corridor before she felt a restraining hand on her arm.

'Wait,' said a voice.

Bobby swung around. Miss WT was gone. In her place stood a tall uniformed figure with a long, smooth face and a swept back forehead and startlingly green eyes. One hand was covered by a strange metallic gauntlet and it was pointing at Bobby's chest.

'Who the hell are—'

'Tilfeth, Special Elf Service.'

'Where's Miss WT?'

'She's still here,' in Miss WT's warbly voice.

'Wow,' Bobby said.

'You carrying iron?'

'Iron? No…'

Tilfeth step forward and quickly scanned Bobby using a kind of wooden spoon with a glassy, bulbous, egg-shaped end. Satisfied, she touched a gemstone at her uniform collar and spoke in a language Bobby had never heard before, paused, and waited for a reply.

None came.

Bobby frowned. Tilfeth spoke again into the stone and once again, stood in complete silence for several long seconds.

'There's no reply from Captain Porter, or Mr Danmor.'

Bobby's intestines did a swoop. 'Are they here?'

'Yes.'

'Is that usual? That they don't reply?'

Tilfeth shrugged.

'Is Pippa here?'

Tilfeth's incredible eyes narrowed. 'Yes.'

'Can you call her, too?'

'No. She does not have communication status.'

'Find out where she is,' Bobby said urgently.

Tilfeth studied her. 'Are you angry about what happened? Is this why you have come back? Are you blaming Pippa for your dismissal?'

'No!' Bobby said through gritted teeth. 'It has nothing to do with that. Look, let's find her.' Bobby took another step down the corridor.

Tilfeth stiffened. She raised the gauntlet. Sparks crackled around the fingertips. 'Walk into reception and keep your hands up.'

Bobby shook her head. 'Oh, for goodness sake, would you just listen? You've got this all wrong.'

'Have I? It is clear you are not what you seem to be. You shouldn't have any memory of this place. Why is that, Ms Miracle? What are you really?'

'She's a witch.'

The disembodied voice came from the corridor they'd just left. Tilfeth swivelled, gauntlet up, fingers crackling and pointing at the doorway as a figure stepped into it.

'Asher?' said Tilfeth, letting her hand drop.

Bobby frowned hard. 'Did you say—'

'I did,' Asher said. 'And I think I owe you an apology.'

'Agreed,' Bobby said. That was a hug-worthy statement if ever she'd heard one, but she resisted. There were things to do. 'And I'm *really* looking forward to hearing it. But it'll have to wait. Tilfeth, where is Kylah?'

Tilfeth shook her head and tried again with the gemstone. There was still no reply. 'She must be in the blue room,' Tilfeth explained. 'It's a comms black spot.'

'It's more than that,' Asher said grimly. 'It's closed to access from outside. I could not get in with my Aperio from New Thameswick.'

'Then we need to get there quickly,' Bobby said.

'Why?' Tilfeth asked, still wary.

'I just have a very bad feeling.'

Asher turned to Tilfeth. 'Get to BOD. And find Professor Llewyn. Tell her to mobilise the raptor squad immediately.'

Tilfeth threw a suspicious glance towards Bobby. 'But—'

Asher cut her off. 'I trust her. Do it.'

Bobby made for the corridor and half turned in time to see the SES officer hurrying towards a globelike structure on the desk into which she thrust her hand. It glowed into life instantly. Bobby didn't hear the message because Asher had overtaken her and was running down the corridor. She followed suit. They looked in on Pippa. The office was empty.

'We need to hurry,' Bobby said.

Asher put his hand out and held her back. 'Wait. I have done you a great disservice by ignoring you in the past. Do me the courtesy now of telling me why you have gone so pale on finding Miss Elmsworthy not here?'

'Because I've found Paula Evans.'

'The missing woman?' Asher asked.

'Yes. Only she isn't missing. She's been here all the time.'

Asher stared back at her in bafflement.

On Pippa's desk, her PC's screensaver kept rotating images of fluffy kittens. Cuteness personified.

'Asher, why do you think all the photographs in the Evans' house were destroyed?'

'Poltergeists can be very destructive—'

Bobby nodded. 'I know, I read the report too. But that didn't happen at the Cuthbertson place or the Loosemores'. So was it random madness at the Evans' or something else altogether?'

'Something else?'

'Have you seen an image of Marie Evans?'

Asher shook his head.

'Exactly. All destroyed. And so were the ones of her daughter, Paula. But then there is always social media.' She pulled out her mobile and showed him the screen. 'These are screenshots from Paula Evans' Facebook pages. There she is, tagged by all her pals from a holiday in Tenerife last year.'

Asher stared at the images of an attractive woman in a bikini seated at a beach café and smiling back at the camera.

Bobby took his silence as shock. 'She's even kept the first letters of her real name. P and E. Paula Evans aka the delectable Pippa Elmsworthy.'

There was no denying it, though Asher seemed set to try. 'But—'

'Premeditated malign haunting,' Bobby went on. 'Tell me if I've got that wrong, but it's what murdering the Bewildered was all about, wasn't it? Parasitism. All done to allow whatever came across piggybacking on a Bewildered soul a chance to jump across into the body of a haunted human.'

Asher was staring at Bobby but he didn't stop her.

'Mrs Evans' poor sister disappeared from a care home and became one of the Bewildered. But what if it wasn't only Mrs Evans' twin that came back when she died? What if something else came with her? Something malevolent that knew exactly what it was doing. It tries to possess Marie Evans but she is weak and infirm and it literally scares her to death. But Paula Evans is there too. She is young and maybe she doesn't scare easily. Maybe instead of frightening her to death, whatever it is succeeds in possessing *her*. And she/it destroys all the photos in the house so as to buy some time, knowing that the DOF might investigate. The possessed Paula Evans mysteriously disappears, only to become Pippa Elmsworthy, all skirts and heels and limpid pools and IT literate.'

'But Matt and Kylah would have obtained photos—'

'Eventually, possibly. But their concern was more with the dead, the Munchers. Paula Evans missing was a police matter, and they dismissed it.'

'Okay, but they'd have screened Elmsworthy for employment—'

Bobby cut across him again. 'Really? CRB checks, references...That's an awful lot of work for what's effectively an extended on-the-job interview. Once the job is offered, fair enough, but all you'd want for an internship is a nice CV.' Bobby shook her head. 'I'm sure there is, or was, a Pippa Elmsworthy too, but I dread to think what's happened to her. This thing that possessed Paula Evans has had time to plan. It all adds up. Think about it. Pippa wasn't here when the Search and Destroy squad ran the sweep. She was conveniently in the hospital. She's been playing us like a hooked fish. And who do you think locked me in the loo so she could complete the *Frankenstein* deal? I'm telling you, this one is a real bitch.'

Asher stared into the distance, frowning as if trying to make sense of Bobby's words. 'But if this is true, it implies significant intelligence and guile. These are not virtues I would associate with the Widicombs.'

Bobby was thinking furiously. 'When I was at Cuthbertson's I was attacked by something called a Sambolith. Could the Widicombs have set that on me?'

Asher threw her an astonished look. 'How do you know it was a Sambolith?'

'My gran told me.'

Asher shook his head slowly. 'You grandmother *told* you?'

'Long story and no time now. Could the Widicombs have controlled the Sambolith?'

'No. It would take someone or something far more powerful and skilled in dark wonderworking to command a Sambolith.'

'More powerful than Stohb? Isn't he the one who was supposed to have crossed?'

'Infinitely more powerful. Stohb was just a foot soldier.'

'So if it wasn't the Widicombs who followed me to Cuthbertson's and commanded a Sambolith, then who—'

'Exactly,' said Asher, his eyes glittering. 'Who indeed, or rather what indeed? Perhaps we've got this all wrong. Made assumptions when we should have looked a lot harder. What if the Widicombs, like us, have been led up a long and winding garden path with something very unpleasant waiting in the woodshed at the end of it?'

'I'm not following,' Bobby said.

The words from Asher emerged viscid and dark, like sludge from a bucket. 'The Widicombs, Stohb included, were all as thick as frog custard. How would they even begin to control a Sambolith, let alone go about trying to hitchhike a lift on the back of a dead Bewildered? Someone, or something, must have instructed them. And that someone might have been very selective with the truth. We know that dead Bewildered were particularly prone to parasitic possession and that the Widicombs were trying to make use of that fact. But what if what they were really doing was marking those Bewildered souls to make it easier for something else to find them as they passed?'

'You mean…'

'I mean that something might have used the Widicombs as a beacon. I bet that in all those arcane incantations Crouch and I witnessed in the caves there was something that would highlight their passage across the void. Make it easier for whatever it was waiting there to spot them. And once it did, it evicted the Widicomb and piggybacked itself on to the Bewildered soul, ravenous for a live victim to possess.'

Bobby frowned. 'But I thought you said Stohb confirmed his success to the others?'

Asher tried to recall the overheard conversation in the Widicombs' underground charnel house. 'They found a message. 'The zealot has landed'…'

Assumptions. More dangerous than sweating TNT.

He looked up at Bobby and growled. 'Gods, I've been an idiot.'

Bobby swallowed hard. 'But it still doesn't explain why Pippa Elmsworthy, or Paula Evans or whoever or whatever she is, is here, of all places. What's the point? What is it trying to achieve?'

'Revenge would do.' Asher suggested. 'Perhaps Gazorch has sent an assassin with Kylah as the obvious target. She was decorated for banishing it in 2016.'

Bobby's brows furrowed. An idea was taking shape and it was a shape she did not care for in the slightest. 'What if it's more than that…' Her voice oozed out in a half whisper laden with dread. 'What if this… *thing*…is going for gold and using Hipposync as its base? Gazorch would like that, wouldn't he? Manifesting here of all places. Real salt in the wound stuff.'

Asher was shaking his head. 'There are complex covenants surrounding Gazorch's banishment. He requires an army of avowed followers before he has any prospect—'

Her look stopped him mid-sentence. A thought, as cold as a crypt, uncoiled in her brain. 'How many followers?'

'A sequilltan.'

'In English?'

'Two million. It'll never happen. It's imposs—' Asher stopped when he saw Bobby's pained expression and the way she lunged towards Pippa's computer.

'HBK_23,' she whispered, frantically agitating the mouse to wake up the screen. It flashed to life and she clicked on Pippa's browser history and then on the topmost address. 'HBK_23. Does that mean anything to you?'

'HBK_23? HBK…' Asher's eyes widened. 'Habihemhock is the name of the summoner demon. The avowed follower of Gazorch the Pantocrator, banished to the Abaddonian plane. But the 16…'

'Is now, this year. 2016.'

The computer screen filled with a YouTube page, a slowly circling wheel of light indicating that the *Kitten Plays 'Three Blind Mice'* video was loading. But Bobby wasn't interested in that. She had eyes only for the number under the grey thumbs up sign. It read: 2,001,056.

'No, oh no!'

'What?' demanded Asher.

Bobby started running. All she'd say to Asher over her shoulder, was, 'Please, tell me you don't watch kitten videos.'

CHAPTER FORTY-FIVE

Bobby could tell something was badly wrong as soon as they reached the top of the stairs and the acrid stench of brimstone caught in her throat. Halfway down, where the hidden stairs turned off, the walls were bubbling. At the bottom, mist roiled around her feet and nauseating red and yellow lights glimmered luridly beneath the door to the room itself. It looked like some kind of wild disco, only here, the pulsing lights made her feel quite sick.

'Keep your eyes averted,' Asher ordered. 'The summoning has already commenced. I suspect that the room beyond the door no longer resembles the one you are familiar with. It will have been joined with somewhere else. A hopeless place where ignorance is king, its denizens eat despair and darkness rules.'

'I always wanted to go to North Korea,' Bobby said. But she dragged her eyes away and almost immediately felt better. 'What do we do?' she asked.

'We await reinforcements.'

From inside the room, they heard a scream. Bobby looked at Asher. 'Really?'

'We have no choice. I am not trained for this and neither are you.'

'But there are people in there.'

'If we enter, it will be a worthless sacrifice.'

Something roared behind the blue door.

'That's the worst karaoke I've ever heard,' Bobby said.

The roar came again.

'That noise comes from the denizens of Abaddon,' Asher said with a shudder.

'I must have missed them. Were they post punk?'

'This is no time for frivolity.'

He was right, it wasn't, and the roar did not sound human. Nothing in the slightest bit funny about that roar. But then laughing in the face of adversity was supposed to be a coping mechanism, wasn't it? Though, come to think of it, she'd not seen one zebra get the giggles when a cheetah was clawing at its haunches.

The next sound, a howling, keening ululation, set her teeth on edge and was as wrong as three plus three equals seven. Bobby wondered if this is what her grandmother had faced that night she'd gone to help a friend. Something so alien and horrifying that even a giant bag of popcorn with extra butter wouldn't keep you in your seat. Common sense was screaming at every nerve in her body to turn and run and hope the thing would pick someone else to tear apart. Bobby wondered if Lucille felt as frightened that night in 2012. The shimmering figure on the beach rose up in her memory. Of course she had. She'd probably heard the exact same unearthly noise. Only a deaf amoeba would not have been frightened. But that was not the point. With a searing pang of insight, Bobby realised that Lucille had known she could not win, not in the sense of total victory. Not against this sort of enemy. But she'd faced it regardless.

That thought brought with it a sudden idea. 'Maybe we're not trained, but I know someone who is,' Bobby said in a half whisper, her eyes shining. 'You can speak to the dead, right?'

'Yes.'

'Think you could give my gran a ring?'

She'd expected scorn, or ridicule, or out and out laughter. Instead, she got shock and wide-eyed admiration.

'But isn't she a witch?' Asher replied and the way his face darkened told Bobby that he already knew the answer.

Bobby nodded and added, 'She prefers the term 'cunning woman'.'

'It is not something I have ever tried before,' he admitted. 'Wit—cunning women that have passed do not appreciate being disturbed.'

'Are they as crotchety in death as they are in life?'

'Ten times worse, or so it is rumoured.'

'Rumoured? Don't you know?'

'No one who has attempted it has been able to accurately report. It is difficult to speak when you have the head of a goat and the tongue of an adder.'

'Ah. Then forget it, as I say, it was just a thought.'

Asher's eyes narrowed. 'And yet, a field will not be ploughed by merely turning it over in one's mind.'

'Asher...I wouldn't want anything to—'

Asher gave her a funny little smile and put his finger to her lips to quieten her. 'I believe I still owe you a cup of coffee,' he said, stepped back and then touched the tips of his middle and index finger against his own forehead.

CHAPTER FORTY-SIX

IMAGINE STANDING on top of a building with your eyes shut and letting yourself fall backwards into the void. It takes a lot of confidence in knowing there's someone there to catch you. If you had a name, it helped. If you had an image of the dead person in your head, that helped, too. Asher thought of the statue in Calumnity Park and so the trip was a short one, though it was to a place he'd never thought he'd visit. Unlike ordinary folk (who ended up occupying a location on the spectral plane near where their death took place), or warlocks (who thought that nirvana consisted of a laboratory full of bubbling flasks, odd smells, and things that went bang), witches, being witches, had opted for a five-star resort in the middle of a tropical ocean, complete with spa facilities, infinity pools, twenty-four-hour room service from young men dressed in skimpy shorts and not much else, running around carrying drinks with little umbrellas in them. There was nothing Chippendale about the furniture, but the same could not be said about the young men. And though wood did feature significantly in their roles, it was nothing remotely furniture-related.

Asher, or at least Asher's astral projection, appeared at the reception desk and rang the bell. The guardian spirit-witch that oversaw this little exclusive corner of Neverland appeared, dressed in a sarong and, by the way she was holding her fingers spread and angled forward like pretend paws, had obviously just had her nails done. She looked Asher up and down. Disdain didn't even come close to describing her expression.

'Let us hope the reason for your visit gives me good cause to refrain from turning you into a worm.'

'I'm here to see Lucille Miracle.'

The spirit-witch's eyes narrowed. 'What meaningless follies in the tides of men would merit disturbing a heroine?' Blue sparks crackled over the tips of her newly painted fingernails. A large black cat perched atop a many-armed statue hissed.

'I'm here on behalf of her granddaughter. I am here at her bidding.'

The witch eyed him suspiciously. 'If it transpires you bear false witness…that you are one of those hacks from the *Daily Inquisitor*—'

'Roberta Miracle sent me.'

The spirit-witch stared at him for a long minute. Asher knew she was reading him. Finally she nodded and pointed towards a pale ash door with brushed metal handles. 'Through that door,' she smiled. 'Be careful, she hasn't eaten yet.'

The door swung open as Asher walked towards it. Lucille Miracle wore flowing robes, her face unlined but unsmiling as she floated across a courtyard to meet him.

Looks exactly like the statue, mused Asher.

'To what do I owe the pleasure of meetin' a necreddo, Mr Asher?'

'No pleasure, I'm afraid,' Asher said and quickly explained. Though it wasn't really possible for Lucille's spectral presence to become any paler, Asher noted tightness around the ethereal mouth.

'Him again,' Lucille said in a way that made Asher very glad he'd made the guest list.

'Roberta was rather hoping—'

'I'll need a ride,' said Lucille.

'It will not be the first time I've assumed that role this month, but it will be the first time I have hosted a witch.'

'Don't worry, I don't bite. And if I did, you wouldn't live to remember it.'

There was no time to come up with a suitable retort. Asher saw Lucille Miracle reach out a hand and touch his face as she stepped forward. A moment later, he'd been crammed into a tiny corner of a room in his mind under a huge and heavy, but not unpleasant, blanket. He could struggle to get out or, on the other hand, he could just lie there until someone else took the blanket off. He could hear voices through the blanket, but they were muffled and far away. But he knew the voices were very angry, so maybe it wouldn't be such a bad idea to stay put for a few moments longer.

———

Asher's eyes snapped open, but the voice that emerged when he spoke wasn't Asher's. It was a voice Bobby'd heard many times as a girl and once, very recently, on a desert island. And as soon as she heard it she felt a hundred times better.

'Well, Roberta. You are in a tizz, isn't you?'

'Gran?' Roberta said, gasping and choking back a tear and trying to reconcile Asher's very male visage with the voice that emerged that was very much her grandmother's. 'Is it you?'

'Yes.'

'Please don't tell me you're going to give me the philosophical pep talk combined with an abstract hint and then disappear again. I don't think I could stand it.'

'No, Roberta. I'm not goin' to do that. But you do know what's behind this door, don't you?'

'Is it the thing that you had to face?'

'Habihemhock. I'm not scared to say his name but facin' him once in any lifetime was more than enough.'

'But you beat him, Gran?'

'No, I stoppered him. Not the same thing.'

Bobby nodded. She didn't understand it all, but it was obvious what needed to be done. *Ah well*, she thought. It might have been fun to have another coffee with Asher. Might even have been interesting to learn a bit more about this witching thing. But faced with an advantageous view of the machine gun nest and the prospect of a hundred or more of your mates dying in a hail of bullets unless you did something, your choices are limited. You can either run and bury your head in a foxhole, or have a go and silently thank the sergeant who ordered you to take that extra grenade from the ammunitions box 'just in case'.

Bobby hated foxholes.

She stepped forward and put her fingers into Asher's waistcoat pocket.

'What are you doin', Roberta?' Gran said.

'Looking for his Aperio. He keeps it in here somewhere. Ah yes, here it is.' She looked into Asher's eyes and saw her grandmother's dancing behind the pupils. 'Is it painful, that's all I want to know?'

The eyes that looked back at her burned with an unnamed emotion. At first she thought it was sorrow, but the tone of Gran's voice said something different.

'You won't get in with that,' Gran said.

'Not through this door, I won't. Come on, I need the loo.' Bobby led the way to the basement toilet and the door Pippa had jammed shut. 'The good news is that I have been in the blue room before. So all I have to do is remember what it looks like, right?'

Asher wasn't smiling. And Bobby knew her grandmother wasn't either. The words that emerged from Asher's mouth in Lucille's voice were fierce and condemning.

'So you're goin' to open the door and face this thing and hope it'll possess you so you can spend the rest of your life fightin' the bugger. So that you can be pitied and injected with drugs and locked away because they'll think you're insane, is that right?'

Bobby shivered and nodded.

Long seconds of silence ticked away and Bobby thought she might wilt in the heat of an unflinching Asher/Gran gaze.

'That's my girl,' said her grandmother.

Bobby frowned. It felt like she'd swallowed a satsuma. 'I don't feel brave or courageous, though. Is it okay to be frightened?'

Asher nodded and Lucille Miracle said, 'Yes, it is.' He stepped forward and pulled her to him in a hug. It felt wrong, but at the same time, she caught a whiff of soap and if she shut her eyes she could easily imagine that it was her grandmother holding her, dressed in her warm candlewick dressing gown all those years ago. 'Did I ever tell you how proud I was of you? How I knew, from when you were a baby, that you were special? Did I tell you how I bit my tongue when my silly son tried to stamp on it all and of how I couldn't wait until you were fourteen and you could do the ceremony legally?'

'Ceremony?' Bobby whispered into Asher's shoulder. She spoke with a trembling lip that tasted of salty tears.

'Yes. Oh, there's a lot of pompous gobbledygook and bits of Latin, and you can dance naked around a flame if you're feelin' frisky and have the photo framed in sycamore, but it isn't compulsory. The best bits for me were the canapés and champagne. People think that all those bits of dagger and bone and the pointy hat are important, but they're not. They're only symbols. Truth is, you don't learn all that much at the Academy. The real stuff—the cunnin'—gets handed down. That's the meat of the thing. Sort of on the job trainin'. Knowin' when to stare someone down, and when to make them think they're winnin' when really they've already lost, and, most important of all, when to run like buggery. And I am so sorry I didn't get to give you all of that, though I think you got more than a bit of it, judgin' by the way you dress.'

Bobby wanted to pull away and ask a question but Lucille Miracle didn't stop. 'But what it's really about is *helpin'*. Especially those who can't help themselves. And knowin' what to do and stayin' calm when everyone else is reachin' for the velvety toilet paper or the sick bag. And yes, it is useful to know how to cure the odd sick cow and give the stroppy bloke next door a rash for a fortnight because he's been nasty to your dog. But the real power is in knowin' what you are. Bein' able to think clearly in the face of the worst thing in this world, or any other world. Actin' just like you're doin' now when everyone else wants to run for the hills.'

'But I don't know what to do,' Bobby whispered.

'You sent Asher to fetch me, didn't you? Who else would have done that?'

'Yes, but—'

'And there's nothin' woolly about what we're going to do next, Roberta. Habihemhock is a match for me. I can't defeat him. And neither can you. But he's an arrogant sod. And Gazorch is a thousand times worse. He thinks he can do whatever he likes to people. Make them hide from the dark and cower at eclipses and give up perfectly healthy young girls and babies just because he wants them to. And though this Habihemhock isn't that bad, he's bad enough. Thinks he's invincible. That's why he thought he could crush me. But there are two of us now.' Asher grinned.

'I'm really scared, Gran. Once you go, I…'

'Who said I was goin' anywhere? But I need your permission.'

'Permission to do what?'

'To help. It's a bit of an intrusion, but it'll just be for a while.'

'Gran, you know I'll do whatever you ask.'

Asher pulled back and smiled. Once again, Bobby felt a rush of conflicting emotions. 'The necklace,' Gran said.

Bobby's hand went to her throat.

'No need to take it off. Hold it so that your fingers are on the knives. Pretend it's a doll's house and you're layin' the table.'

Bobby did as asked. She put up both hands, felt for and held the tiny athame and bolline knives.

'Know that this is exactly what you must do inside the blue room. Ignore everything you see. Let me curse the demon and you hold onto the necklace like this. Alright?'

'Yes, but I don't understand? What do you mean, permission?'

'Will you let me in, Roberta?' Gran asked.

'Let you in? Oh, I mean, of course I'll let you in, if that's—'

It was instantaneous and a bit like scooting up to share a seat on a bus, except this seat was the inside of Bobby's head. Gran was there and it was like wearing a comforting warm throw and having a lit torch of blazing anger fizzing away between your eyes at exactly the same time.

'Ready to pull that pin?' Bobby heard her say. She looked at Asher's lips, but they weren't moving. He'd become an empty vessel.

'Yes,' Bobby thought, and saw/felt/heard Gran nod. Bobby put the Aperio on the hinge side of the toilet door, twisted and pushed it open.

———

ASHER CAME BACK to himself in time to see the toilet door swing shut. He caught a glimpse of the back end of Roberta's leg wearing her grandmother's shoe.

'No!' he yelled and grabbed for the edge of the door, but it was too late. It slammed shut before he could reach it. Cursing, he pressed the gemstone on his lapel and shouted, 'You'd better tell me there's a squad of demon catchers on the way?'

'ETA two minutes,' said Tilfeth.

Turning, Asher ran back up the steps. 'Make it one. The Miracles have gone in.'

CHAPTER FORTY-SEVEN

IT WASN'T blue in the blue room anymore. Sickly red light pulsed on the walls lit by the rotating shimmering convocant in the centre of the room. Steam hissed from cracks in the floor that radiated out from a central oval chasm. Of course, it wasn't the blue room at all now. It was some subterranean hellhole with craggy stone walls. Asher would have recognised it instantly, but it was all new to Bobby. Matt and Kylah hung, suspended by chains hammered into the walls, and they were not alone. They were amongst a collection of dozens of unfortunate beings, many of whom, judging from their expressions, had already lost the battle against hope in this desperate place.

From the gaping maw in the centre of the floor yellow light glowed and wisps of bilious green steam billowed. Next to it, hunched over a collection of elaborately drawn symbols, was Habihemhock, the summoner demon. The sense of wrongness Bobby felt on seeing him made her skin crawl. But the misshapen form moaned incantations and for a moment did not look up. That gave her a second to decide whether to stay or run screaming into the darkness—but she felt Gran nudge her and Bobby Miracle stood her ground. Her brain tried to assimilate the information her eyes were giving her regarding the shape of the summoner demon but it would not compute. Then she saw the discarded body of a woman slumped on the floor. The blonde hair and the high heels told her that it had once belonged to Pippa Elmsworthy, or rather, Paula Evans. It was at that point the demon turned, looked at her, and screamed.

Bobby recoiled and would have screamed herself had she not felt her grandmother's resolve tighten inside her.

Don't let this piece of filth frighten you. Abomination is too good a word for him. And don't forget we know his name. Habihemhock, the summoner.

It possessed no permanent shape. Instead it shifted constantly, a face that was sometimes a black hole, sometimes that of a fish or a bird or a spider or something that had no place on this earth. The air appeared to distort about it as if recoiling from its touch. Habihemhock hissed at her but almost immediately, Bobby began chanting. She had no idea what she was saying because the words were her grandmother's. But one thing was certain. The demon did not like what he was hearing one little bit.

'Ewchallanofanhyncythraulewchallanorfanhyncythraulewchallanorfanhyncythraulewchallanorfanhyncythraulewchallanorfanhyncythraul—'

'I smell MIRACLE.' A banshee screech echoed around the cavern. Bobby saw Kylah look across at her and read despair and hope and a kind of pity in her expression. The summoner demon's breath washed over her. It reeked of decay and the coldest, darkest places under the earth, but still her grandmother kept up the chant.

'—Ewchallanorfanhyncythraulewchallanorfanhyncyth-raul—'

Habihemhock reared up. Instantly twice as tall as Bobby, now a wraithlike figure with no face under a shroud. It bellowed with force enough to rattle a cavern roof higher than light from the guttering yellow candles could reach.

'—Ewchallanorfanhyncythraul—'

Bobby was aware that the thing had started shaking, a blur of movement vibrating quickly and changing with each new wave of motion, so quickly that no discernible shape was evident anymore. She could only stare with a mixture of revulsion and fascination. She was still staring when it flew at her. In an instant her head was filled with a jarring, jagged garble of voices and thoughts that hurled despicable noises and foul images at her.

She felt her knees give way as she gasped, her mind tumbling through the wild chaos the demon pummelled her with as he possessed her consciousness and dared her to defy. She wanted nothing more than to throw herself into the hole in the middle of the cavern. To burn in the oil of the torches. To grasp a blade and thrust it into her own heart.

A fragment of cogent thought appeared like a blown tissue in a gust and Bobby grabbed onto it before it was whisked away by the hurricane of madness whirling through her head. Was this how it had been for her grandmother? Was this what she'd been made to endure for all that time?

Bobby grabbed at her hair. She yanked, squealing from the pain, letting it penetrate through, holding onto the reality of it for another sliver of a moment.

'The necklace,' she heard her grandmother's voice from a long way away. 'The necklace.'

But then she was caught again, her mind a bobbing raft in the turbulent whitewater of some vicious rapids, turned and spun around and unable to think or speak or listen.

'Necklace,' came her grandmother's voice, clear and brittle through the roaring noise.

Bobby knew she was screaming from the pressure in her throat. In the cacophony inside her head she couldn't hear anything of her own voice. But somehow knowing she was screaming helped.

With fumbling fingers, Bobby felt for the necklace and searched for the tiny knives. She squeezed and felt the skin of both index fingers prick and suddenly the roaring rapids in her head became a slick, fast-flowing river. Still too fast to steer with any accuracy but no longer threatening to tip her over into the drowning water.

'You have to help me, Bobby,' implored Lucille. 'You have to help me put this monster down. Think. Think about something. Distract yourself. It will distract him. Think.'

It felt like trying to make yourself heard across a crowded street in a howling gale. Images, horrifying at first, flew past her open eyes as Bobby grappled for control. Think? Think of what? All things? Gran? Yes, Gran. Gran on the desert island. The turtle. Cuthbert and the horror behind the wardrobe, no not that! Has Beans, coffee, Asher, Asher in a coffee shop in Indonesia, Asher with fringing eyelashes darker and longer than hers, Asher with his silly, annoying, loveable over-politeness…

It stopped as suddenly as someone throwing a switch. Instead of the howling wild madness, Bobby could hear only a muted scream that seemed to be coming from a locked box in the corner of…where…her head?

'He's trapped for now,' Lucille said. 'Set the agents free. Quickly. Whatever you do, do it now, my girl.'

Moving was difficult. Every time she did it felt like the lid of the box was lifting a little. It felt that it might snap open. She gritted her teeth. Habihemhock was in the box. Would stay in the box. She got up and moved towards them, gingerly. It was like wading through treacle.

How. How do I free them?

'This is not real, Bobby.' Lucille's voice again. 'Make it what you want to make it.'

She looked up at the unconscious Matt. Iron bands around his wrists attached to spikes of iron driven into the stone. She could not break those. But if it wasn't real, if his bonds were made of string…

She put her hand up to the iron band with bloody fingertips. Though the metal didn't change, it suddenly felt like string. And, like string, she yanked at it and it gave. Once freed, Matt fell to the floor, like a dead weight. Next it was Kylah's turn and then Bobby was hauling them back towards the heavy iron door she'd come through, finding strength from somewhere she knew not where. She attached the Aperio, pushed through the staggering Kylah and yanked the unconscious Matt across, then turned back and dragged Paula Evans' inanimate body through as well.

The lid of the box started to open.

'Gran, what do I do with him? Can I keep him in my head?'

She heard her grandmother snort. 'Not to be recommended, Roberta. But I can't stay either. Once I leave, you'll be at his mercy. But I've got a better idea. Let me take him. We're old friends. He thought he'd escaped when I died and he doesn't seem very happy to see me, does he? There's a cesspit at our place. I'm sure the others won't mind. We'll share him out amongst us. A million cunnin' women should be enough to keep this little bugger quiet for a long time, so long as one of us remembers to think of him everyday and I'm sure we'll manage that. I'll put a note on the fridge.'

Bobby laughed. She felt her grandmother smile.

I'm so proud of you, Roberta.

Bobby saw an image form in her head. Azure sea, the lush vegetation of a tropical island, and young men in shorts carrying trays of drinks. Something roared from inside the box and instantly she heard a snapping in her head, like a ruptured elastic band. There followed a momentary stab of pain between her eyes as the roaring came again and she rode a whitewater flume full of horror and despair. But she knew this was Habihemhock flailing at having lost and that he was receding down into a deep, dark hole that smelled faintly, but unmistakably, of the Bewildered. Receding to be replaced by blackness as Bobby's mind, with her approval, finally gave in and sought solace in unconsciousness.

CHAPTER FORTY-EIGHT

IN THE DARKEST reaches of oblivion, something was screaming. At least it might have been a scream, or then again a howl of frustration. It had no physical form, the screamer; it was more an idea dreamt up by men and given credence, and therefore existence, by them. And just like knowing that the right thing to do would be to stand up on the bus and give your seat to the old lady with a Zimmer frame, the idea of Gazorch existed for men who did exactly that, but surreptitiously emptied the sticky dregs from their can of pop on the seat before they did so. Men with minds as broad as pinheads. There were lots of words to describe such men. Sheep, fanatics, zealots, gullible fools, Gazorchites, or, perhaps the most apposite: gits. In the great scheme of things, gits needed demons because without them there was nothing to hold a mirror up to. But to exist, demons needed believers. And over the years, there was no denying it; one or two of them had done really well in the popularity stakes. Yet it always seemed to end in tears and tantrums, once the mess left by the war had been cleaned up.

Gazorch the Pantocrator festered as it diminished, knowing its star was waning, but that it wouldn't go out altogether. It might twinkle low in the sky for many years until someone desperate enough bothered to look through a telescope and decide it was worth learning about rituals and mass murder and the false promise of the pleasures of the flesh, because their boring, mundane, narrow existence was proving to be hardly worth the entrance fee.

Knowing that, Gazorch tried, metaphysically, to cheer himself up. Momentum was a wonderful thing. A spark could set a city alight. A bacteria could wipe out half the world's population. Miracles did happen…

Those bloody Miracles.

Gazorch the Pantocrator howled again.

———

Nurse Williamson ripped off her plastic apron and peeled off her mask before throwing them both into the yellow plastic bin marked 'clinical waste only'. She shut the door to the room behind her and sighed. She'd be glad to see this shift over. Sixteen hours back-to-back was a long stretch. Still, she couldn't complain about the money. They'd offered her the double shift at three times the going rate. And not through the agency either, which meant those bloodsuckers wouldn't take their cut. Someone must have put in a good word for her.

Still, it was a weird gig. She'd barrier-nursed people before but never seen anyone recover so quickly. And all so hush-hush—they hadn't even told her what the bug was, other than to give it one of those stupid scientific labels. What the hell did HBK16 even mean? Still, the patient was doing well and this was the last hour of her sixteen, thank God.

She sat down at the desk to fill in the chart. At the end of the ward, a door opened and she looked up to see a couple of white coats with familiar faces, Drs Friedman and Powers, striding towards her.

'Evening, and how is the patient?' asked Powers, the female doctor.

'Fantastic,' Nurse Williamson said. 'All observations are normal. She has no temperature and her blood pressure is fine. And she's eating and drinking normally.'

'Great,' said Friedman. 'Thought we'd look in.'

Nurse Williamson nodded. She liked Dr Friedman. He had a

jaunty air about him. None of the downtrodden, don't-ask-me-I'm-too-busy, self-important disdain she usually got. Difficult to believe he was a doctor, sometimes.

'Here, I brought you some tea,' Dr Friedman said. 'And a couple of doughnuts.'

Nurse Williamson beamed and took the offered Styrofoam cup and the pastries which, over the years, had contributed significantly to more than a few of the extra pounds she was carrying. 'Ooh, thanks. You're a lifesaver. I've been gasping for a cuppa.'

'I'm sure you have. And I'm sorry you've been stuck here all this time. We're really grateful for you stepping into the breach like this. There's norovirus on four of the other wards and they've all been quarantined. You've been a trooper.'

Nurse Williamson took a gulp of tea while Dr Powers donned gown and mask, and opened the door to the patient's room.

'So, no odd symptoms?' Dr Friedman asked.

'None. Still slightly confused, I'd say. Keeps going on about some kitten video she wants to see.'

'Mild confusion is not unusual after such a severe infection,' Dr Friedman said.

'Yes, I wanted to ask you about that.' Nurse Williamson frowned. 'What sort of infection is this exactly? I can't find any evidence of pyrexia in the notes.'

'No, you wouldn't. That's because this kind of infection doesn't give rise to pyrexia.'

'No pyrexia?' Nurse Williamson frowned again and then yawned hugely. 'Oh, excuse me. I must be more tired than I thought I was. But I've never heard of an infection which didn't give rise to an increase in…in… temperat—' She yawned again, blinked several times, looked once with slow motion suspicion at the tea and then slumped headfirst onto the desk.

Matt removed the pentrievant from his pocket and slipped it on over Nurse Williamson's drooping forehead. The stone at the centre of the band glowed green. He removed it and opened the door to the other room to find Kylah doing much the same to the patient on the bed. The DOF captain looked up.

'Done?'

'And dusted.'

'She's going to be more than a bit confused after this,' Matt observed with a nod at the girl in the bed.

'It's easier this way. Time to transfer her to the general ward. They'll put her amnesia down to the trauma of her mother's death. Let the proper doctors work that one out.'

'Exactly.'

Kylah slipped off the band from Paula Evans' head and watched the girl look around the room, bemused. Two baby blue eyes focussed finally on the white-coated Matt and Kylah.

'Am I in a hospital?'

'Yes, you are, Paula,' Kylah smiled. 'You've had a nasty accident. Can you stand?'

Paula stood shakily and stepped over to the window. 'Where exactly am I?'

'Southampton. You wandered off. After the accident, I mean. Got a bit lost.'

'After the accident? Did I?' Her eyes looked very big this evening. She stretched and the short gown she was wearing rode up to reveal some fairly negligent underwear.

'Now,' Kylah said without missing a beat, 'if you'd like to follow me before Dr Friedman here does himself an injury? Having your eyes so far out on stalks can be dangerous. Us *doctors* know that sort of thing.'

Paula smiled and made a mildly apologetic face. 'Sorry about the stretching. I'm still a bit woozy.'

'Best we get you into a dressing gown, I think, or you'll woozy any male with a pulse into cardiac arrest. We don't want to upset the hospital's heart attack survival rates now, do we? They can be funny about stuff like that.' Kylah picked a towelling robe off the back of the door and held it up.

Paula pushed her arms through. 'It's weird, I can't remember much. But there is something about kittens playing the piano and yellow lights.'

'We know,' Matt said. 'But that will all change. Your memory'll come back slowly. At least all the good bits anyway. Now, if you'd like to follow us…'

Paula watched as Matt opened the bathroom door.

'Isn't that the toilet?'

'Ah, it may seem like it on first inspection, but it's actually a two-way door.'

'Ooh, I've never seen a door open on the opposite side of the hinges like that.'

Kylah held the door open for her. 'Bye Paula,' she said and guided her through into a ward where the doctors would put her story of having woken up in a strange hospital room down to post-traumatic stress, her father would explain to her about her mother's demise, and she'd have to cope with all of that. She was in for a rough emotional time. But she was alive. Even better, she'd remember nothing about Habihemhock or Gazorch or Hipposync.

Kylah turned to Matt. 'Right, let's get the nurse back to her own bedroom. She'll wake up with a headache and a healthier bank balance.'

'Could be worse.'

They walked out and gently lifted Nurse Williamson between them.

'Do you like her uniform?' Kylah asked.

'It's okay. I'm not a uniform kind of bloke.'

'More a very short hospital gown split up the back sort of bloke?'

'Look, it was very difficult not to notice…things. Besides, I'm in character. If I'd averted my eyes, it would have seemed very weird. Doctors have to be professional about that sort of thing.'

'*Professional.*' Kylah repeated the word so laden with scepticism that it scraped along the floor.

'Look, are you going to help me with this at all?' Matt struggled to get a very groggy Nurse Williams to her feet. 'Only we need to get her back to her room and she is quite a big girl.'

'You're the one who bought the doughnuts. You reap what you sow.'

'Yeah, and if you don't help I'll need someone to sew up my hernia. Can't you cast a levitation spell or something?'

'My name's not bloody Hermione.' Kylah looked around and pointed to a service cart stacked with boxes. 'How about that?'

Matt nodded and grinned. 'Brilliant. Ever thought of running an undertaker's convention?'

They removed the boxes and draped Nurse Williams over the cart. Eventually Kylah asked, 'I'm going to regret this, but why would I want to run an undertaker's convention?'

'So you could call it 'Thinking Outside The Box'.'

Kylah stayed silent but pushed the cart from side to side up the corridor towards the door.

'What's wrong,' Matt asked. 'Got a wonky wheel?'

'No, just doing my best to avoid the tumbleweed.'

CHAPTER FORTY-NINE

He was there already, sitting at the table with two coffees in front of him. He turned around and got up, gallant and polite as ever.

'Hello,' Bobby said, smiling.

'Hi,' Asher grinned in return.

She joined him and sat opposite. She'd come straight from work in a military jacket and a ruffled skirt over black tights. Her pink and white hair was now all black in straight braids.

Asher apologised. 'You look...nice. I hope you don't mind, I ordered for you. Sumatran. I wasn't sure when you'd come...or even if you'd come. If it's cold, I can get you a fresh one.'

Bobby lifted the cup and sipped. Flavour exploded into her mouth. 'Perfect,' she said. 'It's not supposed to be too hot, anyway.'

'So they say.'

The silence that followed involved a lot of intense staring into arty froth from two sets of eyes. It was the kind of silence in which so much furious thinking takes place that harnessing their combined neural activity could probably power a small village for several months.

'So, how's it going—' they said simultaneously, looking up. After an awkward pause, both laughed at their twin ineptitude.

'You first,' Asher said, as she knew he would.

'Well. It's going very well. I'm Hipposync's new Sales & Marketing Director. Matt and Kylah have been brilliant and Mr Porter is back. Even Tilfeth is beginning to warm to me, I think.'

Asher grinned. 'Good to know.'

'And, I secured a day release course at the Le Fey.'

'The Le Fey Academy? Really?'

Bobby Miracle nodded. 'Yup. Matt and Kylah insisted. They say I'm a natural and that I'll probably be able to complete my studies and do the ceremony in twelve months. I'd like to do it, for me and for Gran. So, looks like I'm going to be learning all that cunning stuff properly. I know I've got a lot of catching up to do.'

'Excellent news. Soon I will be seeing you in a pointy hat.'

'Apparently they've been voted out by the Argument. That's what they call the senior circle of witches. They've appointed a style advisor; a Ms Violet Eastwood. I've seen some of her stuff. It's…interesting, to say the least. But somehow I don't think the traditionalists are going to accept a red and green carpet catsuit and a fascinator made of pampas grass as ceremonial garb in lieu of the traditional black dress. She has some great ideas, does Ms Eastwood, it's just that they're not for public release, unless that public takes LSD as a regular prescription. How about you, Asher? How are things going with you?'

'I've been busy. Setting up the BOD's rapid response team. Trying to squeeze money out of the powers that be isn't fun. Blood from a stone, you know.'

'Oh, I think I've got an incantation for that,' she said.

'Really?'

She stared at him. 'No, not really. That was a joke.'

Asher nodded. 'I'm gullible, I know.'

'No you're not. And anyway, I'd heard they'd removed gullible from the dictionary.'

'Really, I had no—' Asher stopped and shook his head.

Bobby grinned. 'I think they've finally put the whole Gazorch thing to bed my side. Matt, who understands these things, got someone to post a series of comments on social media sites suggesting that the 'Three Blind Mice' video had been made after the kitten was drugged. Now it has as many dislikes as likes.'

'That is gratifying. And the killings?'

'Kylah thinks that Loosemore was down to poltergeist activity. Friendly fire from her husband, who was one of the murdered Bewildered, unfortunately. As for Cuthbertson…He made himself a warding cell. Obviously had some cunning. We think his was a true malign haunting. A first attempt by our friend Habihemhock that failed. It was exactly as you thought. He'd charmed the Widicombs such that they sought him out in limbo. Once there, he evicted them from the dead Bewildered and got himself a free ride across. We think he'd been refining his technique for months, if not years.'

Asher shook his head. 'All those poor Bewildered. Slaughtered like cattle.'

'The Evans killing was his lucky break. Tried and failed with possessing the mother and then struck lucky with poor Paula.'

Asher shook his head despondently. 'I missed the clues. The destruction of all the photographs should have told us—'

'What exactly? Poltergeists do that sort of thing, don't they?'

'But not systematically.'

Bobby shrugged. 'Habihemhock was one step ahead of everyone. He knew all about what was going on. He'd inveigled himself into Hipposync for revenge; buried so deep in Pippa no one had any idea. He was able to wander around for two whole weeks doing reconnaissance. He knew Matt and Kylah would investigate and so he monitored from inside. Once we picked up the trail he followed us to the Evanses and tried to get rid of us there with the trogre. Kylah thinks he emerged once in order to trigger the lockdown and plant his convocant in the blue room. Once there it remained undetected until…well, you know the rest.'

Asher nodded. 'He would have sent the geist Sambolith that tried to attack you at Cuthbertson's as well. He must have suspected you'd work it out. Must have known that you were… different.'

'I'll take that as a compliment. And Malachite?'

'They used him for his expertise with the recently dead. He knew all about the Bewildered. They used him to find their haunts. I'm afraid my showing an interest in him signed his death warrant.'

They both sipped their Sumatran Mandheling and studied the decoration inside The Roast.

'It's good to see you settled,' Asher said after a while.

'You too,' Bobby replied. 'Looks like you've really bedded in. Think you'll stay there?'

'Yes, I do…What days are you over on your course? Maybe we could meet for lunch?'

'Lunch,' Bobby said, reflecting on his offer. It was close, but there'd be no cigar. 'Yes, that would be great. I'm going to come over every Wednesday and Thursday mornings as well. A practical class.'

'It sounds busy.'

'Yes, it is. But I'm learning loads. How to read people mainly, how to judge people, how to nudge people in the right direction. Not much magic in witchery, just knowing what to do and when. Matter of timing, mainly and *couching* things in the right terms. And having had Gran in here,' Bobby tapped the side of her head, 'has helped a lot. She left loads of really useful stuff behind. Oh, and thanks for that, by the way.'

'My pleasure. But that's what makes people so wary of witches, I suppose,' Asher observed. 'The psychological aspect.'

'Hocus-pocus you mean?' Bobby laughed. 'Does that include you?'

'Me? I'm not scared of witches.'

'Right,' she said. 'Is it Wednesday *tomorrow?*'

'Yes, it is,' Asher replied.

Bobby waited. This is what they'd told her to do. Plant the seed, water it, and then stand back and let it grow. She watched Asher take another sip of coffee.

'Oh, your grandmother asked me to give you a message, too. She told me to tell you that Habihemhock is in exactly the right place and the other wit…cunning ladies thought it was a brilliant idea. Habihemhock apparently especially enjoys the days after curry night. Mean anything to you?'

Bobby laughed. It filled the room and warmed the air. 'Yes, it does.'

'I can think of no better place for a summoner demon than the Sanctuary. Duana, too, thinks that many other Bewildered were murdered as sacrifices to Gazorch. A way of transferring dark energy to Habihemhock. We should have realised.' He shook his head but then looked up into Bobby's face and the skin around his eyes crinkled a little. 'Your grandmother is a remarkable woman.'

'She is. I've been told your summoning her was somewhat exceptional.'

'Like I said, not many necreddos visit and come back in one piece.'

'But you did.' Bobby took another sip of coffee and waited.

'This coffee really is good, isn't it?' Asher said.

'The best,' Bobby agreed.

'How long is your course going to run for?'

'Couple of years, probably.'

Asher nodded and looked out of the window at the palm fronds blowing in the balmy breeze. It looked, to Bobby, as if he was building up to something.

The barista shouted over to them, 'Anything else?'

'No, we're fine,' Bobby said and *waited*.

'So,' Asher said after another pause, 'if it's Wednesday tomorrow, you will be in New Thameswick.'

'Yes.'

'So, you go home directly afterwards?'

'Usually.'

'But then you will have to come back first thing Thursday?'

'Yes. Kylah has allowed me to use the blue room portway for easy access.'

'Even so, you have to travel into Jericho from wherever you live…'

'Iffley road,' Bobby nodded, and waited.

Asher looked down at his coffee and, after some very long seconds, seemed to make up his mind. 'Since my surgery I have not sought out any kind of…relationship. But you are a remarkable woman, Bobby. I find myself very attracted to you and regret anything and everything I have done to offend you. If there is any mitigation, it is the fact that I wanted to protect you, in the belief that you were an innocent human. I realise now that I got that hopelessly wrong.'

'Which bit: the innocent or the human?' Bobby said, and promptly told herself to shut the hell up.

'A little of both perhaps.' Asher smiled and for once let it be unashamedly flirtatious. 'I have a proposition. The fact is I do have quite a generous apartment. If you wanted to stay over any night…' He paused to give the idea time to settle. 'We could perhaps have an evening meal instead of lunch. I'm not presuming anything but I do have a spare couch. Not that I'm suggesting you should sleep on the couch. I would sleep on the couch and you could have the bed. Exclusively, I mean.'

'That's very generous,' Bobby said. They were both leaning on the table, their faces close. She hoped he couldn't see the way she was smiling inside.

'Good, that's good. I have a cat. At least there's a cat that shares the space with me. Or at least I think it's a cat. Is that a problem?'

'No. Cats are free spirits. I like that. There should always be a cat.'

'Then I'll make sure the sheets are clean. The apartment needs a bit of a once over, so it's exactly the excuse I need.'

'Do you always need an excuse?'

'No. And despite the fact that you have been employing cunning tactics in order that I reveal my true intentions, I did not want to seem too forward.'

'Forward.' Bobby repeated the word, nodding sagely. 'That wasn't forward. This is forward. How big is the bed?'

'It is large enough to accommodate two people comfortably.'

'Then why on earth are we talking about couches?'

Asher blinked, leaned across, and kissed her.

Bobby thought of quite a few things in the next few seconds, but the one that remained with her later was how truly unfair it was that Asher had longer eyelashes than she did.

Maybe there was an incantation for that.

ACKNOWLEDGMENTS

As with all writing endeavours, the existence of this novel depends upon me, the author, and a small army of 'others' who turn an idea into a reality. A special mention to Bryony Sutherland for editorial guidance through the labyrinth. The Hipposync Archives are a work in progress. Special mention goes to Ela the dog who drags me away from the writing cave and the computer for walks, rain or shine. Actually, she's a bit of a princess so the rain is a no-no. Good dog!

But my biggest thanks goes to you, lovely reader, for being there and actually reading this. It's great to have you along and I do appreciate you spending your time in joining and the team at Hipposync and in New Thameswick where anything is possible.

CAN YOU HELP?

With that in mind, and if you enjoyed it, I do have a favour to ask. Could you spare a moment to **leave a review or a rating**? A few words will do, but it's really the only way to help others like you discover the books. Probably the best way to help authors you like. Just visit the book's page on Amazon and leave a few words, or a rating, if you have the time. Thank you!

FREE BOOK FOR YOU

Visit my website and join up to the Hipposync Archives Readers Club and get a FREE novella, ***Every Little Evil,*** by visiting:

https://dcfarmer.com/

When a prominent politician vanishes amidst chilling symbols etched in blood, the police are baffled. Enter Captain Kylah Porter, an enigmatic guardian against otherworldly threats. With her penchant for the paranormal and battling against cynical skeptics, she dives into a realm where reality blurs. Her toxic colleague from the Met is convinced it's just another tawdry urban crime. But Kylah suspects someone's paying a terrible price for dipping a toe, or something even less savoury, in the murky depths of the dark arts.
She knows her career and the missing man's life are on the line. Now time is running out for the both of them…

Pour yourself a cuppa and prepare for a spellbinding mystery.

Id you sign up, you will also be the first to hear about new releases via the few but fun emails I'll send you. This includes a no spam promise from me and you can unsubscribe at any time.

AUTHOR'S NOTE

Once upon a time, in the swirling mists of the last century, my journey into the fantastical began. A devotee of the greats like Tolkien, I found myself drawn deeper into Terry Pratchett's Discworld and Tom Holt's tilt at the modern—the holy trinity of the Ts, if you will.

Two decades ago, I embarked on a series of stories of wonder and the fantastic. Satirising our turbulent modern world with snarky humour by displacing the hapless participants of these tales into situations and places where things are very different. And, come on, who wouldn't want a quick trip to New Thameswick, or have access to an aperio? And all under the umbrella of The Archives.

Blame it on the Bogie (man) came from somewhere, I know not where. Probably from wondering if those people who really do not like to walk on the cracks in the pavement know something I don't. What if people really could slip through? And when I dreamt up Bobbie Miracle, it had to be her story. Her's and Asher's. Plus it gave me a chance to go back to New Thameswick in a lot more detail. Wouldn't it be great if we could?

And a retirement home for witches? Sign here, please.

All the best, and see you all soon, DCF.

READY FOR MORE

Can't Buy Me Blood

Kylah Porter thinks the world of her human partner Matt. But she worries that his skill set is a little too unrefined for a job as a special agent with the Department of Fimmigration monitoring the borders between the worlds.

When a series of vampire deaths in the Fae world is linked to dark wonderworking in the human world, it's clear that a serial killer of the very worst kind is on the loose. With only a group of rehabilitated bloodsucking zealots and a uniquely fragrant bookshop as clues to the mystery, the DOF needs all the help it can get to root out an evil bent on having a foot (or is that a fang?) in both camps.

But will Matt remain a loose cannon? Or can he prove to Kylah that he's worthy of both her affection and her respect once more? He needs to sort himself out and quickly. Because not doing so could have disastrous consequences for all concerned...

Printed in Great Britain
by Amazon